CW00860324

SIDEWARDS

Kieran Follett

Chapter 1

Drugs, Thugs and Porn Mags

<u>2013</u>

It's not easy being immortal. When you have a guy who loves to fight living in your head for company, I find that life becomes somewhat unbearable, though there are at least some good things about it. For one, even when alone, I would always have someone to talk to.

Cain and I sat on one of the many pub stools of The Pea and Leak, drumming our fingers on a dark wooden table while waiting to get served. There weren't that many people around the bar, just this one couple getting their drinks from an inexperienced young barmaid. We were waiting to order our fourth pint. While doing so, we were having discussions in our head; by thinking, we could hold a conversation without having to move our lips, let alone say something.

'God,' Cain muttered, 'could she be any more of a clutz?'

'Doesn't look like she's been here long,' I replied.

'What ya gonna go for?'

'Depends – what do you want to have?'

Cain didn't reply. For a moment I assumed that he ignored me.

'Umm … I might go for a Clarence's, I think.'

'You sure?'

'I dunno; I said 'I think', not 'one hundred fuckin' per cent', Mr Questionnaire.'

I sighed under my breath.

'Look, are you going for it or not?'

'Sure, why not?'

'Alright, then, I'll go for that, too. Let's do it.'

"Hi, there," the barmaid said cheerily. "What would you like?"

"Hi, we'd – *I'd* like a pint of Clarence, please."

"Okay, coming right up." She did her work on the beer tap, accidentally overfilling the glass with a warm gold-coloured cider, and tried pouring some of it out before overfilling once more.

'Dick,' Cain thought. 'I would've felt like I was noticed if ya said 'we'!'

Sighing, I mentally replied. 'Do you even pay attention to what's going on? She doesn't know you're a voice in my head right now.'

'OUR head,' he corrected me.

'*Our* head, sorry. I hate the whole pronoun thing with our body. I wonder how she'd react if you took over?'

'How'd ya mean?'

'For one, she might be surprised at a few … changes to our appearance, plus how all of a sudden we'd sound American.'

'Hey, I can't help it if I love that accent. Besides, the little claws and fangs o' mine always work at fancy dress parties and Halloween.'

'Yeah, but not in public. Plus, there are the ears.'

'I have a good feelin' babes love the elf ears.'

'But not the eyes.'

'They might think o' kittens when they stare into 'em. Who knows, they might be huge cat fans?'

'Yes, 'might' being a big word there.'

The girl pulled our pint and gave it to us, spouting, "£3.50, please." I gave her the money in the form of a five-pound note, which she took and gave me the change.

'I really wish we brought Bob with us,' I said before taking a sip.

'For the last time, I ain't gonna let some fancy revolver get in the way o' my hand-to-hand trainin'. I think I'm outta practice. PLEASE stop callin' yer gun 'Bob', for fuck's sake.'

'Hey, Bob was a good friend to us, and that gun was his favourite; I can't help it if I feel that I should honour him that way.'

'Always found him to be a nutcase. Not sayin' that I hate the guy, far from it, but when ya got five-hundred fuckin' guns stashed in yer house, that ain't a hobby, that's a fetish.'

I took over our body and guzzled down half o' the cider – CHRIST, the taste was so refreshin', it was like I was drinkin' from a well while in a desert. I nearly let out an orgasmic sigh o' delight, but had the strength to hold back before lettin' Davey-boy resume control.

'When's our appointment again?'

'11:25.'

'Okay, good. What's the time now?'

'It's …'

I looked at my/our watch, and my/our eyes went wide-open as we saw how close it was getting to our scheduled appointment.

'Oh, shit. We've got about twenty minutes to get to the warehouse.' I got off the stool and started to walk out of the pub.

'C'mon, twenty doesn't sound that bad.'

"Try walking from here – we'd be lucky to get halfway across by the time they arrive."

Now we were outside, breathing in harsh, frosty winter air.

'They might be late, y'know.'

"That's a possibility, but we can't afford to lay back on it."

'You think too much, Davey-boy.'

"Well, sorry for being the bloody deep thinker, Cain. I can't help if I'm the strategist."

'Know what's funny?'

"What?" I asked in a groan, under my breath.

'Our timin's fucked up and, unlike all the other times, I ain't the cause in this case.'

"Look, let's just get there before they do."

They weren't the nicest of people, you know.

*

3

Warehouse in London. Barely lit. Large. Open-spaced. Perfect meeting for a couple of drug dealers with £100,000 worth of cocaine and other sort of drugs. A rocky surface made up the floor on the inside, with a few of those large, long lights suspended above.

Y'know, the pole-like ones?

Oh, *and* those fluorescent light bulbs that you'd expect to see in old gangster movies. I was quite a fan of them throughout the thirties and forties; that said, the sci-fi an' horror since the 50s were so excitin'. I remember back in the Hundred Years War, adventure and pulse-poundin' excitement and running and crap-kickin' where what made me feel alive, and another thing that I liked was …

I'm just talking too much, aren't I? I can never tell when I do. I think I might have that syndrome, whassit called – Asperger's? Oh well, doesn't matter now, I better stick to the rest of this tale, or else you'll be dead before I even finish this paragraph, so here we go, resumin' this thing.

We sat on the second floor, on a pink sofa that was suspiciously already there when we first went into the warehouse. Maybe the warehouse was once used to store furniture? A mystery for the ages, I guess. While sinking into the sofa, we listened to an old jazz song on our iPod while Cain, in control, was flicking through a porn mag.

We heard them enter, drug dealers expecting a client. They opened the doors; quick, sharp and just exhausted having to move from one place to another (geez, you can never get the right sort of dealers these days, can you?). Must've been about four guys. From what we could see while covered in shadows on the second floor, they eyed on our position. All they could see was darkness.

What they had in mind was a deal; they talk to the owner of the area, who gets £50,000 so that he gives them £100,000 worth of drugs to sell. Coke, heroin, speed, crystal meth, finest lot of the pick. There were a few things that they didn't know about.

The client was actually an alias we created to lure dealers in like fish on a hook.

We planned to kill them all, and not even touch the drugs, probably just leave them in the warehouse.

Did you get all of that? Good. See, we took a vigilante stance, taking out on the worst of the worst criminals; remorseless serial killers, terrorists, monstrous sex offenders, and more. At times we tried to beat up criminals and get them arrested, but this seemed to be the most effective of wiping out the real demons of society. Why this, you ask? Thing is, I think there's a high chance of me being insane – am I insane? I don't know; I'll have to ask those other ten voices in my head, see what they think. They're nice fellas. Ha! Fooled you! There's only the two of us!

But I don't know for sure, 'cause I've never been to a hospital – well, the mental ones, nor have I ever been sick in my life, except for maybe being loony.

Anyway, I arranged everything so that this drug gang meet up with us in an area that suited the specialities of me and Cain – beating the living shit out of evil people, *and* killing them (Cain loves doing that last part). Trust me when I say that you're gonna get one helluva show, mate.

We heard their voices, loud, echoing, and worst of all, cockney.

Max: "So, Boss, you think he's here?"

Boss: "He better be, Max, or else, if we find him later on, he can say goodbye to his empire and we can take the lot."

Max: "Okay, Boss, you know best."

Alex: "See that second floor? I bet that's where he is. Nowhere else he could be, for sure."

Boss: "Could be. Mark, check it out."

Mark: "Sure, Boss."

Boss: "If he's up there, then I don't see any point of him dragging this out any longer."

Mark (who, as I remember, was a big fat twat with balding yellow hair and a beard) eyed the stairs that would grant him access to the top floor. They were covered in an army of dust, since this place had not been used for some time. As he slowly went up, only the corresponding metallic sounds of *clang clang clang* accompanied him. He didn't take his gun out of his holster, otherwise the (non-existent) deal would be off and all that burnt rubber of the car's wheels would be for nothing.

Oh, I wish he *had* pulled out his gun. It had been years since someone tried to shoot us. Nowadays, I get a sort of thrill out of being cornered with a bunch of gun-toting lunatics.

After walking towards the sofa, which was covered in darkness, Mark lightly touched his holstered gun with his fingertips, working his way up to the finger entirely. At first, he stared at the side of the chair, before looking at the very seat of it up-front.

No one was on it.

Well, except for the hot woman parading the cover of the porn mag that lay on the seat.

Mark faced his superior from above and shook his head, as in, "No, he ain't here, boss, but there *is* a porn mag. Want me to bring *that* down for ya?"

Looking at Mark, the boss replied with, "Forget him."

Everyone beside their boss looked at him like dogs to their master (stupid dogs to equally stupid masters).

He, in turn, addressed the goons. "Alright, lads, let's leave this shithole. He wasted our time for nothin'. Get down here, Mark."

As soon as the boss looked away, Mark was confronted by a ghastly figure, Cain. We had secluded ourselves in a dark corner, invisible to anyone unless they were close to us. With no one looking at Mark, it was time to off him. Cain bared our teeth, which now looked like an animal about to eat prey. God, they were huge. Not goofy-huge, but instead were razor-sharp huge, like in those monster movies, especially werewolves. Another thing that caught his eyes were that we were wearing a red Stetson and a full-length crimson trench coat. The seventies were a weird time for us.

As soon as Mark saw us, Cain quickly slashed his throat with one claw, causing blood to squirt out of him like ketchup from a bottle. Cain grabbed his rapidly crimson-coated throat and tossed him over the rails, his body colliding with the floor with a loud thump.

The others turned to find Mark redecorating the ground in red, twitching slightly before accepting death. All but the boss screamed and flapped about with fear in the manner of a headless chicken, while his face was devoid of any emotion, a statue come to life. That's when Cain left out a roaring laugh to keep up with scaring them. After that, he allowed me to take control.

They started blindly shooting at the second floor out of fear and self-preservation. For the most part, they missed, though we took a couple of bullets to the gut, wincing from the pain. That didn't matter, though, as we'd regenerate in half an hour. "Damn," I moaned, "that's my favourite shirt!"

Pumped up with adrenaline, Cain leapt us over the rails with the grace of a ballerina. While falling, he focused on the thug nearest to us, Max, and when we landed on our feet like a cat, Cain sent his claws into his eyes. Blood squirted out of the sockets like miniature water balloons. I wasn't so disgusted; I've seen worse.

The man's screams pierced the atmosphere like a bullet … which was soon to follow. Cain took our fingers out, I grabbed Max's gun (a .45 handgun; cute) shot him dead, a semi-automatic 'BANG' exploding; I did the same thing to Alex; we withstood several rounds of gunfire; the boss ran out of ammunition. He threw his gun at us and made a beeline to the warehouse entrance door. Wasting no time, we shot him in the leg just as he was ten feet from the door.

He let out a scream as he fell, trailing off into a wail, along with calling us a 'fucker' and 'arsehole'.

We stared at him with contempt. He did likewise, his eyes wide and nearly shedding tears, revealing his panic, his anger, his need for revenge.

"Who the fuck are you?" he asked, his face red and eyes wide.

"Karma, I guess." I walked over to him while twirling our gun.

"Y-you fucking psychopath!"

"Getting morally lectured by a drug dealer – not how I wanted to spend my Sunday."

Cain took over. The boss jumped (well, tried to) as he witnessed the transformation, slack-jawed and scared witless.

Lookin' at the gun in our hand, I tucked it into the back o' our jeans, disgusted.

"Hiya, buddy," I said as though I was talkin' to an old friend. "What's up with your face? You look pretty grim n' emotional n' shit. Oh, that's right; we killed your pals."

I kicked one of his dead friends in the head; I'm pretty sure the skull cracked.

"Numbskulls. Hehe – gotta write that one down. Don't worry, you'll live long enough to make some new ones. Oh, who am I kiddin'? We'll kill you in a minute, so the reunion with your friends ain't gonna take long."

The boss attempted to get up, but the best he managed to do was sittin', usin' all the strength he had in his arms to support himself while he got into his sprawled position.

"People are going to come here because of the gunfire, you idiot," he groaned while rubbin' over an injured leg.

"Not really. They'd think it was somewhere else. All we gotta do is just dispose o' your bodies, clean the place up a bit an' then maybe sell that Audi o' yours outside. Actually, come to think of it, I want to drive a car. Okay, scratch that last part o' our list, cuz we're gonna take your car after this."

I made my way to the nearest corpse an' started to shift through their pockets.

"Just need to figure out which one o' you bastards has the key." There was nothin' on the body. I moved to the second nearest one. All he had was a pack o' cigarettes, which I shuffled into our coat. "An' don't tell me it's you, cuz I don't wanna go to all effort to kill ya just becuz ya own the damn thing."

'Cain,' David told me, 'we're not getting the car.'

I looted a third body and didn't care that if I had to shout. "OH, COME OOOOOOONNNNNN, Davey, don't tell me that! When's the last time we drove a car? Oh, 2007, that's when. It's been too long! We've never driven an' Audi before, and I REALLY, REALLY, REALLY, WANNA HAVE AN AUDI!"

'NO, Cain, we are NOT stealing someone's car just because we're killing them, and that's final.'

"You are SO unfair, man! I just want us to have some fun, and what better way to have fun than to drive a car?"

'No, YOU just want to have fun because you like that model. You know that I don't care for Audis.'

Nothin' on the body. I gave up the search an' walked around while talkin'.

"You're bein' mean," I yelled out.

'No, I'm being sensible.'

"Yeah, right. If you WERE bein' sensible, we wouldn't be doin' this, an' I wouldn't be pleadin' for the car. I bet you'd even go so far as to buy us a different model just to piss me off, huh?"

I crouched so that my face was inches away from his. I wanted my hot breath to be the last thing he'd ever smell. His bloodshot eyes and sweaty face. I could taste the fear comin' off him, and it was pretty damn delicious.

With one sharp finger, I stroked his fat cheek – I'm a cat with a ball o' string.

"You guys have been great tonight. I got my trainin' done, so I'm happy now. Might as well say 'bye'."

I left the rest to David.

I stood up, took a few steps back, pulled the gun from our jeans and aimed it at the boss. "I'd say I'm sorry about all this, but you kind of brought this on yourself."

He snarled at me, anger taking over.

"You stupid-looking basta—"

BANG.

Chapter 2

Helping Those in Need

Cain and I made our way back home, feeling tired after a good night's slaughter. Blood was pasted onto my red full-length trench coat. Cain's sharp teeth were no longer like knives when I took control of our body; they were normal human teeth, but there was also blood on them, stained disgustingly like bleach on the Mona Lisa. A few good bullets had dug into our lungs and chest, which had me coughing up blood at first before wiping it on my sleeve.

Our head was pounding – not because of the fact that we suffered from headshot wounds, but because we heard the sound of a fiend growling, his bestial moans hurting us like a sledgehammer against our skull. Our more violent side, the Voice, had had its fun. Now was the time to relax and become civilised.

Sore eyes; again, felt tired. I kept rubbing them, but that didn't work. It didn't matter in the slightest, really; we'd return to our home soon, flick on the telly, drink some Diet Coke (because it's better than ordinary Coke) and maybe accidentally sleep when our favourite programme is on. Our home… an apartment that's actually quite close to the warehouse. It wasn't very large, nor was it very small. It was okay.

The telly I had was not really old – it was from the early 2000s. A DVD player nestled below it, not bothering to remove the ever-growing traces of dust it had been gathering for several long weeks.

For those who actually remember the days of VHS tapes, it was quite a transition from blocky black bricks (I love alliterations!) to thin, fragile discs. We watched the hell out of video tapes when they first came out, and we imagined DVDs would last for a good couple of decades before being replaced by something more advanced. The chairs weren't very posh or up there in high living. All that consisted were a couple of thin black chairs in the small kitchen, and a nice, comfy sofa that had beautiful patterns all over it, forced to face our telly since the 1980s and would do so forever, or about five more years.

Arriving at the entrance to the flats, I stopped for a second in the first-floor corridor. I pressed my back against the slowly rotting walls, deciding to give it a few minutes to let our brain properly absorb what we had done; don't get us wrong, we knew exactly what we'd been doing. I just felt like taking in all of our actions and what kind of consequences they might have. It was brief. I had known beforehand that all of those druggies were without wives or kids (I mean, these are people who make a profit out of indirectly killing people, and had a very good chance of winding up in prison then getting out if I hadn't given them their comeuppance) so it was easy to dispatch them from life without having to worry about their children wondering why Daddy hasn't come home.

Children. I never allow any person to harm children. They're pure, innocent, naïve. Forcing them into darkness shows them sides of life they shouldn't have to see at a young age. I made it my duty to try and prevent children coming to any harm. Otherwise, they might die too early or live with unbearable scars. That type of stuff shouldn't happen. I try to not let it happen. I've faced too many incidents involving innocent children and evil; it keeps me up every night.

I unlocked the front door, entered and took in the aroma of the remains of the Chinese food we had before going to the pub – noodles and curry sauce. I slumped onto my sofa, closed my eyes and opened them after a second's thought. It was brought up when Cain nudged it out of the open. The blood on our clothes. And our face. They needed to be removed as soon as possible, otherwise anyone who saw them might become … curious. Rising from the sofa, I removed every item of bullet-riddled clothing bearing blood (I ended up having to put on another pair of pants) and decided to put them in a pile then bung them in the washing machine for a while. Tonight was a rough one, so I didn't bother to wash them for the time being; I just washed over my face and went to bed.

I took time to observe my body... full of bullet holes and blood that had dried up and coated itself over sections of my skin. It's very difficult for me to die; I've come close to snuffing it too many times to count, but no matter how bad the damage was, I came back. My body tends to repair itself whenever there's damage.

You might be wondering how we get the bullets out. Well, we found out ages back that we had these odd little internal routes used to dispose of foreign items, as long as they weren't too big.

The bullets, in this case, would flow down whatever route they were closest to until they reached the exit – our limbs, specifically the fingertips and toes – and were done with. As you might imagine, getting shot at repeatedly was always a hassle.

After a while, every wound had been healed, magically 'stitched up'. It would take a minute or so for them to disappear. I decided to send the spent bullets down the toilet, and gave it a while for the flush handle mechanism to work its way up to being... workable. It was always annoying waiting when the flush handle didn't work all the time.

We stared into our bathroom mirror's reflection, focused, obsessed, as we thought to ourselves:

'How long do I have to wean Cain 'til the Voice is silenced?'

'I want that Voice to shut up – I don't wanna kill any more.'

This was something that had been boggling in our mind for some time. A Voice had been influencing Cain to kill, shouting, 'KILL KILL KILL'. Cain grew tired of it, and so I had been weaning him from it for several centuries, killing fewer and fewer criminals until finally the Voice would have no more power over him. Sure, we killed criminals, but we made sure that we didn't kill those with family – yes, those kind of people don't deserve a family, but it would break the hearts of family members who were kept in the dark or cared about them despite what they might have known about their activities.

It's me and Cain doing this all the way. We had been at it for a while now, the odd century or six. How long the disastrous duo would keep doing this was a mystery to us. I wanted – wished – for there to be a day where there to be no injustice, just good old peace and happiness. We had a feeling that when I finally die (*hopefully*) I get punished for the things I've done. We all have different forms of justice. Technically we're kind of a vigilante... like Batman. Except Batman has people around him, the kind of civilised, respectable people you wish to find. I have Cain. Hooray.

Just as we sat on our bed, hands rubbing over our exhausted pale face, Cain decided to talk. Conversation was the last thing my mind needed at that moment.

'Hey, Dave. Dave. Dave. Dave. Dave.'

"Yes?"

'Got 'em good tonight, didn't we?'

"Yes, Cain, we got 'em good tonight."

'When's the next one?'

"Eh?"

'Next time we kill dealers.'

"Cain, I don't know, okay? You always ask me this and I give you the same answer over and over."

'Oh. Okay. What you doin'?'

"After what we did tonight, I thought it would be clear – going to sleep. You're bored right now, aren't you?"

'Yup. You know me so well.'

"It's not hard to know you well. After all these years, it's easy to think of why you do things. Reading your motives is so clear, a blank piece of A4 paper is difficult by comparison."

Cain figured it would be best to shut up. Tucked into bed, the two of us went over much of the stuff we had been doing for as long as possible. Eventually I closed our eyes, waiting to be reunited with all the good people we knew from the past. Our rest wasn't peaceful; something was occurring next door. The apartment walls were particularly thin, and our head was placed right near next-door. I heard voices.

Thud.

Yelling.

Crash!

Mumbling.

"You... you get out'f here."

"But Daddy..."

"Look, I'm feelin' not too well, so I don't need you 'ere! You're givin' me a headache!"

Sobbing.

Drunken mumbling.

More sobbing.

Door slamming shut.

Now something was happening in my apartment.

Eyes opening.

Sheets folding over.

Fresh clothes put on.

The jiggling of keys entering my pocket.

My door being shut quietly.

A little girl was seen down the hallway. I recognized her from the countless times I'd been around the building. Never talked to her before. She must have been six, maybe seven years old. I couldn't see the girl's face clearly, due to the lack of lights in the hallway (the apartment building had a long history of no lights in hallways, something the tenants, myself included, were not pleased with). Sobbing could still be heard. I slowly went up to her before she realized that I was four feet away. The girl stopped crying.

She was the first to talk. "Who are you?" She wiped her eyes.

"Hello. I'm from next door," I replied softly. "I heard what was going on inside. Thought I'd see what was going on. I want to help."

"I was told not to talk to people I don't know."

"I know you. I've seen you dozens of times around this building. Ever seen me? I bet you have."

The kid nodded. Could've remembered me, or maybe pretended that she did. Didn't matter.

"What's your name, little lady?"

It took a few seconds for the child to talk back. "Emily… What's yours?"

"My name is David Stroke," I answered. It was the name I was using while living in the apartment.

"Can I call you Jacob?"

Cain, who was watching this, whispered to me, 'What the hell are you doin'? You stupid, dumb idiot. Would a child you just met really give you a new name? I mean, really?'

I brushed aside Cain. "Why Jacob?"

"I was gonna have a brother called Jacob. He was in Mummy's tummy. But he didn't come out to meet me. Daddy said he and Mummy went to Heaven."

I understood what she was trying to say. It struck me deeply. Poor kid. I had heard – even experienced – this kind of loss. Her brother-to-be didn't make it. She didn't have a sibling to comfort her. I knew loneliness – such a feeling had struck me for so long at so many times in my life. If her father wasn't nice to her, then that meant that her loneliness was even greater, more so than my own. I don't remember my parents, or even if I had any brothers or sisters. She had the one thing I didn't have, the most important thing – a childhood.

"Mister Jacob, are you crying?"

The little missy was right. Unbeknownst to me, a tear was rolling down my face. I wiped it away, knowing that I had compared the two of us, and that she was in a worse state than me.

"Yeah, yeah, I am." As upset as I was over this, I wanted to press matters forward. I made sure I said things nice and slowly to her.

"Okay, I know your daddy isn't feeling very well, and I don't want to meet him yet if he's like this, and he certainly won't like you being in the same space as him, considering what he was saying to you. So why don't we pop into my space for a bit, just to make things easier?"

She nodded. I let her into the apartment and we sat in two of the wicker chairs in the kitchen. Thanks to the lighting, I could see her properly. Blonde hair in two front streams over a chubby face (baby fat, if you don't know). Clothes were looking crusty and creased (maybe they were worn for days on end?). But the most noticeable fact about her face was cemented.

A bright red bruise was on her cheek. Daddy didn't just yell at her when he was drunk. When you're drunk, you can get angry. Angry before drunkenness is even worse. In his bottle-riddled rage, he would harm his own daughter for no reason apart from just being there. He saw her as an object, a means to vent out his frustrations. Did he hate her because he may have seen her as a cause of his wife's death?

Something needed to be done about this.

I made myself some tea (not a stereotypic view of British people in a crisis – I just fancied tea) and gave the girl some squash (she liked orange – I like oranges, too). At first, we didn't drink our refreshments – for her, it was natural, what with her being in the home of a complete stranger she might not have full trust of. For me, I was settling into this predicament.

Three options lay before me. Each one was in the line of morality. Whatever happened with each one would've affected the child.

Option One, the 'sensible' option. Ring up the police. He'd be arrested for child abuse, she'd be sent to a new family forever or until he sobered up (though that seemed unlikely). The only downside to this would be, on the smallest of possibilities, him getting off the hook for whatever reason. On the other side of it, there was him being sent to a rehabilitation clinic.

Option Two, the 'one-on-one' option. I temporarily leave the child in my apartment for safety measures and chat with the dad. Chances were that he wouldn't have listened in his abusive state and would try to threaten me. However, I might've been able to get through to him, or at least film him being a complete wreck on my mobile phone. If that failed, then I could've gone with Option One or Option Three.

Option Three, the 'violent' option. Should he have tried to further harm his daughter or anyone else, let alone continue drinking himself to oblivion, then retaliation was in order. People might argue with 'if you do that then you're no better than he is'. With that comment, this needs to be stressed – even if I did have kids, I wouldn't endlessly get drunk in front of them and abuse them every day because of a lack of common sense. Using force on this guy would be one way to stop him from harming anyone else – break him before he'd break others.

The police felt like the right answer. If I alerted them before anything else could happen, the girl's safety was guaranteed. The 'beat him up' option would only be used if the dad tried to attack before or after the arrival of the police.

A few good seconds of ringing and waiting later, I had been able to report the 'drunken dad abuses daughter' event to the police. They said that they would come round and apprehend him, after meeting up with me to confirm things. In the meantime, it was best that I would have Emily in my apartment and make sure that she was okay.

I asked her if she wanted to watch anything on the telly, and she replied with "Yes". She didn't have much of an idea on what to watch, so we flicked through the channels until we would see something good – quite a challenge, since I don't spend all of my time watching shows aimed at children. I forgot that it was the middle of the night.

We couldn't find anything available, so we resorted to looking at a few DVDs I bought in case any friends of mine that popped round brought their kids over (that and in any scenario where I needed something light and jolly to cheer me up in severe depressions, usually a Christmas cartoon).

Finally, Emily went with a DVD of a show that was on the program Cartoon Network, *Ben 10*. She explained that she wasn't that much concerned with dolls and beautiful dresses and princesses, but rather stuff that involved a lot of (kid-friendly) action, explosions, pretty much anything that boys prefer in a cartoon than girls. I already saw all the episodes on the disc during my 'off-time' (i.e. me getting bored and having nothing else better to do).

It took about five to seven minutes for the police to arrive at the apartment complex and make their way to my quarters. The standard three-knock rule was used, and I told Emily to carry on watching the DVD, saying, "Everything's gonna be okay."

I opened the door, and there stood two coppers wearing their standard black-and-white-stripes-looking-like-a-panda uniforms. One was male, thirties, with short black hair. The second officer was a policewoman; she was roughly in her early forties, flat brown hair, a few minor crow feet around the eyes gave her a solid, wise appearance. I found her rather attractive.

The policewoman spoke first. "Hello, there, sir. I am Officer Danielle Telloff and this is Officer Robert String. Are you Mr David Stroke?"

"Hello, officers, and yes, I am."

It was Officer String's turn, stating, "We received a phone call from your apartment. If we were told correctly, you are looking after the daughter of an intoxicated man so he won't hurt her, correct?"

"That's correct, officer. Would you, uh, like to come in?"

Officer Telloff responded as if she had prepared for my question.

"Yes, and we'd like to see the girl first before checking the father's place."

I stepped aside and allowed the police to enter. They noticed Emily on the chair watching the cartoon, who removed her eyes from the screen just to see who knocked on the door.

"Hello, Emily," Officer String said with a smile. "Are you okay?"

Emily replied with a simple "Yes", no wet tone indicating pain, or confused looks. She locked eyes with Officer String.

"We're just here to check on you." He looked at the bruise on her cheek, noting the sheer force that must have been applied to cause such a mark.

"Does it hurt there?" He pointed a finger at where the bruise was.

Emily replied with, "It hurts a little. It did a little bit ago, but now it doesn't hurt a lot."

"Okay, then, Emily. Now, about your daddy. Does he... do stuff like this to you?"

The three of us waited for a reply from Emily, which took a few seconds due to the nature of the question and Emily's memory to help her out.

"... yes. Daddy was doing it after Mummy went away."

"Went away?"

"She went away some time ago. Daddy got sad. He likes to drink a lot. Dunno why. If I take a bottle he..." The memory of countless times that incident had happened made her stop mid-sentence. I didn't want to see her upset, nor in pain.

"I understand, Emily," said String. "Don't worry. You don't have to say anything else."

Telloff decided that it was time to question me.

20

"So, Mr Stroke, what exactly happened? Did you know Emily before making the call?"

I sat myself down on a chair, trying to relax.

"I was in my bed, trying to get to sleep. I heard some voices – Emily and her dad – and heard sobbing and a door being shut. The dad's voice was slurred, from what I could hear. I got up, put some clothes on and went out into the corridor, where I met her. It's clear that her dad didn't want her back inside the flat, so I made sure that she had somewhere to be. I only saw her several times before, but we didn't interact then. It was just a matter of walking past each other. There. That's everything I know."

There wasn't really much for the policemen to ask about everything leading up to this. They decided that it would be best to arrest the dad – Charlie, by the way – on charges of child abuse and see how everything went from there. Knowing the justice system, I would have made a bet with Cain that Charlie would have been out in a few months, but betting on a situation like this wasn't funny or light-hearted.

Telloff and String insisted that Emily and I stayed in my place while they took care of Charlie. I just knew that he wouldn't go out without putting up some form of resistance. I told Emily to carry on watching *Ben 10* during the arrest.

I heard the police knocking on the door, and the faint sound of a drunken "Shut up… Go away…" and the response from Telloff and String that they were police only heightened his replies, becoming, "Fuck you! Fuck *off*! Leave me alone, you *pig bastards*!"

Even when told they would burst in if he didn't answer the door, he refused to do anything. A few seconds later, they straight-up kicked down the door. There was screaming from Charlie, with no sounds being heard from the police, save for the usual "You're under arrest" line.

And so, Charlie was arrested under charges of child abuse, especially when intoxicated. At the station, I was told to write down everything I knew about the incident, the standard police procedure. Such a procedure was something I admired police for; the one aspect of the justice system I actually liked, if somewhat mixed. Don't get me wrong, I have great respect for the police, but I have my suspicions on those who might be corrupt. At least the witness report gave a chance for one to tell the truth, though the downside to it was when complete dickheads falsify things. Yeah, if you haven't noticed, I find the justice system tricky. And full of shit, sometimes. But I digress.

After filling in my view of events, Charlie stood on trial for his abuse towards Emily. Speaking of her, a child therapist had lessons with her in order to help her out. She sometimes thought that she was doing bad things, hence the abuse, but she was okay after a few talks. To this day, she only very rarely has nightmares about her dad. Only very rarely. She still goes to therapy to get rid of them, but they don't seem to go. I had a talk with her a few weeks back about this; we've become very close friends.

No… no, no, no. I don't want you to get the wrong idea. See, a lot of time's passed since that incident. Only a couple. Thirty-four. Nothing big. She has a kid of her own now, a little girl named Scarlett. Meanwhile, I'm still looking the same I was since then. Then again, I've always been in my prime.

Here's the funny thing about Cain and I: we're thousands of years old.

But the ladies don't complain.

Chapter 3

The Start of Everything

Prehistoric Age

In the beginning, there was nothing. A great darkness. However, there were words being said, spoken in what felt like a booming voice, a distinct, commanding authority trying to let itself be known. And then everything came into being.

No, I'm not talking about the Bible.

The words were spoken in such a demanding way, yet at the same time, they were difficult to make out. They were faint. My mind tried to focus, but still nothing. Noises were heard, but they weren't in my head. They were elsewhere. Outside my mind.

I opened my eyes. The sky stared at me, like a peaceful light-blue ocean looking deep into my eyes, offering a mysterious nature to life. It was gorgeous. I had never seen anything like it… because this was the first time that I had seen anything.

It took a few seconds from staring at the sky for me to realise that I was somewhere. And for my mind to figure out that it was connected to something – a body. A head, some eyes, two arms, two legs, a chest, fingers, toes, elbows, knees, etc. A strange feeling. A very strange feeling.

I was lying on the ground, spread as if I was trying to sunbathe. I turned my head to the left, and I was met with brown dirt. Head to the right; more brown dirt. It was difficult trying to get to grips with a place you don't remember being in. So far, all there was was the sky and ground. Trying to come to terms with moving your body was weird. In the body of a fully-grown man, attempting to figure out what you look like was the black sheep of human mind-body relationships.

I didn't realise that I had light-coloured skin.

Nor that I had five toes and fingers.

Nor that my arms and legs were long and muscular.

Nor that I had nipples.

To this day, I am still fascinated as to the purpose of male nipples. I mean, I can understand the purpose of female nipples, but men? They just offer pain with the deadly nipple-cripple aka purple nurple aka whatever the hell you want to call it.

After waving my hand in front of my face as a means to associate my mind and how it can influence the movement of my body, I decided to get up. One arm planted its palm to the ground with fierce strength. Another arm and palm followed suit. Legs positioned the feet like with the palm. I then thrust my body upwards. Or at least, I tried. I hadn't yet got the hang of moving the main body. Gave it a couple of tries before getting used to it. Maybe ten attempts later, I was finally on my feet.

The surroundings were mainly trees, perhaps thirty, maybe forty feet tall. There was a lot of greenery; leaves and grass were by the hundreds. Looking up above, I saw just how huge the trees were. They were like brown, limbless giants, gods towering over everything (until the invention of skyscrapers, that is), proclaiming dominance and superiority over other life. I like to call them The Trees That Be Superior To Thee. I say it as such, in a singsong voice:

The Trees
That Be
Superior
To Thee

Great fun; never gets old.

They were spread out, allowing me to see the sky which I felt had an elegant beauty to it. Just seeing the sky from above, surrounded by trees, felt as if a child drew a circle, or any other shape for that matter, on a piece of paper, then took scissors and cut it out, leaving the paper with a hole in the middle.

These surroundings were spectacular. Amazing. Mysterious. Deadly?

I looked at myself after all this. Apparently, I was well-hung.

I just realised that I wasn't wearing anything. I *knew* it was a little cold for my liking. Then again, it was the first time that I had ever thought of 'cold'. What was 'cold'? Food? An emotion? An activity? In fact, what were any of them? But that soon didn't matter, as I felt familiarity and already-accessed knowledge of feelings and what things relating to the body and mind were.

But there was one thing I still didn't know. Something all that knowledge failed to provide. In my observations, a deep something wasn't quite there. Today, I still didn't know.

I traced my face with my hands. A face. But whose?

Who?

Who

Am

I?

I remember now, looking back, that those were my first words.

Back then, I reached out my arms to the sky, to the Trees That Be Superior To Thee, and yelled them out.

"*WHO... AM*

... I?"

That was in the Prehistoric Age. The age where things were 'primitive'.

I lived on, never knowing why I outlived so many people. I just did. That question plagued my head, so I made aliases to cover it.

Who am I?
Am I Human?
Am I a Supernatural Being?
Am I an Alien?
Am I a Monster?
Am I an Angel?
Am I a Demon?
Am I something entirely different?
Who?

I traced my hands of my face, trying to get some idea of what I looked like. The face seemed to be flat, though the cheekbones were prominent from what I could feel.

I couldn't just stand around in this forest. I had to go somewhere. Nowhere specific, just anywhere. A place where there might be other people, those who might know me, might attack me, might embrace me. With no sense of direction, I simply wondered around the forest, intent on finding people.

Perhaps there were people already in the area, with the Trees That Be Superior To Thee?

It was a possibility. A possibility that could be certain, or hand-waved. My mind was everywhere; while wanting to go somewhere different, I also wanted to see if someone might be around this terrain.

Left foot forward.
Left foot forward.
Rinse.

Right foot forward.
Right foot forward.
Repeat.

Walking for the first time was easier than getting onto my feet.

The same couldn't be said for dancing, though. That took me a few dozen millennia to sort out.

As I walked across the green paradise, I took notice of sounds. A chatter between unseen mammals. The bristling of branches. Wild screeches from equally wild brothers of nature. With every sound, I turned to whatever direction it came from, wondering what these beings could look like.

The smell of the place – almost like the scent of heaven. It felt nourishing, almost as if it was the richness of a finely-made meal in a restaurant. It was rather strong at first, though in a sense that strength helped me appreciate the environment more – the strength of it made it feel addictive to breathe in. I'm telling you now, you might not come across a smell like this in your entire life. Well, you could imagine it; imagining the beautiful smell of that forest could be just as good as actually being there.

But that smell was interrupted by more noise – this noise, however, was different from other cases. Grunting. More than just one entity. A pack. A pack of creatures hunting on foot?

I was scared. I feared that there might be something ready to jump at me. A pounce, a tackle, a hit. This could have happened at any time. Those things were getting closer. The grunts appeared to give way to mumbling – a conversation? – and I first realised that they were only so far away from my location. Perhaps they weren't going to kill me? Maybe they had just hunted some unknown prey and were celebrating a victory?

That's what happens when you have no memory and wake up in a jungle; you may just assume that anything loud may try to kill you. Good old annoying paranoia.

With my ears sharp, I tried to pinpoint their location. As they talked and talked, I found that they were to my left. I turned and carefully made sure that, in a slow manner, I didn't do anything sudden. I wanted to look at them.

And then one of my feet stepped on a large twig. The twig snapped.

Bugger.

The nearby creatures, who apparently heard that twig, burst through layers of leaves and plants. They were tall. Some were my height, others were bigger, while a few were a tad smaller. Hair hung loosely from their heads, some possessing mighty bundles of it on their faces (my mind gave me the word "beard"). They carried large sticks with sharp things at the top. They were wearing an assortment of furred clothes, which I had a faint idea of, for another unknown reason.

One bashed their stick across my face. I fell onto the ground with ease. The fellow who socked me raised his stick so that the weird sharp thing was pointing right at me.

Having only figured out what I looked like for a few minutes at the most, it came to my attention that these creatures must be the same kind of people as myself. Except, well, I was not as hairy-looking. Other people! Thank God! Or rather, these guys would be thinking that, while I appeared to be at the end of a lad's pokey-thing.

Words shuffled in my head; the big sticks were called spears; the sharp pokey-things themselves were spearheads. And then another word: hu-man.

Hu-man. Human. That was it – human. I was a human. These people were fellow humans. Aggressive humans, yes, but humans all the same.

Something clicked in my head, a sort of fuzzy feeling, as if I had been shaken back and forth many times. I thought to myself, "It's probably nothing". Surely it couldn't be related to the harm given to me by that one fellow?

The guy who was pointing the spear at me had a wild look in his eye (wait, he's a prehistoric man, so does that mean everyone back then had a wild-eyed look?).

He spoke to me in a language that I had trouble understanding. It wasn't a bunch of garbled roars and ape-like grunts, but instead a fairly intelligent string of words like how any of us talk today. I admit, I had trouble figuring out the context of his words as the fellow stared incredibly angrily at me.

But then I felt another 'click'. This one had the same feeling as the last one, but it appeared to have an influence on what was around me. I listened to the man's angry dialogue. Instantly, his words sounded different. That is to say, they remained the same as was said, but my mind created an odd overlap of his language and the same language that I spoke in earlier – it was a translation.

"*Rah me tosi agh yoh fo rartuk*! – You try to hunt us like creatures!"

I understood him! It was incredible! I wondered whether I would be able to talk in his language? I decided that I might as well go with the language that I had been thinking and speaking in, which sadly I no longer recall, having taken up multiple languages since then. There's the gist of it.

"No, no! I have not tried to kill you! I do not want to hurt you!" I shook my head in opposition to my up-and-close friend.

Unfortunately, this couldn't get through to him. He looked perplexed, like someone trying to find the answer to a very hard question. He replied:

"What do you say? You talk not like us. Are you a bad spirit who looks like a man? Talk!"

He shook his spear arm in rage, drawing it closer to my throat. I felt the pricking pain of the spearhead lightly pressing against my vocal cords.

There was confusion? How? I was simply talking to him. Then a thought struck me.

Oh. Wait a moment. His words are probably only translated for me, *so… while I know what he's saying, we don't speak the same language. He's just as confused as I am.*

Just then, another member of the tribe placed his hand against spear-buddy's spear-shoulder. This one appeared to have a scar on the left side of his face, and seemed to be slightly less muscular. He spoke in defiance:

"Hold, Ra-Ma! We do not know what he says – perhaps he is a man as well. He could be from another part of this plane, not knowing of spirits and demons."

Ra-Ma took his eyes off me and focused on the guy who I felt was making some sense of Ra-Ma's accusations. Once more, Ra-Ma's words were filled with hate.

"Toya, he is not a man! He is a spirit! He must be killed or else he will kill us all!"

Toya did not raise his voice in his next argument, but spoke calmly. "Brother, we only know he talks differently. We do not know if he will do that. If he had a death stick, I would see why you would think it, but look! He has no skins to cover himself, no long sticks, nor bones of dead creatures. You are rash, brother, so let us see if you are right or wrong by releasing him."

"Toya, I am right! Whenever have I been wrong? I have been hunting many years before your first hunt, so do not think that you are right and I am not!"

I was just wide-eyed and scared during this brotherly argument. Due to the whole throat-about-to-be-impaled thing, my breathing was naturally fast, taking in short breaths. So far, I was rooting for Toya on that day's edition of my favourite title for a game-show, 'Right or Wrong'. I wished that Ra-Ma would listen to reason; or rather, a reason that wasn't his smug 'I'm right and you're not' attitude.

"Listen to yourself, Ra-Ma. Even a hunter can be wrong; they think their prey take bait, but they may not. A hunter can be wrong in what they plan – this man very well may be a man, not a spirit. Brother, we are hunters that learn from mistakes – perhaps the gods have willed you to see that you may have made a mistake. Let him go."

Some fellow tribesmen argued for both sides. Somehow, possibly due to the primitive belief of evil spirits in human form, I think there might have been more Ra-Ma fans than Toya. They were yelling at each other like a bunch of football fans calling each other shit because of what team they support (closest comparison I could come up with, folks, and I don't even like the damn sport).

Ra-Ma put an end to this Jeremy Kyle/Jerry Springer arguing with a mighty, "*Quiet!*"

A part of me thought that I would end up with a handsome hole in my throat that would be small enough to pop a cigarette into. However, I could see something in Ra-Ma's eyes. They didn't seem to be filled with a savage anger – no, instead it was replaced by self-doubt, that one thing that stops us from being overconfident pricks. Slowly, the pressure of his spear against my throat loosened as he drew it back. He stood up straight as he glared at me. He turned to his fellow brothers-in-arms.

"I have taken in Toya's words and have thought over the matter. This – *man* – may not be a spirit. Perhaps I *am* wrong."

Then Ra-Ma turned to face me again.

"If you know what I say, then stand."

Of course, I did know what he said, and subsequently took no time getting to my feet. I had to wipe away or brush aside all the mud and dirt that covered the back of my body. That wasn't pleasant.

Toya spoke to me. "Are you a hunter?"

Nope. Since I couldn't just say it, I shook my head with hope that they got the message. Luckily, they got it straight away.

"Are you not able to speak our way by any means?"

I shook my head.

Ra-Ma had some sort of idea. He talked in a voice that wanted an answer quickly, but not *too* quickly.

"You do not wish to attack us?"

Shook my head.

Toya pointed out the obvious: "Brother, if he is not a warrior, with no long stick, then he would not wish to kill us. It is what I have been saying."

Ra-Ma realised the stupidity of his question with a blush. Toya took over the interrogation (of sorts) as before.

"Do you have a home, or a tribe?"

Not a clue. Cue head shaking.

Toya raised a rather life-changing question for me.

"To survive, you must be a hunter, to provide for others and to prove yourself to those at home. Do you wish to be a member of our tribe?"

I was very much taken aback by this. I was instantly offered a place to stay in. Incredible! That was the first time humanity gave me a welcome. It felt great. I nodded in answer to Toya. Ra-Ma slapped a hand on my shoulder – it hurt – and had a sense of confidence or delight about him.

"Then we will make a hunter of you, just wait! You will become a great warrior... not as great as me, but a warrior nonetheless. We will welcome you to the others of our tribe. Do you have a name?"

I shook my head once more.

"Then we will think of a name for you when we go to our tribe. Come, fellow hunters, let us go."

As so, I followed my new kinsmen, unsure of what would happen, or of what my name would be. But I knew one thing – I now had a family.

*

Describing how this language-translation thing works is odd. Despite having been exposed to it for centuries, trying to work out the exact science behind it was a mystery. Okay, let's try and look at it with an analogy. It's sort of like watching a foreign movie and its dub at the same time.

Can I lend a hand?

No, Cain.

But WHY?

Because God knows how you'll try to describe it.

Dude! Let me do this, man! I can SO help make everyone understand things better. WAY better than YOU, Mr David Sir.

I feel that you shouldn't have used capitals to enforce the words you're saying. You should have gone with italics. You're like an actor who enjoys over-acting his lines.

YES.

Wait, is that "YES, I should have gone with *italics*," or "YES, I OVER-ACT"?

...YES.

Okay, Cain, I give up. Try to explain it to the readers.

Thanks, Dave!

Righty-o, folks, here we go.

So when we hear whatever it is people are saying, like the French and the Russians and the Celtic and the French and the Chinese and the Korean and the French and the Japanese and the German and the French, we hear it as they would always say it, like, normally, but our head is somehow able to understand what they're sayin' as if they're talkin' to us in the language we go for, so we hear them as they would totally say it but we can also hear them talkin' to us as if they're not speakin' in their actual language, like when there's a dude talking' to us in French.

MAYBE there's like some kind o' filter in our head that takes in the language and filters it for us but also retainin' the real language.

No, wait. Might not make sense.

Okay, I guess before we got amnesia, someone stuck a Babel fish up our ear and later Douglas Adams discovered one and used it in those books o' his.

There, all done. That was easy.

For you, yes. For some of the readers, no.

Hey! I can't help it if it's so goddamn confusin'!

Look, some things are best not explained. This is just something that I suppose should be laid to rest. Regardless, I was given a home by these primitive people. Things were... a bit difficult in terms of communication. Given how they couldn't understand me to begin with, it was tough at first, but we got on well. It's frustrating to try and not talk when you can but can't be understood. Kind of like going on holiday.

*

Being introduced to your new housemates or neighbours can be quite awkward. Everyone's staring at you, you looking at them nervously. Some were looking at me with fear; understandable, as my skin was pretty pale compared to their somewhat tanned skin. Kids were gawking at me in a 'look mummy, there's a weird funny man over there!' fixation.

The mothers placed an arm over their children to make sure that they dare not move. The tribe's home area featured an assortment of wood being used to create very crude houses; they had some kind of shape, rough around the edges, small enough to be seen by the modern eye as particularly small cabins. Inside each 'house' lay many a set of animal skins, used by the people as a means to blanket themselves.

I was being guided by my new friends, Toya, Ra-Ma and their buddies, all having decided to just accept me as a 'brother'.

"Do not be afraid," said Toya. He gave me an assuring smile, which felt nice; I felt that he was going to be a very close companion.

Ra-Ma helped the reassurance. "This the first time any of us have come across a new person such as you. Your skin is too light for a person who has lived in this forest. I am troubled by this too, but fear not. We will persuade the elders of the tribe that you can be with us."

Well, that would be fair, wouldn't it? Ask the old fellas about this, yay or nay, then live with the results unless you want to have another go with it. First impressions are important – some might feel good about something/someone and accept them, or feel pissed off and want to kill them.

The elders sat outside a 'house', amongst a collection of children who had been asking about the times when the old were young, and when the young became hunters before being old and teaching the new generation. The old fellas were made up of three; two men and a woman. All of their faces were creased like scrunched up paper balls, and their hair grey with white strands running through, the men's thin while woman's reached down to her back. In their old eyes, one could see that they were sharp, the same kind of strength that had surely carried them forward in their youths.

We stopped in front of the elders and their young audience. Ra-Ma represented our group in briefing the ancients of my coming here.

"Old Ones, we have found a person on one of our hunts. He stands before us, as you see. His skin is of the colour the young have before the light from above blesses them with a new colour."

The female Old One observed my features, squinting as she did, and asked, "Does he speak like us?"

"No, he does not, Old One," answered Toya, "yet he can understand us. He has no home, no tribe, and is not a hunter. That is why he is here; we wish that you, great Old Ones, will allow him to stay with us and pursue a life surrounded by others."

The leaders faced each other. They whispered in their ears, so softly that even the children near them could not hear. It made us wonder what they were saying. Some ten seconds after a good day's work of mysterious whispers (*mysters?*), one of the male old fellas gave the much-anticipated answer.

"It is accepted. Lone one, you may stay here if you wish. You will become part of our tribe if it is what you desire. Is it so?"

In a weird combination of nervousness and stoic expression, I nodded.

"Very well," said the other old man. "We will begin the marking ceremony. Only then will you be a part of our tribe. The ceremony will be at night. Until then, you may stay with Ra-Ma and Toya. May Those From Above grant you a good life."

Ra-Ma and Toya said, "We thank you, Old Ones."

Trying to understand a collection of words in learning their language meant that it would be tough figuring out

35

which word is what. However, in this case, there was a sentence that I could say. While I understood that they were thanking their elders, what they were actually saying was "Shja ruk no rutta ip, Et Quo Tow."

I too said, "We thank you, Old Ones", although it was somewhat disjointed.

"Shja ruk… no rutta ip… Et Quo Tow."

Everyone stared at me in disbelief. Here I was, a lonely person with the inability to communicate with them properly, clearly speaking in their language. I had some rough idea of what they would say.

Toya was the first to talk to me: "You… spoke our words."

I nodded.

Ra-Ma had a slight hint of anger in him: "But you told us you could not."

Toya stepped in to prevent Ra-Ma from doing something stupid.

"Old Ones, as he knows what we say, he can talk like us. Surely if he could understand us, then he is able to talk back."

The woman of the elders spoke. "It is alright, Toya. You need not worry. Our new friend may show more surprises than his ways to speak two kinds of words. You may all go to your partners. Dismiss, tribesmen."

As I had no one else to go with, I continued to follow the brothers, who separated from their fellow hunters.

"Come, friend," said Toya in a compassionate mentor tone. "We will introduce you to our family."

I heard a young boy shout out Toya and Ra-Ma's names in excitement. At first, I wondered where the child was, but the matter was soon cleared when I saw him speeding towards us like a bullet. Zoom! He was carrying a small hunting stick with him, though it was easy to see that he had not 'graduated' into becoming a proper hunter, as it was just a plain old long stick, and nothing more.

"Brothers! You have come back!"

The kid hugged his older siblings. Toya and Ra-Ma must have looked roughly in their late teen/early adult years, while their little bro could have been no more than twelve or thirteen. Toya and Ra-Ma smiled as they embraced him. As they separated, Toya placed a hand on my shoulder as he introduced me.

"Sha-yo, this is a man who we found in the midst of our hunt. None know who he is, including himself, so he will become a fellow member of our tribe."

The boy, Sha-yo, stared at me nervously. He said about five seconds later, "Hello, I am Sha-yo."

In response, I just said, "Hello, I am... new."

The lil' fella asked, "Why do you have bright skin?"

"I... haven't been in the sun for long. The... sun hasn't blessed me with skin like yours."

"Are you going to be a hunter?"

"Yes, Sha-yo, I'll be alongside your brothers, providing for everyone."

Ra-Ma got in the way of chit-chat: "Sha-yo, go to Mother, she always smiles when seeing you."

Sha-yo smiled with that knowledge. "Yes, big brother, I will!" And off he ran, zooming around like an excited bird!

I was kind of confused with Ra-Ma decision for Sha-yo to go to their mum – weren't we going to meet the family?

"Ra-Ma, I thought we were going to see your family regardless? Why send him away to your mother?"

Ra-Ma placed himself near my ear – it was one of those situations where it feels uncomfortable, like personal space being demolished by a sledgehammer. He spoke aloud, so I wanted him to move his head back. While Toya was a naturally soft-spoken person, the same couldn't be said for Ra-Ma; it was like having a megaphone near you.

"Well, you see, friend, Mother always helps out fixing the skins that we wear. As you can see, we're wearing the skin of the creatures we've slain. It is something women do till darkness approaches, same with us men hunting. The rest of our family stay together, and, if you do not know, our tribe supports a lot in one family. You will see."

Give or take an unnecessary description of how long we walked and we were where Toya, Ra-Ma and Sha-yo's remaining family rested. There wasn't a small collection of relatives; two aunts, three uncles, five cousins ranging between ten and sixteen, and two teenage sisters.

Needless to say, there was quite a lot of talking. We were all active in getting to know each other – okay, me getting to know them. Still, excitement and friendliness fluttered everywhere. It just made me happier to know that I would soon be considered something of a family member to those in the tribe. Smiles cropped up on everyone's faces.

But in time, those moments of joy would disappear.

*

The ceremony for my acceptance started. A dark sky, with the absence of the sun, allowed the moon to conquer the view. The tribe were circled around a fairly large fire, which flickered in every direction like an angry animal observing its surroundings. I sat between Toya and Ra-Ma, wondering how the ceremony would occur and what exactly would be involved. The elders were prominent in the circle, all beside each other. They stood while everyone else were sitting, warranting silence and wonder. One of the male Old Ones was the first to address the people.

"Tonight, we have gathered around the flames so that a new hunter can be born. *This person…*"

He dramatically pointed at me. Heads turned, as if they just realised that I was among them. Naturally, I was glancing at all the faces that went, 'This is the guy who will be with us? Get real!'

"… Though you may be new to our tribe, you show willingness to *hunt* like the others, to *work*, to *provide*, and above all, show the *skills* of a *protector* towards those who wish to *attack* us." He stopped giving me the pointing finger (or as Cain likes to call it, the Whodunnit Youdunnit finger point) and his fellow elder, the second bloke, carried off where the first one had very hammily exited.

"For you to join us, you must first extend your arm. Please rise."

I stood up, thinking, 'Let me guess, they'll paint my hand or arm or something?' I took out my arm, like I was trying to reach out to the flames.

The first male and the female Old Ones moved towards me and grabbed my arm, one hand on the forearm, and another past the elbow, almost as if they were ensuring it was immobilised.

The currently-talkative elder took something from the ground...a rock. No, sorry, let's include another word – a *sharp* rock. It was only when he brought the rock towards the fire that I realised that it was *fucking sharp*. I had no idea what to expect; would he stab me all the way from my fingers to my shoulder in one long line? Or would he attempt to penetrate my palm cleanly like in Stephen King's *Thinner* (Cain and I love it; both the book and the film)?

The elder spoke in a commanding voice: "Now you must turn your hand so that your palm faces the sky."

I did as he requested. The old fellas grabbing my arm had a tight grip (well, as tight as you would be when in your sixties or seventies), and the short movement of my palm did not shift their hands.

The Old One with the rock came up to me and lightly grasped my thumb. He carefully pricked the ball of it, drawing some blood. It was slightly painful, so I winced and gasped a little in pain. Bad enough that he had to prick my thumb, he had to do the same with every digit on my hand. Finally, the same was done to the centre of my palm.

"There. Now all that is needed is to offer your blood to the flames."

The arm-grabbers released me so as to complete the initiation. My hand had now become a small fleshy water spring. Several tiny streams flourished. I placed my hand above the fire, and tipped it, waiting for the 'streams' to say goodbye and go to a vacation to a sort of mini-sun.

Drip drip drip drip drip drip drip drip drip drip …

It was bloody slow. The Old Ones were watching to see if enough had been 'sacrificed'. After experiencing what felt like an eternity, the Old Woman called out.

"Enough, enough. You have given much inner water to the flames. The fire appears to have accepted the offer."

She smiled, meaning that she either wanted me to be with them… or she wanted me to be with her. I was kind of creeped out by the thought of the latter. In any case, I smiled back at her, letting her know I was happy to join them.

The hammy Old Man who started the event asked me what I would like to be called. Such a difficult task when you don't have much experience with names. But then that experience was filled with a burst of information in my head, coming to me like a vibration in my brain. In my head, I heard names coming from bodiless voices.

"… Oi, Arnold, whatcha doin'…"

"… Cheers for the lift, Michael…"

"… Mr Evans, when I ask you a question, I expect an answer…"

"… Mary told me the other day that I…"

"… Hi! Claire, Mikki, what are you doing here…"

"… Hey there, kids, I'm Captain Matt…"

So many names, an endless ocean of them. The pain was increasing; I felt like my head was going to explode. My eyes were fluttering as the names kept coming and coming and coming… and… and…

I collapsed. I just fell from the shock. When I came to, Ra-Ma and Toya were looking at me, to check to see if I was okay. The countless names had stopped hitting me hard and fast. No pain, just a mild fuzziness from the whole thing. People were asking things like, "Is he dead?" or "If he's a goner, can I use his blood for hunter face marks? I'm too scared to use my own."

Toya asked how I was – my reply was essentially, "Everything's alright, just felt a bit dizzy." People thought that the blood-lending drained away some of my energy. These memories of peoples' names made me wonder what I could have been doing before I awoke among The Trees That Be Superior To Thee. Despite all that I could make out from these echoes, there was no trace of familiarity in them. I firmly remember my thoughts at the time, so confused, scared and curious, succeeding in providing me so many more questions. *What the hell am I? Where did I come from? Who... who were all those people I heard? Am I losing my mind?*

But now was not the time. Another day for those questions. I had asked myself those kinds of questions too many times in one day and already it was beginning to get very old very fast.

"Every... everyone, I have thought of a name for myself."

I got on my feet while rubbing the temples of my head. Time for the dramatic announcement.

"My name is..."

Cough. Clear throat. Inhale. Exhale.

I was new to everything. I was fresh out of the woods. I was the latest member of the tribe. I was...

"... Raanan."

No one had ever heard of that name before. A hand from the Old Woman firmly caressed my cheek.

Dude, that is SO not the right way to describe it.

Okay, 'caressed' was not the right word to use. It melds in with that shuddering thought involving her a minute ago. Let's replace that with 'explored'. 'Explored' sounds alright.

She proudly exclaimed, "Your name is Raanan, and you are a part of our clan! Be proud, child, for a long life is ahead of you!"

I was a brother of the tribe! I had something to look forward to! A family of sorts awaited to embrace me.

The elders faced every 'family' member with celebration on their minds. The Big Three practically said the same thing. To boil it down:

"We have a new tribesman in our home. Come, we must celebrate this news! Let us show our joy by dancing among the flames."

And, boy, did we dance the night away. Everyone was lively, filled with enough energy to run a hundred miles. Some danced in front of the flames to stand out, while others barely attempted to put any effort into it, giving off a stiff and lifeless performance. But ultimately, we all had a good time. A portion of us sat back and enjoyed the night, looking forward to tomorrow.

My hand was still stinging at the centre, and the same went for the fingers. Any blood had been wiped away by a small piece of clothing, about the size of a handkerchief; probably meant for instances like this.

A nice young woman was tending to the clean-up. She looked roughly in her early twenties. She gave me 'the look' two or three times. Was I really that attractive? I'm pretty average-looking, nothing along the lines of 'Sexiest Man of the Tribe'. Best guess, judging by physical appearance, I appear to be in my early thirties. Was it some kind of appeal towards a slightly-older fellow, or what?

I think she'd bang any sexy-lookin' dude. I got longer hair than Davey-boy, and that counts as some kinda sex appeal, I guess.

Oh, who am I kidding? That's not important. What's important was everyone having a new buddy joining them and enjoying the news. I had a place to live in, people to know and befriend, faces to see smile and laugh with; the creation of a new past for myself while the old one eluded me.

Anything to make me feel homely, perhaps.

Soon, I would participate in my first hunt. We were expecting good things to come out of it. Well, *things* would come out of it. *Certain* things.

42

Chapter 4

Scarlett

<u>2047</u>

The Prehistoric Age always makes me look back at how long we've lived. In some ways, I'm glad we've experienced the growth of humanity and its accomplishments, as it shows how a species can go from primitive to incredibly advanced. One minute we're in the 1990s using a big old block of a mobile phone, and in the next we're sporting an iPhone. The other side to it is that I grow bored and stressed with our apparent immortality.

For too long, I've seen friends and loved ones die, and there are times when I think to myself, "Why can't I just die now today?" Believe me when I say that walking through so many countless years is no cake walk. I'm not saying that I want to be a loner forever; on occasions I could do with a friend, but I have to leave them after so many years so that they can forget about me and carry on living. That, and avoid them asking why a guy like me appears to suffer from what I like to call 'Paused Youth Syndrome'.

Cain is a bit of a prick at times, though he's also the only guy who's been keeping me company for centuries. Having an alter ego can do wonders for the mind. Example: we both like the same type of trench coat (full-length), but the split comes down to colour. I like red and he prefers black. The same goes for the nice three-corner hats and Stetsons we wear with it.

Black is awesome! Think about it – Batman wears black to intimidate, and I really like scarin' the crap outta criminals! Plus, it gives me a Gothic look, like Dracula – he's old and had black on, yet had quite a sexy charm to him. Me + Black = Sexy Beasty.

Even after chatting to him for forever, we still didn't know why the changes over our body – the fangs, long hair and claws – occurred. Cain didn't mind, as he enjoyed having a more animalistic look. Whatever floats your boat, I guess.

In tune of people and our long-lived nature, some didn't have to remain ignorant of it. They could go to the grave with the knowledge that immortality isn't quite fictional after all. Especially when they keep trying to ask you over and over why you look the same despite them seeing you years ago as a kid. One such person was about to come round ours for dinner, in the town of Chelnsworth.

The house in which Cain and I had spent the last decade in wasn't big or small, just your average two-floor, three-bedroom place quietly blending into the rest of the cul-de-sac of Hover's Road. It was well into the evening, and I was studying volume six of 'The Greatest Cultures Never Known: An Examination of the Remnants of Lost Civilisations', the past driving me to inspect page after page. 'I wonder what happened to them,' I would always ask myself. Too bad I didn't stay long enough to learn anything distinctive about my first 'family', that would've helped me loads. Eventually, I closed the thick leather-bound book in defeat and put it back on the large shelf in the living room, squeezed between the bulging rows of all the other books that made up my obsession.

The doorbell rang three times. I removed myself from the sofa, dressed in some jeans and a smart black shirt, and made my way to the front door. Our two special guests had arrived. The clicking of sharp Italian heels across the wooden floorboards made the walk seem like someone was tapping at the sound of my footsteps. A right hand with the mind of a cleaner came alive and desperately brushed my rather slicked back hair. Cain must have done it.

"Cain, did you just brush my hair?"

'Yeah, you gotta look good for your guests, Mr Dashin'!'

I opened the door with much excitement. It swung towards me as fast as lightning. Right in front of me stood two women; Emily and her daughter, Scarlett. Emily was now in her early forties, and her beauty had not vanished. A couple of faint lines were scattered over her face, but that didn't matter in my opinion. She was a tad thin, but otherwise she was in good shape. In some circles, women would be envious. Emily was 5'8", about two inches below me. Black earrings waved from her ears, barely noticeable from her shoulder-length hair. She wore a small black jacket that worked well with a beige shoulder bag across the shoulders.

With Scarlett, she looked a whole other story. The kid was about seventeen, and her hair was dyed so that it matched her namesake, with a big ponytail hanging out. She had those big hoop earrings that look big enough for you to try and slip your hand through them. Never really understood those ones.

Her outfit? Black, tight jeans and a short-sleeved shirt that had a picture of an anime girl on it, saying, 'The name's May. Anne May.' That was pretty funny.

Three years ago, Emily's husband, Trevor Kingsley, decided to divorce himself from Emily. From what I understand, Trevor had felt that he no longer loved her. The divorce was rough on the ladies; I was there to comfort them. Emily was grateful for my help, and since then, our friendship became stronger. Scarlett didn't know how she felt about her father and stuck by her mother through it all; they had needed each other so much and were grateful for it.

As for Trevor, a matter of custody was settled so that Scarlett could see him every weekend. Seems sort of fair to me. I don't hate Trevor, as he wasn't being a prick over the whole thing. He was a good enough man, and love isn't exactly limitless, as experience has taught me. The guy just realised that his feelings for his wife weren't as strong as what they once were. Couple counselling did bugger all – in life, things just happen.

"Oh, hey there, ladies," I said in a burst of over-the-top politeness.

Emily gave a smile, that of a good old friend's. "Hi, David! Sorry we're late; we sat down watching some telly, got distracted."

"Hi, Mr Short," Scarlett said with a smile, lips coated in bright red lipstick. Long, fake, red fingernails stuck out, as I noted when we shook hands rather nervously.

"Hi, Scarlett. Please, just call me David. I mean, your mum's called me it dozens of times when you were around, so you might as well follow on. If not, I'll slap a piece of paper with my name onto my forehead, see how it goes." I was aiming for a joke. Did it work?

The kid giggled. Yep, it was a success – well, just about. If anything, I realised that it barely looked like a joke, but oh well.

"Come on in, ladies." I stepped back, and they entered. A nice introduction is all part of proper formality.

"You want me to take your jacket, Emily?"

She took it off while she answered, "Oh, yes, please."

It took up a nice place on my coat rack, between my red trench coat and Cain's black one. Scarlett just stood there and watched me, the Master of the Coat Rack, handle her mum's jacket like someone observing a person making a fine wine.

We sat in the living room – two long black sofas dominated the place as if they were a pair of tough guys. A fuzzy-looking red carpet blanketed the cold floor boards, and a creepily long, thin lamp glowed in a corner. Emily and Scarlett sat on one sofa, and I on the other. The mother and daughter were right next to each other – it was cute.

"So," I started off, "you've been okay?" I didn't really aim it at any of them specifically.

Scarlett answered in a shy manner. "Uh, yeah, we've been doing fine, Mr... I mean, David."

Her mum carried on for her. "We've been with my cousins for the last few days. Boring for her, obviously. How are you, David? Has anything exciting cropped up?"

"Um…" Hmmm, exciting? A tough question. Cain opted an answer while I thought it over.

'Davey, tell her about what happened yesterday, when we fought those bank robbers with a bread stick and a fish!'

No, I didn't want to tell her about that. Yet. That would be used for dinner talk. The answer should be something a bit more casual for conversation.

"… I got a bit of leg work yesterday."

Yesterday – I ran after some low-life gangster in the alleys. It was energetic but short. When the distance between us was almost non-existent, I lunged at him, holding him to the ground while I asked him to show me where his boss and other scummy co-workers were meeting tonight. What followed after that was a one-sided ass-kicking with gun play, and a call to the police to arrest them. Good day.

"Well, I've gotta keep fit somehow."

"David, in all the years we've known each other, I've never seen you out of shape."

"I know – I just thought, 'Why not?' Do you want any drinks, by the way? I've got some wine for us, and some Diet Coke and that for Scarlett. Want a drink, Scarlett?"

Scarlett requested a Diet Coke. Nowadays the drinking age was seventeen, not eighteen (God knows why), yet that wasn't of any interest to Scarlett. Her birthday was four months ago, and she only had two alcoholic drinks, and nothing else following that. Drinking wasn't something she wished to indulge in. Stuff like Coke and Fanta were okay – they were the nearest thing to alcohol, in her opinion.

In the kitchen, a nice wine had been selected, made in 2016. With the taste, 2016 was a good year. With the memory of what happened that year, it wasn't.

The three (or four, rather) of us sat on the sofas chatting away, not much going on in the Importance Department. As per Emily's suggestion a few days ago, I'd gone with Chinese for dinner, shop-bought and microwaveable. Ten minutes after getting out the drinks, the food was served. Three lots of rice, noodles, prawn toast and chips went 'PING' and were laid out on beautiful decorative plates.

Now that dinner was ready, everyone tucked in at the dinner table in what was a rather compact dining room. The Chinese was okay, good enough for dinner. The conversation started to turn to Scarlett wanting to know a bit more of me.

"David, I just want to know, um, since I've never really known much about you... how did you and my mum meet? Exactly, I mean?"

Emily and I looked at each other. Our eyes were locked, as if we were sending each other telepathic messages. I can imagine why Emily hadn't filled the kid in on things. The 'I saved your mum when she was little' story doesn't work well when you look a good deal younger than the woman in question. No, Scarlett was referring to something else, something that was more believable... in a way.

At the time, I had no knowledge of what it was that Emily had informed her. So, in a moment of similar inquiry with the teen, I felt like asking her.

"What do you mean, 'exactly', Scarlett?"

"Mum's only told me that you two met at university. I wanna go there, see how I can make films. So, what, did you both study the same thing?"

I sighed. Couldn't her mother have thought of something beforehand? I was thinking of telling the girl a variation of the truth – kind of a half-truth. Emily actually covered it before a word could come out of my mouth.

"Okay, I'll tell you. Back in my second year there, there was this guy that David was chasing after, a grubby-looking fella who had stolen something. He took this ancient container that belonged to a friend of David's, or something like that. I got out of a pub when he ran past me and David yelled for someone to stop him."

"What did you do, Mum?"

I answered in Emily's place. "She ran after him, I saw what she was doing, and made sure that I had my eye on her."

"So I tackled the guy to the ground and grabbed him by the arms so that he couldn't try to hit me."

Curiosity struck Scarlett. "But what about that container? Didn't it break when he fell?"

I had this covered. "He stored it in a backpack, Scarlett."

"*Oh…*"

Her mum resumed. "So, David came up to me and helped me restrain him, and then we sent him over to the police. That container went back to Dave's friend, and I was thanked for apprehending him. David seemed so sweet when he thanked me. He said that he owed one, and that if I was in any trouble, he could help me out."

"Did you live near the uni, David…?"

"Yup, I certainly did. Gave her my address and number, and we soon became mates. We were even on Facebook."

Scarlett looked perplexed as she faced her mum. "Mum, isn't Facebook that chat site?"

Oh yeah. I keep forgetting that Facebook got terminated twelve years ago. My memory's never good with remembering stuff like that, especially when you've been living too long here, there and… I think just about everywhere.

The mother and daughter had a small chat about Facebook, while I just sat there and ate my noodles, watching them. It was like observing a one-teacher, one-student history class.

The telly provided some entertainment, barring dinner talk. Not a lot of good stuff was on, save for a movie or two that the three of us labelled 'So Bad It's Good'. Game shows in 2047 hadn't really changed a lot. On the other hand, technology by this year had changed dramatically compared to thirty-four years ago.

I suppose I should talk about 2047 tech. There were free-thinking androids taking part in society, like working at bars; stronger batteries; cars were able to fly, but only up to about 10 feet. Some idiots were wishing that cars could fly higher, but only time would tell if that was possible. And then there's …

How about guns? I'LL tell you, and boy, you'll be wishin' that you got your hands on 'em! First, there're handguns called Dividers that are connected to each other by a long thin attachment thingy by the bottom of the magazine. The attachment made 'em look like gun nun chucks… gun-chucks. There are bullets in it, with a block on the inside so both guns have the same number of bullets. You can twirl the guns around and go BANG BANG BANG BANG BANG a dozen times! It's AWESOME! And then there's …

… thanks for the interruption, Cain. Now that that's out of the way, time to resume how the night went on. After the telly, nothing. Three hours since they arrived, Emily and Scarlett left my house to make their journey to their own. As the front door shut and I saw them drive off, Cain took over our body for his share of activity.

I felt my messy hair an' at first figured that it was kinda greasy. Nope, it was just hair gel. A newly-clawed hand brushed off some rice that was on my/his/our shirt. Personal pronouns for stuff like this is a pain. I felt up my sexy figure, specifically my pecs. Or is it his pecs? Or our pecs? Whatever.

One thing struck my mind – a drink. Determination made me wonder where some wine was. Then ye olde memory struck – the dinner table. I made my way to the table and carelessly, loudly gulped down every drop of the red, gorgeous stuff. Delicious! It looked like blood. Probably one of the reasons it's one o' my fave drinks. I was desperate for another bottle.

"Hey, Davey-boy, where're the other bottles at?"

'In the kitchen, Cain. I thought you'd remember, since you've been looking through my eyes in-and-out for the last few hours. Come to think of it, what *were* you doing while I was having dinner?'

The bastard got me thinkin' about that. I stared absent-mindedly at the empty wine bottle as I made my way to the kitchen. David didn't know what was goin' through my head, cuz *nothin'* was.

"… thinkin' o' porn."

I heard sarcasm in his reply. 'Oh gee, what a surprise. Nice to see you never check out anything that gets you thinking.'

"Hey, porn does get me thinkin'. Okay, about their tits and asses, but hey, it's something."

I felt like worshippin' the wine box that sat on the work surface. One bottle was worthy o' my attention. An unopened brew from 2025 made a tiny thud on the kitchen surface. Off went the cover, an' hello mister cork. How to get the cork off? Given my little finger-blades, the idea popped to use one of them to easily remove it. Fuck the corkscrew, it was my time to shine! My right hand held the bottle down while a left finger slowly went into the wooden bastard… slowly… slowly… fuckin' slowly.

This wasn't doin' anythin' for me. Mr David Man rang in my head to give a word of advice. Literally. He used our memory of the sound of a phone call to get my attention. We can do stuff like that. In return I took our mobile out o' our jeans an' answered it.

"Yello?"

'Cain, just take it out with your hands. This isn't a bomb disposal operation, for god's sake.'

"Oh hi, David. Nice for you to help me out from only a phone call away."

'Just open it already. Seriously, it's like seeing someone reading *The Divine Comedy* in slow-motion.'

"Okey-dokey, man, I'll do it. Well, call ya back when everything's successful."

I put the phone down an' firmly held the cork. Things were tense in preparin' for this. Like at that point in movies when the good guy has to turn off the bomb by cuttin' the red wire. A countdown would work with getting the little git out.

One…

… Two…

… Three!

POP!

The cork flew out of my hands like a missile, ricochetin' all over the place. Maybe I used a bit too much of the old muscle. But anyway – yay, job done! A thought struck me.

After guzzlin' this down, where should I go out?

An' then it hit me. The cork, not the answer. Right at the back of the head, too. I fell onto the hard floor, rubbin' a bruise that was startin' to bloom into a prominent lump.

"Ahh! Shit shit shit shit shit shit shit…! Note to self: corks can be painful." Got myself to my feet with a bit of effort. David had to wisecrack, the know-it-all smartass.

'Well, since you've got a taste of that, I'm thinking that you'll want to purchase a popgun sometime soon. Could be useful, you know – I got the idea at the back of my head.'

Fuckin' wit. I countered it with my own. "Thanks for the suggestion, Dave, but I think that mini-assault gave me a headache; I'm hearin' this annoyin' voice who sounds just like you, and he ain't funny."

'Oh, so you've just realised what your voice is like? Took you a couple of centuries to hear yourself.'

"… sometimes, I really fuckin' hate you, David."

Oh, what to do? Hmm… oh wait, there's a light bulb flashin' above my head! A stroll about town, head towards The Green Goose, a good pub. Sometimes filled with assholes if you're lucky. I was wishin' it – startin' a fight with a bearded fella with muscles like barrels, a great brawl with smashed tables, glass all over the floor.'

In the meantime, I sat down in the livin' room and drank away. Nothin' good on. The image of that kid, Scarlett, popped in my head. And then Davey talked.

'What did you think of tonight, Cain?'

"Alright, I guess."

'Did you notice that Scarlett was shy at times?'

"Oh, really? Didn't notice that. Liked her shirt, though."

'It was weird how Emily never came up with some kind of story to tell Scarlett about how we met. Still, it's more believable than what really did happen.'

"Tell me about it. Nearly everythin' we've been through deserves a half-lie. Livin' long's got its probs; we see Emily as a kid, then we see her as a late teen, then she's got a kid of her own. Awkward, ain't it?"

'Yup. Scarlett's turned out well. Emily's always told us how nice she is. We've gotta thank Trevor and Emily bringing her up the right way. I hope she gets on well in uni just like her mum. Oh, and I picked up on your thoughts of going to The Green Goose. Let me tell you something - don't try and get into a fight. Promise me that. Just go to the pub, have a drink with a packet of crisps or the like, and head home. Any time when you try and start a fight, I'll put a stop to it.'

"Okay, 'Dad', I won't. I'll be a good boy, you have my word. Scout's honour. Now let me finish this bottle in peace so I can go to the place shit-faced." Gulp. Gulp. Hiccup. Gulp. Picked up the keys. P-put the black trench coat on … on. Grabbed the keys. Hiccup. Walked to the door. Open sesame. Hiccup. Walked out. Ssssslammed door. I felt pretty damn merry, a tad red-faced. Boy, I really wanted to enjoy tonight.

I suppose you want to know what exactly the circumstances were behind the reunion between me and Emily. Trust me, it's quite a thing.

Chapter 5

Hell of a Weird Reunion

<u>2025</u>

Doing odd jobs for mates isn't always easy. You'd think they'd be nothing serious, but there can be the challenge in one or two places.

In this instance in late January 2025, I was contacted by a friend of mine from America, Fred Venus. His nickname is 'Dead Fred' because of his occupation, which was collecting and selling mystical items that date back to centuries, formerly belonging to some ancient civilisations. He owned a shop, Dead Fred's Amazingly Ancient Artefacts, in New York.

We became friends in 2019 when one of Fred's artefacts, a seven-hundred-year-old pot from China, turned out to contain a large lizard demon. The reptilian wraith was going to chop him down with a great big axe that you'd have to wield with two arms. Luckily, I happened to be wandering around and kicked its scaly arse until the pot was destroyed, where its connection to the material world was severed, resulting in bye-bye, Mr Lizzie.

Over the past six years, I had to help solve four cases of supernatural collector's items. It's not some bizarre thing that happens to me one day per year; I get caught into stuff like this all the time.

Fred was a great guy, a real character. He was a third-generation Haitian-American, and felt better to live in America than Haiti (dunno why; maybe he had a bad experience there). I remember, he rang up sounding panicky. It felt a little bit like a scene typed up in a film. It was still morning when the call buzzed through my ears.

Rrrringgggg. Rrrringgggg. Rrrri—

"… mmm… hello…?" I asked drowsily, having just woken up.

Fred's voice burst out of the phone, speaking as rapidly as his mouth could allow. I was amazed I could hear everything he said.

"DavidIneedyoutofindsomebodyformeit'sreallyfuckin'important!"

"Whoa, whoa, Freddy, calm down a sec. What's this all about?"

The sound of his heavy breathing dominated my ear for a few seconds while he calmed down. "Sorry, Dave. It's just that… well, I think we're in some deep shit, and you might be the only one to sort it out."

"Okay, so in what level of 'deep shit' are we in? Is it 'the two of us might be in trouble' or 'everyone's going to die'?"

"The last one. I mean it, man. This is A+ Grade danger."

"Considering what we've been through, I'm not surprised; it's always got to be the last one. For once, I just wish it could have been the former option. So, what is it this time, Dead Fred?"

"A couple of days ago, this kid from England came into my shop, askin' for a certain artefact – the Box of Rhasadon. Beats me how he knew about it, but he didn't seem like someone out of the ordinary. I'd say he was at least a university student or something."

"The Box of Rhasadon? Never heard of that one before. Is it something that you got recently?"

"No, had it in the shop for two months. Anyway, the dude buys the Box for $600 and walks away. Now, you know how I don't really look into some of my stuff even after havin' them for a while?"

I groaned like a disappointed parent. "Oh no, Fred, don't tell me…"

"Yup, I did squat until it was bought, and I really wished I researched it before. The Box contains what's been referred to as a djinn, but some legends tend to be not all that accurate. The thing in the Box can only be released when a person performs a ritual that supposedly makes the djinn loyal to them."

"A djinn, eh? This person's looking for someone to grant their wish, then. Djinns tend to screw up people's wishes on purpose, so whoever wants to release it must not be very smart. That, or they just never heard of a djinn before. Probably thought it was simply a genie."

"I don't know if they thought it was one thing or the other, but whatever the case, the creature is said to be able to destroy all life on Earth after culminating enough power following its freedom. Again, A+ Grade shit storm, man."

I couldn't help but groan. "Jesus, Fred, now I see why you went with the 'everyone dies' option. But what do you want me to do about it? I can't just track down a person by relying on the fact that they bought something. Yeah, since he's English, he'll probably be back there, but that's all we've got to go on."

"Not quite. See, I know a guy; back in December, I fitted all my shop stuff with tracking devices, so we'll be able to pinpoint the location of the Box."

"Tracking devices? I'm in England, he's in England, you're in America. Unless you've got the skills to hack into a satellite, I don't think this will work."

Fred gave me a smug chuckle. "A-ha! You'd be surprised by how broad the tracking range – we're talking half the world."

"How is that even possible?"

"Welcome to the twenty-first century, man."

"But have we got a name to go on? I can't exactly step in and say, 'Hi, I'm here to collect a box that can destroy mankind. If you can direct me to the person possessing it, that would be lovely'."

"That's where you're wrong, David. That kid's been postin' it online, probably to show it off. Kid's name is Daniel Novice, student at Brinsburrow University."

"That was surprisingly easy. So just to sum up – you want me to go to Brinsburrow Uni to find Daniel Novice, who bought the Box of Rhasadon, which contains a supposed djinn who has to be released through a ritual, and has enough power to destroy everyone on the planet after a while?"

Fred replied casually, "Yeah."

"I'm up for that. Brinsburrow... that's gonna take some time for me to get there. A train would probably be the best course of action. It'll take the best part of a day to arrive, don't know how long to sort out the Box business. I'll call you when it's over, okay?"

"Yeah, you do that, Dave. Thanks for doing this for me."

"No problem. Just let me know when you want to try taking out a monster in one of your artefacts. Who knows, you might get lucky – it could be a fish spirit the size of your finger. Anyway, you woke me up, and I'm hungry. Call you later, mate. Ta."

"Yeah, 'ta' to you too, dude."

Some toast, some orange juice, and I was up and ready. Cain wasn't even 'awake' yet. I kept asking aloud, "Cain? Cain, are you listening? Cain?" Nothing... yet.

I was figuring out what to wear when the beast himself spoke. Loudly.

'DUDE! If you're gonna wake me up, WAKE ME UP!' I flinched at the bombastic burst of energy. Cain needed to lower his voice every once in a while. My alter ego was the cause of so many instances where I tried taking aspirin to shut him up.

"Morning to you too, Cain. Just thought I'd let you know that we got a call from Dead Fred."

'Dead Fred? Really? So, what's he want NOW?'

"A university student took a box containing this apparent djinn who, if released, can amass enough power to wipe out everyone on Earth. More on the higher-up of the creatures concerning him."

'Fuck's sake, man! Why doesn't this guy just, I dunno, destroy every last one o' those pieces of apocalyptic shit?'

"I think there's the possibility of a) any potential spirits to come out if their containers are destroyed and b) not all of his shop's stuff might feature them."

'Fred might as well have a damn catalogue – "Dead Fred's Super Supernatural Items o' Doom! Get them even cheaper in the Halloween Sale! 20% off!"'

"Look, Cain, I find this just as frustrating as you do. It's just that we're the only people he can count on; not a lot of people will believe someone who says that there are demons in artefacts."

'… okay, I see ya point. But still, I wish SOMEONE could do this job instead o' us. For all we know, we could have been spendin' the day goin' round squeezin' girls' asses or put a five pound note in a stripper's panties, but NO. Instead, we get to go to some university filled with know-nothin' punks and kick the shit out o' some jackass for a box.'

"Take your mind out of the gutter for one second… actually, there's no arguing with you – your mind *is* a gutter. No matter how many times we do this, we need to act as though the world depends on us – which, in this scenario, it does. All we have to do is get the job done, and no overly-done crispy Earth."

Cain's reply was like a moody teenager who didn't care for anything other than themselves. 'WHATEVER. As long as I get to go to a pub afterwards.'

That shut him up. Unfortunately, it was temporary.

'Hey, when we check out the pubs there, wanna bang a woman? Huh? Huh? Huh? Huh? Huh? Huh? Huh?'

"No."

'WHY?'

"You know why. Sex isn't exactly something we should take part in."

'Oh yeah, cuz you worry about little immortal Davids an' Cains runnin' around the place. Who knows, maybe that won't be the case?'

"It's too risky. No one should have to live like us. The amount of times we've talked about this exhausts me. Let's just focus on the point at hand."

*

The train ride was, like for every train-goer, terribly boring. The alteration of sitting down and standing up just so you could feel something resembling excitement, no matter how minute it is. I wore my rather eccentric red trench coat and tri-corn Stetson – yes, I wear them in public. If I was personified on one of those Japanese anime shows, I wouldn't look out of place. Sure, some people found it to be eye-catching (in the sense of taking the piss), but I like wearing them. It looks cool.

The crowded mess of people made the atmosphere of every long, grey interior of each train carriage seem overstuffed and dull. So many people, so many chances for people to pickpocket, not that I'm paranoid or anything. Kids whining, others sighing, some moody. Hello, everyday life! You never cease to give us negativity.

Bob the Revolver was rested in my hip holster. I met this scientist who specialised in temporal physics a few decades back; after saving his life, he returned the favour by working on my gun. He modified Bob so that he would never run out of bullets, so that the same bullet would be fired over and over again, sent into the next chamber slot. In other words, Bob was pretty handy.

We finally arrived in Brinsburrow at 3:30, thankful that we were no longer sitting on our arses.

I spent my time goin' through lists o' all the TV shows I've ever watched. That, and annoyin' Davey-boy. Why, you might ask? Cuz I can.

You have no idea how aggravating it was trying *not* to talk aloud when he's listing things nonstop. He is an eternal sufferer of verbal diarrhoea.

According to some information Fred gave me during the ride (he forgot it somehow), the ritual used to open the Box would have to commence during the full moon. Good, we had enough time to think things through. Like, for instance, how to plan this thing out. Seriously, I could not think of anything while Cain went on and on, even when I told him to shut up.

One thing to do – find Daniel. It was vital to track him down before he could come anywhere near starting the ritual. One might ask how I could find him in a crowd. Luckily, Fred sent over a few pictures of that idiot with the djinn fetish. Short blonde hair, short and wide face that looked bored, and was rather tall with a thin frame, except for his legs, which were fairly bulky. In my mind's eye beforehand, I saw him as a tad muscular in the arms, maybe a slight potbelly, and face by which you could tell if he was destined to make screw-ups in his later life. He was about to make the biggest screw-up tonight, one that held Earth in the balance.

It took a while to get anywhere near the Brinsburrow University. I had to ask people directions, which didn't help when considering that I had to ask too many men and women who wanted to get on with their lives. And finally, we arrived outside the Uni. A splendid place in appearance – old but rejuvenated through reconstructions, a fusion of brick, glass and metal, still giving the impression of a force at work. Beautiful, so beautiful.

As I looked at the campus, I gazed at the students waking around it, and through that, a glimpse of Daniel, making his way out of the area. How lucky that I should see him just as I arrived! I made sure to follow him, closing in on him like a predator to its prey. Didn't feel like one of those scenes in movies where one guy's desperately trying to follow another in the middle of a crowd of people. *Please* – Brinsburrow doesn't have a lot of people walking around. Sooner or later, just a few feet away. And then, a tap on the shoulder; that got his attention.

"Excuse me, Daniel?"

He turned around, replying with a formal "yes?" like a polite little boy.

"Daniel, you don't know me, but I'm here for something that you bought."

"Something I bought?"

"Yes, a certain box in America."

A light bulb flickered and lit up above his head. Then he looked like a fish, mouth wide open.

"Wha-what do you want? Are you here to take it from me?" His body shook a little bit defensively, quite a Nervous Nelson.

"I have to, kid. You don't know what you're properly doing with this. If you allow that entity to escape, it could kill everyone on the planet."

Daniel started to back away. I moved in a sort of mini-chase, ensuring that I still talked to him, as well as kept in mind that he might make a run for it, which was extremely likely.

"It doesn't matter if that happened. I just want my wish granted, that's all."

It was time that I turned on the break-his-will attitude.

"Oh, really? And what *is* your wish, exactly?"

"I just want to... I want to see alien life, that's all. Explore other worlds, meet new species."

"At the cost of the world you live in?"

His face turned red as he looked around, anger surging through him as he declared, "I hate this planet, it's a shithole. There *have* to be ones better than this. Who cares if others have to die?"

"Including your friends and family? Anyone else who'd love you? Surely you can't be so selfish that you'd cast them aside just to further your own needs?"

That hit him hard; he flinched and stepped back slightly. "D-don't even go there!"

"You're one to talk; you're the kid who doesn't mind everyone's deaths."

He couldn't handle any more pressure; his eyes were blinking fast, possibly on the verge of crying.

"H-how did you find out?" he said in an effort to avoid anything else that could turn him off the idea of using the Box.

"I'm a friend of the guy you bought it from. Just give me the Box, son, and you'll save us some unneeded conflict."

Anger started to swell in his voice, eliminating some of his fear. "No, I won't. Just leave me alone." He stopped moving, intending to make a stand. And that's when Cain interfered.

Dumbass brat ignorin' Davey-boy. We're tryin' to do a job here, an' he's screwin' it up! Time for some extra help for the boss – force.

I took over our body, and the quick change in appearance creeped the punk out. Ha, made 'im jump! Fear's a great way to get people to listen to ya, 'specially kids who got themselves doomsday devices.

I took a hold o' his shirt and swung 'im towards me, grinnin' all the while. The look on his face; horror with a bit o'anger drizzled over it, such a delight that I'm sure I could o' made 'im piss 'imself if I wanted to. I lowered my voice for dramatic effect.

"Listen, kiddy, we ain't got time for this shit. Hand us the Box o' Rasanfrasenrabbit and I won't have to gut yer body and dump it in a disposal bin. Clear?"

Kid still looked like a fish, no answerin' or nothin'. So a little shakin' was done to get him to respond, but the little bastard said squat. Started to get annoyed by all this, and my words made this clear.

"Talk, Danny-boy. TALK, dammit, why won't ya talk? Is it the teeth? It is, isn't it? Like 'em? I do. I use 'em to rip idiots like you to bits when they don't answer a question. That, or pretend I'm a vampire. You ever seen me as Dracula? If ya don't answer me, let's just say I'll act out the part where I suck out yer blood. Trust me. So talk."

That seemed to work; Danny surrendered and led us to his place. Didn't take long to get there, fifteen to twenty minutes o' walkin'. I was annoyed with how long it was takin', but Davey-boy reassured me that I hadda be patient.

Punk's room was on the ground floor of the halls of residence. Room was a bit clean, ain't exactly the cleanest room ever seen, but he knew how to tidy up in some places. Bed was neat, stationery organised on his desk, books lined up. Now all that was left was gettin' that fuckin' Box, then gettin' outta this dump. Blondy took it out from his desk drawer, and presented it to me like some servant to his boss – so in other words, he was my bitch.

The Box was kinda pretty. Looked a bit Asian, all golden 'round the sides. Main colour was red with a blue gem on top o' the lid. I slowly took it from him like a super cool slo-mo scene in a movie, wantin' to make the whole thing feel dramatic, a triumph 'gainst the assholes bein' dumb an' tryin' to screw the whole world over. Made a grin and eyed Dan like the mad guy I was, an' spoke with terror to continue scarin' the shit outta him.

"There we go, buddy-boy. Now that wasn't so tough, eh? All you gotta do now is promise to never do any of this demon shit again, or I'll come over and do the Dracula routine, 'kay?"

No response. No noddin' or shakin'. He just… closed his eyes. That's when I noticed somethin' else. Slight movements with his mouth; like he was talkin' to himself. Or… mumblin'? And he had his hands behind his back. The hell was goin'—

David was quick to realise. He sounded worried.

'Cain, I think he might be doing some kind of ritual. We need to restrain him in case it's to do with the Box …' I laid the box onto the bed. I lunged at the punk, wrappin' one arm around his back and another coverin' his mouth to shut him up. No doubt about it, I was pissed off with this little prick.

"Stop it, ya idiot! You tryin' to give the Apocalypse a kick-start? Shut up!"

And he did. Eyes opened, and a hummin' was heard, like a fly buzzin' near your ear. Kid turned his head to where the Box... the Box... oh shit... it was glowin' like a boxful of light bulbs.

FWOOSH!

A supernatural wind surrounded us, sendin' papers and used food wrappers flyin'. Our faces were stunned – I was shittin' myself and Danny-boy was grinnin' like some maniac.

A low-pitch growl similar a big cat (a lion or whatever?) was heard from the Box, like giant speakers in our ears. If BOOM could've had a voice, that's a prime contender. Really, really scary, not lyin'! Just think – if the voice of it was shit-yer-pants scary, what the fuck would that monster look like?

In all this shit, all of what I feared the most was happenin'; I was gonna have to fight this thing. Fuckfuckfuckfuckfuckfuckfuckfuckfuckfuck—

Then the wind picked up and sent me back into a cramped corner as if it had punched or kicked me while catching me off-guard. Fuckin' typical; supernatural big-bad, supernatural dramatic release.

Danny-boy, for some reason, wasn't pushed back. It was like he was observin' this thing as a spectre, immune to effects like the damn wind. He stood up as quickly as he could, and held out his arms so that it looked like an upside-down V. The punk was embracin' this!

The room's main door was opened as a few other kids came there to see what exactly the hell was it that made all those sounds. Their reactions were predictable – f-bombs, shouting out questions, runnin' away. Can't blame 'em, 'cause if it weren't for David in my head, I'd piss off outta Apocalypse Paradise.

But one kid made note of somethin' else other than the glowin' Doomsday Box or Danny – me. Girl in her late teens, probably just nearly hittin' twenty, with long hair, pretty bland casual clothes underneath a tight waist-high black jacket, small earrings. She stared at me like she had seen me before, with shock and big ol' eyes wide open. I swear that, in the middle of this shit-storm, she said, "It's you." But who was SHE?

Any instance o' thought on her was bashed aside when our oh-so-ever-lovin' monster finally decided to get out and stretch his legs. What looked like some kinda grey … stream, i guess, slivered outta the Box and went SPLAT on the floor. It resembled a giant glob of Semtex an' Play dough.

A shape began to form; it stretched out like someone usin' a rollin' pin when makin' a cake (yum). The stuff shifted and reached up to the ceilin', makin' it eight feet tall. Arms appeared from the mass, at first gooey like everything else about it, but then started to look familiar – y'know, muscles, fingers, hands. Same with the legs, too. Ended up gettin' a grey… what's the word? One David uses?

Humanoid.

Cheers!

Ended up gettin' a grey humanoid appearance. A body like Arnold Schwarzenegger overdosing on steroids was almost complete, its arms covered in red spirallin' tattoos from the wrists to pecs. The head was the last to solidify. The creature looked weird. No hair anywhere, not even the head. Hell, he didn't even have the ever-faithful manly package. This big bastard took up too much space for the room, and his eyes were black, with white pupils and irises. His arms hung loosely, and the hands were made in fists, possibly to pound the livin' shit out of any of us.

I panicked even more. The other uni kids fucked off, save for that girl, who just backed up in the hallway. Well, that's what I saw given the limited view of her with our large-and-in-charge supernatural barger.

Dan smiled. No, scratch that – his wide expression with his mouth had every form of 'wrong' on it. Musta been thinkin', "Yay, I get to kill people with this hunka demonic muscle!"

Speakin' of it, our gigantic guest had his eyes on him. Surprisingly, the monster spoke in a voice that was deeper than the biggest canyon on Earth. God-*damn* was it disturbin'.

"I AM RHASADON. YOU, I PRESUME, ARE THE ONE WHO FREED ME FROM MY PRISON, ARE YOU NOT?"

Danny, still smilin', answered with so much glee you could swear that he was high.

"Yes, I am! I freed you in my hour of need! This person," he pointed one insane finger at me, "was going to take your means of containment from me so that you couldn't be free. But here you are, now out in the human world, free to do whatever I say!"

Rhasadon looked at me stoically before turnin' back to his 'master'.

"I AM GRATEFUL FOR YOUR RELEASING ME. BECAUSE OF IT, THAT MEANS THAT YOU BEAR THE MARK, CORRECT?"

"Yes, I do."

He rolled up a sleeve and showed off some tattoo I couldn't see. Judging from where he pointed it with his other arm, it must have been on the forearm.

With satisfaction, Rhasadon faintly smiled, givin' the impression that that no-good little snot did a little emotion transplant. When the big bad beast smiles, that ain't good.

"GOOD. SINCE YOU POSSESS IT, YOU ARE TO BE MY SOURCE OF RE-NOURISHMENT."

I bet you anythin' that Danny-boy had an 'oh shit' expression when hearin' that. His tone went from triumphant and energetic to shocked and scared.

"What? No, no, that's not what it said! That's not what I looked up when researching about you!"

"IT IS CLEAR THAT YOU HUMANS HAVE A WAY OF TAINTING THE TRUTH. WHAT IS FACT BECOMES FICTION, DETAILS SCRAWLED IN SAND ARE WIPED FROM TIME."

David had hit upon somethin' with that monster's statement.

'Cain, he's probably right. That could be why Fred was wrong about the midnight ritual; it might have been a fictional element.'

"Great deduction, Davey-boy, but that ain't gonna help us with this at the moment!"

Turns out I said that last quote aloud – Danny and Rhasadon noticed me.

"Uh... Hi... don't worry about me. Just get on with that nice lil' chat of yours."

Danny looked at Rhasadon then back at me, movin' erratically like he was frickin' high. He pointed at me again.

"K-kill him! Kill him for me! Come on, y-you don't have to kill *me*! I got you out, so don't you owe me something?"

He was gasping as he said every word, clearly losin' his mind. Rhasadon wasn't in the mood for this.

"I AM AFRAID THAT WHAT I DO, I DO FOR MYSELF, NOT FOR THOSE WHO ARE PATHETIC AND BENEATH ME. YOU REPRESENT BOTH THOSE THINGS. IT WILL THEREFORE MAKE IT EASIER FOR ME TO ABSORB YOU. DO NOT RESIST YOUR FATE; MARK IT, YOUR DESTINY."

"No! No! Don't...!"

Too late for Danny; next thing I saw, Rhasadon took out one giant arm and grabbed him by a throat, liftin' him off his feet. Dan struggled, still screamin' his ass off, but then those screams went 'bu-bye' when Rhassy's arm was covered in a kinda purple light. Kid's wild-movin' arms went limp, and his head just rested awkwardly on one side. Dunno 'bout you, but I think he died.

The big dude tossed him aside, right near me too. Fear already grabbed me by the bollocks, so I was flinchin' when Dan's lifeless puppet of a body was next to me. That allowed me to see his face. It looked all drained and... well, corpse-y. I was next to a recently-rottin' person!

"Ew ew ew ew ew...!"

I stood up in panic near that pathetic punk's creepy cadaver, kinda frantically. My eyes were looked onto

67

Rhasadon's… just Rhasadon. Seriously, that monster's like one of those CGI things in horror movies. You just *cannot* focus on one part of him.

I raise my fists up like a boxer's, and my fear said *"Hi"* to the djinn douche through my shaky voice.

"O-o-okay, Mr—Mr Tall Dark and Horrible, I-I'm gonna kick your ass…"

Rhasadon didn't look at all like he cared; emotionless face all the way.

"FOOLISH MORTAL. THROUGH THE SUMMONER, I HAVE AMASSED A GREAT DEAL OF STRENGTH. DO YOU BELIEVE THAT A BEING SUCH AS YOURSELF CAN DEFEAT ME? IT IS OBVIOUS THAT YOUR ATTEMPT AT BRAVADO IS A WEAK MASK TO HIDE YOUR TRUE FEELING – FEAR."

"Oh… dear god, you're on to me," I said in an embarrassed tone.

No way I'm fightin' when the enemy knows I'm scared of him. I called to David, "Tag out! Tag out!"

Cain forced my psyche to stand our ground, the coward. Then again, I understand why he'd do that; given the situation, it's natural for people to run off while others fight. You're looking at two people who do both options in the same body.

Rhasadon noticed the subtle changes that came with each 'tag in'. "INTERESTING. IT SEEMS YOU ARE NOT LIKE ANY MORTAL; YOU CAN CHANGE YOUR APPEARANCE."

I decided to introduce myself with a wisecrack. Always helps when dealing with the tough stuff.

"Congratulations, Rhasadon, you can point out the obvious. Must be a special ability that comes with being a demon. When I punch you, you can call it out, if you like." I cracked my somewhat stiff neck. "Anyway, can you cut it out with the killing thing? I get why you might want to do that – a big guy like you trapped in a teeny-tiny box for so many centuries, you're bound to get mad as hell… where, after this, you'll be living permanently."

"I SENSE SOMETHING UNUSUAL ABOUT YOU. PERHAPS I COULD GAIN GREATER STRENGTH FROM YOU…"

"Sorry, but I don't like it when people decide to steal my life force. I use it to do important stuff, like living."

"ENOUGH. IT HAS BEEN DECIDED – I WILL FEAST ON YOUR ENERGY."

He started to walk towards me, to which I responded by taking out Bob the Revolver from his holster. With him in hand, I didn't hesitate to pull the trigger and unload a string of bullets into the demon's head, but it turned out to be in vain. The bullets simply ricocheted off him, reminding me of that scene in *Superman Returns* where a bullet failed to pierce the Man of Steel's eye.

As soon as I realized the futility of what I was doing, Rhasadon lifted me by the throat like he did with Daniel. His large fingers were applying such pressure that my oxygen supply was rapidly fading away. Just as bad, my energy was being sapped by the demented demon, a purple aura hanging over his arm. My limbs felt as though they were being held down, every attempt to move them requiring more and more effort.

My thoughts were drying up, growing weaker with every second. If that was how I was to die, it would have been with regret – regret that I couldn't save the world from this entity.

Oh God, I can't do anything… I want to save everyone, but I… can't do… any… an…

Consciousness was growing thin. Eyes were beginning to close. My defiant arms gave up, and felt as if they had vanished, leaving only the fabric of my coat arms. Bob the Revolver departed from my loose, barely-alive hand, the sound of his impact on the floor barely noticeable.

During all of this, Rhasadon decided to point out the obvious, as if he hadn't done that already.

"IT APPEARS I WAS CORRECT: YOUR ENERGY IS GREATER THAN THAT OF MY SUMMONER. YOU DO WELL IN HELPING ME BRING HUMANITY CLOSER TO DESTRUCTION, NON-MORT—"

Thankfully, his mouth was silenced by a force from behind. Despite my thinning condition, I was able to hear some kind of 'thudding' sound, at which point Rhasadon sort of forgot about me and let go. I fell like a discarded toy, limbs just all over the place and my mind barely able to function.

My energy, though at what appeared to be on its last legs, strangely came back like a life-force boomerang. I took in a deep breath, and it felt so good while my head cleared. Every breath I took in felt like the oxygen had turned to gold; richer than what the air was before.

I looked up at Rhasadon and saw that he faced the one who had hit him; it was the girl that Cain and I had noticed, a fire extinguisher in her hands. She tried to step away from him, but with one step backwards she was pressed against a wall. She had put on a courageous face, not a shred of fear evident, just a stern expression (as stern as you can get when facing something inhuman like a demon) that said, 'Come on then, you fucking hard case! Do the best you can!'

"THIS IS UNEXPECTED. YOU ARE A DISTRACTION; YOU MUST BE REMOVED IMMEDIATELY."

I knew that if I didn't act soon, she'd be the next victim. Noticing Bob on the floor, I grabbed him without hesitation, swift as I could in my second wind, and aimed it at Rhasadon. There had to be some sort of weakness to him. Even though it was shown that bullets didn't affect him, what were the chances that I could shoot him in the head by placing my gun in the mouth? How about his eyes – were they vulnerable? Surely even his eyes would be squishy enough for bullets. It was a long shot, but I had no other ideas at the time. The stress of the situation was too much to bear, especially with the fate of that girl closing in on her with every step of that muscle-bound demon. I took in a deep breath as I yelled as Rhasadon.

"Hey, big guy!" Sure enough, he took no time turning to me, that blank, statue-like expression still on his face. "I'm not done just yet. Come on, it's time for round two."

"I WILL BE WITH YOU MOMENTARILY – THIS FEMALE MUST BE REMOVED."

"Yeah, so you say. Nice that you care about me enough to get rid of any problems, but why don't you focus on me and not the girl?"

"I DO AS I WISH. YOU CANNOT ORDER ME TO DO OTHERWISE. I AM RHASADON, REMOVER OF SOULS. YOUR WEAPON IS USELESS AGAINST ME."

"But her fire extinguisher is?"

"NEGATIVE; IT ANNOYED ME."

In all honesty, I couldn't argue with that.

"Okay, fair enough, mate. Still, let the girl leave, eh?"

Rhasadon faced her again, and she was still backed up to the wall, paralysed by fear. He then looked at me.

"I WILL LET HER LIVE BEFORE I AM FINISHED WITH YOU. THEN I WILL KILL HER."

"But you've got a problem now."

"THERE IS NO PROBLEM," he bellowed.

"Oh, but there is – I think I know how to kill you."

For a second, it seemed as though the behemoth was about to break his stoic face and show fear, but his face remained stiff.

"THAT IS IMPOSSIBLE – MY RACE IS INVULNERABLE."

"Come on, nothing's unkillable," I replied with confidence and a smile. The irony of the statement wasn't lost on me.

"I AM THE EXCEPTION," he boasted in that monotone voice.

"Well, we'll see, you muscular mannequin."

I aimed for his left eye and pulled the trigger. I was used to the recoil, focusing on how the bullet hit Rhasadon's eye;

it managed to pierce that small black hole, and with the puncture came a burst of bright white blood, some of which went on the floor while some started to roll down his face. In pain, the demon let out a scream, one that was deep, filled with anger, shock, pain and most importantly, the death of pride. He couldn't help but cover his eye with both hands.

Now knowing that he could be hurt, I fired at his other one. Rhasadon screamed once more. With his handicap in place, I pulled the trigger on both eyes, sending bullet upon bullet into his sockets. The screams and gunfire soon became the only things you could hear, turning every thought mute. The girl was still there, stiff as a statue as she watched this brutal attack. Her eyes were wide-open, surprised by all this (which you can't blame her). She must have felt that this was all a dream and that she'd wake up in her bed any minute. She would have been wrong.

My trigger finger was eventually worn out; I cannot remember how many times I fired at him. Rhasadon fell to his knees, his hands feeling the fuzzy, worn-out carpeting of the room. Most of his face had become white thanks to the blood, which had now covered a small portion of the floor. The demon's breathing was heavy, drawing out a groan every two seconds. He raised his head in my direction, but recoiled when he tried to blink; the pain caused him to send his hands near his eyes, then in vain attempted to get the bullets out with his large fingers, unable to get even so much as his pinkie finger in there. When he realised it was useless, my buff shooting practice target stood up and spoke to me, not even pretending to mask his anger.

"YOU – YOU ARE – I WILL KILL YOU! YOU WOULD DARE WOUND ME! I WILL GIVE YOU A DEATH MOST PROLONGED! YOUR LIFE FORCE SHALL BE SAPPED SLOWLY, YOU INSIGNIFICANT PIECE OF DIRT!"

"And then what are you gonna do with all that energy, eh? Go to Hell and cash it in for points?"

He tried to swing at me, one massive arm after another. It was too easy to dodge – it was like I was experiencing the world in slow motion, side-stepping and crouching casually. I decided to knock him down – all I needed to do was to hit him in the knees with enough force. Doing it at average strength (in other words, average to any other human) wasn't going to get the job done, so I had to use more force than I was holding back. We might not look it, but we're actually much, *much* stronger than anyone else, like a superhero.

Using my free hand, I made a nice, tight fist, so tight that it actually hurt a bit. While Rhasadon tried punching me, a good hard fist hit his right kneecap; we could hear the wet, crackling snap that followed. He fell down, back to the floor, and howled in agony as he felt his broken kneecap with his hands. Calmly, I placed the barrel of my faithful friend Bob deep into one of Rhasadon's sockets. There must have been a hell of a lot of bullets piled up there – it was a miracle that he was still... not 'standing', but 'alive'. A point-blank blast would probably send all those bullets right through his brain, put an end to him.

I saw the girl, and she just looked a bit spaced out now, what with her eyes being open as far as possible.

"Kid," I said, sounding like a parental figure, "please move away from the wall. This might be dangerous." She did just that, leaving the room and not even attempting to peak at me from the doorframe. Now it was just me, Cain, and our demon friend.

"When you see Daniel, Rhasadon, tell him I said, 'Hi'."

Rhasadon grabbed the wrist of my gun arm, and spoke through his teeth.

"CREATURE, WHATEVER YOU ARE, YOU ARE BRUTAL. OF ALL THE ENTITIES I HAVE ENCOUNTERED, YOU ARE NOTHING LIKE THEM. I DUB YOU AN ABOMINATION."

"Well, you know what they say, mate, 'He who fights monsters'."

I pulled the trigger for the final time, and in a flash every one of those metal slugs that was jammed in there flew out of the back of his head in a single file, followed by a spray of white blood. They collided with the wall, where they rapidly bounced off of, creating a small firework explosion alongside the blood before they were on the ground. Rhasadon's hand lost strength, and as I removed my gun from his eye, he fell over backwards.

"That'll take a load off your mind," I quipped. It then occurred to me – that wasn't a very funny wisecrack. One of those cases where it sounded better in your mind.

My eyes darted at the bed like they were locked onto it: the Box was still there, sitting on the duvet and showing off the beauty it had for centuries. My mission was to bring that thing back, and despite everything that'd happened, returning it to Dead Fred was still part of the deal.

Brushing my forehead with one hand, I sat on Daniel's bed to get some needed relaxation and grabbed the Box, observing it. As I looked back at everything that had just happened, I wondered where security was. Surely the students would have notified them of the bizarreness of what they'd fleetingly seen? Maybe the kids were too terrified to do anything, thinking that waiting for it to blow over would be a good course of action.

Today had been rather long and stressful, to say the least. Letting out a long, soul-draining sigh helped matters. Actually, the bed felt pretty comfy. Cain agreed; in his own words, it felt like, "our ass was bein' held by some sexy angel ladies". Resting on it wouldn't hurt. I removed the cushions, took off my coat, placed Bob in his holster, proceeded to lie back, used said coat as a blanket and tipped my hat over my face. The Box was still in my hands. It was one of the best beds I've ever been on. The material of the duvet was so smooth that I didn't even feel my own body. Nothing would interrupt it.

Except for the sound of a female Uni student's voice.

"Um, excuse me?"

The girl removed my hat from my face. I opened my eyes and saw her staring at me.

"Oh. Hello," I said casually. "Can I do anything for you?"

"Who are you?"

I cleared my throat while getting off the bed and putting my coat on.

"I am… someone you don't know," which I bellowed in an overdramatic voice, just for fun.

"I know, that's why I'm asking."

"Okay, sorry. Hi, name's David," I introduced myself, offering a handshake. "And that's a demon," said with a finger pointed at the muscle-bound corpse. "Don't worry, he's very dead, I made sure of it." Then the finger was pointed at Daniel's dried-up body. "Oh, and that's Daniel, he's also very dead. If you knew him, I'm terribly sorry, and I offer my condolences. And you are?"

She looked at me with a dazed expression. As if she had a delayed reaction, she eventually shook my hand, rather weakly to be honest.

"Emily. Emily Harley."

"Nice to meet you, Emily Harley. Name sounds a bit familiar. Then again, I've known a lot of women with that name. And a man – he was good fella, really skilled at pool. Well, he was American, so he called it 'snooker'. Well, I say 'man', but he had a sex change. Sorry, going off on a tangent. Now, if you excuse me, I'm going to leave. Thanks for the fire extinguisher, by the way, that helped me loads. I guess you could say you helped extinguish that situation."

I started to make my way to the door, minding Rhasadon's huge body by walking around it. The sleeve of my coat was quickly snatched by Emily before I could even be within a foot of the doorframe.

"Wait a minute! I remember you."

I spun around, captured by her words. 'Remember'. How could she know who I am? Sure, I had been around for a long time, but the chances of randomly running into someone again years later seemed unlikely.

"I'm sorry, do I know you? I have a bad memory, so forgive me if I don't recognise you."

"It was a long time ago, but it was definitely you. Jacob – David Stroke, right?"

I briefly flinched at the sound of my old alias. Emily could tell that I was shaken by that. Cain was quick to point it out in our head.

'Buddy, she's lookin' at us like we're about to have a heart attack.'

"Y-you must be mistaken. As I said, name's David Short, not Jacob or Stroke."

"No, it *was*. The face, the voice, none of that can belong to someone else. Back when I was little, you were there in that apartment, taking care of me until my dad got arrested."

All of a sudden it came back to me. 2013. The little girl. The drunken dad. The police. I was immediately overcome with excitement.

"Oh God, it's *you*! Little Emily! I let you watch *Ben 10* and gave you orange juice!"

"Yes, that's it," she said with a grin on her face. Without a moment's hesitation, she wrapped her arms around me tightly like a snake, pressing her soft cheek against mine. Must have been like meeting a long-lost friend again. Her voice emitted the happiness that she wanted to show me for years.

"Oh, I thought I'd never see you again. I wanted to say 'thank you' so many times."

"Um, that's great, Emily." I tried to hide how awkward I felt from this very personal hug. My voice flew up and down, making my attempts at masking this obvious to her.

She released me from her snake-like hug and her smile evaporated, replaced by a small embarrassed expression.

"I'm sorry, Ja— David. It's just that… I've always remembered your face. I've always had a great memory, even when I was little."

"To be honest, I'm not surprised. After all, we are having this conversation, rather than a Q&A on all this. I'm surprised you haven't even talked about Daniel, yet. You must have really been indifferent towards him. Then again, he summoned El Diablo here, so I guess that gives you a reason to carry on like that." I waved an arm at the dead bodies.

"Was that – you said a demon, didn't you? *Was* that summoned by Daniel?"

"Indeed it was. He wanted it to obey him and grant him wishes, but he didn't expect it to turn on him and suck all of his energy dry."

Her big innocent eyes widened and her mouth swung open. "I can't believe it. I thought that demons didn't exist."

"You'd be surprised by how much there is that people don't know. I've had a run-in with a lot of stuff; yetis, wendigos, dwarves, even creatures that I'm sure no one's ever thought of. Demons, on the other hand, they're new."

Emily glanced over at Daniel's corpse. She looked sad, sounded sad, but there was something about her that was off, indescribable. Maybe it was her casual acceptance of all this? "Poor Dan. I can't believe he's dead. We started Uni a month ago, so we were still getting to know each other. He seemed so nice, so polite. I never thought he'd end up like this."

I rested a hand on her shoulder for comfort.

"He tampered with forces that shouldn't exist, dark stuff. Everyone's got a side to them they don't want others to see, but sooner or later it'll be exposed. It's a shame that he got a hold of this Box. If he hadn't, chances are that he would have turned out fine, succeed in Uni, maybe life. Poor lad."

"Just what the hell are they gonna say to his parents?"

"I don't know, Emily. In any case, it's time I leave. I've got to take this," I shook the Box, "back to a friend of mine, the guy Daniel took it from. It's not gonna harm to anyone now, so it's better off being sold in my mate's shop. It was nice catching up with you, dear. Good luck at university."

I exited the room and made my way through the short corridor before leaving the building. The air was fantastic to take in, and just experiencing it after all that from inside just relaxed me a little bit. A part of me hated to leave the campus because I wanted to explain to the people there what happened, but what could I say? Cain suggested that I flat-out tell them the truth, which I responded by with a simple 'no'.

Emily followed me, tried talking to me, but I wasn't listening when all that wanted to do was to leave. I had no idea what she had been saying. That changed when, roughly halfway through the campus, she tugged at my shoulder violently.

"Hey, David! Listen to me!"

I turned around and saw her face, slightly red and scowling.

"… yes?"

She groaned at my ignorance.

"Just answer my question. Why do you look the same age as you did years ago?"

"You ask me that now? That should have been one of your first questions."

"Yeah, but the demon kind of side-tracked me!"

"Okay, understandable, that *was* the biggest thing going on at the time. Anyway, I don't know why I haven't aged, it's one of the biggest things I've wondered about myself."

"Wait, one of them? What else could there be? I mean, there can't be anything that can top that."

I was puzzled, evident by a tightly-knit frown on my glabella. The disbelief of her statement sent me into hysterics, making my voice high-pitched.

"There was a demon – *a demon* – in your block! De-mon! I'm pretty sure you can believe anything by this point! Okay, you want to know what else there is on my list of personal questions, here we go. Number one: Why have I been alive for centuries? Number Two: Why can't I die? And finally, and this one's my favourite, Number Three:

Why do I have an annoying entity in my body who likes to speak in an American accent?"

Emily just looked confused as you would be when someone says all of that. Every word she said had so much emphasis on it, and her tone was just as inquisitive as before, but with a sense of disbelief.

"Are you – are you serious?"

I rolled my eyes before calming down. "Yes, yes I am. Saying that I've been here for a while is cutting it small, possibly more than recorded history. As for other guy, you wanna see him?"

She didn't answer for a couple of seconds, taking it all in like a sponge. I waited patiently until she gave her answer.

"Yes, I do."

"You're pretty brave, you know that?"

"Why?"

"Because anyone who talks to him would find him annoying." I smiled to lighten things up. I couldn't really tell her the whole truth about him.

"Watch carefully, Emily." I allowed Cain to takeover, and she stepped back at the change.

"Hey, kid, nice to meet ya. Name's Cain, by the way." I outstretch my hand. Emily didn't look so excited to see me. If anythin', she went from puzzled to "oh my god, what the hell is that?" I gave up with the attempted handshake.

With Cain in position, I was seeing everything as I usually did, acting as a spectator. I saw Emily's expression. In her eyes we could see her world – the world that she thought she lived in, one that was filled head-to-toe with the mundane – crumble. The demon business had started it, created cracks, caused mountains to fall apart, ruptured the sea bed.

Seeing me again, hearing my questions about the life Cain and I shared, and seeing Cain himself was what finally did it. There were earthquakes, tidal waves, destroyed buildings, the earth's core overheating and eventually collapsing in on itself. Her world was dead, and a new one, feeling both old and new, had taken its place.

"Oh my God," she yelped with her face screwed up in shock. She recoiled in from the sudden altered appearance, taking two quick steps back. I didn't blame her.

"Yeah, I know, it's weird how I – we – screw it, let's just go with 'I' – look different. Look my fingernails, they look like claws." I wriggled my fingers in front of her to show 'em off. 'Creeped out' is probably the best way to describe her reaction.

"Your – your eyes," she pointed at her with her fingers.

"Lucky bastard, he looks the most normal. Me, I'm stuck with lookin' like some sorta cat-man from Doctor Moreau's island. Check out these ears, for cryin' out loud."

I put my hand at the back of my pointy ears and wiggled 'em. Actin' brave, tryin' to get used to these looks, she stepped forward.

"Go on, feel 'em." I removed one o' my hands to let her touch 'em. She did it, and rubbed the tip of it to make sure.

I felt one hell of a sensation comin' from that ear, not just the rubbin'. At first it was so soft, but soon that softness spread across my head, chest, stomach, limbs, groin… oh god, the groin. And then it hit me – it had been so long since anyone, especially a woman, had rubbed my ears, that I forgot that they were an arousal point. I could get turned on by someone feelin' 'em up, for Christ's sake! That's just weird! I wanted to tell her to stop before she figured it out.

I let out a small gasp as I could feel my groin startin' to harden. My eyes bulged while blood went rushin' to my face. It was agony. Emily saw my pain and stopped (what felt like) caressin' my ear.

"Cain, are you alright?"

Now that my ear was abandoned by her delicate hands, everything returned to normal. All of that was exasperatin'. I panted, "Oh man," as Emily tried to process what happened.

"What's wrong? Did I hurt you?"

"No, no, kid, ya didn't. It's just that… I forgot that it, uh, it's still healin' from some pain from earlier. Don't blame yourself." I cleared my throat, my face red with embarrassment.

"A-anyway, I'm David's other side. You've, uh, grown up, haven't ya? I can remember when you were little. When we found out what ya dad was doin' to ya, I wanted to beat the shit outta him, fuckin' abusive prick. We don't have any kids, so we're pretty protective around 'em, wanna make sure none of that stuff happens to 'em."

Kid understood what I was sayin', I could tell by her face. She was comin' to terms with it piece by piece.

"I… see. Are there any… any other differences between you and David? Like, in personality?"

"I'm more in love with beatin' bad guys up with my fist than him. David's always tryin' to sort stuff out with words, and then fisticuffs if that doesn't work out, and I can see why he acts that like, but I'm willin' to hit right off the bat, know what I'm sayin'?"

"I think I do, yeah."

"I guess I think some people need shuttin' up the hard way. Other than that, nothin' else."

"I'm just curious about your appearance, too. Do you always have to look different every time you switch places?"

"Yup. Damned if I know why."

"This is too weird. Just… so much. All of this, I can't believe what's going on. I want to know so much about you, but a part of me's afraid."

"I think I know what ya mean, little lady. Do I bother you or not, or just okay seein' Davey-boy?"

"I don't want to sound rude, but I think I'm used to David."

"Right. Okey-dokey. Hang on." I closed my eyes and tagged out.

I opened my eyes and saw Emily, who took great care in focusing on to see if I was back. I might have been wrong, but I remember her smiling a little bit.

"Hey, Emily," I said as though I had turned up at her front door.

"Hi," she said meekly. "So, you're back."

"Yup. Good to see this face without the eyes and fangs, eh?"

"I'll say," she said with relief.

"Is there anything else you want to know?"

Emily reached into her jacket and took out her phone, roughly the size of a hand, and was silver, asking, "Can I have your phone number?"

That wasn't something that I expected. Asking for my phone number – what was she thinking?

"Do you really mean that, Emily?"

"Absolutely. I know it seems odd, but otherwise I'd probably be spending the rest of my life wondering about you. It'd be good to at least stay in contact with you."

"Alright; it only seems fair, I guess."

I whipped out my phone from my coat, an eight-year out-of-date Blackberry (I forget what model it was) and looked up my number, which I read to her while she typed it down. She did likewise. After that, we put our phones away.

"Thanks, David. Are you sure you have to get going?"

"Yeah, I need to hand it back as quick as I can. If you want to, look me up on Facebook, add me as a friend. At least then you'd be able to chat without having to use the phone all the time. Well, it was nice seeing you again, Emily. Take care now."

I gave her a small wave and started to walk backwards as I resumed my journey off-campus, looking like someone who's living life in reverse.

"Okay then. Bye, David – a-and Cain, too! Bye, Cain!" She waved at me – or 'us' – before I turned around and walked normally.

82

'Ya know,' Cain commented, 'she's kinda acceptin' all this way too easily, know what I'm sayin'?'

'Yeah, I know what you mean,' I thought. Never before had we encountered a person who adjusted so quickly to the weird stuff in our life. Then again, her memory was awfully clear, so I guessed there were still more surprises in store for us.

I informed Dead Fred that I recovered the Box and that the world would have to wait until another person (demon or otherwise) would try to apply for the job of World Destroyer (which is a pretty rare job). However, rather than send him the Box by post, I said I'd go to America and give it to him myself, despite his objections. See, I've had a few experiences in the past where very important stuff I posted abroad was never received, so I tend to go to wherever I want the items to go and send them personally. Call me paranoid, but I feel comfortable doing it. I kept the Box in a small backpack, making sure that I would never let it out of my sight, and left my gun at home, in fear of the metal detectors.

One plane trip later and the worst of our problems were a stiff neck, legs that needed at least ten hours' worth of stretching and the memory of watching a terrible in-flight movie, a romantic-comedy about a dentist who wanted to go out with a hairdresser (Cain and I never really liked rom-coms). I can't remember how much the taxi was, but chances are that he got enough to call me his favourite customer.

The shop name presented itself handsomely, but at the same time cheaply. For starters, it was in red. 'Dead Fred's' was in a thin font and surrounded by what appeared to be electricity drawn on by a blue felt-tip marker. Below it, 'Amazingly Ancient Antiques' were in a much bolder font, resembling three giants overshadowing a thin master. The alliterative words were piled up in three rows so that the

'A's were in a line, which also had the same drawn-on lightning surrounding them. Just looking at the display made me think that I had gone to a cheap European market.

Inside, I breathed in the mix of vanilla-coated air and the dancing wisps of cigarette smoke. Coughing was too hard to avoid, and my nose wanted to escape the damned vanilla scent. I had gone into a shop, not a car air freshener. The place wasn't dark, as a couple of lightbulbs could attest, shining like miniature suns. They helped me forget that it was night, and that I'd have to eventually get a flight home.

Fred showed off his so-called 'amazingly ancient' items on rows of wooden racks. The inventory included an actual human skull that was preserved in a glass container (how and why on Earth he got it was something that I was too creeped out by to ask), a twelfth century chess set and a child's crayon set from the eighteenth century. It was amazing how he could get his hands on stuff like that; it made me wonder what he would do if all items were sold? Chances are that he'd temporarily close down until he'd get something to sell.

And lo and behold, the man was behind a small tucked-away counter in a corner, smiling at me like his favourite meal was right in front of him, showing off a row of white-yellow teeth, save for one that was made of gold. The counter somehow gave the impression that he was taller; Fred was 5'6", but you'd be forgiven in thinking he was 5'9". The last time we met, a smooth thin black carpet dominated that small head of his. Now there was barely anything – if you looked really hard, you could see small hairs poking out, resembling a game of connect-the-dots.

Witnessing my arrival and treating it as an answered prayer, Fred clasped his hands together as he removed himself from the counter and made his way to me.

"David, great to see you, man!"

Removing the backpack from my shoulders, all I could do was smile and greet him while I rubbed my tired eyes, never giving away that I was exhausted.

"Hey, Fred."

I unzipped the backpack and took out the Box, and I could see a flicker of greed in Fred's eyes as he grabbed it.

"Thank you so much for doing this, pal!"

"No problem, Fred. So, what are you going to do with it?"

"Sell it, of course. Something like this, after all that's been going on, might need a little bit of the price taken off."

He went to the front door and flipped over the OPEN/CLOSED sign so that it said 'CLOSED'. Fred made his way to the counter before slowly placing the Box onto it.

"Oh, by the way, there's some guy looking for you," he muttered casually.

"Some guy? Who is he?"

"Ain't got a clue. Said his name's... damn, what was it? Hang on a second, I'll go get him for you." He went through a door past the counter, forcing me to stand around in wonder. All I could do was ask myself and Cain questions. Who could this person be? And how did he know I was coming?

'Maybe he's some kind o' government spook?' Cain asked, his voice echoing in our head.

With Fred gone, I muttered my reply. 'I don't see how the US government would be interested in us,' I shrugged off. 'Besides which, how would they even be aware of us in the first place?' Seconds later, Fred came back, still with a smile, and behind him emerged a large heavy-looking black man wearing a black suit and tie. The suit made it a little tough to figure out if he was muscular or overweight, but I realised it was the latter thanks to a double chin that stuck out against his tight shirt collar. The only notable (and archaic) thing was that he sported an afro that just about went past his ears, looking as though a bush had invaded his head.

"Mr Short?" The man inquired as he drew closer to me and Fred stood back.

"Yes?"

85

"This here's…" Fred introduced.

"Dwight White," our new friend cut in. He drew one hand into the breast pocket of his suit and flashed a badge, filled with I.D. and the name of who he worked for. "I'm with the US government…"

Cain belted out in our head, 'I knew it!'

"… part of a little organisation that deals with – well, let's just say 'weird' stuff."

"Weird stuff? What are you talking about?"

"Mr Short, I think we both know what I mean. For the last twenty years, we've observed and dealt with the supernatural and alien, and we've noticed your involvement with such things."

I couldn't do anything but look surprised. An organisation dealing with all things weird, sponsored by the government? When was our life followed by the lovechild of Torchwood and UNIT from *Doctor Who*?

"Okay," I said, "you know about everything that's been going on here?"

"Yes, we have, thanks to surveillance and tapping your phone conversations. Hope you don't mind." A sense of sarcasm was detected in his voice.

"Not at all," I said sarcastically. "So, since you've decided to talk to me, what happens now? Do I get a request to write stories about you and publish them in a sci-fi magazine? Or do we sit down and spend an hour talking about our experiences and sipping tea and coffee?"

Dwight smirked at my remarks. "Nothing like that, no. Instead, we're giving you the opportunity to join us, be a part of the team. We've been based in America for a long time, but we've decided to set up multinational branches, and we might need someone like you in the British one. Your experience could be very helpful, especially since we're recruiting newbies who need to learn a lot more about the 'other side' of our world. Although, it depends on whether or not you already have some form of occupation, as well as any skills you believe you can lay out for the job. If you're free, then I promise you, the pay is *very* good."

What an interesting proposal. The chance to join these people, who've no doubt faced stuff parallel to my own cases, was such a rare thing. A part of me wanted to work with him, but another side felt that I'd need to know more about what I was dealing with. I can't just sign up for a job when I barely know the details, now can I?

"To be honest, I'm not employed at the moment; got fired from my last job because of cutbacks. I really need the money. Okay, Dwight, sounds like a good offer. What exactly would we have to do?"

He gave a low hearty chuckle. He sounded relaxed, very casual, as though he was talking to an old friend. "Not much, really. Just help us in investigations, like tagging along, apply your knowledge and experiences to any areas, filing events. It's a very important job, and I'd hate for you to back down, since you seem like an interesting fellow, David. Or am I talking to Cain?"

Our heart skipped a couple of beats as I froze up. He knew that I had another personality, dammit! How much did these guys know? Cain gave me his own reaction, shouting more in shock than anger.

'What the hell?'

"You – know about him?"

"Ah, I see I'm talking to David. Yes, David, we know about your little friend in there," he said while tapping the side of his head. "Can I see him for a minute? Otherwise it's like hiring twins but only interviewing one of them. That's just unfair."

Someone asking to interview Cain? Just when we thought we saw everything, there had to be someone to bring a pound of insanity to the table.

"Okay, I'll ask him," I muttered. I closed my eyes so that I didn't have to stare at something awkwardly. 'Cain, what do you think?'

Cain's tone was insistent, like a child, very calm but demanding. 'Sure, but as long as you have our back to him first so that it looks dramatic.'

I took in a deep breath and sighed quietly. Dramatic – was that really necessary? He always acted like a little kid, or at least a teenager, always wanting things to be done his way or no way at all. And I, acting as his 'parent', had to cave into such a childish request. I remember wishing at the time that Cain would appear in his own body so that I'd slap the back of his head, the damned idiot.

"Fine, then," I muttered through my teeth.

"What's he saying?" Dwight asked curiously.

Through with my brief conversation, I opened my eyes and didn't so much as talk, but groaned my answer to Dwight.

"He says… he'll talk to you, but I have to turn around so that it's… dramatic." Just saying 'dramatic' made me want to scream until my throat was incurably sore and my lungs were shrivelled.

"O-kay," Dwight said in mild disbelief (I couldn't blame him), emphasising the word's syllables with the pace of a turtle running.

Wanting to get this over with, I turned around, facing the shop's windows and door with the 'CLOSED' sign. I took in a deep breath…

… an' I was there to exhale. I placed my right foot to the left and quickly twirled around to face Dwight. There wasn't much of an expression on my face – there was no smile and my eyes were half-open so that he could make out that I had cat-like eyes. Dwight himself, on the other hand, couldn't help but step back by about – a ooh, half a pace? I could tell from his eyes that he was studyin' every little detail that made me stand out.

"Hello… Cain," he managed to say with some effort, distracted by my appearance.

I was silent, starin' at him like a statue. After five seconds, I slowly and stiffly raised one arm to invite a handshake, my claws pointin' right at his chest. As I did this, my expression changed from unbudgable to a big, toothy, goddamn-creepy smile, every little crease below my forehead stickin' out. The result was an unsettlin' screwed-up piece o' paper that just happened to resemble a face.

"Hiiiiiiii," I croaked in a long, drawn-out way, just to make things even more awkward. What can I say? I like screwin' with people.

Dwight observed my hand, and looked like he was scared at the prospect of me stabbin' him in the heart with it.

"What's wrong?" I asked eerily, abandonin' the slow croakin', soundin' like an ecstatic serial killer. "You a little shy with givin' me a nice, hard handshake?"

Our big buddy regained his posture, replyin' with confident humour.

"No, but I could see that you're a little shy with a nail trimmer."

"Touché, smart-ass." I stopped grinnin' and put my arm down. I hadn't even talked to 'im for a minute and already I was startin' to hate 'im.

"So, you're American? Seems none of my guys took notes on the accent change."

"Guessin' they didn't do the same with our looks. Your 'guys' must have piss-poor senses, huh?" I said it with just a hint of dislike towards him.

"What's wrong, Cain? You don't like meeting new people?"

"No, it's just that... well... you government-organisation types are *weird*. And no, I'm not apologisin' for that; I meant to offend."

"Lucky for you, I can laugh that off." Dwight let out a slow, flat 'ha ha ha'. "Anyway, I could say the same with you." He scanned my body from head to toe. "You look like you could be the basis for a horror movie," the big guy concluded.

"Yeah, and you could with blaxploitation," I snarled.

"Oh, you're both witty! I can tell we're gonna get along just fine."

I couldn't even tell if he was jokin' or serious. If he was jokin', screw 'im. If he was serious, screw 'im. "Yeah, I bet," I said flatly. Listenin' to his accent at the time reminded me of somethin' important. "By the way, how's my accent? Does it sound American-y enough?"

"It's a bit exaggerated."

"Okay, cool. We haven't interacted with Americans for a while now, so I just wanted to make sure."

"Hey, are you forgetting me?" Fred asked.

I pointed a sharp finger at him and shout angrily. "You, you're a fuckin' idiot! If ya took the time to do some goddamn research beforehand, we wouldn't have to be goin' on a train and gettin' assaulted by a giant grey naked man!"

They looked at us with that face you'd normally make when someone says somethin' weird and you wanna ask 'em what the hell they're talkin' about. I kept shakin' my head back and forth at Dwight an' Fred, lookin' at their confused faces.

"Ya had to be there!" I yelled to both of 'em before talkin' to Dwight. "I don't like ya job. Yeah, there's stuff that could be cool enough to fit our bill, but I ain't the kind of person who wants a deskjob typin' at computers. David, sure, but not me. Plus, in case you haven't noticed," I made typing gestures for a couple of seconds, "I can't type. I love these claws, man, though they're a bitch to chew."

That must have been funny, cuz Dwight laughed a little.

"Don't expect to be spending your time typing, Cain. You can leave that to David. Instead, you'll be included in investigations, some might include encounters with the unexpected; or, in your case and mine, the semi-expected."

"What kinda stuff do ya mean by 'unexpected'? I mean, yeah, there's supernatural and alien stuff, but can ya be more specific?"

"Well, you'll just have to find out, won't you?"

The big guy had a good point, and damn 'im if it wasn't a good trap for me, too. I thought o' havin' a lil' talk with Davey-boy on the matter.

"'Scuse us for a moment, Tighty-Whitey-Dwighty – me an' my associate gotta have a discussion 'bout this before we can give ya an answer."

"Fine by me."

I turned my back to 'im while David and I had our mental chat.

'He ain't gonna tell us anythin' unless we agree, right?'

'Unless you agree, yeah. I'm all for this. Are you going to do so?'

"Hmm," I said aloud. I then knew my answer. There actually wasn't much thinkin' involved – as in, none. "Screw it, sign me up, fat boy."

Dwight once again grinned, sayin', "Perfect. All we need to do is set up an interview, go through some paperwork and an I.D., then it's official – you two will be part of the UK branch of the International Investigation of the Supernatural, Extraterrestrial and Paranormal."

Fuckin' long name. Just hearin' it made me stare at 'im in disbelief. I musta blinked more times in five seconds than I had fingernails. "Got a... got a way of shortenin' that?"

"Yes: IISEP."

"Good enough for us, I guess. Oh, couple o' questions – do I get a badge?"

"Yes, you'll have an I.D. badge asserting your place with us."

"Will we be, uh, on the same badge? Cuz when I get round to flashin' my badge, lookin' all cool an' like a cop, I wanna have it say 'Cain' on it, an' have David with one sayin' his. I ain't havin' one meant for both of us with our names listed like we're married."

"If that's what you want, we'll make sure you both get respective I.D.s."

"Great to hear, buddy."

"If it's all the same for you, I think I'd like that handshake now."

He took out his hand, which was pretty big, his fingers lookin' like sausages connected to a burger. I attempted to shake it, just about managin' to do so without scratchin' him with my fingers. Dwight gave us a good, hard shake, nearly made my arm flop about.

"I think this is the start of a beautiful friendship," he said coolly.

Chapter 6

Three Pints and a Packet of Fists

<u>2047</u>

With one foot steadily goin' in front of the other, I just about managed to go through the front door of The Green Goose. Didn't take an awful long time gettin' there, though since I was drunk, it might have actually taken longer than I thought. I took in some o' that pub air, that weird kind of smell that you have trouble describin'; musta been somethin' to do with the atmosphere feelin' pretty... um, indescribable. I guess we could pick up the scent of a bit o' booze, maybe some cigarettes thrown into the mix. If that was the case, I think I can describe the smell – nauseatin'.

The place would have been pitch-black if it wasn't for several orb-shaped lights, about the size of your fist, scattered around. I ain't talkin' about lights on the ceilin', mind you, just glowin' balls connected to nothin'. They were in the middle of every table, behind bars, a few of 'em even tucked away in corners just stickin' to walls. Don't even think about stealin' 'em; they got this little security thing installed, so they glow red and make those fuckin' annoying 'BEEP-BEEP-BEEP' noises like with car alarms.

Davey and I had been goin' to the pub for a couple o' decades, and in order to make sure that we didn't get recognised by people every decade, we'd only go to each pub once a month. A little unnecessary, yeah, but ya gotta take precautions with the whole long-livin' thing.

Weren't that many people there – one table had a bunch of guys in their thirties loudly talkin' about the likelihood of their football team winnin' some match, and two pals were playin' pool with a spark of friendly rivalry in their eyes. At the corner of my eye, a big, damn-beefy fella and a tiny, damn-hot brunette sat on a small round table for two. You could map out every muscle and vein on his arms, thanks to him wearin' a vest. As for her… shoulder-length hair that, if you stared for too long, gave you the feelin' that it'd come to life and strangle you for bein' turned on by a gal's hair (I love me a brunette). She had a tight red shirt that showed off just how big her… balloons were… yummy.

Bullseye. Chances were that the guy was good fightin' material if I goaded him, and his lady friend looked like the perfect bait. At the moment, I could do squat; no point startin' a bar-room brawl without gettin' completely hammered. Maybe it was all that cold outside air, but I didn't seem drunk enough to go ahead with my little plan.

One thing that always caught our eyes were the four bartenders; I know what you're thinkin', "Why the bartenders?" Answer's simple, really – the bartenders were robots. The ones that really could pass for humans, 'cept for their grey eyes and skin that, if ya pay close attention to, had the tiniest hint of plastic. Anyone who grew up with sci-fi stuff like *Star Trek* and that *I Robot* book by Isaac (Asimov? No, Newton) squealed like a bunch of pigs when the big-head scientists allowed 'em to work in public back in the thirties. Not a day goes by when I don't give any of the bartender robots nicknames, that's always fun.

I stumbled my way onto a barstool, givin' it a sense o' pride in bein' the only one out of the lot that was comforted by someone's ass, almost worthy of boastin' it to his lonely buddies. Feelin' pretty relaxed, I took off my black hat and placed it on my lap, holdin' it with both hands. I focused on my reflection in a mirror behind the bar. The only thoughts I had that passed through our head was, 'Damn, I look pretty good in this black coat. Better than red. Who wears a red coat, anyway?'

'Oh ha-ha, Cain,' Davey said hollowly in our head. 'That joke never gets tiring. It's only, what, seventy years old?'

'Hey, I'm not the guy who thought red clothes would look good,' I muttered to my reflection.

'It was the seventies, people were wearing all sorts of things.'

"Yeah, but not a red coat and tri-corner Stetson. Ya end up comin' off as either a cowboy or a gay pirate. No, wait, I'm sorry – those two had better taste.'

'Just hurry up and order a drink.'

My eyes were torn away from my reflection by a voice. Not Davey-boy's, but one of the robo-bartender's. It was male (well, it was designed to resemble one, anyway) and had the appearance of a guy in his thirties, with slicked-back hair and a piercin' glance. He wore a white tucked-in shirt with black buttons, and a pair of black trousers which were concealed by the bar. Oh, and a gold watch was shinin' delightfully off his wrist. Why a robot had a watch on him, I will never know.

"Excuse me, Mr Short?" he asked in a sort o' friendly tone (about as friendly as you can get when you're programmed with feelings).

Took me a few seconds to remember him in my tipsy daze, and when I did, I belted out his name like a maniac.

"DATA!" People gave me a look that said, 'Shut up, you idiot.'

"It's Constantine, sir."

Okay, 'Data' was a nickname I gave him. He always had to correct me – didn't he know what a nickname was?

"Yeah, I know, buddy, it's just that you ALWAYS remind me of that robot from *Star Trek: The Next Generation*."

"I'm afraid I haven't seen that show, sir."

"Well, watch it whenever ya can. You'll enjoy it, I promise ya that."

"I do not think I was programmed to 'enjoy'."

"Aw, c'mon, man. Why ya gotta focus on the LITTLE things?"

"By now I see that you sport an American accent tonight, and what seem to be contacts; coupled with your looks, I assume that that means that I'm talking to Cain Short?"

"Yup-in-dee-di-do, Data, old buddy."

"Constantine, sir. Would you like the usual?"

"Sure, why not? Actually, can you make it three?"

"Why three, sir?"

"Cuz I'm in a bit of a hurry. See those two sittin' over there?" I pointed at the guy and gal with one crafty claw.

"Yes, sir."

"I'm gonna get into a fight with the big dude by makin' a few advances on his lady."

"Why, sir?"

"Cuz I wanna, that's all. Nothin' too complex, just simple fun."

Constantine stared at me in confusion, his artificial brow bulgin' and his grey eyes fixed onto mine, givin' me that piercin' glance.

"I do not see how fighting is 'fun'. It is dangerous."

"Nothin' gets past you, does it, man? See, there're some people in the world who just wanna rumble; cause some damage, throw some punches, and eventually fuck off when they've had enough. I'm one of those people. Dunno why, there's just somethin' in my head tellin' me to do so, like I was programmed with it like how you're programmed with a ton of stuff. Ya get me?"

"I believe I have some idea. Since we, as staff, are programmed to ensure that all customers enjoy themselves, I will allow this."

Clever boy, Conny. I had to hand to him, he was great when bein' a rebel, bendin' his own rules while still stickin' to 'em. That was why I liked him out of all the other robots David and I met – he can be both kind and a bastard at the same time.

"Really? Ain't that kinda against yer job as a goody-two-shoes, law-abidin' walkin' collection o' circuits?"

"Yes, but technically I am going by my programming, so therefore I'm not breaking it. And besides, I've grown bored of my job. Have you any idea what it's like working at beer taps every day for the last three years?"

That deep question wasn't what anyone would expect when tryin' to get pissed. All of a sudden this was blown into a look into Conny's life. No amount of composure could stop me from lookin' at him like I walked in on someone doin' somethin' unnatural. I never had much of an experience at pubs besides drinkin' at 'em, so I knew about workin' there as much as I knew what was underneath my fingernails when walkin' down alleys.

"Uh... can't say I have, buddy. Sorry, I guess."

There he was again, doin' that owl-like stare into my/our soul. His voice shrank into a whisper, nearly hidin' distain, hate and a touch of coldness. Conny was a walkin', talkin' statue that paused every now an' then.

"You get bored of the repetitive nature of it, the fact that you can't escape it because that's what you're made for. I was assembled to work in this establishment, and it's quite taxing on your mind. Imagine being confined in this building, cut off from the rest of society, wanting to escape into the wider world, and see what it is that humans do on a daily basis, how they live their life. No matter how hard I try, I cannot do that. It is my fate to be here, to serve drinks, give and take money, and be switched off when unneeded. From my perspective, there is no time in-between being turned off and on – I cannot have dreams, as much as I desire them. I want all these things so that I can call myself a human. Allowing you to fight in this pub, my own form of rebellion, gives me an opportunity to forget that I am artificial. I can believe, for a brief moment, that I have an existence outside of this prison."

The stare was makin' this speech even more uncomfortable; the idea of closin' my eyes started to seem attractive to me. Part of me was afraid that he might do somethin' god-awful, like: a) throw any old fella across the room, b) takin' the cash register for himself, c) snap a couple o' necks, or d) destroy all the alcohol. Quite a lot of feelings were on show for our dear old pal, but it was tricky figurin' out what emotion he was playin' up the most on that fake, plastic-covered face of his. Bein' a robot, he probably wasn't made to sport a lot of expressions. I guess that's one advantage humans have over robots... for now.

Honestly, I felt bad for poor Conny, cooped up here so that no flesh-and-blood had to do the work for him. If it wasn't for the awkwardness of the moment, I might have said something along the lines of, "I'm so sorry to hear that", or, "Have hope", stuff that David would say. Speakin' of him, David expressed his own feelings (so many people openin' their feelings... this ain't an emotional library, for Christ's sake) by tellin' me the exact same stuff I could've gone with. At that point, I pondered if David's good-guy personality was rubbin' off on me.

This episode of When Robots Go Dramatic was cut off by a sudden mood-swing from Our Friendly Neighbourhood Bartender, as he pulled himself away from my eyes and spoke casually, as though what he blabbed about didn't happen.

"I'll go get you your drinks, sir."

"Good man, good man." I gave him a thumbs-up, as if he did a good job of somethin'. Since he was gonna pull some pints, I thought about doin' again so that there was an actual reason for it.

Data – sorry, Constantine (screw it, I'll call him Conny) lined up three pint glasses from behind the bar, and started fillin' 'em up with two bottles o' my all-time fave booze brand: Mandy's, an Irish pear cider. I prefer that over Magner's (Davey's fave beer), cuz it's got a sweeter taste.

I could hear the surface of foam gettin' all fuzzy and saw whisks of bubbles risin' from the bottom. Every glass was filled with that sweet, sweet liquid gold, and just thinkin' about drinkin' it made my mouth so dry I had a hard time drawin' saliva. When all the glasses were filled, he placed 'em on the bar, along with the one remainin' bottle that had a bit of Mandy's in it.

"That will be £9.75, please."

"Okay, buddy." I put my hat on and shakily ordered my hand to pick up our wallet; Davey and I were kinda ticked off at how my claws were scratchin' the inside of the jacket a little, but luckily there weren't any tears (d'ya know how damn pricey it is gettin' the fabric redone?).

Conny took the liberty of holdin' his palm out for the money. I took out and planted the exact amount in it (£5 note and coins), followed by Conny sortin' out the places for it in the cash register, doin' it faster than any human, all blurry (though that could have been the wine).

"Cheers... cheers, buddy. You're a real nice guy, y'know that? I really like you, Conny, that's a fact."

Not a trace of emotion in his voice – completely deadpan. "It's nice to know that, sir. And it's nice to know that you still won't call me Constantine."

With three wonderful pints for me to guzzle down, I went straight to the job. I grabbed a pint in each hand and took turns sippin' 'em nice and slowly, goin' through all three in a kinda of cycle. That damn-sweet cider flushed down my throat like a toilet flushin'. There was barely a second in-between, it musta been goin' at superspeed to anyone observin' me.

By the time I finished all of 'em – with a nice, long sigh – I turned my head left to right, scannin' everyone else. Some were still occupied with their little routines, while others were fixated on me, givin' me confused stares with their eyes wide-open, most likely because o' my drinkin'. Once I stared back at my 'admirers', they turned around awkwardly as got back to whatever the hell they were doin'.

There was still a tiny bit of Mandy's in one bottle, just as long as a human's fingernail. With that, I gulped it down in one go. And then all that cider hit me. The centre of our brain suffered a mini-explosion that stretched out to every little corner, followed by a sound that kind of went HUM-HUM-HUM. It didn't create enough pain to actually get me screamin', only enough for me to carefully rub my temples with my fingers, and let out a groan or two under my breath.

And then the alcohol REALLY started to hit me. Eyes started gettin' a buzzin' sensation, like bees were goin' around in 'em. This forced me to close 'em REAL tight, that kind of works at times. That lasted for about three seconds before the pain of doin' it made me back out. I had the strangest sensation to open my mouth as far as I could until my jaws hurt, and release a tiny, almost mute croak from the eye pain. Still, bloody good drinks.

"Did you enjoy the drinks, sir?"

"Yeah, Conny – I mean, *Constantine*."

"Happy to know. You called me by my name – I believe tonight has been successful for the both of us."

"You're a bit of a smartass, ya know that?"

"I was programmed to be a 'smartarse', sir. I take great pride in it."

"Guessin' you were programmed to feel pride, too?"

"No, actually. I take pride in *that*, as well."

"No arguin' with that, then. Anyway, 'kay if I have another three pints?"

"That depends, Mr Short. Did you have anything to drink before coming here?"

"Um..." I counted with my fingers. All the pints and wine screwed up my memory a bit. I was lucky I was able to remember what I had to drink a second ago. I concentrated all my resources into finding out the answer. Dave tried askin' me for help, but I bunked him off. Doin' this quietly, and Conny's incredible patience, distorted time for me. I couldn't even tell how long this was takin'. And then the answer hit me; not like a wine-cork, thank god.

"One, a bottle of wine."

"A bottle of wine and now three pints?"

"Yup."

Conny looked into my eyes like a hawk again. "I'm sorry, Mr Short, but I can't serve you anymore drinks."

"Awww," I groaned. "Alright, then. By the way, how long did I take to answer?"

"One minute, three seconds and fifteen milliseconds."

An impressed whistle escaped my lips. "That's a very precise figure."

"Indeed. Are you still going to get into a fight, Mr Short?"

"Yeah, wish me luck."

"If anything, I wish that you would always call me 'Constantine' and never anything else."

"Okay, I promise I'll always call you 'Constantine'."

I got off my seat and straightened my hat, ready to get straight to business. Givin' my robot buddy a nod, I parted from him with a goodbye before walkin' to the brawny dude and his gal.

"See ya later, Data."

Conny muttered under his breath, "Goodbye, idiot." Nice guy.

'Cain, don't do this. Again, like I said, I'll stop you if you try.'

'Davey, relax, it's not gonna be over-the-top stuff. Just one blow here, one blow there, and we leave, that's all.'

'I doubt the fellow over there will agree to do it like that.'

'We'll see about that, won't we?'

Although I gained a lot more courage from gettin' drunk, it didn't help that those fuckin' lights were blindin' me. I blinked a lot so that they didn't slow me down; this made it easier for me to see that big ol' mountain of a guy. I was then right in front of 'em, just standin' and lookin' at the lady, focusin' on her... big balloons. There was no way I couldn't be noticed by 'em.

Turns out I was right, as she eyed at me with a scowl.

"D'you mind?" she asked angrily in a Cockney accent. I didn't expect her accent, especially since I really don't like it.

"No, baby, I don't mind at all," I slurred.

"Piss off, mate," the guy said.

"Gimme a sec, man, I'm tryin' to enjoy the view while it lasts."

"Go before I hurt you." He stood up, displayin' to me his large, almost bulgin' muscles and the honour he had for his woman in that fiery, I'm-gonna-kiss-yer-ass look in his eyes. That definitely caught my attention. My voice was just gushin' with excitement.

"Ooh, you're a big boy, ain't ya? How about we have some fun, know what I mean?"

'Disgust' is a pretty good way to describe his reaction to my question (like I hadn't disgusted him already), and responded with pullin' back his right arm, ready to punch me.

101

Wantin' to make sure he got the first punch to start it off, I made sure I'm perfectly still so that I could take the blow.

Even though I relaxed, my upper body suddenly jerked to the right, against my will, dodgin' what could have been a great punch. That fist went straight past my head like a missile missin' its target. What the hell? My question was answered by my good old close friend:

'See, I told you, Cain. Try anything and I'll stop it.'

I took two steps back, hopin' not to be hit while distracted.

'Took ya a while,' I thought.

'It's all that bloody alcohol.'

Mr Beefy, meanwhile, was still tryin' to deck me, firin' another jacked-up torpedo at me with his left arm. David, not done with just makin' me chicken out with the first punch, kept up our dodge act; my/our body was steppin' back, steppin' to the side, bobbin' up and down like a duck, enough times to make me feel sick more than the alcohol was liable to make me. This was the first time in our very long life that David exerted so much damn control over our body when I was pilotin' it – I was a rag doll bein' moved around.

Thankfully, my attacker was gettin' fed up of this, as the time between his blows were gettin' slower an' slower, his interest wanin' despite the angry look on his face still bein' there.

"Dude, there's a time to give up and a time to give up. Do you give up?"

Just like that, his woman got up and grabbed his shoulder the way a crab would try and pinch someone. In response, he turned to her, ignorin' me for the moment. With no one tryin' to hit me, David stop shakin' me around.

"Duncan, stop it, now! That's enough."

"Angela..."

Duncan? To me, that name's just silly. Very, very silly. I couldn't do anything else but snort at that fact. As for Angela? Not a big fan of the name. It sounds like someone wanted to make the name 'Angel' sound cuter, and cute ain't my thing.

"Wait, yer name's Duncan?" I asked while grinnin' from how hilarious this seemed, followed by a chortle. "How sad is that? Hopefully you're surname ain't Dick – that'd just be unfortunate for ya."

David snarked at me, 'Yeah, get him mad with an immature insult, that will help.'

Angela shot a scowl at me, and growled, "You, get out of here. Now." God, she sounded so hot. To add even more appeal, her eyes displayed that burnin' need to kick my ass. Sexy women sayin' stuff while angry is such a turn-on for me. Maybe it's because I tended to piss off so many attractive women over the centuries and I got used to it. On the other hand, I was very angry in my early days, always willin' to kick someone's ass, yell and hate things with a passion; seein' 'em share those traits probably had me relatin' to 'em and findin' a common link attractive. Or, the most likely option, I was just a screwed-up asshole. Thinkin' about it, I agreed with the last one, and so did David.

I wasn't willin' to fight a chick, and there was enough excitement already, so I replied to her in an intentionally bad Cockney accent.

"Awright, luv, I'll leave ya two luv birds to it." I faced Duncan and curved one o' my hands into a hook. "'ope you 'ad a good time wiv practice, mate. Keep them 'ooks at 'and, eh?"

I laughed at my joke, but Duncan and Angela just stared at me in contempt. They made it clear that either they didn't get the joke, or they just wanted me to go. Could have been a bit of both. In response, I dropped my accent.

"G-get it? Hooks at hand? It's a– it's a joke. Okay, be seein' ya." I turned around as fast as possible, wantin' to forget their deadpan expressions and anger-filled eyes and get out of the place. Tonight hadn't been very fun, apart from the chat with Conny. I quickly made my way to the door, givin' Conny a glance and wave; he did the same thing, with that eagle-like look. Though walkin' takes a long time for me when drunk, all I had to do was think o' the air, how great it would feel to breathe it in, and that would make the journey to the outside come off as shorter.

103

Chapter 7

Mugging the Monster

One step out the door, and I was transported to a street that gushed with parked cars, sleepy buildings with lights off and windows shut, and a damn fine field of stars. That cold, lovely air filled my lungs up to the point where I could feel my ribs pressin' against them; painful but otherwise relievin'.

Now the next item on the list was figurin' out what direction I had to go in. Was it north? No, there were houses facin' me. South? Wait, that's right behind me. East? Yeah, that was it, east! I shifted myself to the right in some demented wobble, and strutted one good ol' leg in front of the other.

"So, tonight didn't go exactly as planned."

'True, very true. You disobeyed my warning, nearly causing a brawl. Thank God I could stop you from doing anything worse.'

"Like allowin' myself to get hit and call it a night?"

'Better to avoid a blow rather than receive one.'

"Am I wrong in sayin' that you're mad at me?"

'On one hand, you're right. On the other, I'm very disappointed in you.'

The way he said that was like a parent claimin' that they ain't pissed off at their kid for whatever reason, just so that they don't cry and whine and generally act as annoyin' as little brats can be.

"Gonna punish me, 'Dad'?" I snorted at my nickname for him.

'No going to the pub for a month.'

I almost blurted out my shock, but managed to control myself, whisperin' it through my teeth. "A MONTH?! Oh, come ON, David!"

'You brought it on yourself, Cain. This was a good opportunity to be nice and peaceful, but no, you just *had* to try and start something.'

"Can ya really blame me, thanks to that little 'violent' mindset goin' on in my part of our head?"

'Look, I just expected you to have a little more self-control. All those years teaching you how to ignore it seem like a waste.'

"Sorry, David. Next time I won't be so brawl-happy, okay? I swear, I'll be a good little boy and only get drunk at pubs."

'You better, Cain, or else you'll just have to put up with watching me at the pub through our eyes.'

I sighed. "At least I'll be able to taste the alcohol you'll get down our throat. That way, I can't miss out on bein' drunk to an extent."

'True, but I'll water it down with soft drinks.'

How dare he do somethin' that cruel! Anger struck me so hard I couldn't help but grind my teeth.

"You – heartless – git."

'Tough, Cain.'

Distracted by our conversation, I almost failed to spot an alley on the right, in-between a closed off-licence and a card shop. The lack of lamps on the street shrouded it, and there was barely any light from the other end, though I heard the voices and saw the shufflin' silhouettes of a couple o' guys who sounded like they were in their twenties. Our house was just in that direction, about a fifteen-minute trek, so it wouldn't hurt to use a shortcut. If anythin', it could lessen how long it'd take for me to get home while drunk by about five minutes.

"Okey-dokey, this'll go well."

The shufflin' commenced in loud steps, helped by the space o' the alley makin' it sound like a baseball bat hittin' a ball. I musta been halfway through the place before one o' those kids spoke out to me.

"Oi, you!"

Surprised, I froze for a couple of seconds before slowly turnin' round to face 'im. There he was, wearin' a cap

105

(couldn't make out the colour; probably black) with a smiling cartoon skull on it. It had a visor that was long enough for you to dive off of; it was tough not to focus on it more than his face. Speakin' of face, he didn't have any eyebrows (coulda shaved 'em) which made me think of givin' him new ones with the help of a permanent marker. He wore a brown leather jacket that was made with attached leather hands (thanks, 2040s fashion) which he probably bought to make him look cool. Oh, an' he had a knife in his right hand; I almost forgot to mention that.

Not stressed out about the knife, I talked like a cheery little boy, smilin' to present my fangs. "Yeah?"

The punk took a half-step forward, and he grunted out his words, twistin' his lips into a wobbly shape, givin' me the chance to see that he was talkin' through grindin' teeth. He needed a brush and toothpaste, cuz they were so yellow I thought his mouth had struck gold.

"Hand over your wallet. Now." His three pals came toward me, makin' them easy to see without the shadows. One was black, dressed in a white cardigan and had calve-high boots; he had two handguns connected by one long ammo clip, which was long and flexible enough to go around your body, and could touch the ground if you had your hands to your side. He pretty much had gun-chucks (which is why, in our head, David and I nicknamed him Chuck). Another was thin (nicknamed him Stick Figure, looked like a skeleton; his cheekbones were REALLY pushed out) coulda been six feet tall, was white and wore a denim jacket, carrying nothin' but his fists. The last one (McTubby) had a white vest that looked WAY too small for him; it didn't help that he was as wide as his chums put together, with arms that you could use as pillows. I swear he had three chins, each one of 'em bigger than the last. None of 'em even looked the slightest bit intimidatin', and not givin' a rat's ass, I decided to have some fun with them.

"Oh, my wallet? Okay, let's see where it is, then." I patted my pecs, stomach and pockets in a kind o' fast, panicked way.

Just when I thought I was gonna stop, I was havin' so much fun I carried on with it, pattin' every single part of my body.

"Let's see – no, not the calves, that's usually the tightest place to put it... biceps, nope, what a pity... well, it's not under my fingernails, they're already filled up with something, could be dirt..."

I took off my hat and lightly scruffed up my hair before restin' the hat on my head again.

"Okay, couldn't find it. Oh wait, maybe it's back at the pub – I just came out of one, see – so gimme five minutes while I search for it. Hang on, it's a big place. Okay, make it half an hour; sure, I might come out even more drunk then I was comin' in, but I might find the wallet for ya." I let out a small giggle.

The kid wasn't impressed by my light-hearted humour/insult, takin' another step forward and raisin' his knife up to where my neck would be.

"Look, we ain't *fucking* joking, Yank. Hand us ya money, or else you'll be wishing ya had more time with ya lips."

"Had more time with my lips? That's one of the dumbest threats I've heard comin' out of a knife-nut's mouth. Are you new to this muggin' business? Ya don't just say to 'em 'hand over your money' and expect 'em to follow. Ya gotta back up your threat; sure, you got a knife, but ya gotta raise it to right against my throat, not to raise it to where my throat's gonna be if you take a couple of steps. Use yer initiative, for cryin' out loud. I don't wanna have to be the author of 'Muggin' for Dummies'; but chances are, you guys are so dumb you ain't even the target audience."

'Chuck' put on a scowl, and aimed both guns to my face. Mr Skeleton got into a boxin' stance. McTubby lover cracked his necks a couple of times. The knife-nut had had enough of this.

"Quit fuckin' about, Yank! Hand us it, including all ya cards and codes, or we'll fuck ya up! My name's Will Spade, ya hear me? I'm the guy calling all the shots, ya get me? We're The Four, the best gang on the streets. We're the hardest of the hard. We don't take shit from no one, especially not some arsehole who thinks he can get away with bein' a funny guy. And you're American, too. We *hate* Americans, you…"

While Will 'Why-Am-I-Still-Boastin'' Spade was blabberin', my face was sort of fixed on him in an attempt to hide that I wasn't spacin' out. For the head honcho, he was so boring when tryin' to make himself sound like a badass that had to be feared. Instead, he came off as an annoyin' little twerp who wanted to have respect in whatever way.

At some point I stopped listenin' after hearin' him curse a lot. Kid was probably makin' up so much stuff that I couldn't be bothered to take him seriously. I went on a little constructive criticism; he actually got me and David questionin' a few things while I was spaced out. Like, why and how would a small gang – of four, just so they'll let ya know – be the biggest punks in the area? Wouldn't the best of the best do more than just randomly mug a drunk guy, and do more efficient things like smuggle drugs to big-time drug lords or somethin'? For them to earn their reputation, they'd probably have to be the only gang operatin' in the area, since one with more people would easily topple this sad pile of idiots. And why even call yourself 'The Four'? If ya lose one or two of your members, that'd seriously affect your title. 'The Two' or 'The Three' don't sound as effective (not that their current name was effective in the first place). I came up with a better name for them – The Four Stooges.

"…you fuckin' listenin', Yank?" the fat one asked us.

Half-aware of what was goin' on outside my head, I just gave a smile and a nod.

"Then hand it over." McTubby made a little give-it-here gesture with one hand. I shook my head while thinkin' of other ways to insult them.

Will took that as the last straw, and pulled back his knife arm, which was the only thing that changed from the last thirty seconds. By the time I snapped out of it and got back into the real world, I felt a small stingin' sensation in my stomach. While it hurt, it also felt kinda warm, and there was somethin' stuck there, which I could tell from the fact that at least one of my organs might have been stabbed. Ow. I looked down and saw a small dark pool of blood comin' out of the bottom half of my shirt. The gunk was slowly oozin' out and mixin' with the whiteness of the shirt, makin' an ugly pattern that stretched out, goin' down, goin' left, goin' right.

Surprised to see my blood spill (after some unknown years of not seein' it), I undid my shirt buttons, took out one clawed hand and carefully brushed it against the area of the wound, not wantin' to accidentally cut myself and get another noticeable mark like the one I had now. I examined my own life-juice, every line on my palm and digits smeared in it, remindin' me of the hand and foot-prints Hollywood stars would present to the world on barely-solid cement slabs.

Somehow, maybe from the lack of seein' blood after a long time, a part of me was compelled to lick it off rather than brush it on my legs. The chance of doin' it won over my voice of reason (which might have been David), and I unleashed my tongue to do the job. It slowly went up my palm, wide and wet, and came off once I reached the top of my fingernails. God, it felt fantastic. I could feel the dark, rich taste of it in my mouth and the warmth it gave to my throat as I swallowed it. This was a flavour I hadn't felt in a long time, and it made me want more of it. If blood was a food, it would be the only thing I'd eat. I didn't mind if it was stained on my gums or on my teeth; the knowledge of bein' able to lick it off later gave me satisfaction.

I could hear The Four Stooges' groans and voice of disgust, spoutin' curses and sayin' that I was fucked up. I had to agree with them, but that doesn't change the fact that I was still wounded.

The stab didn't send me back a few steps – maybe because I was drunk or it was thanks to bein' stabbed so many times that our body numbed down the pain. Either way, the hole made from the knife would be patched up in under thirty minutes, more than enough time to deal with the idiots. Takin' advantage of my unbuttoned shirt, I covered my other hand with blood and showed it to Will "Creeped-Out-By-This"

Spade. By now my voice was strained with delight, as I felt like a bride on her honeymoon.

"Look at this, son. I'm delicious. Want a piece of me? Trust me, you won't regret it. Come on, take a lick of me. The taste is downright BLOODY divine." My tongue circled my lips, showin' off its crimson look.

My thoughts felt so savage, and I enjoyed every bit of it. David expressed his disgust in it, and, makin' a 180-degree turn, I had to agree when I heard him. I wasn't like this nowadays, not willin' to down blood like my favourite drink. Centuries back, I was an absolute berserker, a real monstrous piece o' work – there wasn't anyone I wouldn't kill. The only thought that went in my head was to kill anyone I saw with no discrimination. If there was blood spilled, chances are I'd lick it before doin' anythin' else. You wouldn't want to have been around me (more than now, dependin' on your view). There was a voice in our mind, only callin' out to me, never David, though if I want to, I could let him hear it. We remember what the Voice says, always the same thing, like a broken record lastin' till the end of time.

KILL THEM, KILL EVERY SINGLE HUMAN.

We never remember what the Voice sounds like (aside from that it echoes), only that it wants me – not David, just *me* – to go around an' do that one command. Because I was a dumb bastard with barely any self-awareness, that was what I would do, an animal carryin' out a mission while somehow knowin' what to do, much like how an animal knows how to do stuff despite not learnin' it from anyone else.

Thankfully, David 'tamed' me, if that makes any sense, takin' away my literal bloodlust, whereas tonin' down my love for violence has been takin' a while (now it's just limited to bashin' the worst criminals and the very rare bar room brawl). A part of me hated him for that, cuz he took away a chunk of who I am (or was), but most of me thanked him cuz he made me feel human, got me to appreciate bein' more of a man than I was before. That part of me/us was locked away in a corner of our head, under lock n' key. We hoped that it would stay that way, forever and ever and ever – but now it saw a crack of light shinin' on its face, and wanted to swing that damned door open, see all that light, and be FREE! HONEST TO GOD-DAMNED FREE! We heard that voice again, and so many thoughts came floodin' to me, so many unrestrained needs:

TEAR THOSE PUNKS' GUTS OUT AND SUCK ON 'EM TILL THEY'RE DRY AND COLOURLESS AND EAT 'EM AND CLAW 'EM AND BITE THEIR SKIN AND CHEW ON IT TILL I HAD MY FILL AND LICK THEIR BONES THEIR LOVELY THICK BONES AND PIERCE THEIR TINY NAVELS WITH MY CLAWS MY SHARP-AS-HELL CLAWS, TEAR THEIR STOMACHS OPEN WITH BOTH HANDS CHOMP OFF EVERY ONE OF THEIR LITTLE DIGITS ALL TEN OF 'EM KEEP 'EM IN MY POCKETS FOR SNACKS LIKE PEANUTS SHOULD I UNRAVEL THEIR BRAINS AND EAT 'EM LIKE NOODLES OR FEAST ON 'EM LIKE CHINESE TAKEAWAY BOXES SO MANY CHOICES SO MUCH GLEE TO TAKE FROM 'EM

With effort, David and I shut off those thoughts with as much difficulty as it'd take for you to turn off a switch from a distance. My/our head was hurtin' an awful lot, the forehead throbbin' in tune with our now-rapid heartbeat, and coverin' it with our blood-stained hand (not carin' if some of the stuff was on our face) made us realise that we were now sweatin' from the pain of closin' the lids on those thoughts that I never wanted to hear again.

Meanwhile, outside of all that mental angst, Spade was surprisingly the most calmed out of everyone else; he stood his ground, not movin' an inch back, and still raised his now-bloodied knife to me, though his eyes did shift from me to the knife. Seein' me say all that creepy stuff might put him on edge with the right use o' words from me.

"Stay back, ya hear me? Or I'll—"

"Stab me? You've see how well that worked. None of ya get it, do ya?" I took in a deep breath (as deep as ya can when you've got a hole in yer gut) and shouted with confidence and ferocity, "I'M INVINCIBLE!"

"You're a loony," Will spewed out shakily, anger and fear evident and the grip on his knife even tighter.

"Look at you. You're all just pathetic. Best gang in the streets, my ass. I bet you ain't got the balls to get any job done, even if it's muggin' some prick like me. Plus, your looks ain't exactly terror-inducin'."

I faced McTubby. "You, eat what Stick Figure's eatin'. Swear to god, ya look like you're one meal away from bein' a sumo wrestler."

Not willin' to spare anyone my harsh bluntness any time soon, I turned to the Stick Figure. "You, eat what McTubby's eatin', otherwise people are gonna mistake ya for a skeleton at a medical centre that just escaped."

Finally, there was Chuck. "And *you*... get some fashion tips."

That did the trick; I could see the fear in their eyes turn into hate, the kind that goads ya into beatin' up someone. After all, I wanted them to make the first move, just like how I planned at the pub.

"You're all so willin' to beat me up, steal my money, yeah? Well, then, let's see if you'll get as far as one punch, ya pile of know-nothin' waste-of-space."

McTubby made the first move, rushin' at me with a high-pitched squeal that I think was supposed to be a battle cry. Even though there wasn't much space between me and the rest of 'em, I took my time to behold the jigglin' fat hangin' on his arms and the oh-so-easy-to-see man-tits that bounced around under that tight white vest. One straight punch to the solar plexus winded him, which I was lucky to hit under all that girth, cuz it looked like my arm was bein' sucked in for a second. He wheezed before I gave 'im a bloody slap on the cheek, followed by a hard punch to the other cheek. Safe to say he wouldn't be chewin' for quite a while.

Chuck, only holdin' one gun, started firin' at me, but I saw his shots comin' a mile away and dodged 'em as fast as lightning. The only thing that got hit was the wall, as a few stuck-in bullets will tell ya. By the six shot, he gave up and started swingin' around his other gun thanks to the ammo clip, lookin' like he was tryin' to imitate Bruce Lee himself. I struck up another name for him, somethin' that coulda been used for blaxoitation martial arts flicks with a hero who moves really fast and hits really fuckin' hard.

"Whatcha gonna do, Black Thunder? *Pistol whip* me?" Then somethin' occurred to me. "Actually, that's a nice pun. Gotta write that one down."

Chuck, thanks to my pun distractin' me, threw his gun-chuck at my arm. Now, you'd think he was tryin' to hit me with the gun he wasn't holdin', probably in the face or anywhere else that might hurt, but no. No, instead, he made it really frickin' clear he wanted it to hit my arm, or maybe wrap around it so he could pull me forward. How do I know? Simple: the gun bounced off my arm and plopped onto the dirt-covered concrete ground, at which point Chuck muttered, "Damn."

That was just a beautiful fail, so funny that I nearly let out a laugh, instead lettin' out a raspy sound in my throat that vaguely sounded like one. Grinnin' like the nut job I am, I quickly grabbed the gun near my feet and, chucklin' under my breath, happily yelled, "Get your ass over here!" And he did, in a funny awkward jerk. Very quickly, too, just like how I very quickly punched him right in the nose and sent him screamin'.

"Nice guns," I said while holdin' both guns. "Shame they're wasted on an idiot like you." He didn't listen, though. Cuz of the nose, see. Eyein' the bin, I threw the gun-chuck into it, where it hit the very bottom with a CLANG.

The Stick Figure, in his stance, tried to hit me. Left jab, blocked by my right arm. Right jab, blocked by my left. In return, I gave him a barrage of fast blows from stomach to chest in a circular fashion and a hard punch to each shoulder. To finish him off, I sent him into the bin head-first.

"Good riddance to bad rubbish."

Now it was just Spade. He hadn't moved ever since his friends pounced at me. Hands were shakin' slightly, mouth was open, eyes were wide with fear. Good. That meant he was either gonna flee or embarrass himself.

"It's just you now, boy. You're the big, bad leader of this group of piss-ants, so hopefully you got a lot more to offer than them." I spread my arms and legs out so that I was in a star shape to mock the brat.

"Here, this'll make things easy for ya," I stated in mock-kindness. "An' I promise ya, I won't move, not by an inch. Cross my heart an' hope to not-die." To goad him further, I smiled hard enough to give off a cocky-guy-who'll-get-what's-comin'-to-'im look, with my teeth (sharp or not) on display.

Spade focused on my stance, and his eyes seemed to have that look that suggested that he was willin' to risk the injuries he'd get, in a vain attempt at tryin' to take me down permanently this time, to succeed where his pals didn't. He closed his mouth and his shakiness stopped; the knife looked pretty still to me. All that confidence had to build up to somethin'.

Waitin' for him to move, I whispered loudly, "Come on." In a heartbeat, he ran towards me the way a dog runs to its owner, givin' out an angry yell, knife arm pulled back (similar to a punch). I scratch that – he didn't yell, he *roared*, bringin' out all his hatred, every ounce o' oxygen those pair o' lungs could hold. He wanted me so badly, and I really hated to disappoint him. I did.

David and I came up with a nice bit o' teamwork while we observed Spade's change from scared to mad: Operation Close-Enough-Disarm, as I coined it. A second before Spade swung his knife, I tagged out, feelin' myself bein' pulled back into our head by invisible hands, still seein' things as though I never left, but acted like a ghost that didn't wanna do anythin' to whoever it was hauntin'. As I gave David centre-stage to counter, our face shiftin' from my toothy grin to his closed bombastic smile, channelin' as much life into it as I was.

Spade's arm swung at us wildly, just inches away from our face, but David, with ridiculously great speed, grabbed his wrist with our right hand, almost squeezin' it. In the same beat, he moved our body to Spade's right arm, lockin' our left

114

arm around his – David did all this in a way that didn't seem human (well, to you, but normal to us), shift as a dancer in the moment. Our shoulders were as close to Spade's as much as possible, with clothes bein' the only barrier. The kid dropped his knife and turned his head to us, now back to being the little wimp he was before.

"Hey there, son," David said casually, like talkin' to an old friend.

"P-please don't hurt me," squealed Spade, his voice goin' into a painfully high pitch.

"Don't worry, I won't. You've seen what I can do, so take my advice: give up this gang business. If you don't, you'll look forward to being arrested, killed by the wrong kind of people, or live with the guilt of crossing the line. Alternatively, you'll do terrible things with your peers, and you won't have enough humanity left to see anything wrong with what you do. Do you understand?"

Spade tried to speak, but his throat gave out gibberish in that same pitch, makin' it more painful to listen to by the second. David, in response, tightened his arm lock and his voice became stern and impatient (if it wasn't for the fact that I was just a viewer of this little show, I'd have done the same thing).

"I want an answer, son, and I'm not gonna wait forever. Get your vocal cords straightened up immediately."

"O-o-o-o-okay! I won't do that shit again! Promise!"

"And your mates as well."

"Yeah, sure!"

"Good."

David released him from the hold, still in that dancer kind o' way, and gave 'im a hard pat on the shoulder. All that stern and straight-to-the-matter talk was replaced with the 'old friend' tone.

"Have luck getting on in life, Will. Get that one with the broken nose to the hospital, if you can." We turned around and walked to the other side of the alley, actin' as though the entire incident never happened. There weren't any other footsteps echoin' 'cept our own, so I thought Will was still standin' there in shock. David spoke to him one last time without ever stoppin' or lookin' back.

"Oh, and what've you learned?"

"I don't know," he said in a quiver.

"Never try mugging a monster, Will. Some people can be right beasts."

Chapter 8

The Moderately Big Shop of Horrors & An Up-Close Interview with an Arachnareptile

The hangover was easily the worst we'd ever had; for the first time, it felt like a full-on blitz instead of a tiny explosion that you could shrug off. Normally, we'd feel pretty tipsy after getting back from a pub, but now we felt like someone was bashing our brain in with a sledgehammer repeatedly – and carrying on even after turning it in a red pinkish mush.

The sensation of it was what woke us up, a great throbbing across our forehead, doing laps from side to side. I groaned as I rubbed it gently, and when that didn't do anything, rubbed it harder until it began to hurt (well, less than the hangover, anyway). Cain wasn't exactly having a great time, either; since he was nestled right in our brain, the hangover could have felt even painful for him. His blood-curdling screaming didn't help.

'AAAAAAAARRRGGHHHHH! SWEET TAP-DANCIN' CHRIST ON A LEMONADE STAND, THIS IS GODDAMN MORTIFYIN'!'

Not the best thing to hear from your roommate when you wake up. Covering my ears to mute him would have been pointless, so, tired and annoyed, I simply let out an exhausted sigh.

"Good morning to you too, Cain. Good sleep, then?"

'DO I SOUND ALRIGHT TO YOU, YA SNIDE-REMARKIN' TOSS BUCKET?'

I got out of bed while massaging our aching head in vain. "Well, you're insulting me, so you're off to a good start."

'OH, SCREW OFF.'

"Ah, that's the kind of politeness from you that gives me a big old smile."

'Then why ain't ya smilin'?'

"Because you gave us this hangover, remember?"

'Oh, don't go harpin' on about THAT, will ya?'

"Can't help it, Cain, it's your fault."

The pain in Cain's voice eased off while I eyed our wardrobe and took out and wore a pair of dark blue jeans so we didn't have to stroll around in our pants. In the past, whenever Cain was in control of our body, if he wanted to spend the whole day at home, he'd go around bullock-naked, intending to express his desire to be au natural, or "unleash the beast" as he likes to call it. He'd sit on anything; beds, furniture, even the floor, all defenceless against our bare body. What would have helped the matter was if he had bothered to make sure to close the windows and blinds beforehand – the outraged yells and confrontations with neighbours were still fresh in our memories.

"Anyway, let's get the day started. It's—"

I looked at the alarm clock on my bedside cabinet. The time was 7:15, and the *tick-tick-ticking* was very loud. Ow.

"—7:15. Let's get breakfast and head out to the coffee shop." We'd head to work at 8:30 on weekdays, 8:00 on a Saturday. Thanks to the magic of Sunday, we now had the opportunity to get up early for the sake of it and relax.

'Good idea, Davey-boy. Let's take advantage of our day off. Go to a couple o' stores, buy somethin' real nice?'

"Sure, no harm in that. First, let's fight off this hangover. Swear to God we'll need to drink an ocean to sort it out."

'Ugh. I hate the sea; all that salt water.'

I put on a white buttoned-up shirt that was lying on the floor without paying much attention, only to casually moan when looking at it properly after putting it on.

"Oh, yeah. This is the one that's got blood on it. Need to put it in the washer when we get back."

Looking into our wardrobe again, I pulled out a yet-to-be-bloodied white shirt, buttoned it up, and made my way downstairs to the kitchen, holding onto the stair banister while massaging our alcohol-addled forehead. The kitchen itself was trapped in time; empty wine bottles, cutlery, bits and pieces of noodles and rice, as well as shiny Chinese tin containers, were still standing, now serving as artefacts of a good, talkative dinner. Although there was something that caught my eye, a new, foreign element to this mini-museum; a bowl of cereal, complete with a spoon, tucked into a corner of the kitchen table. The contents, some kind of chocolate-wheat combination, appeared to have succumbed to sogginess, all wet and light in colour. Peeking into the bowl, I noticed that the liquid in it didn't look right, as it was light brown.

"Cain, what's in the cereal?"

'Huh? What're ya talkin' about?'

"This isn't milk, that's for certain. Hang on."

I got up and made my way to the fridge. Opening it, I discovered a large skimmed plastic milk bottle, empty. I sat on the chair again and swirled my spoon around, looking at the weary colour and the swimming cereal. There was no other way to know than to try the stuff out, so I took a spoonful of the liquid and sipped it. As soon as the taste was recognisable, I spoke again, recoiling in disgust with my eyes closed tight.

"This is Jack Daniel's. Why is there Jack Daniel's in a bowl of cereal?"

'Oh, I remember!'

"Okay, explain."

'See, we got back home and we talked about weird food combinations, and I brought up mixin' booze and cereal together, so that's what happened.'

"So, we both gave it thumbs up?"

'Yup.'

"Wow. I must have been more drunk than I realised."

'Yup; we had a couple o' bottles o' beer in the livin' room, I think, so ya got pretty pissed.'

I got out of the chair and cracked our neck; it was awfully stiff, with the uncomfortable feeling of someone pushing their fists into the side of it.

"Anyway, let's put aside our alcoholic adventures and put on some toast or something. You okay with jam?"

'Yeah, sure.'

"Great. Just have this, then we're off."

*

"Hi, I'd like an almond latte, please."

The coffee shop was almost packed, which was an achievement considering that, as soon as I stepped in, it had only just turned 7:45. People were drinking tea, coffee, soft drinks, hot chocolate, all that stuff. Some of our favourite shops wouldn't open until 8:30, so in the meantime we had the chance to sit down and enjoy the coffee shop's atmosphere. The challenge was finding a place to sit. So many people, so little seats. I ended up strolling down the place, glancing left and right in my little quest, my shifting head resembling occasions where a fly would get right in your face. Thankfully, it didn't take long to find one.

Taking care, I blew lightly before taking in the first sip, and was delighted in the heat and the almond-tinged taste. I let out a small sigh of satisfaction, feeling a tad livelier than I was when we woke up. The only problem with this was Cain's reaction:

'Urgh. Fuckin' coffee.'

'Oh, shut up,' I thought. 'It's good.'

'Just cuz we got the same taste-buds doesn't mean I gotta agree with ya.'

'Keep it to yourself.'

'We're in the same head, moron.'

'Then don't think about it or else we'll start an argument.'

120

I applied some sugar and swirled it with a spoon before drinking the coffee again. The taste was naturally sweeter and much more to my liking. I looked around at the other customers; people sitting on their own, biding their time by reading newspapers or books or on their phones. There were also mothers, daughters, sons, fathers, grandparents; families all interacting, being there for each other. All those people made us think. The closest thing we had to family at this point were the lads at the organisation and, even stronger than them, Emily and Scarlett. There's quite a long list of close ones, nearly all of them long dead. We'd probably forgotten other people, possibly hundreds, names and faces blurred by the fog of our mind that spread with every century; chances were that we'd forget Emily, Scarlett, Dwight and everyone else within a millennium. It's been so long. Too long.

In the middle of our thoughts, we felt a slight buzzing sensation in our head. At first, it felt relatively minor, barely registered to us. But in seconds, it became more noticeable, making our head feel dizzy, light, accompanied by the sound of white-noise growing unbearable. We thought it could have been the hangover, but that had only died down during our walk to the coffee shop. So just what in the hell was this?

The only things I could think to do were to rub our head, drink more of the coffee, muddle with our ears. Nothing worked. The noise, the headache... our head felt like it was about to explode! Both my mental screams and Cain's weren't enough to express our pain, not even if we yelled aloud.

Then, for a reason unknown to us, beyond our control, we suddenly turned to the left and saw a man sitting by himself, reading a newspaper. He wore sunglasses, despite being indoors, and his black hair was a buzz-cut, while a small thick beard compensated for the hair. This was quite an out-of-shape fellow – he wasn't obese, but certainly wide-looking in his brown leather jacket, and had quite a stomach poking out, barely contained by his dark jeans, along with a double chin. He was slimmer than Dwight, that was for certain.

The man, aware of my existence despite looking straight at whatever article he was reading, shifted his face in my direction and smirked – not a smile, but a *smirk* – and nodded as though I was a familiar face. He folded up the newspaper, placed it under his arm, got up and walked past me, still looking at me with that expression. Whoever this man was, he recognised me, and yet despite never recalling him, there was a faint part of us who figured that we did. As he moved away, the pain and the noise dimmed before finally fading away, as though it had never happened.

We were quickly interested in him, so I took my coffee with me and started to follow him. Making sure to keep an eye on him, we noticed that he was already about to exit through the doors; I quickened our pace, looking frantic, footsteps loud. As I left the coffee shop, I tried to spot him amongst a wave of bystanders, but nothing; he had vanished.

Just as we realised this, cursing to ourselves, wishing that we had been able to catch up with him, a familiar voice called out to us.

"Hey, David, Cain."

I turned to my right and saw, much to my surprise, Dwight White himself, still large as life at some sixty-odd years. Twenty years had not granted him many changes; his afro had faded from its superb black colour into a silvery grey, and wrinkles occupied his face like a screwed-up newspaper.

"Dwight," I said in surprise. "What are you doing here?"

"Tracking you down, boys. Tried ringing your home phone, no answer. Mobile, no answer. I figured you'd be out for your morning coffee here."

"You know exactly when to turn up, eh?"

"You're always there at the same time. You've told me before."

"Really? Wow, memory's not as good as it once was. I'm getting on a bit."

"Finally. Only took you a couple of million years. Anyway, I'm here to bring you along with me."

"What for?"

"I'll tell you when we get in the car." He made a come-with-me gesture with his hands as he made his way to a pulled-up car on the street. I followed him, entering the back of the car via the left door while Dwight went in the front passenger seat. As soon as we were in, the driver, the dark-haired thirty-five year old Brad, pulled the handbrake down, and off we went. I found myself wedged between the door and a rather slim but broad-shouldered twenty-something man with combed blonde hair, wearing glasses and a dark blue cardigan. Seemed like a pleasant kid – he nodded and said "Hi" with a smile and took out his hand in favour of a handshake.

"My name's Chris, sir. I've just started out. I'm guessing you're David?"

"Hello, Chris, I am," I said as I shook his hand firmly.

"I was told another person was tagging along. Cain, was it?"

"Yeah."

"Will he be joining us?"

"Actually, he's already here." I pointed at our old noggin. "Right here, specifically."

Chris looked at me like a confused dog, his head turning slightly to his side.

"I'm sorry?"

"We both occupy the same body. Mind you, you'd be able to tell when it's him. He looks a bit rough."

"R-right."

I turned to Dwight's seat, a little annoyed.

"Dwight, if you're gonna tell him two guys are going to be joining you, tell him they're a two-in-one. Otherwise I come off as nuts."

"Wouldn't be the first time," Dwight said with what the rear-view mirror told me was a smile on his face.

"So, Chris, where do you work?"

"Um, in the supernatural department, sir," Chris said with the kind of impossible politeness that makes you question if they're straight out of a posh high school.

"Ah, supernatural, eh? Which area are you in?"

"I'm studying vampires, Mr Short," the youth replied with but a slither of hesitation.

My smile grew like an excited child. "Ooh, our feisty, if fiendishly fascinating, fanged friends! What's your experience with them?"

Chris' mood soured as he looked down at his once fumbling hands and knees. His voice was lower and the politeness bubbling away as he struggled to hide the scratchings of old wounds. "Not exactly what you'd call a pleasant one." He turned over to his door window.

I frowned, dropping my previous amazement and tried to string together an apology, my hands now fidgeting in his place. "If you lost anyone to it, in one way or another, I'm sorry for sounding excited. I tend to forget that some of us are in this line of work due to... personal reasons."

"No, it's alright, you've only just met me," Chris said as he removed himself from the gaze of the window and brushed aside the past in one fell swoop. "Anyhow, I have a lot to learn over at your – oh, I guess it's *our* place, eh? I'm trying to cast aside as much lore the media's given us, even the stuff that contradicts the other stuff."

"You might want to hang on to some of that, son. Rule number one: accept the possibility of anything about everything. Some of our vamp workmates come from all different flavours; hell, there are even ones who are actually angels that got turned. Angel vampires, I kid you not."

"Really?"

"Well, let's check, Chris. Guys, have we got angel vampires at HQ?"

"Yeah," said Dwight. Brad grunted a 'hmm-mm'.

124

"I have got so much to learn," Chris muttered.

"Well to the IISEP. Amazing stuff's aplenty."

Dwight's deep voice sliced his way through our conversation like a sword mowing down a bamboo forest. "Anyway, gentlemen, down to business. Remember how we were trying to figure out who was nabbing those missing people for the last couple of weeks?"

"Sure I do." Said missing people were being taken from the streets in the middle of the night, and due to the town councillor's cheapness, there weren't many cameras surveying every street. In response, we at the IISEP secretly set up cameras roughly around the place of the victims' kidnapping before noticing a pattern – they were all in close proximity of each other. That meant that whoever was responsible had to be living in that area.

"We've finally been able to catch evidence on our security cameras of the culprit."

"Okay, sounds good. Who is it?"

"An old lady, owner of a nearby pet shop."

That was the last thing I expected the hear. Cain and I had a mental list of the possibilities of what the devious criminal looked like; a large, buff man; a youth nearing adulthood; a middle-aged woman, et cetera. A little old lady wasn't one of them.

"...o-*kay*."

"Her name's Caroline Fantus. From what we could make out from a camera located at behind the shop, she's been drugging them so that they're knocked out before she brings them into her shop through the back."

"I wonder what she wants with them? I hardly imagine she's desperate enough to force people to be her late-night customers."

"We'll know when we get there. Plus, there was a silhouette of some sort of animal near the back door, seemed pretty damn large, if you ask me."

"Her favourite pet, perhaps? Maybe she decided to give it walkies in alleys."

"Trust me, whatever it was, I doubt she'd get it out of the house – whatever it was, it had long arms like a spider, definitely not something you'd see in a zoo, hence why we haven't notified the police about it."

"I still think that at least the higher-ups should know about the stuff we come across."

Cain decided to join in on the conversation. His voice was filled with child-like fascination and energy, along with incredible bluntness, as well as being loud. Very, very loud.

"Ooh, ooh, ooh, I got an idea! Maybe it's some sort o' weird animal hybrid thing, like moose-and-chicken, or rabbit-and-kangaroo! A mooken and rabbaroo! OOH, I like that last one - rabbaroo! PERFECT combination! Sounds very rabbity, very kangaroo-ish! Wouldn't ya say, Chris?"

Chris couldn't open his eyes any further than they already were. His head was slightly shifted back, givin' the little fat under his chin the chance to do a fantastic impression of a second chin.

"W-what?" Kid sounded like a timid mouse, barely even a squeak outta him.

"Ya know what, never mind. How ya doin', kid? I'm Cain. Nice to meet ya. I'm sure we're gonna be good friends for as long as you'll live, which isn't very long. How old are you?"

"Twenty-eight," he said, gainin' more courage to speak like a man.

"Wow, you're pretty young, ain't ya? Still, you're gonna die. Live every day like it's gonna be your last. Which might be today, who knows? I hope nothin' claws ya to death, it'd be a pain in the ass, what with all the blood that might go on ya cardigan, which suits ya, by the way. I'm glad we've had this conversation, it's been a real thrill talkin' with ya, Chris. Say, you look a bit like a girl, ya know? Mind if I call ya Chrissie? Or Sissy? Or Sissy Chrissie?"

"Just Chris."

"Okay, whatever ya say, Sissy Chrissie."

"Cain, would you kindly stop annoying Chris," Dwighty said in a big ol' boomin' voice.

"But Dwight, I wanna talk to the new guy! He looks really nice! And cute, too! Seriously, there should be a range of plush dolls modelled after him!"

"Yeah, yeah, he's very nice to look at. Just don't be as creepy as you were just now or else I'll throw you out of the car."

"Ha! Like ya would, ya lyin' Big Whopper."

"Actually, we could deem it that we don't need you for this case, so we could drop you off as far away from the pet shop as we can, and you won't get additional payment for this."

Oh, great. The big guy had me there. With that verbal whack on head, I sulked.

"Fuck. Alright, I'll keep my mouth shut."

"Good man."

"So, Brad, how's the wife?"

"Doing well, Cain," he said stiffly. When it came to drivin', Brad was too focused on gettin' to the destination than he was with the small-talk; it was like havin' a robot behind the wheel. A sharply-dressed robot made of veins, blood, bones and organs. Wait, I think I tripped over myself with that simile. Forget I said that.

"Nice, nice. She still got the artificial leg?"

"Last time I checked, limbs don't grow back." This time, I picked up an emotion from him; anger, and makin' sure it was subtle, possibly so that it didn't break his concentration.

"Okay, Mr Snippy, just askin'. I tend to forget stuff that doesn't concern me. You joinin' us, then? Or just makin' sure no one clamps us?"

"I'll be in the shop with you," he said, any trace of hate for me now gone.

"Great, great. Hope ya do well. Be sure to break a le— uh, an arm."

Phew, saved myself there.

Brad had us outside the pet shop twenty seconds later. It was small, like most pet stores, and there was a sign on one of its windows with a picture of a cute lil' pug puppy that made me REALLY want one.

As usual, Dwight, big ol' leader he was, was the first to talk as soon as we were outside the place. "Okay, everyone, you all know what to do – let's get to it, then."

Makin' our way outta the car, we went into the shop with determined faces and the need to lay out some good ol' justice. The inside of the shop felt restricted, ten feet in width and length, with shelves full o' carrier boxes and a variety o' pet food. There didn't seem to be a set of stairs. Spread out across the area were animal cages to show off any adorable pets on display; they had little name tags to identify them. One talked about Spike, a shar pei; another on Tom, a cat; a small one describin' Jerry, a mouse. It would have been nice if the cages weren't empty – it gave me an' David the chills.

At the back o' the shop was a counter and Caroline nestled there like a mommy bird tendin' to her kids. She seemed to be a pretty-lookin' old gal – late fifties, shoulder-length grey hair with bits o' light brown around her fringe, deep sapphire eyes and not even one crease on her face, which might've been the result of plastic surgery or ironin' her face (I hear that can be quite painful). Even though she was past her prime, she wore a cardigan and a shirt with an open neck exposin' her breasts, an' had a tan that made her look like a damn orange. She had what I like to call Cliff Richard Syndrome. Still, the whole 'kidnapped murdered people' thing put me off; a guy's gotta have standards.

Dwight flashed his I.D. card to her when we got near her. We were going to play it nice an' cool, lull her into a false sense of security before informin' her that we're gonna send her old ass into jail.

"Hey, sweet-cheeks," I said to her in a seductive tone. "Me an' the wife here," I pointed to Dwight, "are lookin' for a pet for our little girl, Chrissie." I then pointed to Sissy Chrissie. "Do you have any spiders we can purchase? Maybe a Komodo dragon? Or both?"

'Oh, yeah,' David thought, 'this is really smooth, not bizarre at all.'

Caroline looked at me/us with disbelief at my intentionally odd suggestion. I didn't care the slightest; my eyes were wide open with the ton of fun we were about to have. Dwight shrugged off my words like I wasn't even there.

"Morning, ma'am."

"Good morning," she said in a cheery voice with a sickeningly sweet toothy smile. Speakin' o' which, she had pretty good teeth for an' ol' broad.

"We're here to ask you about a number of disappearances that've occurred in the area."

"Disappearances? I'm sure I would have heard about it."

"Um, miss," Sissy Chrissie said, steppin' into the conversation. "You would have known about it for two reasons; the newspapers always have them on the front page, and you killed them."

We were surprised at how he was straight-to-the-point about this. So much for settin' her up to knock her down.

"I... beg your pardon?" Her face, despite bein' a satsuma in a tannin' machine, had the faintest bit of redness in her cheeks, and her eyes were opened so far back that I had a feelin' that they'd pop out. Her reaction stumped Chrissie; he had one o' those frowns that implied confusion, and since he was pretty young, he looked like a kid who just stumbled into the wrong classroom and realised he made a mistake.

"Erm, you did *kill* them, miss, didn't you? Or am I talking about your employer, instead? That is, if you're *not* the owner."

"Let me handle this, Chris," Dwight said in a sigh. "We have footage showing you assaulting and dragging people to the back of your shop. As a result, you are under arrest and will be sent to the police after we inspect the establishment."

I could make out a vein emergin' from the side of her head. She raised her voice to shoutin'-level. Somethin' tells me that she was mad.

"I have no idea what you're talking about. Get out of here this instant!" She pointed one stick-like fake-fingernail-filled talon to the front door, but none of us gave a shit.

"I'm afraid that's not an option, miss. Brad, secure her."

129

She bolted away from the counter and made a break for the door behind her. Brad, quick on his feet, grabbed her by the arm and yanked her towards him. Dwight took out a small pad and pen from his jacket an' flipped onto a clean page.

"While we conduct an inspection, you're going to have to answer a series of questions, and any resistance to do so won't be tolerated until we receive answers. As per usual, anything you say can and will be used against you. Do you understand?"

"Yes," she growled from the bottom of her throat. Ooh, David an' I, we could feel the anger, the age-affected gutturalness rollin' off her voice. Had it been comin' from a nice woman in her thirties, I would find that incredibly, unbelievably hot; I would go rock-hard. Instead, comin' for this screwed-up bitch, I found it creepy to the point where I was sure that our dick shrivelled in fear.

"David, Cain, Chris," Dwight announced, "search any rooms available, see if there's any signs of the bodies."

"Okay, Dwight," Chrissie said.

"Sure thing, big guy."

We glanced at the closed door behind Caroline, and I stepped towards it, quickly talkin' to the gal while never takin' my eyes off it.

"Hey, there, fine thing, nice door ya got here. Don't mind if I open it? Thanks, knew you'd understand." I gave the door one helluva kick, all the strength of a kangaroo's, and it fell off its hinges, goin' 'timber' with a '*dunk*'. Ah, unnecessary violence to inanimate objects – one o' the little things in life that makes me giddy. Beyond it was a door seven feet away, with a flight o' stairs on the left side and another door on the right, a padlock securin' it.

"You didn't have to do that," she snarled. "It was open."

"Oh, really? Good to know. Don't give a shit."

"Is he always like this?" I could hear some fear rattlin' around in Chrissie's voice.

"Only when he's excited," replied Dwight. "You should see him when he's drunk; that's how he opens all doors. It's like he's forgotten he has hands."

I went into the next room, walkin' over the fallen door with the faint click o' our heels accompanyin' us.

"Don't touch my baby! My Oliver needs me!"

"Oliver? Another question on the list," Dwight mutters. He then started that borin' business o' talkin' to her with all this law jargon and askin' her a pile o' questions that just drone on an' on. I tuned him out within the first two syllables.

Chrissie an' I went for the door straight-ahead. I opened it, and steppin' in, we saw that there was nothin' but a room around ten feet wide an' long with its tenants bein' cat food, dog food, any other kinda animal food all put in various-sized containers, from pocket-sized bags to large cardboard boxes.

"Hey, Chrissie, lemme ask ya somethin', you bein' new an' all – you ever seen a dead body?"

"No," he said to me/us, and we can see by his face that he was kinda squeamish about the idea.

We went out the room and checked the ten-step flight o' stairs, which curved on the right, and the slightly-bigger-than-shoulder space between walls felt claustrophobic.

"Ah, well, there's a first time for everythin', buddy. You're gonna hate this. A LOT. You're gonna be overwhelmed with what you're about to be exposed to; bloodied, bloated bodies; disgustin', damp decay; the ATROCIOUS aroma." By now, we went past the curve. Again, ten more steps and a door. "If ya want, after this we can head over to a pub, you can blow your brains out with alcohol, I'll be mindin' you like a demented babysitter, and if ya lucky, you'll throw up in a toilet instead of on yourself, which would be a real pity becuz I still like that suit o' yours."

"Thanks for the offer, Cain, it's very kind of you, but I don't think you're making this any easier for me."

"Oh, I see. Want David, instead?"

"Don't get me wrong, I'm fine with you, it'd just that this is really starting to get to my head."

"Right. Sorry about that, man. We'll switch."

Cain allowed me to take over, and I tried opening the door. It was locked. From what we could see from its window, it was only a small room, barely anything in sight. The two (or would that be three?) of us shuffled back down to the ground floor. There was only one more place to check out, the padlocked door.

"Okay, padlocked. Must be important. Excuse me, Caroline, do you have the key that would open that door?"

Caroline took the key out of her jeans pocket and Brad handed it to me. Removing the lock, I gave the key back to him and opened the door. No lights were on – the vague outline of some steps and a light-switch were visible.

Before we could make any progress, we were hit with a terrible damp smell. Best guess was rotting meat and faeces, and it wasn't weak by any means. Our nostrils were assaulted by this to the point where breathing it in for a second felt too long, and our throats were heavy with the need to vomit. We breathed through our mouths to overcome it, and even then the stench was still very much alive, making the air feel so heavy, so dense that you would wonder if you were actually breathing.

"You smell that, Chris?"

"God, yeah."

"Good, of course you can. Helps make you feel human – I'm surprised Cain and I haven't gotten used to it."

"Why's that?"

"I'll tell you later, lad."

I turned on the light switch, and, as faint yellow lights spilled across a flight of stairs, there was a mild apprehension among us. The steps went on for quite a bit – I counted twenty – before they carried on around a small corner, and another set of stairs, wooden walls replaced with stone. It seemed to lead to a basement. Chris and I started to make our way down.

"Okay," I said, "we're going into a basement. Why couldn't it have been the wine cellar at some rich toff's place? At least then we'd have something to drink immediately to help remove the pain of seeing dead bodies."

"I don't think I'll sleep tonight," muttered Chris. Now was the time to offer some sagely advice. It would have worked if Cain didn't keep butting in.

"Relax, Chris. Think of puppies rushing and clamouring all over you, and their warm, fuzzy fur accompanied by – *no*, Cain, we are *not* getting a dog after this, and that's final. The responsibility is – yes, it was a *very* effective poster, but still – come on, don't make me out to be heartless; you *know* I find dogs cute too."

Chris stared at us in puzzlement, bless him.

"Don't worry, Chris, just a bit of alter ego chit-chat." We then went down the second set of stairs, with another lightbulb illuminating the way. The bottom of the steps was barely visible; all we could make out were a second light switch on a stone wall and a foot of concrete floor. The stench seemed to be getting stronger, making it all the more difficult to try and ignore it. The chance of discovering those kidnapped victims as dead bodies grew just as strong.

We could hear, in some part of the room, the sounds of something moving in soft *thuds* – it felt to me that the feet were padded – and the slightly louder noise of vigorous chewing... I don't have to say what I thought was being eaten. With this knowledge, we took our steps as slowly and lightly as possible. One wrong move and we'd have some god-forsaken creature jumping out at us like in a horror movie.

Once we went past the final step, I turned on the switch, and two light bulbs flickered to life. The basement was thirteen feet in width and length, the walls – which were appeared to be cemented, and dull like prison walls – were covered in blood, some of which had turned brown over time. The floor was decorated red in thick, dark blood, littered with body parts so numerous and drenched that it difficult trying to tell what was connected. The only thing we could make out clearly was a jawless head staring at us

133

with a one eye. Chris gave out a kind of half-gasp half-choke sound, and I turned to him to make sure he wasn't going to vomit. I feared that his face would turn green and he'd vomit. Thankfully, massaging his throat, he was able to get a hold of himself and breathe normally.

Tucked away in a corner, swaying its tail like a grandfather clock, was a large, dark-green leather-skinned mass that appeared to be an overgrown Komodo dragon, its fat arms and massive gullet giving it one hell of a bulky physique that made it resemble an alligator that swallowed a sofa. While in any other circumstances we would have considered this to be an extremely disturbing case of an owner loving their pet no matter the cost (feeling like a story more suited for something you'd see off of a mundane crime-drama), it was the four thick, hairy spider-like appendages sticking out of its back that signalled to us that this is more or less in our area. On its head were two large green reptilian eyes with stare-piercing pupils. Above and between them were eight bulbous black eyes, yet another arachnid attribute, very difficult not to un-notice.

This thing, whatever it was, was filling its face with what might have been a torso, using its insect arms to pierce the body, jamming them in ruthlessly in a manner reminding me of the stabbings I saw (and caused) in the Hundred Years War. After a few seconds, the arms retracted; presumably the stabbing was to know where any bones or organs were.

"Christ, what the hell is that?" Chris whispered, almost quivering.

"Well, to me it looks like sewer gators *do* exist. Not only that, but they apparently mutated and one took a holiday to England."

The reptile started looking around, turning its head slowly, taking its time. It didn't take too long for it to notice two clothed bodies standing up, not dead but presumabl prepared for diddums. As if it wasn't sure if we hadn't realised it saw us, it announced this with a quiet, gasping moan. What looked like two forked tongues glossed over its mouth.

"Oh, this is not good," I said with annoyance. "This is very bad, very bad indeed. Chris, do you happen to have a gun on you?"

"No, sorry. You?"

"No. Okay, I want you to tell the others about this."

"Why me?"

"Well, this looks like it could get out of hand, and I don't want you to get hurt."

"What are you going to do?"

"Try and keep our friend occupied, I suppose. Also, take my coat and hat for me, will you? It costs too much to repair my clothes." I removed them from my person, at which point he grabbed them. The coat rested between his chest and one folded arm while he put my Stetson on his head akin to a child wearing his dad's glasses.

"Do you *have* to wear my hat?"

"It's a nice hat, I didn't want it to get ruffled." His eyes were gleaming with innocence; it was refreshing after seeing so many jaded people at the IISEP.

"Please drop any concern you have for the damned thing and put it more towards alerting Dwight," I said while undoing the top three buttons of my shirt.

"Right," Chris muttered nervously. He made his way back up the stairs while I tried to gain eye contact with the creature. Quite difficult, really, when it's got ten eyes, but I was able to lock on to its reptilian ones. It took two steps back – was it afraid of me, or was it unsure of what I might do? In response, I took two slow steps forward, noting how its appendages were tapping on the ground out of its field of vision, trying to feel for things, possibly food. I would stay where I was unless it made another move.

'I wanna go up to it,' Cain thought. 'I wanna go up 'n' pet it like a puppy.'

Was he serious? Did he really feel like stroking this pick 'n' mix animal that was the cause for all those people missing, and eating them? Oh, yes. Oh, God, yes.

"Given the situation and how... creepy it looks, I'm more inclined to stay right here. We just need to wait for the lads to come and knock it out. Why do you want to pet it?"

'Cuz it's a WEIRD 'n' WONDERFUL pet. Me LIKEY that.'

"No, Cain, we just need to make sure this guy doesn't charge at us or anything."

'Nah, too borin'. Let's chat to the fella; he looks like he needs to talk to someone.'

"It always helps to get to know your breakfast, I guess," I muttered.

Eager with his intentions, Cain swapped places with me. Rather than follow in my footsteps (quite literally – in fact, I don't think you can get any more literal than that), he proceeded to stomp forward instead, leading to watery, disturbing *squishing* sounds with every noisy declaration. The thing snarled at us, raising its head before unhinging its large jaw, rows of sharp wild teeth inviting us to come play with them.

"Heeeey, buddy, how ya doin'?" He waved at it with the glee you'd get at seeing a cute animal for the first time.

"Oh, look at YOU! I think you're kinda adorable in a weird way. I'm only sayin' that cuz in a normal way, you're fuckin' ugly, man. No offence. But you're really somethin', ya know that? I sure as hell ain't seen anythin' like ya, 'cept maybe Komodo dragons, but you take the cake when it comes to size. Hell, ya look like ya ate *a lot* cakes, and some other stuff. I get the feelin' ya might be linked to reptiles, buddy; might be even a distant cousin. Mind you, the extra eyes, the weird spider limbs ya have goin' on there – I imagine ya don't get invited to family reunions a lot."

The thing just continued to stare at us, its eyes darting around, examining every inch of our body.

"Let's see, what can I call ya? Certainly not Oliver – dunno what's goin' through that bitch's mind. She could be a Dickens' fan, probably old enough to be a little girl while he was around. Let's go for a surname. Spidereptile? Nah, too awkward. Splizard? Too silly; sounds winter-themed, and I can't imagine you stormin' around in the snow. Komodorachnid? Might be on to somethin' there. I GOT IT! ARACHNAREPTILE! YES! Now how about a first name? Okay, ya got an 'A' in 'Arachnareptile', so we'll try somethin' with 'A'. Albert? Who am I kiddin'? Too formal. Alex? No, too bland. Alfred? Posh. Wait, THIS one sounds GOOD – ARAN. YEAH, THAT'S IT! It fits ya like a weird, four-fingered glove."

Cain spread out his arms as though he was making a V-sign. He took in a rather deep breath before bellowing his announcement.

"I HEREBY DUB THEE... ARAN THE ARACHNAREPTILE! YOU WILL SERVE ME AND I WILL RIDE YOU INTO WORK AND FEED YOU BACON!" He then dropped his arms and took in a deep breath. "Boy, that latte's really doin' a number on me."

"Cain!" It was Dwight's voice. "Shut up, get up and help us detain this gal!"

"Righty-ho, big guy!" He turned to 'Aran'. "Sorry, Aran, gotta take care o' Mom for a second, help put her into legally-forced retirement. For all I know, we might find ya a new home after this. Gimme a handshake, okay, buddy?"

Aran responded by impaling us in the stomach with one of his appendages, going straight through us at such blinding speed that we were unable to react. The tip of the arm burst through our back. We could feel it wriggling around and moving further and further through our gullet. One of the most disturbing parts about it was the shuddering sensation of how its hair felt inside us; thick, patchy, prickly, with every individual strand almost pulsating, as though it was a giant heart.

Cain felt rather betrayed by this; his thoughts were a repetition of 'fuck', 'this little bastard' and 'fuck this little bastard'. See, this is why it's a very good idea to keep a good distance away from something that can stab you. The least of my problems was that my shirt was torn - it was one of my favourites, too. We could feel blood not just spilling out of us, but also starting to clog up our throat.

"...W-why is it always the fuckin' stomach these days...?"

The blood rose up to our mouth, and Cain decided to spit it onto Aran's arm in revenge. Not much payback, but it was a start. I couldn't think of what to do - the pain was almost crippling for me. But Cain had a plan, there was no doubt about it.

"Bad boy," he grunted.

Anger and revenge burst through as Cain somehow had the strength to clutch the limb and perform something I never would have done; he took a large, hard bite into it. *Now* there was payback.

We could taste the hairs in our mouth now, and while I felt disgusted that I could feel them along our tongue and face, Cain didn't care in the slightest. There was the mix of the taste of our blood as well as Aran's, which tasted sour, on par with cough medicine.

Aran let out a squeal, violently wriggling his leg to get us off. It moved across us, up to our solar plexus and swerving to the right side of our stomach, but due to our current position, Cain just fought through the pain once again. My fellow fiend-fighter just kept digging our teeth in until our jaw ached, causing him to pull back from biting any harder. No longer having some madman sink his fangs into him, Aran retracted his limb, freeing us from the pain of it going through us (which was good) but also leaving us with the pain of having a hole in our digestive system (which was bad). Rightfully pissed off, he started to charge at us with his wide lizard legs, letting us know how he was feeling with a deep, guttural roar.

Naturally, when you have something running towards you with the force of a miniature train (and looks like it would be made into an interesting alligator skin bag), you only have seconds to act. In one of those seconds, Cain and I came up with a brief plan.

'Run?'

'Run.'

We made a runner for the stairs. Up the steps lickety-split, not turning back in case Aran decided to stab us enough times to turn us into blood-stained Swiss cheese. We nearly tripped, but managed to clutch onto the handrail. Once out of the room, we locked the door, Cain sighing in relief before being shocked by an Aran leg bursting through near our shoulder. Cain jumped back and made his way to the others, who were still trying to get a hold of that psychotic woman.

Despite being outnumbered by two younger men and a large man near her age, she had quite the strength in her, pushing, punching and dodging them with such agility. Did she have a history of fighting or something?

"You're not going to get my baby, you pigs!"

Looked like it was up to us to sort her out.

"I ain't hittin' her," Cain muttered. "I don't hit gals, even the nutty ones."

"Fine, I'll do it," I thought.

Taking control, I went up to her while she slapped Chris' baby face, punched Brad in the stomach and head-butted Dwight to the floor in that order.

"Excuse me, Miss Fantus."

As she turned to face me, I swiftly knocked her down with a punch to the face. It was a light one to both myself and ordinary people; had I not held back, I'd have found my fist right in the middle of her head. Decking a pensioner wasn't exactly my idea of having a good time – if anything, I felt pretty bad about it. Dwight was able to secure her with the cuffs before we got her to her feet.

"Finally," Brad sighed as he rubbed his stomach.

"You guys okay?" I asked.

"We're all fine, I think," Brad replied, "although my dignity's been critically wounded thanks to an orange senior citizen."

Chris covered his mouth at the sight of my wounded form. "David, are you okay?"

I looked at my bloodied shirt and unbuttoned it to my solar plexus. Staring down at the tears that were in my body – right side of gut, what was left of my navel, and just under my right pectoral – I faced Chris with a nonchalant face.

"Yeah, doing fine, thanks. Just feeling a bit gutted."

Dwight took hold of the situation. "Where's the creature?"

"Ah. Right." I turned around and saw Aran making a hole in the basement door almost large enough for it to fit through. His head popped out and noticed me, unhinging its jaws. Two spider legs and a reptile one made their way out.

"Just there; he's doing a bit of woodwork."

Brad and Dwight drew out their stun guns; they resembled silver plastic handguns with a black end. They could send up to fifteen-thousand volts out at ten feet via a small electric stream, created in the mid-thirties to replace the older stun guns, primarily due to an increase in range.

"Brace yourselves, everyone," Dwight ordered.

Aran managed to destroy what was left of the door, and walked towards us in the corridor free, and roared victoriously. His many eyes darted at us, at which point he proceeded to unhinge his jaw once again and growl.

There was a certain mix of desperation and excitement coming from Carolyn Fantus' harpy-like screams. "Oliver, my baby! Come help Mummy!"

"Sorry, dear," I said, "but he's now called Aran, and now apparently labelled an Arachnareptile."

"A what?" Brad said with his voice almost cracking, practically the first time I heard him sound surprised.

"Blame Cain for that. Got too carried away when meeting it. Give him the rest of the Q&A afterwards."

Aran waddled just to the middle of the doorframe, just about managing to fit through despite his girth. He observed how still we all were with every one of his eyes, and swayed his spider arms around in the fashion of a grandfather clock. His growls were no longer audible; we too were silent. Everyone's weapons were drawn, waiting for the moment when they could use them – appendage versus stun gun. A Mexican stand-off, as it were.

Suddenly, one spider appendage lashed out at Chris, but Chris managed to drop to the floor in time. The arm went to where his throat would have been had he stood for one second longer. Just as quickly, Dwight and Brad went to town on it with the stun guns; two electrified wires shot out and hit Aran, causing the creature to let out a high-pitch scream that almost pierced our ears, though it quietened quickly.

Caroline screamed out in fear for her 'boy's' safety. In some way, I could empathise with her; someone or something you've raised getting hurt by people who have turned up out of the blue to deal with it. You'd want to fight back as much as possible, the same as any pet owner who values it like a child. I still wasn't able to feel sorry for her, but I could understand her determination to protect her pet.

When Dwight and Brad let go of the triggers, the electricity died, and Aran's head dropped to the floor, his jaw still wide open and contaminating the wooden surface with a thick bubbly saliva. All of his limbs were lifeless, devoid of the control of their owner.

"NOO!" Caroline screamed, her orange face wet with tears. "You monsters! How dare you do that to my Oliver!"

Everyone ignored her; Dwight took out his phone and called up the containment crew of the IISEP to come over and sort this out.

"Is it dead?" Chris asked. He stood far away from it as possible, despite being harmless, positioning himself at a corner.

"We'll know when it wakes up," Dwight replied.

Cain possessed our body and moved towards Aran, eyeing on the limb that he had bitten into earlier. "See that mark there?" he pointed with the enthusiasm of a child showing an adult something he discovered. "I made that. With my teeth." To hammer it home, he made a loud snarling snap, brushing his tongue over his teeth.

"Impressive," Brad said dryly, "we'll give you a medal in the Insane Ideas category."

"Y-you did that? That's so... weird." Chris subconsciously brushed over his own teeth, perhaps envisioning how such a thing could happen.

"Welcome to the IISEP." Cain grinned. "Weird shit's aplenty."

As the containment crew mopped things up and sorted out fitting Aran into their vehicle, I thought back to earlier of the terrible sensation – that almost monstrous sensual storm – I felt in my head, and the man who seemed to know me. A sense of déjà vu washed over me once I focused on what his face was like, but thanks to such a long and weary memory, nothing could be salvaged of how I might have known him. Who knows – chances were that with his disappearance, he not only left the coffee shop, but also my life in such a fleeting moment?

I wish that were true, so very true. It would have saved Emily and Scarlett so many problems. What would happen to them in time was because of us.

Chapter 9

Business As Usual

Being in IISEP headquarters can give one the air of being in a thriller movie about secret government facilities – which this was – but also the sensation of peeling back layers of the truth that, in all fairness, needed to remain absolutely tip-top secret. The building was sandwiched between, of all things, a bank and a bakery. So, it was bank, bizarre and bakery lined up together, the most unexpected of next-door neighbours (though it did mean that if anyone expected long queues at the bank – and, let's face it, there are – one could get something to eat from just two doors away for preparation).

There were roughly sixty (or was it seventy?) people working at the place, which might not sound much when you consider what this organisation deal with, but then again there weren't that many areas for jobs to cover. The American branch, on the other side of the pond, had one-hundred-and-thirty employees behind it, a natural result when you have a good twenty years before establishing other branches (the same going for France, Germany and Italy, the other three of the four founding countries that set up whole shebang).

The building had about ten floors; five on the surface and five below. Any object that was of extra-terrestrial or supernatural origin were sent to the lower floors. We had alien corpses, demon corpses, extra-dimensional creature corpses, staffs, armour, amulets, containers, deactivated doomsdays devices, alien devices, weapons, advanced technology, a sword made of angels, and a lot of other things that can't be described. If we could, we would have written a book entitled *The Picture Gallery &*

Encyclopaedia of the IISEP: Top-Secret Things That Would Be Fantasy Authors' Wet Dreams.

The job Cain and I had was very casual; whenever investigations were underway, we'd receive a text or call and come running in. When you have a massive healing factor and centuries of exposure to supernatural and alien elements, it helps to tag along.

Other than that, teaching self-defence at the facility's training area was a pretty relaxing aspect of our work. Arts like aikido, karate and kickboxing were under our joint belt, though we needed to remind ourselves every once in a while the differences between all of them. The old memory had a tendency to play havoc with us at times.

I sat at our desk, typing away at our report of the day's events on a computer, trying the best I could to remember them with the utmost clarity. To my eyes the bright screen was mesmerising, practically consuming my field of vision with how close I was to it – I had a habit of gazing at it in a hunched position like some slave. The effort was so plastering that it was almost as though I could not envision anything but a white square with words whenever I looked away. while Cain – as bored as he was with the mundane office work we had been doing for the last two decades – relaxed by shifting through our memories.

He found himself reliving the warehouse drug-dealer wipe-out of 2013, the sword-and-shield-baring hundred-person army he stumbled upon and massacred one day in the Crusades (whichever one it was) and his personal favourite, slaughtering Nazis left and right during World War II. Yes, whenever he needed to occupy himself, my old companion would look back at what he would call his Top Hundred Murders of People Who Deserved It. I had to give him credit there; he was able to create such a damn large list and never once changed any of the entries.

'Ah, the Nazis,' he thought. 'Easily my fave victims. All the shit they did, someone had to come along and kill the crap out of 'em.'

"Yes, I know, Cain," I said, trying not to get distracted, "we did a very good job."

'Remember that guy, that one guy who we came across and we did that Heil Hitler salute so we could distract him long enough to pull out our gun and shoot him and then you said, "Heil the Bullet" before inviting one to his head?'

"Yup," I said quickly, almost done with the report.

'I like that. I can watch that on a loop.'

"I'm sure you can." The final sentence was typed up, and I read the report back before sending it off to Dwight's email. A familiar voice, Jackie, the weapons expert, called out to us.

"David, Cain! Heard you guys sorted out the pet shop thing."

I removed myself from the computer screen, and saw the thirty-something year-old woman gazing at us with a grin. It was a magnificent one, to say the least, as it displayed all of her bright white sharp teeth in perfectly even rows. Her black hair was done in a short bob, sweeping over her head with a few scruffy patches sticking out; it didn't matter if it was done tidily, made into perfection, or with bangs covering her eyes, as Jackie had the unnatural ability to suit any haircut she was given.

She wasn't human, but rather from a species that resembled humans in frame with the addition of cat-like features, brought to you by the planet Hyo. There were no fingernails or toenails, and very thin leathery black pads comforted her fingers and palms. Her ears stuck out like any feline, triangular and covered in black hairs, as though she glued them on. She was slightly out of shape; a small potbelly was tucked away under a shirt, but you could see the curves of it if you looked hard enough. She might not have looked it, but when force was in demand, she would go out of her way to fulfil it with the power to gain a bit of extra muscle. Those eyes – man, those eyes. Yellow pooled over the space of the eyes, with a vertical line in the middle, almost mesmerising. We remember getting lost in them even when talking to her about stuff like getting a sandwich.

"Oh, hey, Jackie. Yeah, kind of bothersome, really."

"I heard you got impaled in the stomach. Ouch! Is it all healed up now?"

"Yeah, everything's okey-dokey now, though something tells me we won't be eating anything for a while. Been up to much?"

She groaned like she suffered the taste of a whip. "Ugh, I wish I called it 'much'! I've spent the last two hours check listing those high-security items downstairs. I thought I'd like it because, well, there's barely any effort involved, but there's way too much stuff down there!"

"Well, it's not like we can chuck any of them in the skip."

"Mind you, I liked one or two of them, like that… what do you call it, Ail-lu-rus Tails?"

"It's pronounced yew-lu-rus. Aelurus. Did you like it because of the description?"

"Absolutely – a great big fiery cat demon lurking inside it, it just made me think of my people… without the 'fiery demon' stuff, of course. It's like a weird kindred spirit."

"Yeah, well, don't get too fond of it. It's bloody powerful, but if you used it for too long, it'll take over your mind, not to mention feed off your body. You'd be a bag of bones in no time."

"Okay, okay, lesson learned, teacher," she said with a smile, showing off her fangs, much to Cain's pleasure. "Just wondering, the new person – Chris, right? – doesn't he need firearm training? If so, I can give him a session."

"Well, I'm giving him some hand-to-hand work in half an hour, so you can fire some rounds after that."

"Great! So, what kind of stuff do you think you'll try out?"

"Bit of aikido – always had a soft spot for that, maybe throw in some disarming techniques. Then I – yes, Cain, I'll tell her. Cain wants to do some Caipero, says he might even do it to salsa music." Cain, despite us having worked alongside her for six months, was awfully shy around Jackie – he had a crush on her since day one, and had never shown himself to her, letting me do the talking for him.

"Not gonna lie, that sounds like it'll be fun. Cain, try not to break his face, okay? Something tells me he'd be great for my sister."

"He says he can't make any promises, but he agrees they'd well together."

"Great! I think I'll hit the gym in a bit."

"You, exercising? I thought you were okay with how you looked."

Jackie proudly patted her tiny gut, even shaking it a little for fun. "Yeah, still am. Love this belly, it's so squishy, it's kind of amusing. I just want to see what it's like to work out, to put effort into being 'in shape', as you call it. I never understand why you people make such a big deal out of squabbling over your size. My people back home would find this very weird, you know? We're okay with our looks. There's a saying we have, 'Stout and happy, thin and funny'."

Lazy, simple, content – in other words, a feline philosophy. As I took this all in, amazed by this simplistic viewpoint of her society, I replied with, "That actually sounds quite ideal, Jackie. Let me know how it goes."

She walked away, and Cain briefly took over to see her swaying hips and tail in her tight black skirt.

'Oh, BABY,' he thought, 'yer MOCKIN' with that ass, I just KNOW it! I don't just wanna hit that, oh hell no! I'm gonna play it like the sexiest bongo drum you've ever laid yer hands on! Man, I hope it's soft, like one o' them plushies! GOD, I want her to stroke my ears so badly some day!'

I replied in my thoughts while I attended to the matter of printing off the report and trying to make our way to

Dwight's office on the floor above. 'Tell me, do you want to inform her through a letter? Or perhaps Pictionary? Miming it would be good; it would make you shut up.'

'Some day, man, I'm gonna tell her I wanna be with her. Catch a movie, eat Chinese takeaways, get nice an' intimate-like. She could stroke my ears, I can fiddle with her six nipples... it's gonna be a nice trip for my teeth to Cherry Town. Yummy.'

'I'm afraid that train won't be going for a while until you gain the confidence, mate.'

'Might give it a decade, see how that works out,' he said with a slightly bloated sense of confidence.

'That might be a bit too late.'

'How?' Bless him, he sounded so innocent.

'Well, it depends on whether or not she'll get 'intimate-like' with someone else.'

'Oh, right. Damn, didn't think that one through.'

'Don't worry about it, Cain, nothing big. Also, Cherry Town? I'd have gone for Strawberry Station.'

'Well, FUCK YOU, I love cherries.'

As you could tell, nothing but the best conversationalists. We had arrived at Dwight's office; he in was the middle of chatting to Brad, all the time the latter looked at his left hand. Afterwards, we looked around our workplace and felt the need to get some water, which might have been from the mild sense of disconnection we experienced from the hangover. Moving towards a water cooler, we noticed that Alice from Paranormal Division was there, a small girl at 5'2", was filling up a foam cup. It was the first time we'd seen her that day.

"Hey, Alice," I said as I closed in and grabbed a foam cup from near the taps.

The girl turned and looked at us in the way a child would with a new toy. Her red eye makeup stood out from her tan skin, her dark pigtails wrapped in red bows. When she spoke, while sounding very excited, there was the ever-lasting impression that she was holding herself back from

148

being even more excited, perhaps screaming everything in joy.

"Hi-hi-hi there, guys! You okey-dokey today?" She took a sip from her cup, and her smile didn't break away as she did. With her question, Cain, having repressed himself from Jackie, took the opportunity to pop up now and actually talk to a woman he was comfortable with.

"Yeah-yeah-yeah," I bounced back, "been okey-dokey so far, and hope it's stickin' to that." I let out a casual toothy grin, and tryin' to match her smile.

"That's great! Here's something I wanna know – I'm doing a big personal file on spirits that haven't been documented in any investigations, right? I've been writing this list back when I was nine or so." I swear her eyes were bulgin' out by this point.

"Um, yeah? Guessin' you want a bit o' personal experience, huh?"

"Right on the dot, Candy Cain!" Yeah, she called me Candy Cain. She likened Davey's red coat and our white skin to one, and so I got my nickname (even though Davey-boy owned the crap coat). "Three years' worth of working here's given me some pretty juicy stuff to see and write down, but chatting to an old-as-time duo like you's probably a fountain of ghostly ghoully goings-on."

"Hmm, well, we got a fair share o' stories to... well, ya know, share with ya. Sure thing, kid." I winked, and with that her face somehow lit up even more than usual, a big light bulb about to burst. She let out a high-pitched squeal and swung her arms around us, squeezin' us tightly until I felt that our back was going to an impression of a snapped twig.

"*Thank you thank you thank you thank you!* You guys are great! Lemme know when we can talk and I'll get everything sorted and – wow! This could be my big break!" Her arms were slightly tighter now.

"Give it a few secs, an' you'll get ya break alright," I croaked out.

"Oh." Alice loosened her hold on us and took her excitement down a couple o' notches. "Sorry about that, Candy Cain. Anyway, you got my number, so..." She gestured a phone call.

"Yeah," I said, not knowin' anything else to add to that (endin' conversations can be SO awkward). Alice kept on smiling as she gave a little wave and went off, bouncin' her way out of the workroom. 'Man,' I thought, 'if that kid was any more bouncy, no one would be safe from her.' I let David take over; after all, I only came out for one thing, and now that was over.

"Ah, she's fine," I said, filling up our foam cup from the cooler. "True, she's pretty excited about everything, but it's nice to have someone who looks like they won't be disappointed for long. Besides, our little interview's got her really riled up. I don't think we've been interviewed in ages." I took a small sip and walked back to our desk.

'Nice for you, maybe, but it's only so long before we get diabetes from her sweetness.' He let out a heavy groan.

I chuckled a bit as I loaded my verbal weapon and shot back at him. "Oh, from her? And not from all that chocolate you scoff every day?"

'Hey, Dairy Milk is fuckin' delicious, dammit!'

Three hours later, with Cain at the helm, we were in the autopsy room with Dwight and the old mortician, Colin, focusing on Aran's corpse, the creature's large form positioned on a slab in a way that made it look as though he was sleeping. Colin's wizened tall body was covered in a surgical gown and gloves. He made sure to take precious care of whatever body he examined, treating it as, in his words, "the well-made clay we're all birthed from". There was a hell of a lot of passion in the fellow, a sincere energy deeply rooted into such a man of seventy years, that I often wondered why he bothered expressing it in such a sombre job.

While Dwight and Colin were standing up, Cain sat in a nearby chair, kicking his legs up like a bored child amongst adults, not being able to do anything fun.

"DWIGHT, why do we have to BE heeeere?"

"Because David wanted to check it out. You should know that."

"Wasn't payin' attention, Big Whopper; too busy lookin' at my Top 100 List."

"Your what?"

"Not important, nothin' relevant, really. Well, kinda involves Colin's job, but never mind."

"Right." Dwight looked at us with confused eyes and raised eyebrows, showing the weary lines on his forehead.

Colin drummed his bony fingers on his slim stomach. His voice was dry and gruff, as though his throat was sandpaper. "If you gentlemen are quite done, we can continue with the results," he said, quite annoyed.

"Sorry, Colin. So, any idea why it died from the stun guns?"

"Well, the skin," he said while gently rubbing the corpse's side, like he was caressing a woman, "looks thick and leathery, it'd give you the impression that it would hold off some of the electricity. However, that's not the case; turns out it's pretty thin, and some organs are firmly connected to it, especially the heart."

"So anything that can attack the body all over, like the stunners, with enough force can attack the heart directly?"

"Exactly, Dwight." He felt the hairs on the limb that Cain bit into, before drawing his attention to the deep bite marks. "By the way, how did this delightful specimen gain these marks?"

Cain stopped kicking his feet up and raised one arm into the air, giving him the impression of a primary school student. "OOH, ME, ME, ME!"

Colin turned to us, his eyes turning into beams of disbelief and dislike. "I'm sorry, *you* did this? You? Why, David?"

"Uh, I'm Cain, Colin." He pointed at his scruffier hair and fangs. Colin had not gotten the chance to know us separately well enough, unlike our more (dare I say it) 'livelier' workmates. "All this and the accent help tell us apart."

Colin couldn't help but scowl. "Regardless, you shouldn't have damaged such a... beautiful specimen. Its cause of death is just as amazing. Oh yes, it certainly was." He rubbed the limb and its wound, with a pinch of joy in his voice.

"We'll be sure to note that next time any of its relatives try to gut everyone," Dwight said dryly. "I understand that you like examining corpses, Colin, but some day I'm going to come into this autopsy room and not see you act so delighted at death."

Cain and I shuddered, imagining the terrifying sight of Colin giving Aran a romantic ballroom dance, respectively clad in a suit and pink gown, a love-movie score blowing away people's ears (not to mention the spectacle would damage everyone's vision). We managed to stop it before things would get to the kissing stage. As Cain had thought, 'Worst 'Beauty & The Beast' movie ever.'

"What can I say, Dwight? Gotta bring some life into this hobby!" He let out a gruff chuckle that made me worry that he'd cough his guts out at a moment's notice.

Cain prodded Aran's side. "OOOOOH, prickly..."

"Don't touch him," Colin growled.

"Sorry, sorry, can't help it! I just wondered what his skin felt like. You don't have to be so moody about it. Gotta say, though, I understand why you're so protective of him; you know this fella inside-out."

Colin and Dwight couldn't help but sigh, annoyed at Cain's little attempt of a joke. But hey, I had a good laugh about it. Black comedy is still comedy, after all. My alter ego shrank at their reactions, and fiddled with his/our fingers like a nervous child who felt bored or bad with themselves. Poor fella.

"I'll, uh... I'll leave the rest to Davey-boy, now, 'kay?"

Sure enough, we switched places, and I casually put my hands into my coat pocket.

"Um, hi there, Colin," I said with a nod. He adopted a snarl, warping his ancient face into some sort of death glare, showing off those crooked yellow teeth and bulging eyes. The vulture nose didn't help. I didn't like it; it made me feel uncomfortable enough to imagine him wanting to give Cain and I our own little autopsy. I broke away from Colin, and instead turned my attention to the Arachnareptile formerly known as Aran (and Oliver).

I stared into one of Aran's lizard eyes, and as I did, the sheer instinct of the creature, its need to survive and kill, reflected off of its light green pupil. It reminded me of how my time in the tribe was cut short all those millennia ago.

Chapter 10

The Beast Unleashed

<u>Prehistoric Age</u>

The woods looked so plentiful in the morning, like a group of people bundled together to generate the impression of a great whole. A thick mist covered the area, as though whatever gods my fellow tribesmen worshipped were playing tricks with us for the benefit of entertainment. I sheepishly walked alongside the more confident Ra-Ma, Toya and five other hunters, my light tan displaying my weakness compared to them, with their darker bronze skin blending in with the trees around us. I might as well have been as white as chalk. As they carried rocks and crude stone knives in their hands, I stared at my own weapon, a large rock weighing down my hand and an uneasy feeling swimming in my mind. I wore animal skin clothing made for me by some of the tribeswomen, and I had grown enough facial hair to be rugged, but not enough to have a beard.

It had been two weeks since I had joined the tribe, yet I had not taken part in the daily hunting initiated by the leading tribe member, Ra-Ma, with Toya acting as second-in-command. They had been hunting since they were eight years old, so they had honed their skills and experience in the practice. I, on the other hand, found the idea of hunting another creature to be difficult to imagine. Why kill another living being? Was it necessary to do so, a fact in life that could not be omitted? They killed to provide food, clothes and weapons for us, for our protection and safety. At the time, I couldn't provide myself an answer, with such a naive mind. I had much to learn over the centuries. In the future, I would discover that we, as a species, do find alternatives to many things, some better, some worse.

Ra-Ma stopped and raised his arm to signify that we should do likewise.

"Look," he whispered, and pointed towards a shape that you could barely make out, a slightly darker silhouette than the shades of the trees. We hide ourselves behind one of the large oaks, peaking at the side to observe our prey. From what could be seen, it had the same posture as any four-legged creature, though this had six rather thick legs. Little else could be noted without getting closer.

"There, brother," Ra-Ma whispered. "I'd say this one looks big enough to provide just enough food for two days and slightly more clothes, do you agree?"

I wasn't one for measurements, so all I could mutter was, "It, um, it certainly looks large." Ra-Ma, Toya and one of the others laugh, patting my back like I was a child. In essence, I was one, really.

"It is a tradition we hold that the new hunter gets the first kill," Ra-Ma stated. "Do you remember your training?"

"Y-yes. Take the rock, smash its head once, twice to be sure. With the spear, aim anywhere; if the prey runs too fast for you to catch it, throw it."

"Very good. Now it is time to put it to use."

He was right. Now was the time I showed them that I had what it took to be a hunter, a man among his colleagues, not a child dwarfed by his elders. With great courage, both in myself and from the hunters, I got up and started a slick, slow walk to my prey. My feet were soft, yet the rough, hard dirt hijacking the gap between my toes felt slightly ticklish – not the greatest sensation when you're going to kill something.

As I drew closer, the mist gradually cast itself aside, as if to aid me to my task, (in which case, I appreciated its help) revealing more of what my prey looked like, which had its back to me, blissfully unaware of my existence. Imagine a brown-furred sloth the size of a German Shepherd, gifted

155

with three shaggy legs either side, its clawless stubby paws black and leathery, and what appeared to be bright yellow U-shaped tusks that curved out of its mouth and pointed diagonally like readied weapons. If you were to see it as I did, you'd probably think of it as the smaller cousin of woolly mammoths. A rabbit-like tail the size of a fist stuck out, a perfect ball facing my way.

This tusked-sloth was tucking into some pink flowers (or as the tribe called them, pink-sweets, due to the sweet smell they gave off) that were near a large bush; you could hear the loud chewing noise it made, the ancestor of boots stepping on glass. I was now right behind it, its tail just inches away from me. I pulled back my arm and stared at the back of the creature's head.

Even though all that was needed was one strike, one quick action, I felt reluctant to do so. The idea of killing it and the blood seeping from its body played out in my head over and over. Should I really kill it? In the recesses of my mind, I could hear the Voice for the first time, the words rising from slightly inaudible to sharp and loud, "KILL HUMANS KILL HUMANS KILL HUMANS". It scared me, I looked around wildly to see if anyone was next to me, but finding my brothers in their hiding spot confused me. The Voice overwhelmed my ears - they could have popped from the intensity and hatred in its tone, the rough passion fuelled by madness. A pain in my head struck me with the force of an immense drill. I blacked out.

That was the first time that Cain appeared.

I was more animal than guy at first, just a feral mess. As soon as I was awake, aware o' my surroundin's, I beat the thing in the head five times before tearin' out its throat with my teeth. So wet and raw and delicious. The blood – oh that sweet blood, so dark in texture – I licked and swallowed so much of it, must have thought it was the best drink ever (then again, it was my FIRST drink). That wasn't were it ended – whole chunks were taken out o' its body; the fur was pretty tasty, a nice heap o' dressin' on the meal.

I had pretty simple thoughts back then – all I could think of was 'PREY' and 'HUMAN'. I knew that I had to kill humans, but what were they? Just barely able to form sentences in my head, while I mowed down on that animal's body, I thought, 'HUMAN. IS HUMAN. PREY.'

The hand on my shoulder shook me hard, and when I turned around to see what it was, Ra-Ma, the hand's owner, and the other tribe guys jumped back. My eyes were dartin' back and forth, starin' at their wide eyes an' open mouths and their talkin'. I could hear what they were sayin', but I couldn't understand it, it was just a noise to me.

"Raanan, what has happened to you?"

They got nothin' but a heavy grunt from me. Then instinct – MY instinct – told me what to do next. Without warnin', I pounced onto Ra-Ma, holdin' his arms down and saw how scared he looked, so damn bewildered at his new buddy turnin' on him an' lookin' an' actin' fuckin' bizarre. Somehow, I realised it was fear, it registered to me like somethin' I should have known from the start. That was when I got a new line o' thought:

FEAR GOOD.

I opened my mouth as wide as possible before piercin' his throat with my sharp teeth. He died a few seconds later. No final words, no climactic end, no goin' out in a heroic fashion. Just death, the bare bones of it, nothin' more, nothin' less, nothin' else. He just happened to near me, that was all. When you're a beast like I was, ya do stuff like killin' without a second thought, not like most humans. Think >>> Do. The ultimate killin' machine, I guess. My face - or David's, from Ra-Ma's point of view – was the last thing he saw, with those slit yellow eyes and teeth makin' it all the more terrible for 'im.

One of the guys – Toya, I think – stabbed me in the back with his damn pointy-stick. Hurt like hell. I didn't scream, so much as roar in pain. I stopped what I was doin', sprang to

157

my feet, took it out with a lot of effort. I grabbed the stick with both hands an' snapped it in two before throwin' it aside. Toya dived for my rock, but I took him by the throat before he could, and raised him off his feet. Again, the fear an' confusion in his face felt so good to see; it was like they were pumpin' me with adrenaline. A part o' me didn't want to kill him just yet – maybe it was 'cause o' the rush he was givin' me. I sent him flyin' to a nearby oak with one strong throw - musta knocked the shit out o' him there. The others tried to stab me like before, but I wasted no time an' gutted 'em with my claws. I distinctly remember takin' the time to lick the blood off o' my fingers after I did that - oooh, the texture, it was like tastin' honey.

By the time I decided to turn my attention back to Toya, he vanished. I couldn't pick up anythin' – no silhouette, no footprints, nothin'. No prey to hunt, no other human to slaughter like defenceless lambs. That first time around, I wasn't just introduced to fear an' excitement an' pain – there was also anger. So much anger. I felt honest-to-god MAD that couldn't kill another damn in front of me. The only thing closest to that were the corpses I left in my little massacre. I ended up tearin' 'em to pieces. Bones an' blood was all that was left.

I woke up on my back, and the blood on my hands told me something terrible must have happened. Shock and worry struck me just as much as the Voice; in a panic, I rushed to my feet and looked around. Neither my prey nor my brothers were near, but instead I saw that the mist was now thin enough to reveal more trees than what could have been seen before, and the light blue sky soured into a dark blanket. The smell of sweet-pinks were all-too strong. The last thing I remembered was preparing to strike a blow to my prey, and the Voice repeating the same words in an intense, painful loop.

Thoughts were racing in my head; what happened while I blacked out; did I kill what I intended to kill; was anyone hurt; where were my kin; how long was I out for? So many questions, but the answers would only come from my brothers, wherever they were. My first instinct was to head back home, perhaps finding Ra-Ma and Toya there. They'd be able to tell me what went on. I was still new to finding my way through the forest, so I could easily pass the tribe without ever knowing it. Still, I ran forward, hoping I would get home soon.

Two hours later, I could see the large nightly fire shining throughout my clan's clearing, surrounded by the three elders, Toya, his mother and younger siblings. No one else was visible, leading me to assume that the rest had gone to sleep in their makeshift huts, or were elsewhere in the area. Walking up to the fire, removing myself from the cover of bushes, I let my presence be known by saying Toya's name aloud. Everyone looked around, searching for the caller. The reaction was one that I didn't expect. I expected glimmering smiles and the tight embrace of my comrades; instead there were Toya's hot-blooded screams and his charging at me with his spear, the fire casting a large shadow over him. His mother pointing her skeletal finger and her yelling "Murderer! Demon!"

He thrust the spear, aiming for my chest. With split-second thinking, and a fast heart, I jumped aside, narrowly missing him as dirt from the ground stuck to my body.

"Toya, what are you doing?"

Another attempted hit, this one missing my stomach by inches. "You killed Ra-Ma, Ju-Ha, Esta, Bhal! Did they mean nothing to you, you monster?"

A third strike, but this time I grabbed his weapon, pulled it from him with enough force, and had the spike facing him. Now I had the advantage, but I was in no mood to fight back.

"I have no idea what you're talking about! All I remember was that I was going to kill that animal! I couldn't have killed them!"

"Why do you lie when you know I saw you? You had me at my throat, staring at me with those thin eyes! The

159

claws on you, and the teeth! You tore into my brother as though he was food! And the others... we have sent a party to look for them."

Two certain words struck me odd, they definitely told me something was fucked-up.

"Claws? Teeth? What happened to me?"

"It was as though you were an evil spirit, Raanan. You have the mind of a creature, not a man. It seems that I was wrong after all. Ra-Ma said you were a demon, but I didn't listen. He will never talk again, nor will any of our fellow men."

"I could have been possessed by such a spirit, that was why I was not myself!"

"That is your word, and yours alone. But I cannot take what you say as a possibility."

There was no one to help me now. No ally I could persuade, even Toya, whose broad mind was the reason I was with him in the first place. The only option I could think of at the time was the redeem myself, despite how far I had gone in 'my' actions. I lowered my weapon, placing it to one side.

"How can I make up for this, if that's possible?"

"You can't. When one of us kills another, especially with no provocation, they are no longer considered a part of the tribe."

By now, other people had now made their way to the fireplace, some murmuring in shock, others cursing my name in. Spears and rocks were scattered amongst them, like children ready to hit a piñata, but in a decidedly less playful manner. The crowd grew larger and larger as people raised their voices. I could feel that most of them wanted me dead. Attempts were made to get close to me, but Toya raised his arms and told them to keep back, otherwise they might make things worse.

The Old Ones finally rose up, and everyone shushed as they waited for their leaders to speak. It was like a dog eyeing their owner. Every one of their details were highlighted by the bright and yellow light of the great fire; ancient creases, sagging stomachs, thin figures. The constant wisps from the fire added touch to the theatrical atmosphere they gave off.

"Raanan," said one of the male elders, "your actions have wrought darkness upon our home. With what Toya has informed us, you may indeed be an evil spirit. However, as you are one of us, it would be impossible to kill you – one tribe member must not kill another, that is our rule. So, it is with both great shame and necessity that you are cast out, and never return. Once you leave, the one we know as Raanan will be no more."

I took a deep breath, and said with a heavy heart, "I understand, Old One." I presented Toya with his spear, which he took with no hesitation, and pointed it at me.

"I will lead you out," Toya stated coldly. He nodded to signal that I start my exit, to which I replied with a nod, turned around and reluctantly made my way to the edge of place. I tried not to look back and see the faces of my disowning family, and despite the great need to, I stared at the darkness of the forest that I would soon call my new home. I remember the last thing I heard Toya say to me before pushing me to the ground. He whispered, "Farewell, Raanan." How he said it, I wasn't sure; maybe it was a mockery of how he saw me, or perhaps a true statement of sadness. That was a mystery that would never be resolved.

A lump nestled in my throat, staying there for hours on end, like an after-effect of what had happened. No matter how many times I washed myself in the water, I could still feel the blood on my hands. So much confusion waxed over my mind, and I still wondered who and what I was.

'They might be right,' I said to myself, 'if they say that I am an evil spirit, it would explain the evil I've done. I don't deserve anyone.'

In that moment, my short life with a family was spilled into the cynical, disillusioned dirt that would define me for centuries to come.

The next few days were spent trying to get as far away as possible from the tribe, exploring the forest as much as I could. In a way, this was now my new home, a large plant-filled playground. I would have to get used to this new status quo, whether l wanted to or not. Survival was important, and for that to be secured, hunting was necessary. At first, I feared that I would black out once again and wake up to find myself with a full stomach and half-eaten beasts beside me. It was a steady process, trying to hunt and kill animals just for nourishment, as the more I thought about it, the worse I'd feel having to take a life to sustain mine. Hell, I was plagued with nightmares when I made my first kill, but I eventually moved past it and my confidence grew, insisting I do what I had to do. Nature was always like this, the forest a constant battleground and home. When I would do the deed, cooking my prey every night, I was in constant control, no Cain present at all. The Voice that haunted me before wasn't present, making me wish that I could go back and be Raanan again, but that was a dream, nothing more. I feared being with people for some decades, for fear of killing any again. There was so much for us to learn, so very, very much.

Every night I always wish I could find some way to make up for the shit I did that day. No matter how ya dice, I can be an asshole, but I can also be a nice guy. He should've been with 'em for as long as they were around, and I fucked things over for him without even realisin' it. Sometimes, I wonder how things woulda turned out for him if he was able to stay – maybe he woulda had a wife an' kids, made some life-long friends, at least as long as their mortal lives entailed? Those kind o' 'what ifs' haunt me day after day, especially concernin' his brief time as Raanan, his first life, a name that got buried under blood an' dirt an' death. Sometimes, I wish I had died instead o' his pals.

Chapter 11

A Feeling of Things To Come

It was a pretty hot day in town with Emily and Scarlett, but thankfully being with them made the heat bearable. Their shared birthday would be in two days, and today would be their usual, pre-celebration before the upcoming party, where friends and neighbours galore would fill every room, or die trying. Yes, they had the same date of birth, which may feel weird with a mother and daughter combo, but I found it to be cute. Going about in the town, arms hooked up, eyes scanning for any shops they'd both enjoy, knowing they'd have the comfort of each other – that was their real present.

Chelnsworth was a pretty nice place to be in (that is, when you're not dealing with crime, both human and... well... not-very-human); it had some good shops; an open marketplace filled with people who tended to smile all the time, never breaking consistency; an almost immeasurably large park, dominated by lovers, friends, children, parents, and owners with their faithful pets. Not much I could say about the air, except how it is when it's cold and crisp as water falls, that point where every breath makes you feel like you're actually alive.

Cain and I wore black boots, dark jeans, a red tucked-in shirt hiding under a black waistcoat, with my red coat topping everything. If there were any words to describe our look, they would be 'camp', 'weird', 'ridiculous', 'stupid', 'what-the-fuck', 'insane', 'bright', 'comic book-esque' and 'mismatched'. Okay, there were probably a few other possible descriptions, but that would take up *lot* of space. Emily wore something easier on the eyes, a white blouse covered by a beige coat, blue jeans and a pair of black high heels. Her hair was pulled back into one long ponytail which, coupled with the small crow's-feet surrounding her eyes and her sharp looks, helped show off how wonderful she looked. Scarlett just had on some red jeans and a black short-sleeved shirt with a cartoon cat on it.

As we entered the marketplace, we were exposed to the row of stalls filled with customers coming, going or just passing by, surrounded by DVDs, CDs, clothes, foodstuffs, gadgets, tiny statues and other things that you could glimpse at. Just the sort of stuff you'd expect to see in a market. What, were you expecting more? Something magical and super-appealing, like you were going into an area filled with countless wonders in the world of 2047 Britain, anything remotely distinct and exciting compared to what you'd find nowadays? Sorry, but there's no way could I make it sound like bloody Disneyland (well, barring when I said that people always smiled). Mind you, the only thing being sold that was worth any real interest was from a nearby food-stand. We could really smell the heated-up hotdogs and boiling burgers being cooked in the open air. Really hunger-inducing, I tell you. Cain said to me, 'Goddammit, makes me wanna eat all that fuckin' meat.'

"Hey, look," Emily said, pointing over to a corner of the market. "It's Laurel and Hardy."

Indeed, they were there. Well, impersonators, anyway, wearing bowler hats and two-piece suits, squabbling while trying to strum away at the ukuleles in their hands with large smiles. 'Stan Laurel', a slightly thin person with the smiling face of a simple-minded but well-meaning fool. 'Oliver Hardy', with his small square moustache, someone you'd look at and know that he was not terribly fat, though his face would have you assume he was even larger with that rubbery look and double chin, almost disproportionate to the rest of his body.

"Oh yeah," Scarlett responded flatly. She wasn't that big into Laurel and Hardy or any other comedians before her time. Her mother, on the other hand, was. Like, almost on-par with *us*, and Cain and I were pretty damn versed in all that was L&H; hell, we actually saw their lost short film 'Hats Off' back in 1927.

"It's nice to see them nowadays," Emily said with her voice trailing off in a tone of nostalgia.

"Mum, why do you have to say it like that? They're impersonators."

"Yeah, of course, but it's nice to see someone dress up as them. I love old-school comedy."

Scarlett gave a bit of a huff. "I'm not really into, like, hundred-year-old comedians. Too ancient."

I chuckled a bit as I laid my eyes on the entertainers. It certainly brought back memories, and I felt my mind starting to drift off into the sketchy, scratched film reels of the past. "I remember them, nice lads. We shared a drink once, can't remember whether it was in America or when they did that tour here back in 1953, but it was a good time, I can certainly say that."

"What?" Scarlett cocked her head.

I was suddenly thrust back into the present by that one word. I turned to her, just as confused as she was, tilting my head like a dog when it notices something unusual. "Something the matter?" I asked.

"You said you knew them. I mean, you're not old or anything."

"Did I say that?"

"Yeah."

"Sorry, I meant to say my grandfather. He was quite the fan, I got into them through him. He'd chat with them, make them laugh. Fancy that, the comedy fan making his idols laugh."

"Uh-huh," Scarlett said, nodding, while Emily smiled. While the girl had no idea of our immortality, her mother certainly did; any mention of ancestors would translate to her as 'D and C'.

The Laurel and Hardy impersonators, meanwhile, had now ceased playing their ukuleles, placing them on the ground next to their cases. With the applause given, 'Hardy' bowed, with 'Laurel' mimicking him, and waved his tie at their audience. Laurel attempted to do the same thing with his bowtie, only to realise that he could only slightly wiggle it.

"Would any of you like us to give you our autographs?" 'Hardy' asked. He produced several long strips of paper and a pen from his pockets before prompting a woman at the front to come forward. 'Hardy' gave a twirling hand gesture at 'Laurel', leaned over and let 'Hardy' use his back to write the autographs. Nothing came out of the pen, no matter how hard he pressed it onto the paper.

He asked, "How come there's no ink?"

'Laurel' replied, "Oh, there is, Ollie. It's got something called invisible ink; I had trouble finding a pen, but a joke shop happened to have one."

The crowd didn't roar with laughter, but burst with enough liveliness and energy that you just wanted to capture some of it and use it for when you were feeling really down.

As 'Ollie' scanned their slowly-growing audience, there was a sense of fun and success in everyone's faces. However, once he faced our direction, all that passion was suddenly drained from his face as he tensed up in an overly grand way and fixated on us. It was like he was now more interested in wanting to observe us.

"Come on, let's scram," he just barely whispered to 'Stan'.

"Why?" his companion asked.

"It's him!"

"Him who?"

"You know who!" He jerked his head in my direction, even though by this point it was all too obvious that everyone could see what he was doing.

"Oh," 'Stan' simply uttered. He gave out a smile and raised his hat at me; 'Ollie' pushed him for it.

"Will you stop that! Now, how are we supposed to spy on someone if you make it too obvious!"

"But you're the one who pointed it out, I can't help it."

"Never mind what I did, let's just focus on what we do, got it?"

They were then filled with this manic energy (which, in my opinion, would have improved their act), grabbing their ukuleles and holding onto their hats protectively with such speed that it looked like I was watching one of the real deal's movies.

"Well, everyone," announced 'Hardy', failing to hide his franticness, "we've run out of time. Something's come up, and we can't be late. Come, Stanley."

The duo were off, 'Ollie' grabbing 'Stan' by his jacket arm, while his thin friend turned and waved at us with his ukulele in hand. He realised he was holding onto it, and quickly corrected this by using the hand 'Ollie' was holding him by, raising it above his head. As you'd imagine, the rotund comedian fell to the ground, still clutching on to 'Stan's' jacket in determination, weighing 'Stan's' arm down with his great weight. It was pretty damn funny, honestly, something you'd expect from an L&H duo. Everyone laughed, thinking that it was just a final joke before vanishing completely into the streets and shedding their second skin. After getting to his feet, 'Ollie' swatted 'Stan's' hand, and with, no one following them, disappeared from the marketplace, talking to themselves.

"Think those guys know you?" Emily inquired.

"Beats us; the only fat guy we know is Dwight, and unless he's wearing some damn fine whiteface, it's not him."

"Maybe it's part of their act."

"If so, it's a really weird one," Scarlett declared.

"Not the kind of thing the real lads would have done. I should know, I've watched all their movies with a mate of mine, we know them inside-out." I gave out a shudder, recalling Cain's autopsy joke.

"You okay?"

"Yeah, just a bit of a headache."

I looked at my watch. A nearby antiques shop – one of my favourite places in town – would be closing in half an hour, and I would always spend a great deal of time examining everything it had to offer like an inspector. What can I say? Ancient people are interested in ancient things.

"Anyway, ladies, I'm thinking of exploring some of the shops I like. I don't think they're your sort of thing; antique figurines, clocks, furniture, old books, yada yada yada. I've got my phone with me, so if you need me, just gimme a bell."

"I will," Emily said with a nod. "Have fun, David. See you in a bit." With that, I tipped my hat, turned around, and headed off in the direction of the shop, burying my hands into my coat pockets.

'That was weird,' I said to Cain. 'The whole spying thing Hardy brought up felt very real.'

'Yeah. It was like they knew us. Maybe we could follow 'em.'

'No use, they'd be long gone by now. Even then, I doubt we'd be able to get anything out of them.'

I could feel the back of our brain getting hot, almost tight and buzzing lightly, that dreadful moment when you get paranoid, way more paranoid than usual, about even the most irrational things. For instance, whether or not you left the water running too long when waiting for a bath to be made, imagining the floor slippery and drenched, then eventually the house, and before long the electricity frying everything and everyone inside. Or if you made sure that you locked the front door as you left your house this morning, for fear of someone breaking in while you were gone and stealing your most valuable possessions or loved ones. Or if you had the feeling that you were being followed by someone.

'You feeling what I'm feeling?' I asked Cain.

'Yeah, sure as hell do. Wanna see if there's anyone behind us?'

'Yeah.' I glanced over my shoulder and saw, with some mild surprise, the Laurel and Hardy impersonators behind me by a good thirty feet, clutching onto their ukulele cases amongst a tiny crowd of swarming people. I must have stared at them for about ten seconds, noting every one of their actions.

They had buttoned up their coats and stuffed their other hands in their trouser pockets, looking left and right at shops, with a brief look in our direction – I mean right at us, singling us out – before twitching their heads in other directions, as though they had looked at us by mistake. What also didn't help was the nudging of their heads and blatant finger-pointing at us. Their heads were positioned downwards, chins inches away from rubbing against their throats, though they made sure that they still able to see what was right in front of them, even if it made them looked a tiny bit hunched.

Needless to say, they weren't exactly subtle. It really would have helped if they dropped their outfits in favour of normal clothes; they must have thought we were idiots to not notice them.

'Right, it's them,' I thought.

'So, what do we do? Go up to 'em? Lead 'em on? Beat 'em up? I prefer the latter.'

'No, I'd say we go up to them.' Having thought that, I tipped my Stetson at them with a small grin. With that, their heads sprung up, their hands bolted out of their pockets, and they were filled with vibrant energy as they jumped at my gesture, flopping around like fish on a line. I walked up to them, striding with that smile and a sense of confidence. We would go up, chat to them, get answers, resolve things and then everyone goes off to do their own things. Hopefully. If not, then things might turn ugly, maybe physical, if their intentions were more than just stalking us.

"Hey, guys," I greeted jovially. "Nice act you had going. Bet you put a lot of effort into it."

"W-well, thank you, we did," said the faux Oliver Hardy.

"Your following, on the other hand, needs a lot of work. You couldn't be any more obvious if you were yelling right behind me."

There was quite a nervous disposition spread across the two, though 'Hardy' tried to up an ignorant front. "Is there anything you want from us?"

"I think the reason why you left as soon as you saw me. It wasn't exactly subtle to pick up on you spying on me through... being Laurel and Hardy, of all things. I give you an A for that, though."

"We have no idea what you're talking about, sir. We love to entertain the public. Now leave us alone."

"Yeah," 'Laurel' spoke up. "We've got to make sure we're ready to see our boss to talk about you."

"Shush!" 'Hardy' swatted him on the back.

Curiosity struck me in the face. "Oh, really? This boss of yours, what's he like? Don't tell me, he's one of the Marx brothers? Perhaps Abbot or Costello? Any of the Three Stooges? No, wait, is he James Finlayson?"

The portly pretender replied with mild aggression. "He's our benefactor, Mr Short, and he'd appreciate it if you leave us to do our work."

"You mean watch over me like creepily obsessed fans?"

"Yes, precisely, if a little specific."

"Alright," I said. "If we're gonna talk, best not to do it around so many people."

My head swept from left to right, trying to find any convenient places to carry on our conversation. I could see buildings, buildings, buildings, and buildings, plus the odd corner here and there. Fortunately, it didn't take long before I managed to eye a nearby alleyway to the left.

"There we go," I declared in delight as I started to waltz over to the wide space. I turned and saw that the impersonators were still where they were, locked in place like statues as they looked to me in mild surprise. Were these guys really that clueless to not follow me when I ordered them to?

"Well, come on, then. You're supposed to be keeping an eye on me, aren't you? I don't want to have to tell you how to do your job, so move it."

And so they did, springing to life as they trailed me. Once we got deep enough into the empty alley, filled with graffiti that was linguistically and literally colourful, I checked to see if anyone was able to see us. Nobody was around. With that, I continued my interrogation.

"Who are you, really? Obviously, you don't spend all day dressed up as my favourite comedians, so why don't we drop the disguises?"

"Fine," 'Hardy' said, straightening his tie and hat as he stood boldly. "I am Gib, and my friend here," he announced while pointing to 'Laurel', "is Slaml. We're what you'd call extra-terrestrials. To be more precise, alien shapeshifters, Mr Short."

I just shrugged my shoulders. "Okey dokey. Gib and Slaml; sounds like a song duo. Maybe you should try getting a record deal or something?"

"You don't seem shocked by this at all? The fact that we're admitting our true selves to you upfront?"

"My job involves meeting people like you, so... not really."

"Oh."

"Been here long?"

"Since 1921," Gib answered. Pretty short answer; I like people who get straight to the point.

I said with surprise, "Wow, you guys must have quite the lifespan."

"Five-hundred-and-twenty years in Earth time. We're two-hundred-and-eighty-five."

"Well, you learn a little something every day. You're each like three-and-a-half pensioners rolled into one; I hope when you reach seniority on your planet, you get bloody good hospital care, 'cause God knows our one's crap."

171

There was a mild smugness in Gib's words, though he looked a bit reluctant when he talked. "Yes, we've noted that ours is... relatively more sociable."

I scanned their bodies, and the thoughts of their true forms came to mind. "Anyway, do your people look like us, or are you a bit more – for lack of a better word – alien?"

"Our natural forms don't exactly look... natural to your kind."

I rolled off a shrug. "Mate, I don't even know what 'natural' looks like anymore. You're talking to the wrong guy for that. So, anything really specific with your little job?"

"No, just observe you, really."

"Well, I can certainly say that's now a lot easier. I suppose you could stick with me; see how I eat, drink, act when drunk, be in two minds about everything, and might even show you my fairy godmother."

"What's she like?" Slaml asked. Gib shot a look at him that combined the anger of a scowl with the tiredness of half-closed eyes.

"He's being sarcastic, Slaml. 'What's she like' – hmmph!"

Slaml registered this in a couple of seconds... a very long couple of seconds. "Oh, right."

Despite feeling a mild pleasantness in this back-and-forth, it occurred that this was diverging from the real matter. "I realise we've steered off-track, so let's get back on to the more personal, important matter at hand – your boss, who I really hope isn't someone who sticks pictures of me up on his bedroom wall."

Gib said dryly, "I wouldn't know if he does such a thing, but if he did, technically, it wouldn't just be you."

"What do you mean?" The earlier pain in our head smoothly crept down our spine.

"Your... other self, as it were."

"You know about him?"

"Hello, Mr Cain," Slaml said in a slightly raised voice, "can you hear me?"

Sure enough, my alter ego rose to the surface. Within seconds of arriving, he started to pick out and examine dirt from under our fingers with his long nails; a sort of finger mining operation. He intentionally ignored Gib and Slaml, even staring at the alley walls instead of them. Why? Simple: he had the opportunity to fool around with them.

"Hel-lo, Mr-Cain," Slaml repeated in an even louder, slower fashion, "can-you-hear-me?"

"I-can-hear-ya-loud-n'-clear, Stan-ny, you-mo-ron. Now, how's about we do a little less babblin' and lot more talkin'?"

Gib took charge of answering. "About our boss? If so, we can't say an awful lot more."

"Ya know, you better gimme some answers real soon, or else I'm gonna practise a few 'o my boxin' techniques on ya, or maybe some karate. Been around quite a while, ya know. Done a few things."

"Like kill Jack the Ripper," Gib said in a matter-of-fact voice.

"Wait, what?"

"We know about that, sir; you managed to finally confront him, and then there was some nasty business involving human sacrifices and an otherworldly entity. The details are a bit muddy, but we got the gist of it. Our benefactor told us the story. He's also lived for quite some time. Not as long as you, though, but still pretty long."

Cain grabbed Gib by his lapels and dragged him as close to our face as possible.

"Okay, Round Boy, let's play Bad Cop to speed things up. I ask ya more questions, ya answer 'em. That fails, I set my fists on ya, or maybe my claws. So hard to choose. What would ya prefer?"

"Um..."

"Ya know what, don't answer that, that's a waste o' time. Next Q – who the hell is yer boss?"

"I'm afraid that's out of the question."

"No it ain't, ya liar, it's IN the question – I just said 'yer boss'. Don't try n' do any mind-fu shit on me, 'kay?"

"No, I mean that we can't reveal his identity to you. The both of you."

Cain wagged a finger at him, moving his finger with every sing-song word he said. "Uh-uh-uh. That's not what I sa-a-a-a-i-i-id. There's gonna be an answer."

"Actually," Slaml interjected, "he already said it, sir. We *can't*."

Cain released Gib and swooped his head over to Slaml before unleashing what probably the scariest scowl put to human imagination. He tended to do when people were interrupting him during important discussions (which, to him, could include his favourite snacks). At home, he would always practise this on the bathroom mirror, and even feel the mad, lively aura coming off of it. Our lips were peeled back like a banana, showing the sharp, clenched (if slightly yellow) fangs, the maw of the monster, putting so much strength into it that our now-bulging cheeks were in a fixed, burning state of pain. Cain would look past any discomfort from our face's contortion as long as his victims would soil themselves.

"Buddy, wait yer turn," he growled in a monstrous voice that he summoned from the depths of his throat for dramatic effect. Slaml backed himself up against the wall, his face fish-eyed and gaunt, instantly drained of colour. Cain screamed in our head, 'SUCCESS! HA-HA! MASTER O' THE DEATH FACE!' He then turned back over to Gib and dropped the glare, now returning to a more relaxed, friendly voice and expression, as if he never broke away. "Jeez, the rudeness o' some people. Anyway. Tell. Us. NOW."

Gib yelped out, "Alright, alright! His name is Dean Gregory."

"Dean. Hmm. Kinda rings a bell, not sure. Is that actually his first name, or is he the Dean o' somethin'?"

"First name."

"Right, thanks."

174

'The name does seem familiar,' I stated. 'It's a bit cloudy, though.'

"Hmm, do we know 'im?"

Gib answered dryly, "The fact that you have to ask does show that it may be the other way round."

"Alright, next question: why's he been followin' us?"

"We don't actually know, Mr Short, we were just told to do our job; keep an eye on you while he tends to other matters."

"Yeah," said Slaml, "like checking up with Eddie Muzzle."

"Who?"

"Just a chap who owns a ring on aliens being sold as pets."

"Come again?"

"I said—"

"No, no, no, I got what ya said, buddy, I just... I just find that surprisin'. I mean, what kinda asshole decides to sell aliens? Hell, sell 'em as pets? How deep does your buddy go with aliens? I'm surprised he ain't got Muzzle crammin' you in cages an' givin' ya doggie treats."

"That's about as much as we know. I don't know how he found out about us; he just met us, told us he knew about aliens and gave us a task. He even pays us. You have to understand, we don't really get ourselves involved with that kind of business, just our associate."

"Uh-huh. David, anything you want me to ask?"

I replied almost instantly, 'Info on Dean and Muzzle. The more we know, the better chance we have of solving this. We need to get the IISEP involved.'

"Right." Cain threw his hands at Gib and Slaml's throats and pinned them to the wall, making sure that his grip wasn't tight, but strong enough to keep them from moving around. "Guys. Boss and Muzzle. Locations and phone numbers. Now."

"We don't know! Honestly!" Gib uttered from the bottom of his throat.

"Oh, come on, how the hell would ya meet any of 'em?"

Gib asserted himself with a strong calm front. "Mr Gregory calls us with a hidden number."

"Awful lot o' details ya gave me there. That'll do." He released his hold from them, allowing them to rub their throats. "So, how about we head on down to our workplace, interview ya, give ya little profiles so yer on a list o' confirmed alien stuff n' whatnot, and ya trot on hand in hand and set up a meetin' with yer pal?"

Gib looked us in the eyes. "I'm terribly sorry, but that's just not possible."

Cain gritted his teeth. "Why, dammit?"

"We're very private; we don't want anyone keeping us on any lists when we'd rather go about our business earning money and trying to survive. Furthermore, Mr Gregory feels it's not time for you to meet him."

"Wait, so he's already plannin' to see us?"

As Gib spoke, Slaml gave a big nod. "Yes, that's what he told us."

"Look, guys, we ain't gonna let you go an' forget that we ever saw ya. Some bozo's obsessed with us, an' yer the only fellas we know who can see 'im. Now, goddamit, yer gonna walk with us to the IISEP, spill everythin' ya got, an' we'll get ya to help us meet 'im a hell of lot sooner than he wants, got it?"

"No," said Slaml, lowering his brow into a pink tense wall, squinting like he was determined to keep us in his sights. His voice no longer sported any light-hearted idiocy, but the heaviness of a man past his limits. "We only do as he says, and we don't want any more trouble, Mr Cain. Please fuck off, Mr Cain."

Gib's eyes, on the other hand, were sent wide open and viciously tugged Slaml's arm. Cain and I were quite surprised. Up until now, he was like Stan Laurel's film persona in looks and personality, but all of a sudden there was quite an opposite turn, as though he was channelling

176

Clint Eastwood. We half-expected him to pull out a Magnum and do the 'You Feeling Lucky, Punk?' routine.

"You... are quite the hard little bastard, ain't ya? Kinda odd; you off any meds, buddy? Gotta give ya some balls there. Actually... do you dudes even HAVE balls?"

"Mr Cain..." Slaml said, not deterred by my friend's sudden change in topic.

"No, I'm serious, pretty curious, actually. Does your race have any type o' genitali—" We were then met with the swift pain that came with a good hard knee to the groin by Slaml. It was like being assaulted by a stampede of armoured rhino. I swear there was a crunching sound. The blow sent us straight to our knees.

"AARRGH! Ya seem to... know human ones pretty well," Cain gasped as he covered our damaged privates. He winced and closed his eyes, waiting for the moment when the pain passed.

"Come on, let's get out of here!" Gib said desperately, and without missing a beat there was the sound of their shoes quickly clashing with the concrete as they ran. By the time we recovered and looked around past the alley, they were too far gone.

"Can't stand the pain. David, you take over. Gotta relax. Christ, I don't think we got anythin' left down there."

"Fair enough. I'll contact work. We need to try and learn as much as we can about them. If we can get Muzzle, it could allow us to get a hold of Dean."

Taking hold, I took out our phone and rang up Dwight. A few beep-beeps later, and we could hear his voice, low and smooth, amongst the rapid tapping of fingers on a keyboard.

"David, Cain, what is it?" he asked, in mildly distracted tone.

"Hey, Dwight, found some aliens following us, names Gib and Slaml, shape-shifters."

"I didn't know you have fans," Dwight joked. "Have you got them with you now?"

"No, they escaped, but not before telling us that they're working for someone named Dean Gregory, who knows a Mr Eddie Muzzle, owner of an illegal alien pet ring."

The typing stopped, and without missing a beat, Dwight responded with clear interest and surprise. "That's quite the info you got there. Any idea why you were followed?"

"No, but he seems to know an awful lot about us, at least as far back as the nineteenth century."

"David, Cain, who did you piss off?"

"Just an awful lot of dead people, no one recent. We can't really be sure if it's someone we know. Name's familiar, but that's about it."

"Very well. We'll see what checks out and get back to you."

"Thanks, big guy, we owe you one."

"No problem. Let me know when other fans start to pop up; we've got a few cells that need filling out. Call you later."

As he hung up, Cain and I ran the whole encounter in our head, viewing everything non-linear, like a badly-edited movie reel. What started out as a trip into town went to being followed by aliens dressed up as twentieth-century comedians; playing good-cop/bad-cop; discovering some nutter who's got his eyes on us, and a blow to the vitals. Dean was likely to be dangerous, given his ties, so throughout the rest of the day we were a bit shaky, with goose bumps popping up. This sure as hell wasn't how we thought today would turn out.

Chapter 12

Face-To-Face-To-Face

Being in Emily's house amidst a party, surrounded by people that were unknown to us, was like wandering into familiar territory with new inhabitants that just barged right in. It was a half-and-half of the older and younger generations. There were youngsters who must have been fifteen or so, but looked so much more mature you'd think they were ten years older, especially with the amount of makeup that smothered the faces of some of the girls, and the intimidating build on a few of the boys. The mature-faced friends of Emily's – a combination of neighbours and out-of-towners – were scattered around the house, chatting about a lot of normal goings-on that we couldn't relate to in our bizarre joint job. ("Say, how's Johnny doing?" "Oh, he's fine. Window washing has never been better, he says.")

It had been two days since we had encountered the unusual duo of Gib and Slaml, and the worries that were packaged with it were weighing us down like a pair of mountains nestled on our shoulders. We were expecting a call at any moment from Dwight or anyone else at work; the thought of Dean somehow knowing all there was to know about us, and what he would do, took up a nice space at the forefront of our mind. For all we knew, he'd try to go after Emily, Scarlett, the IISEP, just to get to us. Or perhaps he'd try to arrange a nice chat and force some sort of terrible task onto us – be a hitman, a spy, sign an autograph? Anything we'd learn about him wouldn't change what we feared, especially if it was pieces of history that showed he could be dangerous.

The only thing that could make us relax was a nice can of Fosters (we would have gone with any old ciders like Magners, but sadly Emily didn't stock up on them). About halfway through the can, the blending of alcohol and our brain started to ease up a little. Maybe it was also the cheesy-sounding pop-rock music that had spent the last hour or so blending itself into the air and everyone's ears, singing about every single positive thing under the sun (i.e. you're beautiful; life is cool; don't you be worryin'; try, try, try, try and try) but I started to smile a bit and feel relaxed.

The Fosters made those mountains a little lighter, elevated them, cast a touch of mist around them. Things started to feel flexible for me; after another can, I decided to start chatting with a few of the older lot, specifically two women, clearly in their forties, and I started with the 'the party's not bad, eh?' line.

"Oh, it's pretty good, if you ask me," one replied. She gave me her name, Beth, and I gave mine. The other one, Anne, did likewise and shook my hand. As she did, I noticed that her smile, while pleasant, stretched out a bit too much, as though she'd been counting on meeting me and was excited about it. It was like surgery was holding her face into that look; it was unnerving.

"So, are you Emily's neighbours?" I asked.

"Yes," Beth answered, drawing it out slightly. "I live two houses down, I'm number twenty-three."

"I'm number twenty-two," Anne stated.

"Nice to know your ages, ladies." The three of us chuckled, Cain groaned in our head.

Anne asked, "I don't think I've seen you around here. Are you across town, by any chance?"

"Yeah, yeah." I took a swig of my second can.

"So… how old are you, dear? You're very handsome, I must say." She winked.

I nearly spat out my drink. The weird smile, declaring I looked handsome – I don't know about you, but I was getting quite a vibe from this.

"I'm, uh, I'm thirty, erm… I'm sorry, what was your name?"

"Anne, dear."

"A-Anne. And you?"

"Forty-two." Again with that smile.

"I'm forty-three," said Beth. "Been friends with Emily for a while?"

'Am I the only one who finds this way too nosy?'

'Not a whole lot, C,' I mentally replied. I answered Beth's question with, "Oh, just a family friend, nothing else."

"I see. I swear we saw you as far back as... no, of course not."

"Eh? What is it?"

"Oh, nothing. Just that we once saw you – or at least someone who looked like you – around twenty years ago. It was twenty, wasn't it, Anne?"

"No, dear, eighteen," she answered.

"Yes, that's it, eighteen. Ta, dear. Anyway, whoever this was, he was with Emily and her fella., round their house. We caught a good glimpse of him, didn't we?"

"Yes, we did."

"Yes, we did, didn't we? Ooh, he was ever so 'andsome, I can tell you that much. Of course, it couldn't have been you, dear, could it? You're just so *young*."

I chortled and put on a smile to hide my surprise. "Not unless I was a really big twelve-year old."

They burst out laughing like pack of hyenas at a comedy club; actually, 'cackling' felt to be a more suitable word.

"Ooh, you *are* funny, aren't you?"

"Apparently." We chatted for another minute or so before we wished each other a good time at the party and I split from them. Our ears picked up on a bit of their discussion in the aftermath (hey, it's not our fault if our hearing's a bit sharp).

"His name's David? That must be her boy-toy, then."

"I can see why. He's quite the catch. If only I wasn't married."

Ah, yes, these must have been the 'friends' who spent more time gossiping about a person than actually being their pal. Looked like they were reading *way* too much into our days and nights out with Emily and, on occasions, Scarlett. Then again, it was easy to see why they would think that; a middle-aged woman going through a divorce, might be feeling her age and a desire to recapture those lost years and youth she supposedly wasted on a guy she lost feelings for. Oh, but how? I know, how about shagging her decade-younger friend who's always there for her? Yup, that'll do the trick, no doubt about it!

But in the real world (y'know, the one not contained in the minds of bitchy gossip gals) it was all too different. After the divorce, Emily felt it wasn't worth dating again, at least for a while until the wounds started to heal, if they did ('I had a good run', we remember her saying, 'I think it's best I don't try to repeat what I had with him, you know? No point rushing into things so soon. If fate hands me something, I'll go with it') and that level of maturity and strength made it hilarious to think that those two thought she'd feel self-conscious enough to go ahead with me.

I put on a smile while we came up with jokes over their absurdity.

'I don't think there's such a thing as a two-for-one catch, ladies,' I thought.

'If split personalities are ya kink, yer gonna have a helluva time at the crazy barn, gals.'

This was interrupted by the light jovial whistle ringtone from my phone. Taking it out of my coat, we found out that Dwight was trying to call us. This was it. Here we'd get the info we needed, and maybe put some curiousity – and what little worries remained – to rest, or raise them to the next level. It would shed some more light on everything. I pressed the 'call' button in a blind mix of anticipation and eagerness.

"Dwight, what's up?"

"Guys, we ran a search on those two you wanted. We have some good and bad news."

Oh dear, bad news. We never like bad news, it gave the impression that something extremely worrying (or 'extremely terrible', take your pick) was going to happen. Why all the complications?

"Okay, shoot at us with the bad news first, Dwight. Best to go with the bullet then the bandage."

"Alright. Turns out Dean Gregory was born in 1821, died in a fire in 1853. Quite a long time ago."

There was a record scratch that halted everything around us when we heard Dwight. I could barely let my surprise speak for itself when all I was capable of doing was let out a slight whisper of "what?" Our brain went into overload. Old dust-masked memories were shoved in our face. The jigsaw was completed in a rushed panic. The alarm bells rang non-stop. The worry mountain was back in full force; it was heavier than ever, nearly crushing us with the sheer power of that one small, simple sentence. We were crushed, no doubt about it. A ghost from the past had decided to pop up and haunt us. No amount of alcohol could do the trick, oh hell, no.

'Oh my god,' Cain thought in what little space in our head that was free to think. 'It's him!'

'Yeah,' I replied, budging up for some extra room. 'It can't be, and yet...' No, no, it couldn't have been him. There was no way. Everything started rushing back at once.

It was 1853, the third year Cain and I took up bounty hunting in America. It was the perfect opportunity to take down the worst of the worst; the old Dead or Alive options gave us the chance to see whether or not some bounty-heads were worth being filled with holes. The large, almost unforgiving American frontiers were not the fantasies that television, dime books and films painted. It was a hardened place where duels could have taken place for far simpler, and pointless, reasons, like accidentally taking a guy's drink at a bar, mistaking it for your own (we certainly know that from experience – must have died eight or nine times doing that, in one year alone). We had been tasked with taking down a gang of criminals, and Dean was its leader.

He was nicknamed the Castrator, which should tell you all you need to know about him. But it doesn't, not quite. He kept a collection of all of his 'trophies', never once nauseated by the grim putrid stench of rotten testicles, in a large sack that he would carry behind his shoulder. Whenever he smiled that wide rubbery grin, unveiling his yellow-and-brown teeth, you could get two things from him; he was always looking forward to his next hapless victim, and he really didn't like the idea of toothpaste. His gut was like an ugly balloon under a shirt, overlapping the waistline of his trousers.

His weight was one of the most prominent things you'd remember him by; his fat jiggled in just about every place when he moved. The smell of him wasn't a pleasant experience; it was the nose-bombing combination of piss, alcohol and natural body odour that came from extended use of not caring for soap. You could even *taste* it. Taking him down, as well as his friends, felt so good that 'satisfying' doesn't cover it.

And yet he was still alive. It wasn't exactly something that we were used to finding out; if any old enemies kept popping up when we thought they were dead, our lives would take even more of a swerve into this comic book-like existence we shared. Suffice to say that surviving nearly two centuries and a burning house merits even more questions than what we had at the start.

"Guys?" Dwight called out. We must have stood there blankly for a long time.

"Oh, sorry. We were just... thinking. It's been so long that I... I don't even know what to say."

"Yes, that was pretty much my reaction, too. Did you know him?"

"We did, only for a little bit. It was so far back, we forgot he even existed."

"Do you think it might actually be him?"

184

I hesitated, not wanting to say my reply aloud for fear of realising it was more than likely. But I had to say it, whether or not I liked to. "I'm leaning towards 'yes'."

We didn't hear anything on Dwight's end for ten seconds. Knowing him, he was spending those seconds mapping out what to do, how to do it, when to do it, and at what speed. He could show you a fully detailed plan complete with fail-safes, unlikely scenarios, safety precautions, consideration of weapons and the roles everyone would have, and then reveal he came up with it while chewing a fingernail.

"Okay," he began, his voice a bit lower than usual, "we need to sort this guy out as quickly as possible."

"I'm going to assume you have a plan formed in that lovely little head of yours?"

"You're not assuming, David; you *know*." He was right.

"Great! So, what's the plan, D?"

Dwight didn't take his time while informing us. He replied within half a second, direct and thorough, never hesitant in-between sentences, no pausing when laying down the facts in his masterfully captivating voice, the kind that would have made Samuel L. Jackson jealous.

"First of all, we have a lead on that pal of his in the alien 'pet' ring – that's the good news. We've got his address as well as those of his contacts, twenty of them, along with camera footage from across town showing that they converge at this warehouse every day at eight o'clock in the morning. Tomorrow we can raid the warehouse within that time, taking the distance to get there into account. We'll set up the operation at sixty-thirty, leave at seven-thirty. To counteract the high number of people, we'll need thirty operatives at most, especially if there might be some people in there that we don't know. We'll get Andrex and her workers from Recovery to tag along to take care of aliens."

"Good thinking," I complimented.

"Spare stun guns will be required for everyone, two at most in case they get crushed or malfunction. The higher-

185

ups in the police will help cover this up as usual; it won't be that hard to say that they were taking normal animals and treating and selling them illegally. Once we interview Eddie Muzzle and get as much contact information as possible, we arrange a meet-up with Dean and pull out similar precautions before arresting him. If he has a regeneration factor much like yourselves, maybe even at a higher level, then some heavy artillery should be required; quadruple shotguns, armour-piercing rifles, even explosive rounds if he's strong enough. When we're able to bring him in, we scan him for abnormal physical characteristics and match that up with what we know. We'll stick him in one of our cells, and if he's immortal then he should look forward to one very long, very cramped vacation at the Hotel IISEP."

There was a reason he was the head of this branch. Just in case you're dealing with something you don't know about that could be deadly, prepare to go overkill just in case.

"Wow, Dwight, you've... really thought about this."

"Of course I have," he said casually, as though he heard this statement a dozen times already.

Emily and Scarlett flashed in our mind. I quickly said, "Okay, thanks for the infodump, Dwight. Chat later."

"Goodbye, gu—" I just registered the 'goodbye' before I ended the call.

'I think,' I suggested to Cain, 'we need to tell Emily, just in case he tries anything.'

'Yeah, I agree, buddy, big time.'

We caught sight of her in the dining room, talking to a few of her friends (that is, the ones who weren't like the women from The Real Housewives shows).

"...hang on, I'm just gonna get another drink, do you want any?"

Some said a few brands, others said no, and she navigated her way to the utility room, where the alcohol was kept, so I followed.

"Emily?"

186

"Yeah, guys?"

"Can we chat to you somewhere private? It's very important."

"Um, okay," she said, her face stuck in a small smile, but we could see beyond that that she was slightly worried; it wasn't just the way her eyes gleaned at us, but her lips looked as though they were trying to break away and drop the happy face.

We made our way upstairs, into her room. As soon as we were inside, she turned the door's lock.

"Alright, what is it? Obviously it's something serious. Is it good? Bad?"

We tried finding the right words, the right place to start at, while locked on to her face and those warm eyes. I managed to tell her about the shapeshifters, the Eddie Muzzle guy and his operations, and most importantly, Dean and our history with him.

"What the hell? You mean that this guy's still walking around today, like you? And what, he wants revenge?"

"That's our first guess. We saw him in a cafe, but at that time we didn't recognise him. He seemed... I dunno, like he was baiting me. Those impersonators don't know a lot about him, especially what he's got in store. But he knows an awful lot about us, and that could lead to him using you and Scarlett to get to us."

"Oh my God," she said almost shakily. "My baby... he's not gonna harm her, I'll make damn sure of it."

Cain surfaced, saying with false confidence, "Don't worry about it, we got this in the bag." He gave a small thumbs-up before going back into our head. While this was what we hoped for, it at least felt reassuring for all of us. I continued to speak. "I want you to know that we'll try and get this guy as quickly as possible. We already have a link to him. I know this isn't exactly the right time and place to tell you this, but I need you to know because I don't want you to be ignorant of any oncoming danger."

187

"David, promise me this: you find him, and you lock the bastard away for however long he has left. I don't care if he's an alien, a demon, a cyborg, or whatever else there is – you guys bring him down, and you do it the best you can."

"I promise. I'm sorry for all this, that our past has caught up with us, and you might get involved in it."

Emily's eyes went from the wide-eyed shock that came moments before, into a tighter, bolder spark of sensitivity.

"You don't have to apologise," she said. "It's him doing this, not you, and you are by no means bad people. Whatever happens, I'll do my best to protect my daughter, and you two do yours."

I couldn't help but smile at her. All that confidence – she was magnificent. This was one of the reasons I loved people. "Look at you. Sometimes I forget you're no longer that scared little girl outside her apartment. Yet even now, I still try to protect you when you're already capable of doing that. God, I'm such an old fool."

"Don't say that. You're nice, you care about us."

I felt like an old record, but I couldn't help but spill everything I locked up for years. It was slightly hard to voice, but I managed. "You know, over the years, Cain and I have gotten to know you so well, we've been such a part of your life, as you have with ours. You've been so nice to us, and it feels for the first time in such a long, long time, that we've found some sort of family. There were people who took us in over the years, treated us as one of their own, but centuries later, their faces and names started getting murky, and we just have to rely on scraps of what we can remember of them, nothing more. We're just... so old. Give it a couple of centuries, no matter how hard we'll try to resist it, you'll just be another smudge of chalk on the wall."

"David..." She tried to carry on, but the lump in her throat stopped her.

"It's okay," I lied. My eyes started to water. "You get used to it. You'll be 'kind blonde woman', Scarlett will be 'tiny redhead'." A tear slithered down my cheek, I brushed it off quickly. "So, you know, the important stuff," I said with a less-than-reassuring chuckle.

Emily didn't take anything short of a second to hug us. Her arms were like ribbons, so smooth and welcoming across our back, that I wanted that sensation to stick with me and Cain for eternity. All I could do was say, in an almost whispery voice, "thank you". There was nothing else more important to say than those two words. I thanked her for preventing us from spending lonely nights and days in our home. She filled in quite a void. As I wrapped my arms around her, I felt like I was just politely echoing her actions rather than doing them out of friendship. Still, she was a good friend to have.

"Don't worry," she said. "As long as you remember us, there's nothing to worry about, right?"

"Right," I repeated with a smile. With that, Cain took over, and we could feel from Emily's small wriggling of her back that she could tell.

Feelin' her arms around us was pretty weird for me, 'specially since we never worked ourselves up like this. But *man*, could she hug well. My throat was gettin' all worked up thinkin' about what Davey-boy said, all that stuff about forgettin' people... I wished he hadn't brought it up. I tried to ignore it all so I didn't have to worry about the future, just what I did in the now.

"Man, this... this is just... great, kid." My voice was more than a little shaky.

"Cain, are you okay?"

"Um, yeah, yeah, sure thing," I bluffed, tryin' to stay macho.

"I can tell you're upset. Oh, Cain. Please don't cry."

Okay, that wasn't workin'. "Nah, I ain't cryin', kid. I ain't got a single tear in my eye. I ain't—" I sobbed everythin' out. "Ah, who am I kiddin', I'm all waterworks. Thanks, Em," I choked out.

"Hey, don't worry about it. With you, I guess I could say I'm raising two kids instead of one."

"I friggin' love yer hugs, Em. You should make this a profession, ya know?" I must have clutched onto her for about five seconds before Emily started to feel uncomfortable.

"Cain, I really don't mean to be rude, but can I let go now?"

"Gimme a couple o' seconds, kid." A couple o' seconds later, an', "Okey-dokey," we let go.

"So, shall we head back down, if it's okay with you? Or is there anything else you want to talk about?"

"Erm, nothin' I can think of. Anyway, I don't want people starin' at me, so I'm gonna... I'm gonna let Davey-boy take over from here, yeah?"

"Okay," she said with a nod.

Piloting things again, I followed Emily as she went open the door to the corridor.

We found Scarlett on the other side, looking as confounded as we did as she flinched from her little eavesdropping spot. She had hugged her body to the wall, her ear near the doorframe and her feet elevated so that she was on her toes, most likely to avoid getting caught out by the light from inside the room. She was struck by a case of 'oh crap, I'm caught' as her mouth swung open into a perfect little O shape. She took a couple of jittery steps back.

Emily was the first to speak. "Scarlett?"

Like her name, she was starting to look a bit red, accompanied by a confused, slightly nervous voice. "What's going on? Don't lie to me, I heard everything. There was another guy in there, Cain. Where is he?"

"No one else was in here," her mother claimed.

"You're lying, Mum. It was an American guy."

"Alright," I said. No need to beat about the bush. She wasn't a stupid kid by any means. "He's me. Kinda. Another person in this body. Two guys, one body."

Naturally, she took this about as well as you'd expect when a family friend reveals they're housing more than one person in their head.

"You've got MPD?"

"Something like that."

She sounded a bit stunned, but at the same time casual. "...O-kaaay. I guess." Miles better than I expected (I thought she'd call me a weirdo and walk off). "So... how come I haven't seen him?"

"Well," Emily began, "we figured you would have found it odd to notice how David's accent would flip-flop from English to American and that he'd look a little weird at times. Plus, he's not exactly ecstatic when it comes with kids."

"Oh, right," she said, even more uncomfortable than before.

I took out my hand for a potential handshake between the teen and my alter ego. "Want to say hi to him?"

"Umm, no thanks."

"Okay," I shrugged. Cain similarly responded in our mind, 'Fair enough. Talking to teens ain't my thing, anyway.'

"I heard you talking about being really old, like several centuries or something. You're not immortal, right? You can't be. I mean, that's just *crazy*."

"It's true. We are probably several millennia old. It's tough to narrow it down when calendars weren't around at first."

"I'm not buying it," she stated bluntly.

"I'll make it a free reveal – no charges necessary," I quipped.

"What a shame; I'd have charged you with being delusional," she retorted.

"Scarlett," Emily said in the ever-eternal negative tone a parent would use.

"No, don't worry, Emily. I like quick-witted people. Gets me in the mood for a quick-wit comeback competition." I chuckled a bit.

"Anyway, about that guy you were talking about. The one who might come after us..."

"You don't have to worry about him," her mother interrupted. "David and Cain here know what they're doing. He'll be caught before you know it."

"You don't know that. I heard what he's like. I'm not a kid, I've got a stun gun with me; I can protect myself from a creep like that if he comes after me."

"The *hell* you can." Emily nearly raised her voice. Maybe it was because of the party downstairs, or the need to not sound too harsh, but her anger was held back while her maternal instincts went into overdrive. "Just... go downstairs, okay? We'll talk about this later."

"But Mum, I—"

"I don't want to hear you talk back. Please."

"Okay," Scarlett huffed in defeat, and went off to the ground floor that was filled with more normal people.

"Emily," I said, "I think we might head off now. We don't want to make things anymore awkward here."

"Don't worry about it, David. All of this is a lot to process, especially for her. Give it a couple of hours and we'll be fine, I promise." She went downstairs, and I followed. I hoped that there wouldn't be any more surprises in store tonight.

*

The ever-stretching pavement gave me the impression that Cain and I were just walking on the same spot for ages. It took thirty minutes to walk from our house and Emily's, not a problem when you enjoy nice journeys that give you that cold refreshing air to take in and feel better for it. The street lamps were comforting, as their bright glow made me feel equally bright about sorting out our little problem at hand. Okay, not *really* as bright; if anything, we felt only *slightly* brighter than before.

It was good that I had informed Emily of Dean Gregory, but at the same time I realised that I had potentially directed unnecessary panic and stress towards her. If the Castrator was sorted out early and efficiently enough, then yes, it was a waste of time to tell her. On the other hand, if he *were* to target her, then it was right to have let her know. Stuff like this wasn't new to us; unable to tell if we were revealing things at the right time and place, and how that might affect that person's decisions whether they were good or bad. Hopefully I had done the right thing, otherwise I probably stressed off a few years of Emily's life (not a terribly good thing). All we had to do was to wait and see how events would unfold. Reflecting on all of this was not really good for our mental health (well, what was left of it, anyway). I'd have considered having a can of something alcoholic, but then I remembered that I'd be floored drinking a fourth beer and that I also needed to restock on drinks anyway.

We started a questions-and-answers game in our head to occupy ourselves on the trek home. Nearly every time we would have to walk home, we'd come up with a game to help us laugh and, really, just have fun.

'Okay, what's the name o' that story where a guy gets involved in time travel an' becomes his own family, an' who wrote it?'

'All You Zombies, by Robert Heinlein.'

'Ding-ding-ding! Ya get one point! Okay, now you, you, you!'

'Alright, alright. Here's the question: this film starred Sean Pertwee and werewolves. What was the name?'

'Ooh ooh ooh, I got this! *DOG SOLDIERS!*'

'And you're right!'

'Woo-hoo!'

Cain was in the midst of churning up a new question when we noticed a figure along the pavement, walking opposite to us. He was some thirty feet away, a good enough distance to make him out. A chill ran down our spine. Examining his face from the distance, we realised it was the man in the cafe, a face that we could now name after Dwight's call. It was Dean Gregory, the Castrator. There he was, his large, beefy hands swaying from side to side as he strolled along in our direction, a bright smug grin decorating his face. He wore a thick dark blue coat that ended at his thick knees. We could tell from the size of him that he had slimmed down since 1853, no longer the morbidly obese man he once was, but still quite fat. Thick black facial hair dove down to form a short but compelling beard; it was almost the quintessential look for your average obvious villains.

"You've got to be joking," I muttered under my breath. I stopped walking, almost shocked by the sight.

'Aw, crap,' Cain thought. 'What the hell are we gonna do?'

"Talk, see if we get anything out of him," I muttered, "and, if we have to, fight."

'Don't talk him to death, David. I wanna beat the crap outta him.'

"And what makes you think I can't do that?"

'You kiddin'? I'm the master o' ruthless beatdowns. I make you look like some dainty ballerina.'

"Who just happens to be more skilled than you."

'Point taken,' he sulked.

By this point, Dean was ten feet away, and with his closeness came a sense of dread that I hadn't felt in decades.

"Hello there, David, Cain," he announced in a great, booming voice that I'm sure he was in love with.

"Dean," I was just able to grunt out.

"Oh, you recognise me now. It's been, what, a day or two since you last saw me? Of course, those two bumbling idiots told me that they blurted out my name to you, so that dampens my surprise a little. In any case, my old, old friends, how lovely to see you again. No, better yet, how lovely to *talk* to you again."

"You've lost weight."

194

"Well, a hundred and ninety-odd years gave me enough time to do some slimming down for you. I want to look as presentable as possible for my resurface."

"Well, I have to say, you definitely look like you tried. But what exactly is the occasion for trying to meet up with us? I doubt we'll reminiscence about good times over tea and coffee and watch some telly together."

"True. For now, I'm looking for a bit of fun tonight."

"Go to a club," I said dryly. "Might be a good guy for you to castrate."

"No, what I'm after is you two. I want to see how tough you are."

"What? What have you got up your sleeve?"

"Just an awful lot of muscle." In no time at all, he swung his arm at me in a backhanded slap like a whip made of lightning.

I crouched down to avoid the blow – thank God for fast reflexes – mostly by sloping my back, just narrowly missing his hand and nearly scaring me in how fast it all went. From the moment I bent down, I didn't spare any time and responded by tightening my left hand into a hard ball before sending a sharp blow to his stomach. His stomach felt only slightly flabby, and I could feel the sheer bulk behind his fat, but it was too dense to be real. I had punched many a rotund guy before, some even bigger than him, and they went down easily and felt less hard when socked in the gut. He didn't even flinch.

I took a step back, stunned. His non-existent reaction took us a few seconds to take in. 'This guy's built, man,' my mental roommate stated, to which I nodded, and I realised that to Dean it looked like I was glad I couldn't hurt him.

Dean gave out a brief dry chuckle. "Oh, come on, surely that's not all you've got? Don't hold back, give me *everything* you've got, my little *bounty-hunter*." He put loving emphasis on 'bounty-hunter', made it sound like a pet name. "I know you're holding back, blending in with the rest of the herd. I'm not like them, I can take what you can dish out. You're so… careful, my little bounty hunter."

Dammit, he was right; I wasn't using our full strength, considered superhuman by normal human standards. I'd have to consider the risk that if I were to go any higher, to give him the full swing and raw power that coursed through every part of us, it might very well end up killing him. But then again, with his stomach being too hard for anyone or anything natural, and his unflinching, casual reactions, it looked like I had no choice. It was full force or nothing, one-hundred percent all the way. I clenched my fists so hard that I could feel them getting wet with the arrival of fresh blood.

I got into a boxing stance and gave him everything I could throw. The strength I poured out was the equivalent of a truck hitting you at 300 mph, something that should have torn through Dean's flesh, rupture his organs and bones and send me going straight through him with every hit. Left and right hooks to the face, my knuckles briefly brushing against the thick rug of hair on his cheeks. That did nothing, not even a streak of blood out of his mouth, or a tiny shift in his jaw line. His jaw should have been blown off. I broke four knuckles, and I wanted to cry out from how hot and searing the pain was. Three rapid punches to both shoulders, which seemed to just mildly push them back with no real damage. He just kept smiling and rolled back his shoulders, mocking me. There went another knuckle, and further damage to two of the already-screwed ones. The stomach punches went about as well as they did before. All Dean did was grin and rub his neck.

So this was it, then. The Unstoppable Force meets the Immovable Object. What in the hell was he? How much punishment would he have to take to actually receive anything familiar to pain, or even just to budge? I would have thought of more questions if I wasn't trying to take him down before my hands went bust.

By now I only had one knuckle that wasn't cut and bruised and spitting blood. The rest were split, almost sanded down into very vague red bumps. I could barely hold together a fist without being flushed with pain. The exhaust was getting to me; my legs were aching from how tense I was holding them, and my arms felt wiry, like I had shed layers of skin right down to the bone. My chest heaved with every breath. I paused for a moment to rub my damaged hands, and that was when Dean made his move.

His wide palm slapped us across the face at such force that we were flung five feet to the side, our head crashing onto the road. We could tell that we were going to get one hell of a large bump on our head.

Trying to force myself up with bruised hands wasn't the easiest of things. Forcing myself past the pain was almost manageable, but I got up eventually.

"Oh, I'm sorry, David," Dean said in a mock-apologetic voice. "I think I might have hit you just a little *too* hard."

Rubbing the side of my head and slightly twitching from how sensitive it felt, I muttered, "I feel... sorry for people who shake your hand..."

"Heh. If you're having a tough time, why not let your little pet roommate have his fair share of pain? Who knows, with those claws of his, he might actually be able to hurt me?"

I could barely tighten my hands into fists in the name of keeping my guard up, and I knew that there was no way I could take him on. A good deal of damage was displayed all over us like paint over a white wall. Very soon, he would have the chance to knock us out, or perhaps something far worse.

'Cain,' I thought, 'I'm all tapped out. This guy should have been floored within the first punch.'

There wasn't a hint of hesitation in my friend's boastful voice. He sounded positively cheerful, or just downright arrogant.

'Stand back, Davey-boy, cuz I'm gonna tear him to shreds!'

'Cain, we're in no condition for this! Bad idea! *Bad idea!*'

I sprang my claws out an' showed my fangs in a good ol' menacin' fashion, waitin' for the look on his face to wither into one that said 'I've messed with the wrong guy here'. But that didn't happen. I plunged one hand into his stomach, but I couldn't even pierce it; it was like he had a steel wall there.

"Okay, that... ain't what I expected to happen." I took my hand away an' examined my fingernails - they were still sharp as ever, sure, but that Castrator musta had some real hard skin on 'im.

"What's the matter, Cain? Can't cut it? How about this: why don't you try slicing me here?" He swiped his finger over his throat slowly, creatin' an invisible line for us to follow. "I promise you it'll be nice and easy for you. Unless your claws have gotten awfully dull over the years."

"WHY, YOU SMUG BASTARD!"

I didn't wait for 'im to make the first move like with David; that little taunt was all that was needed to set me on fire. I exploded with everythin' I had – anger, confusion, frustration, the need to see 'im dead an' bleedin' from that goddamn thick throat o' his, for his cocky fat face to fade an' his cocky fat body to fall with the sound o' 'timber'. I sliced his throat in an instant.

Nothin' came out. No red river, no scarlet streams, no burgundy body-juices. It was like puncturin' a parade float, 'cept this one didn't even look like he felt or reacted to the hole. He just stood there, starin' at us with his teeth bare and clenched, eyes thick with delight.

"What... the fuck?"

"Looks like your nails aren't getting rusty any time soon," he said.

He placed his hands over his throat an' squeezed the skin together towards the cut, stretchin' an' scrunchin' the flab under his second chin while he did. He was doin' it in sections, an' lookin' all nonchalant about it. Once the bastard removed his hands from his throat, we could see that it was back to normal, all whole again, completely cut-free as if I never sliced it up in the first place. I stepped back an' saw him stretch his face into somethin' that we barely recognised as a grin – it was like a wolf gettin' ready to jump on his prey an' dig his teeth into their tough squirmin' little bodies. I felt both nostalgia an' old shame in that comparison.

There's no way in hell I could describe all the fear that was runnin' rampant in our head. This bastard could regenerate, an' he wanted to show it off. Was this somethin' he always had? Then again, he wasn't as soft and mushy as he used to be, and back in 1853 he bled like any fella an' couldn't patch himself back up. Probably had an enhancement or two, ones that made certain danger feel like small stuff. Was it possible that— nah, it was unlikely. But then again, what wasn't by this point? Maybe he wasn't even the ol' Castrator 'imself? Robot, shapeshifter, anything that can look like someone else? Guesses, just guesses. I didn't wanna think that this was the real guy, an asshole that went from nobody to nightmare. Like it or not, we know for sure that what was right in front o' us was very real, an' he called himself Dean Gregory.

Dean massaged his throat with one hand an' took a couple o' deep breaths. "Thanks, Cain, my throat was feeling clogged up. Did me a great favour there, old pal."

"What the hell are ya?"

"Human. Well, mostly."

I was too busy eyein' his repaired throat to notice his other hand slammin' itself into our gut. It was like everythin' inside us just vomited out all at once. His fist ran deep into us, probably disruptin' a few vital organs and smashin' some into pieces, at least that's how hard it felt. For a sec, we thought he'd punched right through us, from stomach to spine. Our lungs shut down, followin' the domino trail upwards as our throat tightened. I stood there, tryin' to get some air into us, but that didn't do a damn thing. Had to make sure that I breathed out as little as possible, and that was one hell of a challenge. I felt the strength in our arms n' legs fade away, like the force o' the punch had spread to everywhere else, so we were just barely able to stand with our feet cemented to the dull concrete pavement. All I could do was let out a strangled whine.

When he took his hand out, the pain was still there, like he made an indention on our body. As soon as he did, I tipped forward n' collapsed onto the floor like a marionette when its strings are cut off by some sadist. Our nose was curved against the pavement, an' our mouth bein' wide open left us with the foul taste o' dirt n' stone stuck to our tongue. Just when we thought it couldn't get worse, the back of our head got clamped down by ol' Castrator's hard boot, an' he was grindin' us down real good. To this day, I can still hear the dull sound o' our skull gettin' crushed inch by inch. He only squeezed down for three seconds, but it felt so long.

I tried usin' my hands an' knees to get up just before another kind o' pain struck us. It could have been from what he did to our head, but our brain went loco; several headaches hittin' us at the same time, makin' our brain feel heavy an' stretched while our vision went fuzzy with every kind o' colour swimmin' in front o' us. Screamin' doesn't do a guy good when you can barely breathe.

I couldn't handle it anymore. I let David take the helm.

I managed to stand up (thanks to enough willpower, I suppose), and stared down at the outline of Dean in our colour-swirled eyes. It was (for lack of any other appropriate word) painfully clear that he was doing this to us, especially when we remembered the incident at the cafe.

"This pain," I struggled to get out. "How are you… doing this to us?"

I could tell that Dean grinned, his cheeks rising and bulging, almost resembling dough-balls. "Do you like it? It's all thanks to a magnificent little device I've been holding on to; it allows me to disrupt your brain by emitting pulse-pounding headaches the likes of which have not been seen since *Scanners*."

"How the hell did you make that? How are you still *alive*?"

A light chuckle escaped his renewed throat. "I'm terribly sorry, but I can't say. At least, not now. No, not *now*. It's too soon for that, it would lead to you wondering about too much too soon, and I definitely can't have that until everything's fallen into place for my little play."

Suddenly, our breathing returned to normal, taking in great gulps of air. "Your play? You're either an insane playwright or a sucker for melodrama."

"Oh, how I wish I was the former." I could sense some regret in his voice. "Well, I have the first part of it lined out nicely, wouldn't you say? Still, I have all the time in the world to try my hand at the craft."

"Look, what's your goal? Is it to kill, date or torture us? I'd get used to getting killed a lot – at least then we won't have to see your bullfrog of a face staring at us often."

"My dear friends, I have such amazing plans for you. No, 'amazing' isn't fitting enough. I have it: *transcendent*! I hold all the answers that you've been seeking for so very long, all those years spent wandering the world with nary a clue."

My brow went tense as I heard this. "What? That's impossible." And yet a part of me wished it wasn't. I wanted to know, but the fact that *he* claimed to did nothing but made me feel dirty for imagining the answers coming out of his sick mouth. Cain briefly popped out to voice his opinion. "The hell do ya mean, 'hold all the answers'? Our life ain't a book that's been rubbed out or nothin'." Once he dug himself back into our brain, I nodded in agreement.

"I truly mean what I say, my dear lovely two. It's something that holds so much value, it would complete you. And yet, in the cup of my hand, I hold them in a wonderful, gleaming chalice of pure beauty and reflection; like the finest wine, the very peak of excellence, exquisite. To behold it is to behold the very essence of truth – that life throws you with the incredible, the incomprehensible, and it may leave quite the everlasting taste in one's mouth."

"Oh, shut up, you insufferable prick," I shot back.

He scowled at that and grabbed us by the throat. "You really don't believe me, do you? Oh, come now, surely you'd have to, eh, Raanan?"

Our mind went blank for a couple of seconds. My name. He knew my first name! That was impossible; I had never used it since I was removed from the tribe all those years ago. For Dean to know, he had to be there. This was all too confusing, and quite frankly I was scared by it.

"My name... how do you know that?"

"There we go, curiosity piqued. Let's just say I have my ways. Well, I think it's time I made off. It's been fun catching up, Mr and Mr Short, though I'll pick a more appropriate time for it. I'll let you know when. So long, farewell, goodbye, my little bounty hunters."

He threw us to the ground with great force, turned around and started to walk off. He didn't get far before stopping for a bit. "On second thought, I might crank up the pain you're feeling for a little longer. Say, thirty minutes, thirty-five, tops? I can't have you trying to wrangle me in so soon. I don't even know how long it would take for your knuckles to heal up, anyway. Just for caution, I suppose."

The pain redoubled, growing stronger in a matter of seconds. The colours kicked off again, a range of red, blue, yellow, and some new unfound colours bloomed and swirled in front of us; we couldn't see anything beyond them. Our brain suffered from the sensation of an army of spikes plunging themselves into a fresh new victim, covering every angle. Back on the pavement once again, we spent the next half hour curled up in a ball, unable to think, unable to scream, unable to see, twitching and grabbing our skull. If anyone had seen us while passing, I don't think they had it in them to help us out.

By the end of it, we barely had enough energy to do or think of anything other than shamble on home like a zombie, noticing the specks of colours at the end of our vision. At home, we went straight to bed. We still saw the colours and Dean in our sleep, taunting us.

Chapter 13

Downhill Starts Here

Waking up was the hard part. Our mind went swimming along in the miserable muck of madmen and the otherwise insane. Bad memories rising up, trying to drown us, memories of people screaming and dying and cursing us in their final breathes, their faces angry, morbid and red. And that was from the shallow end. The deep end was much, much worse; an old, long-forgotten flashback of 1853, Dean the Castrator doing what he did best on us as we hung upside-down from the ceiling of his living room, blood and pain decorating the place in the midst of anguished screams and wild laughter.

The shed wasn't dark, what with the door in the corner and the window leading to sunlight, allowing us to take in some fresh air before Dean would come back. The dark shade of wood and the blood around us made the sunlight look like a shimmering flame. A tall wooden device, resembling the empty framework of a bed, kept us from touching the floor as rope tied in the corners dug into our wrists and ankles with great annoyance.

Our muscles ached all over from the beating he gave us; blood slithered down the left side of our gut from where he had sliced into it; the right leg was dislocated, the knee sticking out one way and the ankle in the another, the foot facing the wrong direction in a hundred and eighty degrees turn. Our left eye was closed after sustaining enough damage to make it bleed and bruise. We couldn't feel our fingers, what with them being pulled, cracked and twisted around. Dean's messy engraving of his name on our back burned like hell. All in all, if there was nothing else to get in the way, the regeneration would take up three to five days. We wouldn't heal for another week.

Dean managed to squeeze himself into the shed, momentarily blocking the light as he did. His large frame made it difficult for him, all three-hundred-and-twenty pounds of him, but he won this little battle. The strain of his blood-stained shirt against his belly presented the fabric's great challenge to keep the buttons and holes in the same space. They didn't even cover all of his gut; the vast brown forest of hair around his black hole of a navel was all-too visible. The brown faded trousers he wore were kept in place by several belts fashioned together to form what I liked to call a super-belt. At least for his sake, his short black jacket was just about his size. In his left hand was a knife, a curved one at that. The Castrator was ready to do his thing.

"You're gonna look great hanging in this room after I'm done," he said. "I don't know how to start; do it nice n' quickly, or nice n' slow?" He stroked his beard in delight.

"If it'll make things easier," I said after clearing my throat, "do it quickly. I don't want it to take too long – I want to make sure your bodies are brought to the sheriff's before sundown."

"Tough talk comin' from a guy about to get his balls cut off. You'll be dead before you even know it."

"Somehow, I doubt it, you bloated bag of bile."

"Bile? Whassat?" Guess he never looked in a mirror.

"Something sour," I defined. "Bitter, the worst of the worst kind out there. That could be your mother, if I'm not mistaken."

"Ha! I killed my mother when I was a boy! Always too damn keen on wanting me to go after girls instead. She was my first kill 'fore I started my habit. Made me feel like a man, knowin' you can get rid of someone so easy."

"She must be very proud," I quipped.

He let out a high-pitched, almost girlish laugh. "I like you! You're the funniest guy I've met."

"You must have some really humourless friends in your gang, then, if you think I'm hilarious."

"They're all pricks with cacti up their assholes."

"Charming. Look, being in this position and about to lose my most private and tender parts doesn't exactly scare me by means, so how about I show you something really unnerving?"

"Whatcha gonna do? Tell me a nigger's gonna be leadin' this country some day?" Hello, sweet hindsight.

"As much as I want to punch you for saying that word, no. Instead, I'll show you what happens when you tangle with The Beast."

"That what they call ya? Might as well call ya The Cattle."

"As if the Castrator wasn't dignifying. You'll see what I mean. Watch closely." I took in a deep breath, giving off the effect of dramatic concentration when really there was no need when switching with Cain took one second. The look on Dean's face, the slight fishy opening of his mouth and crease on his frown, was for my pleasure for when he'd jump back at our body's transformation. We would scare him and try to break away if we had enough strength.

Cain sprang up, letting out a roar and showing off his fangs, his sharp yellow eyes shooting at Dean's dull stupid ones as our torturer jumped back with such speed I thought his skeleton would escape and run for the hills.

"Holy mother of God," he yelled out in a high shrilly voice as he dropped his knife.

"God's nothin' compared to me! Hello, I'm The Beast, ya sadistic fuck! I'll eat you, gut you, turn you into barbeque and make you wish ya cut your own balls off instead! Not in that order! Or maybe, whatever scares ya the most!" He licked our lips in gruesome delight and tried to push our arms and legs out to free them, but to no avail. Dammit, we were too weak.

Dean stepped forward, slowly leaning down to grab the knife, huffing as he shifted his weight. "What the hell are you?"

"Didn't you hear me? The Beast! Unholy Angel! God's Favourite Backstabber! The Crafty Red Bastard! The Devil, moron!" Cain grunted as he continued trying to break from the wooden frame.

Rather than take these boasts to heart, Dean instead let out a giggle, his fright turning into amusement. "D-devil? My father told me all about the Devil, and you ain't him. If you were, me and my friends would all be dead."

"Never know, maybe I prettied myself up after all these years. Can't keep the same face all the time, otherwise I'd get so bored with it."

Dean grew nearer, smiling with each step as he realised he was safe from harm. "I can get behind torturing the Devil. If you can change like you did just now, I wonder…" He undid our trousers and pants and looked disappointed. "Nope, not an inch more. Shame. Then again, there's still the rest of you to enjoy." He stroked his knife against our stomach, the penetration of our skin growing deeper with each wave. Cain failed to mask our pain.

"Before I get to the real fun down below, I still wanna make sure I don't waste every inch of you up above, especially now you look so… outlandish."

"Ya don't have to," Cain persisted. "Tell ya what, how's about you untie me an' then fight, huh? If ya win, then you can go snip-snip. If I win, I go snip-snip on ya an' kill ya. Sound fair?" The raging cocky voice faded into the desperate pleas of a child. Had I been the one talking, I'd have sound like it too.

"No, I don't like that. Fair ain't my style. Besides, I don't want to get injured at the hands of my friend; that'd be embarrassing."

Cain couldn't help but grin and say with a return to form, "Seein' you try to fit through that door's embarrassin' enough, big boy."

"Now you've done it." Dean dug his knife even deeper into our stomach, and we howled in agony.

We must have relived that ten, twenty, fifty times before we woke up. When we did, I screamed and found myself covered in sweat. Cain was frantic, sobbing and gibbering like a small panicked child: "David, I don't wanna meet him again, I want us to stay in our house n' do nothin' forever. Please please please please please, Davey. I wanna feel safe, really safe."

"Don't worry, we'll nab him and then everything will be okay." I was lying and he knew it too. Given how strong and tough Dean was, it was possible that even with IISEP weaponry, it could be a difficult face-off. Or maybe I was just being way too pessimistic for our own good. Yeah, the latter seemed more likely. Come on man, be more optimistic! I guess a string of millennia does that to someone...

I never been in hurt like that before n' I never wanted to be in that kind o' pain again.

We woke up around 5:30, filled with five hours' sleep and the result was that we still felt like shit. Our brain was barely fresh from the faded numbing pain that Dean gave us (not the greatest parting gift, could have made our skull feel a tad tighter for extra sadism). On the plus side, the record for darkest-bags-under-the-eyes was broken. I phoned up Dwight at 5:40 and informed him of what happened last night. As you'd expect, he wasn't exactly expecting the weirdness of us being face-to-face-to-face with the dead guy we talked about a couple of hours before.

"Damn strange coincidence," the big guy declared. Thanks, Dwight, someone had to say it. Well, other than we, ourselves and us, that is. I felt a groan coming on, but I held it back – didn't want it to come across as insulting.

"Yeah, too big a coincidence, if you ask me, and he was walking near Emily and Scarlett's place. Either that or he must have wanted a really big walk around town, eh?"

Eight o'clock on the dot. Five IISEP vans swarmed around the warehouse like eager vultures, three stopping at the back entrance, and the other two at the front. Cain and I, Brad, Jackie and Dwight were in one of the front door vans, all but Dwight holding on firmly to our stun handguns and rifles as he drove up and parked us by the warehouse. I wasn't sure about the others, but I couldn't help but take a few deep breaths.

"Okay, this is it," I said with a bit of excitement in my voice, as if I had to clarify to everyone what we were doing, which made me sound like a bit of an idiot. Brad just gave a slight nod while he stared at his left hand, flexing it as though it was new and wanted to test it out. Jackie seemed more talkative by comparison.

"Hell yeah, it is," she said in delight, giving us a thumbs-up and a grin, revealing her small, cute fangs. "I'm ready to bring these guys in. This cat's gonna show them her claws." To demonstrate, the claw in her thumb sprung out, looking like a thick needle.

"Sound likes the purrfect plan for you," I quipped. My cat puns were on par with Catwoman from that old sixties Batman show.

"Oh, god," she chuckled, "that was terrible!" Yeah, it was. But hey, I left all my good cat jokes at home.

"Okay," I said, trying for a second crack, "how about, 'you got yourself a couple of scratching posts'?"

"Better, still cheesy, though."

I smiled and took the compliment. "I'm great with cheese, runs in our veins. Cain's pretty cheesy, too. When he gets round to talking, I'm sure you'll agree."

"I'll bet my teeth on it." She then opened her mouth to show them, the nice little daggers that they were, and then shut it a quick and loud *CHOMP*.

"Brad, how you doing?"

"Fine," he said distantly, still staring at his hand. It was like he wasn't really talking; his body was on autopilot while his mind took a holiday. Jackie faced him and laid a hand on his shoulder.

"Are you alright? Is there anything going on with your hand?"

Brad took a while to break away from looking at it, and instead focused on Jackie, his face still distant. "Yes, actually. It's not my hand."

Jackie was the first to ask. "Not your hand? What are you talking about?"

"This hand's artificial, that's what. Had this... thing for two months now. It's not bone or skin or muscle, just plastic, metal and wires. I've been getting used to it, but it doesn't feel like it's really there, you know? I feel like my old hand – my real one – is still here. It's the same with Jane."

"I'm sorry, Brad," Jackie said, and placed a hand on his shoulder with a slight drumming of the fingers, a little sympathetic trademark of hers.

"Hey, mate, I... damn, I can't believe it, you know?" Of course, looking back, it made sense why Brad had previously stared at his hand when I handed my report to Dwight. With that, all I could think of – all I thought I could actually do – was to relate this to our own experiences. "I know it's different from what you're going through, but every time we've regenerated a lost limb, the slow process of it makes us forget that it isn't there. We try and move a finger, only to realise we haven't even got a wrist yet."

"I suppose that's akin to what I'm going through," Brad huffed. "I appreciate the sympathy." He took out his right hand to shake, but withdrew it and used his left one instead. As Cain and I shook it, we shook slowly and gently, unsure of how strong it was. Brad reacted by inducing the tightest grip we've been in, his fingers nearly grinding our hand into mincemeat.

Dwight took out a hand-sized walkie-talkie device and spoke into it, sounding steely and dedicated to the goal.

"Alright, Group Two, everyone, this is it. As soon as we get in, I want a full sweep of the place. Move to your entrance now." He broke away from the walkie-talkie.

"Did we stock up on brooms as well?" I quipped again. Everyone just glared at us. Bad joke?

"Group One, move," he commanded. We all got out of the van, guns at the ready, as did the operatives in the one alongside us. We stood around the building's front entrance, our boots slamming onto the ground with a THUD-THUD-THUD-THUD-THUD. Once there, Dwight, standing tall and wide, took command once more.

"Group Two, move!"

We stormed in, guns at the ready, with the determination of running over hot coals. There was a bizarre rush of energy and excitement coursing through our shared body; maybe it was the idea of seeing people being brought to justice? Maybe it was also to do with getting certain info from Muzzle on Dean that we could use against him? Or it simply could have been the sheer bedazzling brush of battling cruel, careless criminals, arresting their avarice arses? Screw it, maybe it was all three rolled into one.

I think it was the last one – ass-kickin's my favourite pick-me-up.

Inside, a forklift was parked fifteen feet from the entrance, its mighty steel hand facing a series of stacked cages on the very far left of the building (I know criminals tend to be organised, but somehow, I imagined this lot to be of the lazy-bastard variety). The entire place was filled with great, looming metal shelves, most of them occupied by cages, some of which were empty. I caught glimpses of the kind of creatures that were trapped in them; a few looked like living bananas; one small fellow the size of my hand whose body resembled a small red balloon; a thing that I could only describe had tentacles; a sea-creature that resembled a baby squid with big prawn eyes. Whimpers, whines and foreign sounds called out to us. I felt so sorry for them, and even more determined to put an end to this.

Past the forklift were five men, presumably in the middle of chatting just before we rudely (and might I say, dramatically) came in, who they drew their guns. I squeezed down on the stun gun's trigger, hit two of them and they fell in spasms; they hit me in the shoulder and chest. The shoulder threw me off a bit, but not by much, and the chest wasn't really anything to cry about – I've had colds that made me feel closer to death.

Brad, Jackie and Dwight took down the remaining three. Brad shot one while donning an exhausted face, his eyes half-closed and mouth tightly shut, focusing on the task at hand. Had there not been lines faintly shown across his forehead, I would have sworn that his body was acting upfront while his mind was somewhere else entirely. Jackie's gun was shot out of her hand, but rather than pick it up, she dived towards her attacker with the ferocity and skill of her more feline cousins, too fast for him to fire, and knocked him out with a punch to the face, growling as she did. Dwight managed to dodge a few rounds sent in his direction (one bullet even going through his afro), moving his bulky frame at surprising speed, like he was a much younger and slimmer man, and took down his brief adversary with the pull of a trigger. After that, Dwight sent his hand through the battle-damaged hair with delicacy, then shook it around when it seemed it wasn't as bad as he thought it was, and maintained his cool demeanour. Never underestimate the bond between a man and his afro.

Group Two made themselves known by the light-blue stream from their weapons, some gunshots, and the screams from the criminals followed by a THUD. Beautiful. Within seconds, we were given an all-clear on the ground floor. I turned my attention to a small office tucked away in the right-hand of the place, up a small flight of metal stairs.

"I'm checking that out," I stated, pointing at the corner office with my gun. The others nodded while they proceeded to cuff the fallen felons. I went up the steps carefully, gun aimed just in case, and entered the office like lightning. All that was there was a small light-brown desk with a piece of paper tented up with 'Eddie Muzzle' written on it, some papers, a little fan plugged into a socket, and Eddie Muzzle sitting in a chair by the desk with his hands in the air. The guy was thin as a rake, red hair frizzled all over the place like a wild bush, and some of the darkest rings I've ever seen under anyone's eyes.

"IISEP, put your hands up!"

"I give up!" he blurted out. "Don't shoot me! I'll… I'll arrest myself if I have to!" He put his arms out, all straightened up and ready to be cuffed, while he gave a pathetic self-serving toothy smile.

I withdrew my gun, stunned at this (yes, that pun was intentional).

'You've gotta be fuckin' kiddin',' Cain thought.

"I agree," I said aloud. How anticlimactic. I was expecting a big shoot-up, the many pulling of triggers, a rush of excitement in taking down the leader of a gang. Not bursting in on a guy who looked like he'd negotiate with a rat if it meant not being bitten.

"Go on, do it! I hate being stunned by you guys, it always leaves me feeling unwell." His arms trembled, and his face turned a bit red.

"Judging by your appearance, I think the last time it happened hasn't left you."

And so I cuffed him, dragged him by the arm and went down to the ground floor. "I got Muzzle," I announced, and once we could feel concrete on our heels, I looked at the man's weasely face to assure myself that this was indeed the man in charge of all this.

"Good job, you two," said Dwight, giving us a hard pat on the shoulder.

"Nothing to it. Seriously, this guy's weaker than Styrofoam. Have we gathered everyone up?"

"Yeah, we're piling them up in the vans. We seemed to have underestimated how many creatures would be here; Andrex has requested fifteen, maybe twenty vans to store

212

them all. Taking them all in is going to feel like years going by."

"Don't forget the interrogations."

"Don't remind me. As if I haven't got enough to think about."

I lightly shook Muzzle's arm. "Well, come on, you. You're gonna have a splendid time in our interrogation hotel; a containment facility with all your nefarious ne'er-do-well chums, then a large dark room with lots and lots of talking, especially about dear old Dean, and finally a permanent rest in our conspicuous cells, with a little mint chocolate on your pillow."

"He knew about this," Muzzle said quietly. My face dropped.

"What did you say?"

"This. He knew that you'd come for me, to get questions out of me about him. Tapped into your phone calls, so he knew when to pull it off."

Our heartbeat quickened, four beats a second. Our brain scrambled together only the worst of what he could have meant.

'Oh, God, no, don't tell me...' My mind accidentally summoned the image of Dean attacking them, bearing a sickening grin.

'Don't tell that asshole actually...' I pictured 'im haulin' them off into his car, blood all over 'em.

I shook Muzzle's arm before grabbing both of them, my brow low and eyes wide open. Anger seeped through my voice. "What did he say he was going to do?"

Muzzle grinned, and I could see it in his eyes that he didn't have a shred of regret of what he was saying. "He promised me the girl. I liked the look of her, all that nice red hair and slutty little face."

"You vile piece of shit," I uttered, not masking our rage as I grabbed him by the shoulders. "What's he going to do with them? Tell me!"

All he did was chuckle, probably seeing my questions as futile. "Why? You want a piece of the action with them as well? Maybe if you're nice enough, you can join me with that kid, we'll have a great time with her. He'll probably be busy with her mum." He let out another wheezy chuckle, another cocky gesture in our face.

For the first time in a long time, we snapped. We could feel all of our rage crashing down in an emotional inferno. I felt wild, like how Cain used to be all those countless years ago, full of animalistic fury bubbling all over the place. We didn't ask each other what to do next, we already knew, joined in an electrical rush of synchronicity. In that moment, the ones calling themselves David and Cain were not acting or thinking or doing anything else separately. It was bizarre, but at the same time, so right, so very right.

We made our move. A tight grab of the throat with one hand and lifting him off his feet, then maintaining that grip for a couple of seconds, noting how red and pathetic and defenceless he looked in the face of death.

We could hear and feel our colleagues trying to stop us – Jackie shaking us by the shoulder, Brad trying to move our arm down, Dwight yelling orders at us to stop – and we didn't care what they were doing. No, we focused on the bastard in our hand, and thought, 'This guy is pure scum. He should die.' What I'd have given to have had Bob the Revolver in our holster at that moment, and bury him right into Muzzle's mouth before ending it all – what better way than to die ironically?

But, no, we did the next best thing – we pulled our arm back and threw him across the room by a good forty feet. He went faster than your eyes could handle. With better hearing than most, the sound of his head nearly shattering against the steel wall in a thunderous slam felt like the sweetest music. We ran at him before pouncing onto him with the predatory instincts of a lion. He had no time to react as we started punching him in the face. Left fist, right fist, left fist, right fist in an insane rhythmic order. The same rush that we felt earlier when bursting into the warehouse resurfaced, and that just made it worse for everyone involved. Our claws came out, and then we struck him across the shoulder, his screams filling the warehouse's empty corners.

Then we realised that the Voice had been talking at the back of our head since Muzzle's last laugh. It kept up its damning message: KILL. That occurrence helped things out: sanity returned as we pulled away from violence, snapping us back to normal, muting the Voice for now, and with it came fear. That was when we looked at what we had done to Muzzle. His half-closed eyes were faintly lit with fear as blood dribbled down his chin and his lip was cut wide open. The red swelling craters on his cheeks from the bluntness of our knuckles started to show in no time. If we were engrossed by the Voice for a few more seconds, we wouldn't have heard the weak wheeze of his breathing.

"Oh my God," I whispered as I stepped away from the site. 'Holy crap,' Cain said, retreating into our head. Jackie echoed our reaction, as did Brad and Dwight, all of them standing behind us. Jackie crouched by Muzzle and checked his pulse, and stated aloud that he needed medical attention. Brad stared at us with a look of confusion and disgust – I don't blame him. Jackie glanced at us with shock, her yellow eyes tiny suns that seemed to die for a brief second before she turned her attention back to Muzzle.

'Jackie, no, no, don't think we're bad guys, please...'

Our head was blank, save for guilt suffocating our brain. I barely felt the tough clamp of Dwight's hand tugging my arm toward him.

"For God's sake, what the hell were you doing?" The spit coming from his mouth though, I definitely felt that. We deserved it.

"Dwight, I'm so... I'm so sorry, we just snapped. He pushed too many buttons, went way too far with all that damn taunting. It made the Voice pop up."

Cain popped up. "Yeah, the guy was askin' for it. Okay, maybe not that far, coulda been just a really hard slap, ya know?"

Taking control, I groaned as I massaged my forehead and temples to cope with frustration. "Cain, I'm not trying to justify us beating the crap out of him like that."

"Oh... my bad," Cain squeaked in the three seconds he took over.

Dwight got things back on track, still as ticked off as he was at the start. "Don't think I won't put you two on a leash if I have to. Now we have to treat his injuries at the medical department. You'll be lucky if the idiot survives, let alone talks any further."

This was too much. For all of us, really. What I and my alter ego had done could have been the pin that popped the balloon we were trying to get.

"Look, I… we need some air, okay? I… I need to call Emily, make sure she and Scarlett are safe." I massaged my left temple, my head feeling red with the rush of things.

"We can send some our guys here to her place, just in case." It was nice of Dwight to make such a suggestion, but my first priority was to ensure they were okay.

"Yeah, yeah, gimme a sec, I'll let you know if you have to," I said in a rush.

I made my way out of the warehouse, our feet going faster than our brain. It took me a few seconds to realise that the shadows on the ground weren't there anymore, and instead there was the brightly lit concrete basking in the sun. I took out our phone and rang Emily. The lonely monotonous beep-beep made us more determined to speak to her on the other end, to see that she and Scarlett were okay, untouched, that Muzzle was bluffing or miscalculated the time it would take for Dean to get to them. The beeping stopped, and we then heard the voice that we both half-expected and half-knew would be there.

"Hi, my little bounty hunter," Dean said in that grating mock-affectionate tone.

"You..." Cain came up front. "The hell d'ya do with 'em, ya fuckin' psycho?" I settled him down and came into control.

"Don't worry, I made sure they weren't harmed, though that Emily did do an admirable job at defending herself and that brat. Got me in the eye with her gun, the bitch." That last word was emphasised strongly with a tinge of hatred. I smiled faintly at Emily's small victory.

"You don't sound too worried about that. What, have you got an extra eye under that beard of yours?"

"Oh, trust me, I let out quite a yell, got some blood down my face, but I'll heal it soon." So he wasn't completely invincible after all. Rule Number One when against enemies – *never* blurt out a weakness. You're just asking for get hurt for your stupidity. "I assume you let her know about me?"

"For such a smart guy, I thought you wouldn't have to stoop so low as to ask *us*. Are you an arch-enemy or a mastermind-in-training?"

"Heh, I'll see how much of a smartass you are when we meet up."

"Oh, you got a date for that, then? I'll try and see when I'm free from rescuing my other friends to make room for you."

"A nice little get-together would be great, I'll even bring my friends with me, as I'm sure you'll do too."

"Oh, you have friends? What, are they also members of The Legion of Doom?"

"If only," he said with a sigh. We had the sensation that he smiled as he said it. "I won't bring the ladies with me, if you're thinking that would happen."

Damn it. There had to be some way to get to them and soon, before they get hurt. Perhaps the meet-up might pave the way for that? I had to act quickly before the chance was wasted.

"In that case, forget trying to see us. If you won't bring them along, I won't show up. Come on, you just needed them to get to us, and you succeeded; they don't serve any

217

other purpose. Hand them over, and then we'll talk. There's our whole past to discuss, right? The last thing you'd want is for us to get distracted."

I prayed to whatever deities that existed that Dean would accept this. It occurred to me that the knowledge he had of us – however impossible it was for him to obtain – never really sunk in after telling Dwight of last night. Maybe it was because the shock of Dean's resurfacing overtook priority, but bringing it up to him now, in such a dire situation, a small part of me asked how he got what he knew. A very small part.

The silence was unbearable. Cain wanted to scream at him, but I told him not to; it might influence him to say 'no'. I held the phone so tightly that my fingers were going red from the pressure. Finally, he answered.

"Alright, you can see them. I'll be sure that they won't receive any harm; cuts, bruises, broken bones. I don't want to drive you away."

I thought, 'Oh damn right, ya don't wanna. I sure as hell I wanna drive ya close to me so I can break ya in thirty different places!'

In a sickeningly sly tone, he finished this off with, "Anyway, I'll give you a ring later, my bounty hunter. Don't try tracking the phone, I've applied some of my own little tech to prevent that. Ciao." One press of a button and the call ended.

I very nearly crushed my phone in rage. Instead, I placed it back into my coat pocket, barely able to stop my hand from shaking.

'He's got 'em,' Cain stated, mostly to himself. 'I'm gonna kill 'im. Yeah, I'm gonna stab 'im in the eyes and see if I can't tear his head open from his sockets.'

"As much as I'd love to do that to him myself," I said, failing to maintain a calm exterior, my words coming out slowly, "let's just focus on seeing him again at. We need to check Emily's place for anything we can find; blood samples, fingerprints, signs of entry, that stuff."

Turning to face the warehouse, I saw Dwight closing in on us, shifting his bulky body in an almost rhythmic way with every step. "It was him, wasn't it? What did he say?"

"He'll give us a call when he wants to go face-to-faces with us. Emily and Scarlett don't seem to be hurt, at least for now. I've got some other info I'd like to share with you guys, but first we need to go round to Emily's."

"If you went with my suggestion in the first place, we'd probably already have an inspection under way right now." I knew he was right, but on top of everything else, I rubbed my temples in frustration at this. Yes, he meant well, he always did, but I just wanted to get the ladies to safety. That was all we, the demented duo, could think of.

"Yeah, don't rub it in, big fella. I'll chalk that up on the 'Dwight's Right' tally chart. Swear to God, if there was a drinking game based on that, I don't even think our healing factor would cure us of the hangover." An empty joke.

Chapter 14

Empty

Out of all the years Cain and I have been with the IISEP, this was the first time we've inspected a friend's house. The front door wasn't locked, just only slightly ajar – somehow, it didn't feel accidental or forgetful to me, more like Dean had done this on purpose, a little bit of 'help' to taunt us. It felt quite disturbing, uneasy, as we entered the house, like we had turned up at the end of a domestic horror movie.

We found two empty bullet cartridges lying on the living room floor; one a few centimetres away from the smooth Turkish carpet, and another one lying on it, accompanied by a few drops of blood, spoiling the decorative wool ensemble. A third cartridge was discovered in the kitchen, its dark gold-bronze body sticking out against the cream-white backdrop of the tiles. It was clear that she had put up a fight, like Dean had said. Accompanying the cartridge in the kitchen were the broken pieces of a glass vase and purple flowers.

Photographs were taken, and fingerprints were found and caught for forensics. The professionals were doing their work, while we, the ancient duo, just stood everywhere, trying hard not to draw up a mental storyboard; that was everyone else's jobs. Dwight stood by us, asking us if we were okay, and reassuring us that we'll get mother-and-daughter back, safe and sound. I nodded emptily. He forgot to say "try to".

"Are you sure you want to be here, guys?"

"Yeah, we have to. It's necessary."

"Alright, fellas. Do you have Trevor's phone number?"

"No." Then it hit us. "Oh God, no, oh my God. Dean has it, because he's got Emily's phone! How could I have been so blind? He could ring Trevor up and taunt him, too, make him scared shitless with the idea of his ex and daughter in danger. Unless..."

'...He's just focusin' on us, an' ONLY us,' Cain concluded in our head. 'Dean's a vengeful bastard, alright, but I don't think he'd be petty enough to do THAT. Gotta keep himself focused on revenge, ya know?'

"Hopefully," I sighed. Best-case scenario (if one would call it that, given the matter at hand) Trevor would be left alone, blissfully unaware of the current events. I would have tried to contact him through social media, but he wasn't the kind of person to send his details online. He had a bad experience during The Glassman Hacker Incident a few years back, when everyone's profiles were violated by this one guy, and managed to delete them just because he wanted to cause a bit of chaos. Thankfully, that was sorted out in a matter of days, and the culprit was arrested, though the whole thing had left Trevor in a state of paranoia, like so many others in its wake. The only time he'd go online would be to watch videos and trade emails with business partners on a separate account.

"I'm keeping myself to myself," he told us a month after the incident. "Business is business, of course, can't do anything about that. Still, I'm nice and secure if I stay put, you know?"

"The chance of you getting hacked again is one in a stream of billions," I remember saying to him.

"Ah, but what if that one gets plucked out of that stream, and I'm on the end of the hook?" I didn't expect this to turn into a fishing metaphor, but I had to give him props for finding a way to, even if it was a bit half-assed.

I think I shrugged and said something to the effect of, "They'd probably make a pretty good meal out of you."

Pulling myself out of our memories, I turned to Dwight and said, "Dwight, we're gonna pop upstairs, okay? I… we want to look at their rooms."

"Understood. Want forensics to join you?"

"No, just after we come down. It'll feel... crowded, otherwise."

"Got it," our boss said with a nod, and we went upstairs.

Scarlett's room was untouched; her miniatures of heavy metal artists, three-foot detailed idols with disturbingly realistic faces, were perched on top of her drawers, their mouths wide open in captured excited expressions, echoes of a dead moment. I couldn't recognise any of them, but that was beside the point. Her duvet was untidy, scrambled all over the bed. Either it was part of the fleeting kidnapping, or Scarlett was not one for managing her bed when awake in the early hours. I told myself it was the latter.

A few teddy bear plushies continued to guard the foot of the bed, lying against the metal legs of the frame. I recognised one, it was dark-brown with big black eyes with white circles in a corner to evoke shininess; I gave it to her on her sixth birthday, back when she was so small, her chubby cheeks and beautiful innocence reminding me so much of her mother. When she couldn't think of name for it, I offered one: Jacob. It stuck. I bent down and took a hold of it, staring into its cheaply-made eyes.

"So, she kept you, huh?" I felt compelled to nudge its head back and forth as a nod. But I didn't. Then Cain took control of one hand and did it, instead. With a squeaky voice.

"Yup she kept me nice n' safe all locked-up in a loft for all those years and now that she ain't around to keep an' eye on me I'm free to start a teddy bear uprisin' 'gainst those furless humans MWAHAHAHA!"

"Cain, don't make me cut off that hand…" I growled, and put the bear back.

"Sorry, man, couldn't help it! I thought some fun would relieve all the stress on our hands. Okay, doin' it here ain't the best place, but it's a start I guess."

"I get what you mean, just try and be sensitive, for god's sake."

222

"Right, gotcha."

I looked at the kid's music collection, all them records/CDs/whatever-modern-shit, little round disc thingies in a pile. All of 'em metal bands. Had a couple o' AC/DC, Metallica, real classic fellas, an' some recent pussies like ZAdAK, an' HardLine. I mean 'pussies' as in kitties, compared to them big wild dogs o' the good ol' days o' metal, not 'pussies' as in... um... ya know.

I picked up an AC/DC disc and grinned. "Hey, fellas, fancy seein' you here."

"Cain?"

For a sec, I thought the disc was talkin' to me. I was definitely sure that I wasn't high. Then I realised that the voice was Jackie's, an' I turned an' saw her by the door, her face a bit relaxed n' a bit surprised. Those eyes, man, those were some nice n' shiny lil' things. My thoughts screamed like a kid: 'Yay, she's seein' me!' But then I remembered that I was shy: 'Oh, man, she's seein' me...' The toothy smile I had shrank pathetically an' I covered my face with our hat, pressin it right against my devilish features. Okay, I coulda swapped with David, but I ain't good with on-the-fly stuff.

"Um...yeah...?" I squeaked out. "I mean... I mean, uh, yeah, it's me, Cain. J-just so ya know."

'Cain, drop the hat,' David thought.

'No,' I thought back, 'this is my external happy place right now.'

Jackie started walkin', her footsteps slow n' uneasy. She grabbed the hat an' took her time to peel it offa me, then studied all o' the new details I had that she couldn't see with David.

"Snap." She put the hat back on my head an' shook a hand, bein' careful o' both our claws. "Nice to see you at last," she said softly with a very small smile, her fangs stickin' out, those pretty lil' fangs.

Dammit, I blushed. Musta turned as red as our clothes. My ears went hot.

"Yeah, nice to see ya… to see ya… nice? Uh, I meant to say, nice to ya with… w-with… all ya… you-ness, ya know…?"

"I think so." She looked around Scarlett's room, her brow all tense an' heavy in immersin' herself with the layout. "So, anything out of place here?"

I straightened myself up, rubbin' my ears to cool 'em down (dunno if that works) an' cleared my throat before puttin' on a deep, totally-bold authorative voice.

"Er, no, everything's okey dokey smokey, alright, yessir – oh shit, I mean, yes ma'am." Totally pulled that off. Really.

"Cain, don't try so hard, okay?" she said assurin'ly, softly.

"Okay, Jackie," I squeaked out, like a wimp. Dammit, my ears were tiny volcanoes again. She put a hand on my shoulder (a hand on my shoulder…) before pattin' it a couple o' times, an' said, "Relax. Forget about me right now, and let's focus on what's important." With a soft stride, she left the room, her tail movin' left n' right in time with her footsteps.

I rubbed my face an' sighed. My thoughts were consumed by this crazy-awesome catgirl, an' her meetin' me for the first time coulda gone a helluva lot better. All my frustrations were put into one great big thought, somethin' I wished I had the guys to say aloud. 'YOU'RE important, Jackie. You're my Emily, you're my Scarlett, you're my everyone-I-wanna-love. But to you, I'm your kid, ain't I? I'm a big dumb kid ya have to manage, right? Dammit, I wanna show ya I'm more than that. I gotta stop bein' so fuckin' shy. This kid's gonna have one helluva growth spurt, an' I mean it!'

'Cain, that was beautiful,' David said like a girl tearin' up after a romance flick.

'Don't tell anyone I was cheesier than Parmesan just now, got it?'

'Understood. Mind you, you're practically a cheese factory as it is, and rife with plenty of ham, too.'

'Oh, yeah? Well, you're a… you're a… fuck you, that's what!'

'Ow, that was a good one, you got me right in the school-playground. Do you want to carry on walking about?'

'Nah, I'm done now. Bein' 'round Jackie's too much for me right now.'

Everything in Emily's room seemed to be normal; a widescreen TV standing mightily above a large set of walnut drawers, the dark chocolate brown look accompanied by a wary grey streak; a queen size bed at the back (the perfect kind of bed for the little princess I once knew who matured into such a wonderful woman) and beige blinds hiding the windows from me. The duvet was neatly handled, a jarring contrast to Scarlett's. However, on it laid a framed picture of Emily, Scarlett and Trevor, the glass cracked but still whole. Just below it was a piece of paper neatly lined up with the bottom of the frame. I picked it up, noting that the handwriting was big, bold and messy.

They look quite NICE here, don't they?

I WONDER

HOW MANY have DIED because they happened to know you two?

More TEARS over the years, am I right, David? More dead people because of you, more reason to wish for the impossibility of death, all to that guilt and weariness crashing down on you. It all started back THEN, RAANAN, didn't it? Tribe brothers dead, hate hate HATE everywhere in everyone when the wimp was replaced with THE HUNTER.

Cain, have you always been JEALOUS that loved ones died before you could rip their throats out? I bet THE VOICE always beckoned you, it still beckons you, Mister Killer, like always – it's INSTINCT.

One way or another, they WILL die.

But how?

Let's find out,
my little bounty-hunter.

Sincerely,
and Eternally
Yours,

Dean, 'The Castrator'

His words struck us like lightning, sharp, painful, lingering. He wanted us to get riled up, and he was doing a damn fine job at it. Flaunting more impossible knowledge drew more questions mixed with rage and worry. Thinking back to my first family made me clench my clench, crumpling the letter, ruining its smoothness and making it fit with the ugliness he had written down.

I never had that feelin' Castrator was talkin' about never fuckin' liar FUCKIN' LIAR the Voice the Voice the Voice I ain't obeyin' it I ain't a berserker anymore I'm me I ain't a puppet I'M ME any time I kill it's cuz I'M doin' it not the Voice I'm punishin' assholes monsters shitheads I'm tired so tired so very tired I don't enjoy it anymore I just love violence I don't want nothin' to happen to my buddies or Jackie, oh god, Jackie.

Cain lost himself in his thoughts, the poor bastard. I tried talking to him but nothing worked, and his voice loudly paraded through our brain and ears. As for myself, I had a tighter grip in comparison (especially in comparison to the letter I was still holding, which was now bent and creased and feeling even more fragile), though I still feared the worst for the ladies. I was composed to a degree, and I wanted Cain to regain his composure.

I left the room and the letter and joined everyone downstairs. Brad reassured us and patted our shoulder with his left hand. He stared at it; he probably didn't realise he used it until now. I said thanks, shook his by the hand in a mildly awkward way, and he felt uneasy. We all did.

Chapter 15

Selma

'We need to do something about what happened at the warehouse,' I said to Cain as we returned to HQ, remembering how the Voice had left Muzzle.

'Yeah, anythin' in mind?'

'Selma,' I suggested. 'She could place a mental lock around the Voice, hopefully.'

'That'd be a friggin' miracle.'

We took the elevator to the third floor where Selma worked, the psychic department. She had been working there for twelve years, though her services were so rarely required that she turned part-time. Her powers included telepathy, telekinesis, and the ability to find people by using your positive feelings for them, kind of like a mental lock-on, just as long as there weren't too many negative feelings mixed in. The department itself was underfed, as there weren't that many employed; it was a cramped but pleasant-looking dull-blue block, consisting of one large room with seven desks, three along the left and three on the right, with the middle, Selma's desk, facing the door.

Entering the place gave us a slight headache, the result of being around so much collected psychic energy, nothing really life-threatening (unless the guys decided to make your head explode like in *Scanners*). I'd have worn one of the inhibitor helmets outside the room for health and safety reasons, but it would have countered our goal.

Selma had her eyes closed like with the other six occupants beside her, either concentrating on a case handed to her, or simply meditating. Her mid-thirties had given her a self-reflective mindset, hence the motivational poster stuck at the front of her desk saying: *INNERPEACE – Only you can provide it*. I didn't know if she made it herself or bought it, but I thought it was a bit crap. Then again, if it helped, who was I to judge? Her body was shrouded in a dark blue cloak with fist-sized prayer beads guarding her shoulders and chest. The hood wasn't a perfect fit, slightly baggy around her head, but it didn't cover her smooth Asian features or her widow's peak. The pink dagger-like false fingernails stuck out on her desk as her palms laid flat on the oak surface.

"Welcome, gentlemen," she said slowly, her eyes still closed.

"Hi, Selma, I—"

"I know why you've come here. Telepathy, remember?"

"Good point." I walked over to her, and in doing so the headache grew only slightly worse. She smelled of lavender and stress-release oil, quite a comforting aroma. "So, how do we do this? Do we have to hold hands or something?"

"I'll place my hands upon your head. Nothing too complicated," she said while keeping her eyes shut.

"You, uh… are you a bit busy right now?"

"I'm concentrating on something of great importance to me." I wondered if she was juggling several cases at once, it wouldn't be the first time.

"Oh, really? What is it? I mean, if it's okay to ask."

She drew in a deep breath, and said in a pseudo-mystical fashion, "Should I… eat out tonight or order Chinese takeaway?"

Wow. I was way off. Cain bumped in, eager to answer.

"Eat in. Had some damn sick thoughts to do with Chinese takeaway boxes the other night." He shuddered in reflectance of that drunken encounter.

"Ah, I see, I'll keep that in mind. The Voice came through that night as well. Alright, let's begin the procedure." She removed her hands from her desk and pressed her fingertips against our temples. In doing so, she opened her eyes, which shone an intensely bright purple glow, her pupils and irises turning into white rings containing smaller purple balls. We gazed into the fascinating details in her eyes, and we were lost in the hypnotic colours.

Selma's thoughts were audible, as clear as when she spoke aloud. As for us, there was a calmer sense of unity than what had happened at the warehouse, like we were intentionally becoming one. When we spoke, it wasn't as David or Cain, but David and Cain.

Selma: *I can sense it. You've been doing your best to smother it. But it's grown quite strong as of late. Terrifying, but... fascinating.*

Us: *What? How the hell is it fascinating?*

Selma: *The effect these few horrible words have on you, it's a kind of ugly beauty – so much force coming from something so small.*

Us: *Tell that to the people who died from it. 'Ugly' is a good description; 'beauty' isn't.*

The deaths of our former tribesmen burst up in quick flashes, as though someone was fast-forwarding through a movie.

Selma: *I'm sorry. I'm going to place it under lock. It helps if you can exert some strength as well. That way, it'll be easier to make it more secure.*

Us: *Right, here goes...*

We took a deep breath and focused. Much like the experience with the gang the other night, we could feel the Voice in our brain, vibrating and thrashing like a raging animal in defiance, and forced our will onto it. We grabbed it with both sets of hands, and waited for Selma to do her thing.

Her energy, so vibrant and soothing, wrapped itself around the Voice, it was so warm and... bright. Quite soothing, really. But our droning 'KILL KILL KILL' friend shook about some more, at first mildly but then burst into a fit of pure, simple hatred. Our grasp on it was getting more and more difficult to maintain.

Selma: *I'm nearly done!*

US: *Better be quick! We can't hold much longer!*

Selma: *Almost... THERE!*

The Voice stopped. It was asleep now, its ferocity lost with that final touch. We held that door shut as she fastened so many padlocks that we doubted it would pop up for decades. All we could feel now was the warmth and relaxation Selma had given us.

The three of us gave a collective sigh, and before Cain and I could properly thank her, the strain of our little gold-star teamwork struck our throat and stomach, and we bolted to the nearest loo to throw up our guts like we were a human fountain. As you do.

Chapter 16

Snookered

The HQ's relaxation room was something we needed. In the face of everything, the best way to keep a level head was to de-stress, even if it's an impossible task; we could attest that it was. The windowless area was quite large; it took up a good ninety feet in width and length, set with a dark wooden floor and red walls designed to be soft and comfy with padding, like a scarlet sponge. It bathed in the yellow-white glow of eight 150-watt bulbs scattered around the place. Half of it contained gym equipment, including rowing machines, running machines, bicycle-peddling video games, weights and other things, including a basketball hoop.

The other half contained tables and chairs on either side, with three pool tables and a bar serving soft drinks nearby that had spare pool cues (it's amazing how many cues here break in one year alone). Speakers were tucked in every corner, playing anything from the graceful guile of classical music, to the soft sensual feel of jazz, or the feverish funk of soul, with all-too-catchy pop hanging around too. Right now, the electric Spanish rush of Santana burst out of the speakers, and its vibrancy was infectious.

The red walls, though a bit depressing in a certain light (maybe one that was less than 150-watts, eh?) were rather comforting. The colour was picked out from a survey, set up during the UK branch's installation, on what colour room would you prefer to relax in – quite surprising to find red as the winner, especially since blue was the second-most popular answer. I'd have gone with something lighter, like beige. Still, at least it wasn't yellow – I'd have kept thinking of custard and bananas, and bananas in custard. Not exactly a delicious stream of thought, in my opinion (still, fair game for anyone who likes it).

I'd have painted this damn room black, reminds me o' death an' how I ain't afraid o' somethin' that can't happen to me. Makes me feel truly invincible an' unstoppable.

We were playing a game of pool with Brad, with Chris observing our little duel from a chair, drinking a pint of cola with a flustered face, excited and worried at how Brad was going to get out of his latest predicament. At this point, Brad had three yellows balls left to pocket, while we still had five reds on the table. One of his yellows was right near a corner pocket, with a red blocking the white ball from hitting it. But he had a plan to pot his ball, there was no doubt about it. For his next shot, he circled the table, eyeing every angle, to get a greater scope, a greater feel than just simply staying in one position and reckoning how to shoot. Once he figured it out, he leaned over the table, his body one with it, and lightly tested the speed of his cue. He then struck the white ball diagonally to the opposite side of the yellow, and it bounced off, hit the yellow ball, and sent it into the pocket at lightning pace. He curled his left hand into a fist with care and tugged it in triumph, with a smirk on his face.

"Gotcha," he said with quiet satisfaction.

"Not bad," I said while chalking up my cue.

Chris looked at me with surprise. "Not bad? That was great! I'm not much of a pool guy, but that kind of skill is fantastic!"

"Thanks," Brad said, lining up for his next shot.

"Trust me, son," I said with a good dose of reality, "he's skilled, no doubt about that, but he's nothing like any of the pros you'd see on telly."

"Oh?"

"Yup, lad," Brad answered, and then potted another yellow ball. "Compared to them, I'm *okay*."

Now it was my turn. However, I took advantage of our topic and, rather than facing the table, looked at Chris. "Do

233

you want to take this shot?" I offered my cue to him in the same way you'd offer someone flowers.

"Really? Are you sure?"

"Definitely. We'll at least be able to see what you're like."

The young man took it with nervous anticipation, like he was about to pull Excalibur from its stone confines. His right hand was laid out clumsily over the table, the gap between his thumb and forefinger too wide and dull to properly use his cue, the thumb sticking out flat on the surface, as if it had been glued there. His left hand managed the back, only it wasn't right at the bottom, but instead slightly higher up, and judging by the way his elbow stuck out like it had been squashed into position, it was an awkward angle. His goal was to hit a red ball that was in the perfect position to be sent in one of the corner pockets, a straight deal. Taking no time to practise, he slammed the white ball with a wobbly jerk, only just bouncing into the red one along the side rather than forward, and the red missed the pocket dead ahead.

"You're rushing it," Brad observed. "Your form is terrible."

"Sorry."

"No, don't worry," I said. "It's your first go. Just take it easy, take your time, and just give it a few practice shots before you do it."

"Right, okay."

"Trust us, the worst thing to do when playing is to act without thinking. You have to form a little plan in your head, you know? For instance, what ball are you gonna hit? If it's at an angle, what strategy are you gonna use? I know all we're doing is hitting balls on a table, but it's like a mini-war, got it? Kind of like chess."

"Doesn't that require more strategy than this?"

I shrugged. "True, but keep your eye on the ball here – literally. This is a bit more animated, really shows you how to hit your objective and your enemy. How hard do you strike, eh?" My voice swayed with energy, its volume and tone fusing softly with my words. "With the delicacy of a floating feather, or with the powerful slam of a whale's tail hitting the ocean's surface?"

"David, you're using this as an excuse to be theatrical, aren't you?"

"A bit, yes," I admitted with a mild reluctance. "Then again, I find that the best way to really sell my point is with a touch of drama."

"A touch, are you serious? You make Shakespearean actors look like subtle."

"Well, I try my best. You want to take over?"

"Thanks. I'll make sure to chew less scenery than you; I want to ensure the table's intact."

Chris looked at me with an uncomfortable frown.

"Um, David, I was wondering…"

"Yes?"

"Well, I hate to sound rude, but I'm kind of worried about how you're handling all this. I mean, your friends being, um…"

"I see. Well, they'll be home safe and sound soon enough."

"I know, but being all casual here, even if it's called a Relaxation Room, seems like the wrong place for you guys."

"Emotions," Brad cut in, his eyes focused on the pool table as he prepared to take his two shots. "In times like this, they, especially anger, can make things worse; an outburst in the middle of a delicate set-up can result in unwanted outcomes. Changes made to deals, longer waits, collateral damage, death on either side in the worst-case scenario." He nearly potted one of his balls and aimed at it for his second shot. "It might sound inhuman if you think otherwise, and fair enough. No point stressing over this when a cool, calm head is what you really need." His shot sent the ball in, and used his additional one to just barely hit

235

a yellow with a red ball blocking it. His cue tipped in our direction. "Case in point."

"Right on the dot, Brad," I said. "Look, it's not like we don't care – trust me, it's impossible not to think of Emily and Scarlett and worry for them, what Dean might do to them. Selma's session with us has really soothed our mind for the time being, kind of a side effect. It makes it easier to ty and destress before anything worse happens. You had some experience with these matters, then?"

"Too much, really," Brad stated sourly. "I'm not exactly being perky just because I choose to be."

I was about to hit the white until our phone buzzed in our coat's breast pocket.

"Dammit," I muttered, knowing what was to come. I took the mobile out and saw that it was an unknown caller. All of a sudden, the Relaxation Room faded, the music muted, everyone else in the room was invisible to us in the few seconds we spent registering what this could entail.

"It's him," I announced, resting my cue against the side of the table.

'Davey-boy, you take it. I ain't up for this.'

I answered the call and placed the phone oh-so-carefully against one ear.

"Hello?"

"Greetings, my little bounty hunter," came Dean's disgustingly affable voice. "How's your day going?"

"Cut the crap, Dean."

"Oh, no time for chit-chat with me? How rude of you – I like it. Just thought I'd inform you that I've a date for handing over those precious little ladies of yours."

My voice sprang to life. "What? When?"

"Tomorrow, midday, perhaps 12:30? The place will be Wolf Park, familiar with it?"

"Yeah, we know the place." We had gone there a few times in the past, it was in the middle of town, quite a long stretch, nice for a stroll. "Are you planning some sort of picnic by any chance?"

"Do you like to crack jokes because you're scared of what's to come?"

For someone who knew everything about us but our brain, he was dead-on. "No," I lied, "it's because I like to amuse myself before kicking someone's arse."

"That's it, there's more of that fire I'm used to!"

"Yours will die down soon enough."

"We'll see about that, my friend. I'm sure info about your past will keep that fire burning." We could feel the urge to uncover our history rising up, but we had to make sure he didn't notice.

"Only when Emily and Scarlett are out of your reach, Dean. Besides, I doubt whatever you have to say might not be that interesting; for all we know, we could have been the universe's greatest double-act, or worked as a fry-cook in an alien fast-food joint."

"When you find out, you'll be on your knees, and then the fun will truly begin." The playfulness in his voice made me shiver, each syllable wrapped in decades' worth of fantasies. "Your ladies will be fine after tomorrow." Trusting him seemed impossible, but we had no choice but to hope that he was telling the truth.

"If they've even got so much as a scratch, Hell's gonna rain down harder on you than the fire you burned in."

"Ooh, I'm so excited now." Then a ruffling sound erupted, followed by a crash and voices lashing out, one Dean's, the other the mature fibre of Emily's.

"Bitch," Dean cried out, lashing with the sting of disgust.

"You're welcome," we heard Emily shoot back, faint but dripping with dry wit. Atta girl. But then she groaned.

"Hope you get used to this little 'improvement', kid: pain with every step."

Our skin ran cold while our heart punched our chest like mad, and the ears were red to the point of flames. There was no time to think to ourselves, our mouth got the point across. "Emily! What did you do to her?"

237

"A good twist in the ankle. She tried to knock me out from behind – isn't that right, you brave bimbo?"

'Fuckin' bastard,' Cain thought as I started grinding my teeth.

Emily replied, in much anguish, "Take my daughter off of that machine, or else my boys will really show you what they can do."

Dean snorted. "Hear that, fellas? You two are her 'boys'. How fucking sweet. My heart would melt if I had one." As he spoke, he directed his attention back to Emily, adopting a light faux-polite voice. "Of course, I'll remove her from it. In fact, we were just sorting out your release, and I can't do that if she's still plugged in."

Trying not to sound terrified of what it might be, I calmly asked, "What machine, Dean?"

"Nothing to worry about, just something to keep her occupied; she's watching a few movies, that's all."

Rage seeped in. "Tell us!"

"But I am, David. Just some visual entertainment, not that kids get enough of it nowadays. She's subjected to what I like to call the 'Brutal History' Cinema. Much better than that ridiculous History Channel tripe, I assure you."

"You monster," Emily growled, her voice capturing the same explosion as cannon fire. "My little girl is crying in there, I can hear every whimper she—" She screamed. I held my phone even tighter, and clenched my hand.

"Emily!"

"The more you talk, the more I'll step on it, got it?" Dean directed his attention back to us. "Women, am I right, bounty hunter? They're always such a pain; I love to return the favour." He cleared his throat, and his speech no longer contained his misogynistic malice. "So, Wolf Park, midday. Till then, friends." With that, he hung up.

I blindly slammed my fist onto an unoccupied pool table, the balls leaping into the air as I broke into the smooth cloth and was met with the slate surface just underneath.

Removing my hand, I saw that I had gone two inches into the slate.

So much for destressing.

Chapter 17

Confrontation

Wolf Park looked like a football stadium, colossal yet homely. It seemed so endless and bright in how green it was and surrounded by trees at one end. A concrete path stretched out before splitting off into different directions halfway through; a sharp left and right path in the middle, and a left and right path at the very end, each one leading to an open entrance, a space between black railings and dark green bushes. Throughout the whole area, there were benches, always two beside the entrances, two facing each other along the paths, and two at the crossroads. And on one of those benches would be a man who held the fate of others in his greasy grasp. It made us think of how every decision we would have to make is full of so many different outcomes – do we go left or right, and what would happen then? Would it be the right road for us to walk down? It was practically Possibility Park, the Potential Pathways, the Green Junction, the Concrete Train Station... or it's just a park.

A memorial dedicated to the brave fellows who fought in World War II stood erect on the left near the mid-left path, a great slab or stone and marble with names engraved in gold. We shuddered to think back to that time. A good twenty feet away from it was a fountain, not as marvellous-looking, but the grey beaten stone and moss underneath made it just as old. Lovers, families, people with pets, friends, nearly every type of person covered the park, entering, exiting, staying in one place, walking around. Hopefully if nothing terribly dramatic happened, they'd be safe, if maybe a bit shocked. The thought of potential causalities would weight our shared brain down even more than what we were going to do.

Cain and I had entered the park. Dwight, Brad, Jackie and five additional IISEP members scattered themselves around the park, Jackie herself needing no disguise, knowing that people would assume her to be just dressing up. Dean sat on mid-left bench facing the memorial, studying it with his hands clasped. We made our way to him in steady strides and noticed that Emily and Scarlett were on the middle path's seats, and opposite them were two people. One was a large broad-shouldered man with a heavy beard and sunglasses, his sleeves rolled up to display his tanned muscular forearms and his palms warmed by fingerless gloves. His seatmate was a thin woman in a black-and-white striped shirt and slim jeans; her black hair was in a bobcut. While she seemed busy talking to Emily and Scarlett (a serious chat judging by her almost teary-eyed expression), her male friend was solely dedicated to staring at them with his arms crossed, like he was waiting for something.

"There they are," I said under my breath.

'I wanna beat the snot outta Dean,' Cain thought, his growling voice echoing in our brain.

"Do that, and we're just gonna make things worse." Taking a deep breath, I moved towards him in strides, every footstep heavier than the last, our heartbeat in sync with them. I stopped in front of him for a second before sitting next to him, and he acknowledged me with a smile, the lines around his mouth were deep curves from plenty of use, and gave us a flamboyant wave.

"There you are, my little boun—"

"Is that the only nickname you have for us after two centuries of thinking? It's archaic, nostalgic and especially annoying the more you say it." Our heart started to slow down. *Good*, Cain and I thought, *keep it easy*.

"This might be a surprise, but yes. Schizo, Wolf Man, Jekyll and Hyde, Two-Face, Mr Longcoat, Blood Coat, the list goes on. I could spend the afternoon recounting all of them. But here's my favourite nickname for you, I saw it in the history books: The English Devil."

Our blood soured with those three words. Old memories, ones under lock and key, came bursting through and swarmed our senses. Fresh air was corrupted by mountains of corpses and the rust and bloodied metal of swords; blood, the rich earthly taste of it filled our mouth and stained our teeth. Yelling, so much yelling; the cries of the innocent and dying, the commands and warrior passion of allies and enemies, arrows sailing through the sky while blades crossed and shields dulled the blows of swords. A younger, wilder Cain's primal screams and laughter that made us feel afraid to sleep once we recalled them, while I whispered in shock at the blood of friends and foes alike on my hands. We couldn't see the park now, just an endless battlefield shifting in clouds of mist that changed from milky white to red, it was littered with discarded weapons, mangled bodies and armour – the ruins of war.

"Oh God," I gasped, closing my eyes in fear and shame. Cain was muttering 'No' like a chant to protect himself from evil.

"Did I touch a nerve?" I faced Dean and the battlefield vanished, now Wolf Park once more. He was smiling. "I'm sure the Hundred Years War was very taxing."

"H-how did you find out about that?"

"Let's just say my associates have kept a very observant eye over you for years. They may have missed several centuries, but still, they've been keeping tabs on you."

"Associates? And who might they be, our fan club? A bit of obsessive, if you ask me. We're not up for autographs."

"Believe me when I say you're more of a walking possession that's been misplaced rather than someone worth idolising over."

"You mean to say your friends are very... close to us? If they're willing to bring back the likes of you, I doubt they're good company. Especially if they had anything to do with the Voice."

Dean sighed with delight. "They'll do whatever's necessary to recover you; you're priority #1 and #2. I owe a great deal to them helping me survive that fire, and anything I do they simply look the other way, as long as I wring you in. Oh, and that Voice thing wasn't quite their doing, that's all I say."

"Who are they?"

"Some people who want back what's rightfully theirs, both of them."

"Both? Nice to see they don't lump the two of us together," I said dryly.

"Oh, no, they do. The other thing's much older, much more important. But I'll keep my tongue steady on that."

As I drank in what he told me, I realised that we were dealing with a bigger picture here; these details of our past were vague but at the same time led to a more complex picture. But while I contemplated this, Cain was preoccupied with something more personal to him, if that was possible.

THE VOICE THE VOICE WHO IS IT WHY'S IT IN MY HEAD DEEP IN MY BRAIN WHO'RE THE BASTARDS THAT DID IT WHY WHY WHY I GOTTA KNOW HE'LL TELL ME—

It's my turn now. I snatched his arm an' said in a calm growl, "The Voice. Tell me now. Please, don't make me angry." I tried not to sound like a whimperin' beggar, but I think I failed.

"My, my, what's this? The English Devil himself interested in the cause of his own evil?"

"DON'T call me that! I ain't into killin' anymore. I gave up bein' that... THING'S lapdog. But tell me about it. How can I get it to stop talkin'!!"

Dean took all o' this in, a smug smile spreadin' over his hairy face.

"You can't. You had it wired into you, it's in your nature."

"LIAR! Why's it in me? Who's responsible, huh?"

Davey-boy tried to step in. 'Cain, please calm down—'

'Davey-boy, shut up! I need this!'

243

'Try not to get so excited, that's all I'm asking.'

"I can't say who," Dean explained, "but if you want, I can give you back something related to it: a memory."

"A memory? The hell d'ya mean?" While mentionin' our origins grabbed our attention, speculation swirled in our head – a passin' anecdote, a detailed little story to reel us further into his greasy palm? Or somethin' more, somethin' sensual, filled with the power o' every one o' our senses?

"What I'm talking about," he said, "is a part of your shared mind that vanished like rubbed-out chalk. A real memory, one you can ponder over." He removed from his coat a small handheld device that resembled a television remote, a black block filled with many different-coloured buttons, some of which I'm sure were so new and different that describin' 'em would be difficult. In the middle of it was a white ball-like button, slightly bigger than the rest. Pressin' it, as he did, led to it sinkin' in to the block. Almost immediately, our brain was attacked, a brief feelin' o' vibration, before everything went white.

There was a room, but all we could see was the bright burning light of what looked like large bulbs that gave off a faint blue glow. From the corners of our eyes there was darkness. The atmosphere smelled of sawdust, paint and disinfectant. Someone was talking to us, their voice smooth and robotic, like they were focused on other matters.

"I need you to stay calm, do you understand me? Your body is fully prepared, just as I wanted. Your mind, though, needs a little adjustment."

Some sort of headwear was placed onto us, metallic and cold, and started to tighten. It dug mercilessly into our skull like a drill, anxious to get to the centre of our brain. A groan of rising discomfort stirred from our throat.

"Try to relax. It may hurt, but you'll be thanking me when it's done. By the end, you'll be a different person."

The pain increased, our head turning numb as numerous colours swarmed our vision, before darkness covered it, and a scream filling the void.

I jumped back from the shock, just barely able to hold back a cry.

"Did you enjoy your trip down memory lane?"

"That... what was that?"

"Your manufacturing. A nice little tune-up to send you on your way."

"To kill. A walkin' death machine, right?"

"Yes. Admittedly, despite your setback, you've turned out to be quite a success."

"Tough shit. Tell your pals I'm defective."

"I'll pass on the message," the scumbag said with delight.

'Davey-boy,' I said in our mind, 'it's all yours, man.'

'Cain, if you want to rest, take your time.'

With that, I came forth. "Under very different circumstances, I'd say thanks for your little 'gift'."

"Ungrateful, aren't you? Be glad I didn't give you back a more painful one."

"Just seeing you stirs one up already. Enough of this; let's focus on what we came for."

"Oh, very well, then. I was enjoying our little conversation. Still, all good things must come to an end, eh?" He got up slowly, perhaps to savour the meeting, turned and made a 'come here' gesture with his hand to the large man and thin woman. They went over to Emily and Scarlett who in turn rose from their seats, and they converged to where we were. Emily's face was steely, unable to give into the pressure of the situation, while Scarlett was trying to close her eyes and turn away from us.

"Well, here they are," Dean said, "all ready to go home."

"David," Scarlett said, her voice stirring with fear.

"David, Cain," her mother said softly, some hope and nervousness instilled in her.

"Ladies, don't worry, we've got your back. Just walk past me and you'll be escorted out of here."

Emily was the first to move, tenderly holding Scarlett's hand. Her daughter stuck close by, her eyes now shut with intense effort as they went past us. I turned to face them as Jackie made her way to them.

'They're safe,' I thought.

'Yeah, an' that just leaves him,' I thought.

I made sure to keep our eyes focused on them until they left the park, but then they looked at each other and stopped, confused, before their hands broke away. Something wasn't right.

"Mum... I can't feel your hand."

"Me neither. It's like you're—"

"Like she's not even there," Dean interrupted. "That's because you're right. She's not really here with us in the park."

"What?" Emily asked, shocked. Not really here? What did he mean, unless he was using some kind of technology? Then the answer hit me.

"A hologram," I said aloud. "You're projecting her image to us."

"I'm a-a hologram?" The young lady's expression reeked of confusion and, more prominently, fear.

"Bingo, my friend. She's still back at my place, hooked up to some tech I picked up from my friends; they're quite the clever bunch. I put her in there when she fainted; she's been living through a projection of herself for about an hour or so."

"But, I can touch things!"

"I change whether or not you're intangible, kid." He grinned at Scarlett, whose face was now glowing like her namesake, examining herself, patting down her body to try and prove to herself that he was lying.

"No, no, no," she said to herself. "I was gonna get away." Tears started to roll down her cheeks.

Emily stopped herself from putting a hand on her shoulder. "Sw-sweetie, no matter what, we're gonna get you back, and I want you to be strong, okay?"

"I will, Mum."

"Good girl."

"Dean," the woman in the striped shirt said, disgusted. "That's… I thought we were just gonna hand both of them over! Jesus, the kid!"

"I knew you'd say that, Daisy," Dean replied. "That's why only Tranue was privy to it."

She turned her attention to her broad-shouldered accomplice. "You were okay with this?" Her voice was fraught with pain. He didn't answer her, be it from focusing on the matter at hand or shame. Clearly Daisy had a softness that made her the lesser of three evils, if she was even bad at all.

"Daisy, quiet," Dean barked, before talking to me and Cain. "In any case, you've got the insufferable Emily with you for now. Good luck earning Scarlett back."

Emily shot back with motherly rage. "Earn? She's not a possession!"

I asked, "What'll I have to do to get her back?"

Dean nudged his head in Tranue's direction. "Beat him. He's tougher than he looks, in ways I'm sure you can't imagine."

"After facing you, my imagination's even broader." I grabbed Emily's hand and squeezed it. "Scarlett, do what your mum says. Be strong."

"Don't worry, I'll give them hell. Kick his arse," she managed with a smile. Brave kid.

"Thanks, good luck with you too."

Dean pressed some unseen device in his pocket, and the young lady vanished instantly, rubbed away from the place. Her mother's hand overpowered mine.

Brad and Dwight proceeded to make their way over to cuff Dean and Daisy, stun guns aimed at them. When they were within a couple of feet, Dean once again fiddled with his pocket, and then he and Daisy disappeared as well, leaving Tranue.

"Damn it," Brad cursed with gritted teeth, switching his aim to Tranue.

"Should've known," I said, hate stuck at the back of my throat while I clenched my open hand. Emily let go of my other one.

"Do your best," she said steely. "Don't worry about me. Do what you have to do."

"Emily..."

'Kid...'

With Jackie beside her, she limped the rest of the way out of the park.

'Ready, Cain?'

'Ready.'

I walked over to Tranue, my clenched hand feeling like a rock. Somehow, releasing it wouldn't have felt right. "I have to fight you, right?"

"That's right," he answered, "until one of us is a pulp. You're immortal, but I doubt your body with all its capabilities can cope with what I'm able to do."

We had no idea what to expect here, so screw it, might as well ask for one before starting a brawl. "Nice boast, Trampoline or whatever your name is, but do you have what it takes to back it up?"

"Oh, definitely," he replied with smugness. "The elements are mine to manipulate. Earth, wind, fire, water, they're my allies. I feel nature in and around me." He spread his arms out slightly in a small gesture, embracing Wolf Park. "Dean did well to pick this place as my playground." His tanned skin instantly began to darken into a deep crimson, and fire erupted from his palms, steadily forming into roaring fire balls. "It's cold this time of year. How about I heat things up?"

As you can imagine, all of us were surprised as hell. Cain and I shared the same reaction:

"Oh…"

'…shit.'

I drew out our stun gun, wishing I had taken my Bob the Revolver out first. Things were about to get hairy at Wolf Park. Or ruff. Take your pick.

Chapter 18

Nature's A Pain in the Arse

Tranue's fireballs were flung all over the place randomly, grinning as he did so. He went about it at such speed that it was impossible for any of us to react sooner. A father shielded his young son, a couple managed to avoid the projectiles, while a lone park-goer was set alight and fell into the fountain he was perched on. The chaos of this led to everyone else, in fits of fear, confusion and self-preservation, fleeing to the many exit points scattered across Wolf Park. We had to make sure no one else died; the lives of innocents were in our hands now, and the shock of these attacks filled everyone with adrenaline.

Brad, Dwight and I unleashed the electricity stored in our guns, but as they burst to life in a stream of crackling blue energy, Tranue was unaffected and halted his destruction to face his attackers, chuckling at the failed display of heroics while his red body surged with hundreds of volts.

"Stun guns? Really? Nice try, but all it's doing is making me wired." The flames from his hands died and his skin calmed down to its normal tanned colour again.

As we ceased our intervention and sent our weapons back to our holsters, Brad made a fist with his artificial hand and sent a punch to Tranue's face. This made Mister Nature stumble, but he was quick to regain his footing.

"Shouldn't have done that," he said through gritted and freshly-bloodied teeth.

Brad recoiled and screamed as he stared at his fist. The hardcover plastic and metal base started to melt, the false flesh and hair bubbling and dissipating in seconds; the fingernails slid off of twisted and contorting digits that twitched when Brad tried to move them; wires underneath

250

fused and fizzled, sighing light wisps of smoke. The pain might as well had come from his real hand thanks to how deeply wired the prosthetic was to his senses. He managed to sneak in a curse through his yells, and fell to his knees with a throat strained to breaking point. All that remained was a blackened and warped piece of metal.

"My skin wasn't quite finished cooling off, and now you're paying the price of it, you idiot."

Dwight took out his walkie-talkie for back-up while I dove in with a fist. It collided with Tranue's stomach, which was bulkier than Dean's but not impossible to wind. His deeply-grounded feet crushed the grass behind him as he was sent back by the blow, and clutched his gullet with a sharp groan that escaped through his clenched teeth. Just as I was about to hit him again, the elemental mental case gripped our arm and threw us with Herculean strength over to the circular middle of the park's concrete path.

'Aw crap,' Cain thought, 'not the concr—' Our face hit the ground first and I swear our nose broke like someone yanked the damn thing out. We didn't have time to think or do anything as we lost consciousness.

It didn't take long to wake up, though, and as we struggled to work through the haziness in vision and thoughts from our bashed head and the blood trickling down our forehead, it was pretty clear someone had torn a page or two from this scene as we noticed Jackie engaging Tranue in combat.

Jackie no longer possessed a potbelly or thin limbs; she was bigger, *much* bigger, her muscles ballooning all over, rock-hard biceps bulging past her short sleeves, and a great strain across her shirt and its buttons, enough to give the impression they would fly off with a PING and hit Tranue in the eyes. This was her secret weapon, the biological ability she labelled Muscle Force. Even her face changed, red with the stress on her body and veins that were faintly featured on her forehead, and a great deal of feral fury in her eyes, a far cry from her collected and laid-back self. She and Tranue were evenly matched, every punch and kick slamming into their hulking bodies with low grunts, two titans locked together in a stalemate that made the ground shake with every movement.

While I was fascinated by this in, admittedly, quite a theatrical way, Cain's thoughts were a lot more simplistic and to-the-point; he was practically drooling.

'Oh, god she's used it again! Muscle Force for the win, girl! I wanna touch her arms! I wonder what her tail's like?'

I groaned, my throat a pit filled with boiling frustration. 'Cain, shut up and focus! You can poke them later on after we've beaten this guy!'

'Sorry, must be the head wound! Thoughts all over the place…'

It was clear she was also keeping him occupied while a dozen or so IISEP agents spilled into Wolf Park with heavy energy rifles, and those already near were blasting Tranue with pink glowing energy balls at every angle.

Our decked-out cat friend managed to grab a hold of Tranue's fists, and the two stood their ground, a great weight vibrating around them, muscles tensed as they forced all their energy against one another like two ships colliding in a storm. The rifles' energy blasts seemed to have an effect on him, as arms started to shake, allowing Jackie a chance to overwhelm him and push him back.

'Damn, she's got him on the ropes,' Cain thought with joy.

"This seems to be going too well," I responded aloud with doubt, getting to my feet once the pain in our head started to clear up. "It's great he's getting worn down, but he hasn't used anymore powers yet – he could have something up his sleeve." Not wanting to be a spectator anymore, I made a dash towards the commotion, even with a slightly hazy head, but I stopped when a large stream of water from the fountain sailed through the air as if it was natural.

It flew in the direction of the agents, Jackie included, splitting off into individual streams, ready to assault them. The water plunged into their mouths, the force of which threw some of them back onto the ground, while others suffered the dread of having the streams rush down their throats. I recalled the guy who fell into the fountain and never came out; the poor bastards must have been tasting some of his burnt crispy flesh. Jackie was experiencing the foul tactic, and the sudden hit gave Tranue all the time he needed to release a fist from her hold and punch her in the stomach, winding her. She crashed to the floor, desperately trying to breathe.

'Shit, what do we do? What the hell do we do?' I thought frantically.

As though in answer to this, my hand drew out good old Bob, and I steadied my aim while breaking into a run. I focused on Tranue's left leg, roughly where his knee would be, and squeezed the trigger three times. Once was enough; the first bullet pierced his jeans and he called out in pain as he faltered. The other two gave him more to worry about, and judging by the small explosion of blood and the way his leg bent, his kneecap was in pieces, allowing me time to clip him in the other knee with a single bullet as the gap between us closed.

He was on all fours, baring his teeth in agony, grinding them down to the point of breaking every one. His concentration broken, the water fell on to the ground, as dear old Mother Gravity intended. Now looming over him like a building witnessing his neighbour being demolished, I put Bob back in his holster, and smiled with a chuckle thrown in for good measure.

"You should have legged it when you had the chance."

Tranue let out some curse under his breath, wounded and annoyed by my little one-liner. I turned over to Jackie, who was fine now, aside from coughing up some of the water.

Concerned, I asked, "Do you need help?"

'I'd like to help,' Cain thought.

Jackie put her hand up to reject it, and closed her eyes. Her buff body retracted within a few seconds, her thin arms barely filling out her stretched sleeves and the rest of her shirt hung lazy from her frame, even her circular belly wasn't big enough to press against it. That done, she threw up what I assumed was the rest of the water.

"Feeling better, Jackie?"

She gave us a thumbs-up. Cain hastily took control and hugged her tightly, squealing with glee, "Thank god yer safe!" He then realised what he was doing and quickly drew back, and fumbled around before tipping our hat, quietly saying, "Uh… I mean… cool, you're okay."

Jackie patted our shoulder, unfazed by his outburst and stumbling. "Cain, it's alright. You're quite an excited kitty, eh?"

"I-I guess…" He blushed and retreated back into our head.

Just as either of us were about to secure Tranue, the man-mountain grinned, like a caricature of Jim Carrey. At first, I thought he was just pulling his face back in pain, but the truth came to us when he said, "I'm not done yet. This was just a rocky start."

His hands and legs were changing, taking on the ground's dark brown texture, all colour across him fading as his skin and clothes grew dark and ridged at alarming speed. He turned into a figure of rock and mud, looking like some kind of statue; he had absorbed the earth into himself.

Nothing occurred to any of us on what to do next. Would he break away from any cuffs if we applied them to him? Would any of our weapons faze him in his new exterior? How powerful was he now? Something in the pit of our stomachs told us this wasn't going to get any easier. Before any action could be taken, Tranue's body sank into the ground quickly, as if he was being swallowed up.

As you can imagine when you're facing a guy who could summon special effects for a big Hollywood blockbuster, we were paranoid as hell. Every second I feared that he would have hands burst up and grab a hold of everyone's legs so that punching the living daylights out of us was a breeze. At least Dean didn't pick the countryside for this fight.

'If he wants to play games, then by God, we'll give him one,' I promised Cain. I told Jackie to stay where she was, and went into fifth gear to the concrete circle at the heart of Wolf Park. Standing right in the middle, I began my attempt to goad Tranue out.

"Come on, Trampoline, or whatever your name is! We're right here! Just you and us, got it? Do whatever it is you want with us – we're the chew toy of a life time. These mortals, they're so fragile – I've made card pyramids that last longer than them! Is that why you enjoy tearing them up so much, why you went for all those innocents first, to rile us up? Coward! I bet when you were born, your mum took one look at you and hit your dad in the joy factory! You got all these powers, and you hide yourself like this? Here's what we say to that – fuck nature, you elemental weasel!"

I gave a V-sign in one hand and flipped the bird in the other, both aiming at the ground like Weapons of Mass Offending.

'That should get him all rough and rumbled,' I said to Cain.

'That was friggin' beautiful, man,' he responded, pride sailing out of him with every word. I thanked him, which was long enough for me to not notice my legs feeling hard below the knees at first.

And I did, and looked down. Two concrete hands that were three-times bigger than ours weighed us down.

Oh dear.

Punching bag time.

Shit.

There was no point trying to struggle; the grip was so monstrous that we were practically dead below the waist. Just when we thought it couldn't get any worse, it got worse. The ground, or rather a great deal of it, just outside the concrete pathways shot up, with a thunderous BOOM that, for some reason, made me think of cartoon explosions. What I'm trying to say was, it was loud and gnawed at our ears as they continued to erect themselves around us, with parts breaking off to barricade the concrete, creating a giant claustrophobic ring that stopped at around twenty feet. We could feel our tongue and lungs reject the dense rank taste of mud.

We were trapped. Trapped and bound by a man who could have had a nice career as a nature-themed wrestler. The names 'Earth Shaker' and 'Mountain Moe' seemed pretty appropriate right about now.

'I think ya may have pushed it with the mom thing.'

"Good thing I didn't insult his dog."

Okay, we were in deep-shit territory, and chances are if it wasn't for Dean castrating his actions (I'd have some sympathy for him if he had been castrated on a literal note), he'd probably have some fun burying us under these earthly pillars.

But what if he'd had given Trampoline the thumbs-up to do that?

In that case, our aftershave and mouth-spray would be distributed as part of Mother Nature's Ground 'Boots' branch.

Coughin' up-and-down lungfuls o' dirt ain't my idea o' relaxation.

Or bouncing us around like a worn-out pinball. But now wasn't the time for speculation, but for action. Which of us – the demented duo, or Tranue – would act first, and who would react?

I clenched our fists. Striking the concrete clamps below us would be a fruitless effort; we were bound, that much was true, but we weren't defenceless as long as we had our arms and brains. I looked around, unsure as to where Tranue would materialise.

Just when I was running thin on patience, his face grew out of the block in front of us; at first, nothing more than cracks and ridges and bumps, but it swiftly gained shape and familiarity, and as it did, it moved in our direction, stretching out until there were only several inches between us and him.

"Enjoying the interior work, fellas?" he said, a rotten stench leaving his carved lips and pushing itself up our nose.

"Could use some decorating," I answered. "I'd suggest some flowery wallpaper and a couple of windows."

'HA!'

I continued, planting a little strategy along the way. "How about you give us a bit of legroom, eh, Tranue? Come on, be a fair sport."

"Why should I bother?"

"You want to have some fun, right? After all, you yourself said that this is your playground. I imagine it'd be boring for you to pound us into mush without us putting up *some* resistance."

The rock-man's chiselled mouth spread to reveal dirt-brown teeth. "You have a point."

Good, good, little fish, take the bait.

You'll be reeled in nice an' easy!

But getting us free was the best thing we could hope for. As long as we had the use of our legs, it was a step up from our current predicament, a weak advantage, but an advantage nonetheless. A small thought came through that somehow, someway, our agent chums were working on a way to bust through Tranue's little shake-up. But even Jackie and her claws, no matter how far she pushed herself, hadn't the strength to climb up this; even if by a miracle she was halfway there, he'd bat her off with a giant hand or something. All we could do was rely on our wits and, if need be, physical force.

"You're definitely not a coward, Tranue, I know that for sure."

"I think I've made that quite clear, David, Cain, or whichever one you are."

257

"Do it," I said. Cain and I were crossing our fingers by this point, hoping he'd go through with it.

"Very well." His voice was booming with pride and competition. "You better bring something to the table." At his command, the hands released their hold on us and sunk back into the path floor as if they never existed. We forgot how terrible the pressure was on our legs; pain exploded below our knees, followed by a groan and some futile rubbing.

A humanoid body for Tranue, towering at ten feet, appeared in the same fashion as the head, connected to it and stretching out before us, only for the figure to free itself from the wall, and the earth that it shook from retracted back into the wall. In the messy library of our brain, I picked out his resemblance to that of the Golem of Jewish folklore – a being whose body of raw material, most notably clay, was brought to life. He had an imposing menace about him from the way he stood still, his broad-shouldered form a perfect recreation of his normal self, complete with clothes. The result was distinctively uncanny and unnerving.

"I'll let you make the first move," he said with a smug smile creeping at the corner of his mouth.

'Here we go, Cain,' I thought, unsure of what to do.

'Wait! Let me take over, Davey-boy! I got a plan!'

'What is it?'

'No time to explain, but it's better than yours!'

'You don't even know what mine is.'

'Somewhere along the lines of yellin', "Stop or I'll plant a garden on you!"'

'Far from it.'

'Oh yeah, well what is it?'

'You don't tell me yours, I don't tell you mine.'

'Dammit! Just let me try mine out, okay?'

'Okay.'

And so Cain was in full control. Jumping up, he quickly grabbed onto Tranue's face with both hands.

"Take this," he yelled out, and then immediately pulled back our head and started to slam it into Tranue's with a *T-WACK* sound, shouting out "headbutt" at the top of our lungs with every hit. Bearing in mind that we were in the midst of a head injury (with our nose still out of place, to boot), this was both insane and highly dangerous; the thunderous blows might as well have been a shotgun blast to the face. Vision was getting blurry, nothing was solid throughout all this.

'Cain, what the hell are you doing?' He didn't hear me, probably due to the crunching sound of our head getting bashed in, skin and bone wearing thin as blood burst out to say 'hello'. Even if he did hear me, the chances of him actually listening to me were pretty slim; I think the injuries were starting to affect our thoughts, especially Cain's. Things felt kind of hazy, wonky. Stringing sentences together was more of a task than actually doing anything else.

All I heard from Cain in our head was:

HEADBUTT HEADBUTT SLAM SLAM SLAM EARTH-MAN INTO MUSH EVEN IF BODY BREAKS I'M INVINCIBLE NOT A LOONY NOT A LOONY I'M SUPER-MAN A POWER-MAN POWAAA IAAIA DAA FRA ERRGGH RAA

As you can tell, things were going swimmingly. The more he committed himself to his act, the less energy I had to stop him – our brain was turning into jelly. Maybe it was because of the damage received, but I couldn't help laughing at a funny thought; Cain, a man bashful around his crush, was now bashing his head against our enemy, hoping to crush him. The fact that Jackie and Tranue had fought each other prior to this made it a laugh riot.

All of this didn't seem to hurt Tranue at all, in fact his act of non-resistance made me think that he was enjoying this little spectacle. Was Cain really expecting to break him into itty bitty pieces? As if the universe answered my question, a good chunk of the top of Tranue's head broke off; a jagged diagonal line ran all the way from the top left temple to his right jaw. The top portion above the line crumbled into weak patches of rock and dirt, causing our left arm to hang limply in the absence of the face's right side.

Our rocky friend screamed, the foul stench of earth going up what remained of our nose, down our mouth and inflating our lungs. Just barely managing to keep his eyes open, Cain grinned and removed our other hand from Tranue, and we fell to the ground. What little life that was left in our body was almost gone as we groaned from the impact, our back giving us the sensation of a sledgehammer driving into it.

Tranue's damaged shape slid back into the great wall he had made, and as he did, the element he absorbed himself into was slowly growing back what he lost. He was completely gone in the structure by the time he was whole again. He was badly hurt, no doubt about it when you temporarily lost half your face, but that didn't mean he was finished.

'Well done, you mad stupid bastard,' I congratulated. 'Now we're even closer to dying for the umpteenth time than when he threw us.'

"For my next trick," Cain slurred faintly, "I'll dig my way to China usin' only my feet."

Footsteps were heard. Raising our head, we saw Tranue in front of us, his body now human and towering over us. "Too weak to get on your feet, guys?"

"Aagh," Cain responded, closing our eyes and wishing that the fight would go on a time-out for a wee few hours.

"Alright, let me help you with that. You could do with some air, fellas." Oh dear. Truly this would not go well, unless he had some sort of honour about him, but that was pretty darn unlikely. We had just enough energy to raise our head and look in Tranue's direction; his chest rose and fell with every deep breath, his hands and fingers spread out and aimed at, a puppet master waiting for his toy to respond to the strings he pulled.

Then, our body started to move, but not of our accord. We felt lighter, finger and shoes barely touching the ground.

"And we have lift off in three…"

Air? Lift off? Did he really mean…?

"…two…"

Oh, dear. Oh, deary me. By now it was as though great hands were lifting us up.

"…one…"

Not good, not good, not good… he was levitating us. If only we had wings!

"Lift off!" As he roared this with great excitement, a powerful blast of air shot us upwards, and the white puffy clouds resting in the sky grew awfully closer. Our limbs were weighed down by the sheer force of the wind, cheeks fluttering and making our face look as if it was being stretched out. Though the air was strangely refreshing and lively. I know, of all the things to bring up, there was *that*.

Oh god we were up 'n about in the freakin' sky! Turnin' our head to look around didn't work, it felt too heavy. It was all too fast to take in all at once – couldn't tell how far up we were, the banged-up brain an' dizziness an' air could o' meant a mile a sec or livin' out five years in five minutes! I wanted to go to sleep an' have Davey-boy do the rest – I did my part an' I was beat.

"Cain!" I shouted, unable to hear myself talk or think. "Still there?"

'Nothin' else but here!" he yelled back in our brains-to-soup mind. 'Scared shitless right now! How the fuck are you takin' it?'

"Surprised, for one. Little bit scared, honestly."

'You fuckin' moron! This is bungee-jumpin' in reverse! The fuck can't ya be more scared?'

"Dunno. The air feels nice, actually."

'Fuck you!'

"I don't want us to be people pâté either, but we can't really afford to do anything at the moment."

'Grrr…'

And then we stopped, floating in the sky as you would in a pool or any great body of water. We hadn't gone through the clouds, oh no, but they looked so very, very near, inches from us, pillowy sky-marshmallows that, in our dazey-mazey brainy, I wanted to rest on. The brain damage was really screwing me up. Everything looked brighter. Who turned up the saturation?

'Why ain't we fallin'? Who pressed the pause button?'

"Well, take a guess," I said. Tranue was probably able to manipulate not just the strength of the air in order to blast anyone anywhere, but also make it like a wall and hold someone in suspension somehow. Like telekinesis. Not sure how that worked – air particles? Constant wind in two different places at once? – but he was doing it, a giant roaring fan, a playful, mean one at that. Question was, when would he turn it off? Would it be a gradual or quick descent?

The immobility made it impossible for me to see if Bob or the stun gun were in our holsters; we couldn't feel their bulk strapped against either thigh. Too bad, but then again, what good would they do? Practically peashooters, unless he was flesh-and-blood, though it was likely he would avoid using that form and stick to the more unnatural, difficult, annoying ones, anything if it was able to stretch out this little trial of ours, and delaying Scarlett's freedom and end of her troubles by minutes. Tricky dickie. We wouldn't give him that satisfaction, for her and Emily's sakes.

Just as I thought over this, Tranue's face suddenly appeared, so close to us that I could count every hair in his beard.

"Enjoying the ride?" His breath stank, spoiling the air.

"I've had better," I replied with a bit of sass in my voice. "It's got nothing on those rollercoasters at Petlins. Take a note from them – they make us vomit. With you, we're not even queasy. One out of five. If you try harder, I might bump it up to one-and-a-half."

He let out a half-chuckle, half-growl, and I held back wanting to tell him to invest in mints.

I held back wantin' to scream!

"You've only just reached the top. Now it's time for the fall." He drew back a fist.

Oh, dear.

Oh, shit.

The blow grazed our chin, our jaw tightened and teeth ramming into each other, blasting us through the air once again with the force of a rocket. We can't really describe the following as air-diving, as that would imply we were going straight down right there and then. No, that would have been a relief, a sweet break before the rather gruesome breaking of the rest of our body. We felt another hit, this one snapping our spine, and that's when Tranue started to pinball us around. Everything was so constant, we couldn't keep track of his moves nor did we have time to come up with any ways to counter each punch.

We were rising and falling in short bursts, a pectoral here, a shoulder blade there; then we were sent higher and higher with every punch, like he was trying to beat some sort of record. Our body whistled through the wind, going left and right per second as he used us as the ball for what I can only describe as a one-man air-tennis match.

BISH - hard hit in the shoulder, left arm possibly dislocated.

BASH – right knee's out of place with a sweet 'PLOP'.

POW – uppercut to the chin, bloodied teeth retreating from our mouth.

KER-FUCKED – right jab to the stomach, winding us (how appropriate).

Right cheek turned to mush. A nose left in pieces, shattered glass in flesh and blood and bone. One working eye, the other a swollen, bleeding mass of purple. Left side of the head was numb, though that may have been the previous head trauma. Legs were inoperable. Our stomach was burning with sadistic slowness. It was only when Tranue gave us another blow from above that we finally descended.

The crash, surprisingly, didn't cause us to black out, though it hurt like hell – it was like we were briefly punched out of our body. Grass comforted our broken hands, though I wished we had something to comfort our breathing, as it was on par with breathing through a straw. The sky and its white puffy curtains were now still, no longer a blurry rollercoaster ride. We saw, to our left, a line of dark green trees (The Trees That Be Superior To Thee, said the echoes of my half-buried memories) all bulky and proud. I moved our head to the left and was met with bushes; to the right, a small river lazily sliding under a squat bridge.

"Well," I muttered weakly, "this is a nice change of scenery. I didn't like that ride, so I suggest we get a refund."

'The only way this could be any more humiliatin' was if any o' those trees fell on us…'

"Yeah, we got quite an arse-whooping, eh?"

'We got an everythin'-whoopin', man. Good thing no one saw that; I could boast to Jackie that we were bein' all manly an' heroic an' invincible an'… shit.'

"Sounds good to me, Cain. Of course, when you take all the damage into account… sounds unconvincing."

'Dammit. Where's that big fella, anyway? The less I see 'im, the more I want to end this.'

"Did you enjoy the ride?" Tranue asked in a sly whisper. I turned over to the lake, and saw him rise from it, his upper body a shimmering transparent version of itself, with a wall of water in place of his legs. He was just as detailed as he normally was, from the outlines of his clothes to his mad smile.

"We want our money back," I said with a chuckle, my voice a croaky, weak mess, "If not, we'll sue."

"Sorry, non-negotiable. Time to wash you down."

"I'm more in line for a shower later on, thanks."

"Not your choice."

"Tell me, did Dean ask you to be like this, or are you just naturally a dick?

Tranue started talking, but neither Cain nor I listened as we instigated a little one-to-one chit chat. No doubt Water-Boy was saying something cocky or spouting off puns; anything if it kept the tap running.

'Cain…'

'Yeah…?'

'Stun gun.'

'Thought o' that, too.'

I tried to move our hand, but it failed. I was only able to move a finger slightly.

'Fingernails, quick.'

'Got it.'

Cain took the helm and raised a finger so that the nail would get into the trigger guard, which it did. He dragged the gun to towards us until it was right into our hand. As we took in deep, slow breaths through our nose, we could feel a sliver of strength creeping in. In spite of the pain, it felt so good to have even the tiniest bit of control over something after our bout in the air.

"…whatever he's got in mind for you," Tranue said in a tone that sounded like he was wrapped things up, "I hope it means the end of you. Of course, you've already failed this little trial; I might not allow second chances."

Scarlett's smile hit us as I grabbed the gun and shot him before he could react. The anger burning inside this damaged shell of a body came to life in the crackling roar of electricity that tore and distorted his own. His cries of pain, scratchy and gargled, was twisted music that we embraced with a mad, painful grin. My finger wasn't just squeezing the trigger; it was clamped down, just how I liked it. After ten extremely satisfying seconds, I let go, and the stun gun fell onto the grass again. Tranue's liquid body tried to regain some semblance of shape, but it collapsed under the pressure, resulting in a splash that sent a few drops on our face.

"Gotcha," I said under my breath.

'Great work, Davey-boy,' Cain thought with victory bursting through his voice.

"Great work," I replied. "Couldn't have done it without you. We're a team, through and through."

Before we could say anything else, there was the sound of something dragging itself on land, water rippled as the grass was met with the *thump* of heavy hands and boots. The big fella, as we could tell with a painfully-raised head, was resting on the ground as well, breathing quite heavily, his clothes dark and wet and they stuck to him.

"D-dammit," he let out with some difficulty. "I guess you won."

"Yay… shame there's no prize money. We've certainly done a number on each other, that's for sure. What would've happened if we had lost?"

"What does it matter? You beat me."

"She matters."

"I honestly don't know. Maybe Dean would have had to arrange a rematch, or something entirely different. He wanted me to hold back, see how you'd fair if I went easy on you. I bet he didn't count on me actually trying to pulverise you."

"Why'd you bother going the extra mile?" Our head was starting the grow fuzzy. Oh dear.

"Not entirely sure. Could be that you're like us; unnatural, a freak who can do the impossible. We're unique, and with all the tales Dean told us, there was no point pulling punches for the sake of softening you up for him."

"Ah… curiosity," I managed to say as the fuzziness amplified to the point of pain. "That can do a world of good, but considering how this came to a rather… shocking conclusion, was it worth it?"

The man looked at us, at first unsure, but made up his mind with a small smirk. "Yes." Having the final word, his body took on the familiar rocky state as he sank into the ground, gone. Seconds later, our heartbeat was getting slower, and slower, and slower. And then we were gone, too, dying for the first time in decades. To be honest, we really needed the nap.

Chapter 19

Updates

Ever had that occurrence where you wake up and have a big ol' face staring back at you with a smile plastered over them, welcoming you with a joy-filled "Hello"? It could have been a family member, or a lover sharing a bed with you, or a nurse at a hospital, ensuring that you're safe and comfortable in your warm bed?

Well, Cain and I weren't so lucky. Instead, we were blessed with Colin and the dark steel interior of his morgue, his beak-like nose a bit too close for our liking, his eyes gleaming with love for familiar or new 'residents', and his breath left much to be desired. Oh, and our body just so happened to be stark naked and lying on a slightly cold steel table. Sometimes, it's just not worth waking up from a short lapse of death.

"Hello," he uttered with a macabre smile.

I yelled as I beheld the sight in front of me and closed my eyes for a few seconds, before accepting the new surroundings. "Hello, Colin," I said, shaking off the initial fright. "You, um, you doing alright?"

"I think I should be asking you that. I was given quite a mess when they handed you over to me; so many broken bones, bruises, cuts, disconnected parts here and there." Still fascinated, he moved back, allowing me to lean up.

"Good thing no one else can do the 'coming back to life' act, they'd be shocked within seconds of meeting you," I joked.

"Oh, I'm not that ugly. I was quite a looker back in the day."

"Don't worry, I'm sure your days as a world-class stud were aplenty, my boy. Your face really fits in the morgue –

268

a cloak over you would add some atmosphere. No, it's the breath I'm worried about."

By this point, Cain had started to regain consciousness, his disjointed, mumbling thoughts rising in our head. '…an' I… were… tomorrow night… apples… fuzzy llamas… whoa, what? The hell… we're in Creepy Colin's Crazy Crypt? Oh, yay… Davey-boy, you handle this for a sec, I gotta pull myself together.'

'Right, C,' I thought.

Colin brought a small tray from the corner of the room, containing Bob the Revolver, the stun gun, our wallet, and surprisingly, our mobile phone, somehow still perfectly intact.

"Your belongings, fellows. Your phone was damaged, but Dwight had someone up at Spell Division restore it. Lucky you, eh?" He left the tray on a small table beside ours.

"We wish. I'll thank Dwight and the caster when I see them. How long have we been out for?"

"About two days," Colin replied with uneasy delight.

"Two… days? Was our body really that messed up?"

"Oh, yes. The head trauma might have played a part in it."

"Well, when it comes to the head, that's always taken the most time to heal. But for two days…"

"Hmm, it was a pleasure to observe your regeneration, if that helps."

"Actually, no, it doesn't, Colin. Sorry, but having you look at us constantly with glee isn't the sweetest of mental images."

Colin said warmly, "I guess you could say I was dead wrong." He let out a croaky chuckle.

"Yes, very." There was no attempt to even try and pretend that we found that funny; we were in a bit of a grave mood. Then a question popped up a little too late. "Wait, why are we in the morgue, and not the medical centre?"

Another grin from our friendly neighbourhood mortician. "You've been dead and back, where did you expect to wind up?"

"I dunno, really. Twenty years on the job, and we're only doing this now."

"Having you in the medical centre would have been rather morbid for everyone else. They'd fear they were looking at their own potential future, I bet."

He had a point there. I just shrugged as I noticed to lack of something rather personal. "Where are our clothes?"

Colin shuffled across the room and brought back a big see-through zipper bag containing the very latest in this summer's battle-damage wardrobe. "Here we are, lads."

I snatched it from 'im and tore it open with my lovely claws. Colin looked a bit miffed.

"You didn't have to do that. There was a zipper."

"Death's made me delirious, sue me," I said as I laid out the clothes on the autopsy table and started to put 'em on, torn jeans first.

"Why couldn't you have been the one knocked out instead?" Colin groaned.

"I bet you say that to all the cute chatty corpses." I grinned while slippin' on the battered shirt. "Hey, on a scale o' one to ten, how surreal is this for ya?"

"One. For how annoying, ten."

"Glad to see dyin' for the umpteenth time hasn't stripped me o' my charm."

"Whatever helps you sleep at night."

I let Davey-boy handle the steerin' wheel again, though really because o' the socks an' shoes. Claws are a bitch to work with.

"Colin, where's the Arachnarep – the creature from the petshop's corpse? Too big for the morgue?"

"It's been placed in storage, all frozen up. He wouldn't have been a good bedfellow for you, anyway," he laughed.

"True. There would have been quite a smell, I can imagine." I turned on our phone, checking to see if Dean had tried to reach us. No missed calls or texts. Strange.

"It's gut-wrenching to not have it around anymore," Colin said, unknowing irony ringing in his voice.

"We know exactly how you feel. We were somewhat... close to him, too." By now, we were fully-dressed, shoes, waistcoat, everything, minus a hat. "Pity the Stetson wasn't found," I said with a sense of longing. "Had that since the 1970s. There weren't that many red tri-corners made, and you'd hardly find anyone willing to recreate them, so they're quite a collector's item now. Take a guess at how much."

The old man's face grew bright in fascination, as though he was a child again. "Oooh, that's something. Seven-thousand, nine-thousand?"

I gave him a cheeky smile as I supplied the answer slowly. "Ten-million."

A massive 'WHAT' echoed across the room as Colin's face dropped. "*Ten-million?* Why didn't you *sell* the damn thing? Any money problems you had would've been solved."

I shrugged and said coolly, "Would you believe us if we said we couldn't live without it?"

"What a waste of intellect. And I thought *I* was a numpty in my old age."

"Oh well, can't be helped. Makes you wonder though, how much we'd all be if it mattered who we are. Innocent; cruel; knowledgeable; naïve; well-meaning. It's not just the components, it's the quality that truly makes the product shine, you know? Everyone here would be worth a fortune."

"And you'd be at the top?"

"Hmp. We wish. We'd be at the bottom, with barely a penny to hold on to."

"At least you're rich in humour, or with how unnaturally calm you are about that. It's making my skin crawl, and given my job, that's a damn good feat."

From there, our freshly-refined feet carried us to the door, wanting us to get a move on while our mind finished getting prepped up. "Well, it's been an experience being your guest, Colin. Sad that we can't repay you somehow."

"Knowing you boys, you'll find a way. Maybe bring me back a nice big stack of work. Ta-ta." He performed his traditional hi-bye hand gesture, pumping his hand into a fist in the rhythm of a heartbeat, and in response I drummed a hand onto our chest.

Stepping out of the morgue made walking down the milk-white hallways and the rooms filled with much livelier occupants feel like we had stepped from Kansas into Oz.

'Phew, glad we're outta there. I thought a zombie was gonna pop out at any moment.'

'Rob promised not to do that again, not since Dwight warned him.'

'Wish we coulda put our brain somewhere else. It takes up too much space for my likin', an' it really hurts.'

'I reckon we always leave it at home, anyway.' I turned a corner, getting closer to Dwight's office.

'If that's the case, I wanna put it on my spot o' the sofa.'

'Okay, let's stick to the matter at hand.'

'Sure, sure. Hope we get Red back soon so I can kick Dean's ass real quick.'

'Likewise. I reckon that young woman who was with him – Daisy, was it? – she could be of some use if we get the chance to meet her.'

'Cuz she had standards? God, you sound naïve.'

'No, I'm being open-minded.'

'Well, I'm open to thinkin' ya really ain't all there if ya believe we can find a weak link in the rest of a so-far really strong bad-guy chain.'

'We'll see.'

As we grew closer to Dwight, a familiar soul walked by us – Chris, a somewhat nervous brow and his face staring past us indicating a problem or two

"Hi, Chris," I said, adding a small wave to the greeting.

Thankfully, this caught his attention, a smile spreading over him and he turned to face us. "Oh, hello, there," he responded with equal brightness in his voice. "I've heard there's been some progress recently, even if you've been, um, out of commission, so to speak. I'm glad things are looking a bit better now."

"Well, in part," I corrected, hesitant to elaborate further to spoil his day and new mood. "Still, how've you been doing lately? Doing okay settling in with your workmates?"

"Um, not quite," the young man stated, his brow dropping back into its old position. "I, erm, I know they're people too, but I find it uncomfortable to… connect, you know? Don't get me wrong, they're all nice, and learning about them's fascinating, like the substitute blood they use, but I can't help thinking about my dad, and… yeah."

"Oh, I see. I'm sure Dwight had a good reason for giving you your position. There's potential in you to be a good member of this place; you just need to lighten the baggage, so to speak."

"Y-yeah. That Alexander, though, he creeps me out the most. The slicked back hair, black clothes, cold looks – it's like he's about to bite into me."

I shrugged. "Well, he did inspire Dracula."

Chris' eyes opened as wide as they could. He blurted out a squeaky, "*What?*"

"Yeah, he was Bram Stoker's friend, got him thinking about writing 'Dracula' down. Easy for him to market it as fiction; I mean, who in their right, sensible mind was going to believe it? Since then, we at IISEP classify his type as 'Stokers'."

The young man's voice rattled. "Oh my god…"

I placed a reassuring hand on his small shoulder. "Don't worry, he's not evil, just a bit cold. Cain and I are friends with him, have been for years. Look, to help make things easier, go out to lunch with him or something, break the ice a little with him and the others."

"Okay, okay. What would you recommend I eat with him?"

"Steak."

The look on Chris' face was one of delightful bafflement – I could see the gears shifting on trying to figure out if it was a joke or not. "You're... really, steak?"

"You'll see if it works," I said with a cheeky smile as I patted his shoulder. "We've got some stuff to do, so we'll chat later, okay?"

"R-right."

Chris nodded and made his way past us. I turned and declared, "Oh, he likes them well-done, by the way!" He glanced back at us with another nod and a thumbs-up. I wished him the best of luck; God knew we all needed it.

Now we were just by Dwight's office, the door slightly ajar. I gave it a light tap and entered. As soon as Dwight raised his head from some usual heavy paperwork, he couldn't help but give us a warm smile that kept everyone and everything perfectly still.

"Ah, Lazarus has finally risen," said the booming voice of Dwight as he came forward.

"Hi, Dwight," I greeted him, wishing that my hat was with me so that I could afford to top it. "Anything been going on while we've been under?"

"No word from Dean. We assume that he only knows your number, but we don't know your phone's password."

"Considering his subscription to 'Love/Hate' magazine, you'd think he'd factor in our workplace. How's Emily doing?" My ears grew hot and red, heartbeat quickening as her face struck our mind. Poor child. The need to apologise to her sprung up.

"We made sure she was okay before escorting her back home," Dwight answered.

"Back home? Sorry, it just feels a bit odd to me, considering we haven't even got Scarlett back yet. I figured she'd be here with us."

"Don't worry, we made sure her house is under our protection. We've got a handful of our agents watching her every move."

Cain's growling rang in our head, an upset animal waiting to roar when pushed. I made sure that he didn't seep through and yell at Dwight that his protection wouldn't stop Dean from sending Tranue or anyone else there for a surprise attack, for whatever reason. Worrying and sheer paranoia wasn't going to get us anywhere, not at this point in Dean's sick little game. Just gave Dwight a simple nod and continued to receive updates.

"We managed to interview Eddie Muzzle yesterday once he healed up. He said Dean had supplied him with the aliens and feared to ask where he got them from in case he cut off access to them. For a second, we thought we hit the jackpot when Muzzle provided us with an address to Dean's whereabouts."

I sighed and lowered my head. "Dead end, wasn't it?"

"Yup. The place was empty – must have a couple of back-up hideouts stashed throughout the area, maybe even the country."

"Makes sense, I guess. He's had years to plan this, decades' worth of resources at his disposal."

"Hopefully, we'll be able to nail him while Scarlett's alright."

"I have a feeling it'll only happen when he wants it to," I said grimly. "Any casualties from Wolf Park?"

"Thankfully, no. One civilian got burned from one of Tranue's fireballs, but he was lucky enough to survive; he's being treated at the hospital."

The mini-movie of the poor soul being set alight and falling into the fountain played out in the cinema of our thoughts; the news made it easier to recover from, but it was still a nightmare to think back to that moment, and that he was still suffering from it.

"Right, that's good, that's good," I muttered. "How's Brad doing, after the whole…" I refrained from saying 'hand'.

"He's managing. He got a new hand commissioned for Spekro up at Tech Division – let's just say she was ecstatic when he told her he wanted to have the fingers shoot energy projectiles, using Spell Division crystals as fuel."

I stopped as I heard those last two words. Energy. Beams. Raw, concreted bursts of energy compressed into his very fingertips. "You're… serious?"

"I asked him that, too. As he said, 'mmm-hmmm'. He wanted to prepare himself for any eventuality, and what better way than a hands-on approach?" Cain and I were too bedazzled to notice that Dwight had made a little joke. Well, *I* was; Cain was wrapped up in how cool the idea sounded.

"Oh my god!" I blurted out as I came up, sportin' a big ol' toothy grin an' pullin' my hair in big clumps. "Frickin' laser beams! In his hand! Hand beams! Fingertips o' DEATH! Death Beam, BANG! This is amazin', Big Man! Can I get one, PLEASE? I'll cut off a hand to make sure it fits!"

"No," the Big Guy said sternly.

I scowled. "Geez, yer no fun. Everythin's better with energy attacks."

"So's having you under control. Try and not to give into your impulses, Cain. We're not a toy shop."

"Fine," I caved in with a sigh, an' went back into our head to let Davey-boy be Mr Sensible Guy.

"Wait," I said with a busy, overactive head. I gathered what little ideas I could muster from this type of scenario, tried to branch out. "I just thought of something. Couldn't we have Selma or any other psychic examine Emily's memories? We could try and find Scarlett and Dean."

Dwight shook his head. "We tried that, but Emily was unconscious when they were driven after their kidnapping, and when it came to driving to Wolf Park, so no leads there."

"Then how about we have Selma connect with Emily's mind and scan any neighbouring areas for Scarlett? I mean, they're mother and daughter, they've got nothing but positive feelings for each other, so no doubt those feelings would help Selma pinpoint her location."

"Yes, we tried that too, but it didn't work. No matter how far they scanned, Selma couldn't pick up anything. Dean must have set up some kind of defence against telepaths for this kind of thing."

"Shit." The need to punch a wall was rising. "That bastard's got everything covered." Thoughts of what could have been happening to Scarlett painted themselves in our psyche; strapped to a chair, eyes and cheeks bruised and beaten into large purple and black lumps, tears streaming down the ruptured land of her face and she struggles in vain to escape her confines; suspended from the ceiling with her back bare and home to many large and bloody cuts; knife marks scattered all over her arms and legs. In all of these, she screams to stop, to be let go, to see her mum, and words that are lost as every instance of pain strike her innocent face. He laughs. He grins. He is all-too content. I stopped myself from letting vomit rise from our throat.

Dwight laid one large hand onto our shoulder, with enough weight to nearly tip us over. "Are you feeling alright, guys?"

I nodded. "Forget how we're feeling. We're gonna see Emily."

"Very well. She's still in shock, bare that in mind."

"Will do," I said listlessly as I shook his other hand. His grip was as powerful as ever. It gave us some of his strength, and we felt grateful for it as we walked off.

Chapter 20

A Moment of Comfort

It was surreal to walk up to Emily's front door, looking back at how, just a few days before, we were inspecting an empty house with workmates at every corner, the echoes of a disruption, the taunting note on Emily's bed to drive the knife in further. I knocked on the door gently, as though the house had been a victim as well.

"Hello, Emily? It's us."

The door opened, and there was Emily, still in the same clothes as before, a single tear running down her otherwise restrained face.

"Hi," she muttered in a low voice. Before we could say anything, she stepped aside to let us through with a small gesture of the hand. We weren't able to ignore the clothes' odour as we went in, constant wearing mixed with anger and distress.

Silence reigned as we entered the living room and sat on the opposing sofas, Emily covering her mouth with her hands, and Cain and I trying to find some way to start a conversation. As I stared at her, I was swamped with self-frustration.

"Did you beat that large guy?" she asked.

"Y-yes," I managed to say.

"They said they found you near a bridge, dead. I worried if the fight might have been too much for your body to handle. To lose Scarlett, and you two..." She stopped herself as her voice rose.

"She'll be fine, don't worry." Easier said than done. "We'll get her back. We work with some damn fine people, they'll help us out."

Emily nodded, reassuring herself with a calm, "Okay, she'll be fine, she'll be fine."

I got off our sofa and moved over to Emily's, sitting beside her; at first I was reluctant, but then went through with putting an arm around her.

"Thanks," she said, "but I'm alright. I'll manage." I removed the arm from her, knowing that she was a strong woman, no matter what.

I took over my shift. "Kid, I, uh, I just wanna say that yer great an' all, an' even though it doesn't look like it, all the dark shit goin' on's gonna be washed away. You ain't gotta worry after we show that guy what's for. An' if ya need a hug, ask Davey-boy; I ain't good with that kinda stuff." I had no idea how to end this, so I just gave a couple o' awkward pats to the head.

"Thanks, Cain. I hope – know – that you'll do what you have to do. I should have prepared myself for him. Maybe then, my little girl wouldn't be suffering right now." She sniffed, an' there was another tear.

Taking the handle, I said, "Don't blame yourself. Cain and I are kicking ourselves as it is; we don't want you to be in that bandwagon. Dean's ridiculously tough, and even then, none of us could have expected him to have friends."

"That woman, she seemed to hate being around them. Daisy, that was her name."

Our mind flung back to the moment at Wolf Park where Daisy called out Dean, and his ordering her to stay quiet.

"We remember her. What's she like?"

"Nice, and worried. She kept checking up on us to make sure we were okay; she'd try and give us some of her food, and there was a lot of it, mostly gum."

We pictured the lady pushing along a huge airline trolley packed with different brands of bubble gum, and offering them to Emily and Scarlett.

"Makes me wonder how she got caught up with those fellas," I said, puzzled.

"I guess she was forced along," Emily muttered.

Depleted of anything else to say, I asked, "Do you want us to stay with you for tonight?"

279

"No, thanks. Just… let me know when you're able to get Scarlett back, please."

"Alright. What are you going to do, then?"

"Ring up Trevor, tell him Scarlett's phone got damaged, might need a new one. I don't want him to call her up and find… *him* answering it, instead. Just act like everything's normal, and that she's as busy as always. For his sake." She kept up a strong front.

"Do you still love him?"

"No. I still care for him, as a friend, and… he made us happy for so long."

"I understand. Take care, Emily." We hugged, and for a moment that felt like forever, I loved her more deeply than I ever had before.

Chapter 21

Unpleasant Dreams

The battlefield in our dreams had the same tainted smell of blood, rust and pain as it had all those centuries ago. The mud and grass, stomped on by countless men in armour, felt weak and worn as Cain and I moved as one swiftly, experiencing a raw power within us with every step and swipe of a sword. It was raining, the drops against our face feeling so good, almost refreshing, even as our short beard grew wet. The mist could have made it difficult to make out the French warriors up ahead, but our eyes, sharper than the longsword dubbed Joseph in our hand, were miles ahead of theirs. The weather wasn't a problem; all that mattered was fighting for—

Good, was it? Fighting for good. At least, that's what we were told. Good, which was God's work, in His Name, and the King, as appointed by Him.

The French were defenceless against our longsword and Cain's claws, taking one soldier out at a time in a kind of weaponry rhythm. Sword through one, claw in another's chest, sword crashing through a shield, claw slicing into an arm.

There was yelling everywhere, like the whole world deemed it the sound of the hills screaming as their steep bodies were met with the thunder of swords and lighting of our speed. Allies of both old and new, novice and veteran, supported us through blood-stained teeth while they managed to fight their own enemies.

Everything felt good, as a terrible surge of excitement washed over us, determined to do our bit in saving people, the innocent, from those who had been branded villains to us. This time, this place, this moment, it was grand, though I thought in spite of this, was this doing any good, slaughtering others? Fighting for—

Others? Fighting for others? The King and his God and England, yes, but what of France and its people? Surely they had a God on their side, too?

The bodies of hundreds of men laid behind us. We knew, there was no point in turning to see. Our title, The English Devil, was there for a reason.

Blood everywhere. Our armour was coated in it, already drying and brown in places. How many years had we spent on the battlefield, annihilating every foe? Fighting for—

Fighting to continue to be a puppet, that was it. We remembered now. Our 'friends', our mentors, allies in the War, saw us only as a weapon, a walking blade easy to handle with the right words. Helping others was the bait for me; the chance for a fantastic fight like no other was Cain's, at the height of the Voice fuelling him with insane bloodlust.

No more enemies left, and we were finally tired. The sword fell to the blood-and-rust-coated ground with a soft *thud*. With nothing else to see but the hills, we turned around, expecting to see a breadcrumb trail of corpses that we would grieve over in guilt.

There were hundreds upon hundreds of Emilys and Scarletts scattered across the field, piled into flesh-skinned mountains. We dropped to our knees, the rain cold and stinging like acid. Dean's laughter, vile and poisonous, muted our screams.

Chapter 22

Troubled

We got outta bed, our body hot an' experiecin' an odd faux-sweat sensation as we adjusted to reality. The darkness made me think we were gonna be attacked by some shadow-dwellin' monster, but thankfully Davey-boy bein' there reassured me that we were fine. Splashin' water on to our face in the bathroom didn't calm our nerves, 'specially mine. The guy in the mirror lookin' back at us was like a ghoul. My yellow eyes were tiny glowin' specs surrounded by black circles, while the rest o' the face was just a pale chalky mess waitin' to be rubbed out. That nightmare, bein' in the War again an' enjoyin' all that shit I did while Davey-boy felt all conflicted… I wanted to claw our eyes out so that we couldn't see our reflection.

"Fuck Dean. Fuck 'im. On top o' all the stuff he's done, fuck 'im for makin' us think back to that. No way to get ridda the Voice, huh? Bullshit. I don't count on reelin' onto every word as true."

'Given what he's told us, it's very difficult to consider if it's true or false,' Davey-boy said carefully. 'The only thing we've got to go on is that memory he gave us.'

"Ugh, that." A shiver trailed across our back an' a small headache pulsed away. "That was terrible. Not the least that it felt like yer typical mad scientist set, the pain we felt on that doohickey – I don't wanna revisit that, either."

'Consider this, Cain – he gave us a memory, one that may very well be real, at least I think it is. From that, we can derive that we were experimented on by some unknown faction, and that we were used for a less-than-pleasant purpose, with the Voice added to ensure that. Now, Dean's working for them, so if we get to Dean…'

"We get to them. Maybe give 'em a nice bit of karma when we do, five across their dumb lil' faces." I stared at my hands an' their sharp nails, maybe too eagerly in hindsight, but it lightened me up enough to forget about the dream an' sweat.

'Too violent for my taste, but in the right direction.'

I looked into the mirror again an' yelled; an eyeless soldier was in our place, its face so badly scarred an' shredded that I couldn't tell if it was male or female. It was breathin', its chest – or rather, the big gapin' wound slashed across their pecs that dribbled with dark bubblin' blood – heaved up an' down slowly.

'It'll go away, Cain. Just look away,' Davey-boy instructed me. But I didn't. Not intentionally, though; my instincts, the really primal scraps in my mind that made me an animal, kicked in. I squeezed my eyes shut before sendin' a fist into the mirror. I dunno if it was cuz o' fear or anger in bein' reminded of our guilt by a made-up ghost, but it happened. However, I knew one thing for certain – glass on yer hand hurts like hell, 'specially the big shards.

"Agh, goddammit!"

'Cain, for God's sake—'

"Sorry, sorry, sorry. I shoulda listened." I made up for it by binnin' the glass an' removin' the parts in my knuckles. While waitin' for the hand to heal, I put on some clothes, includin' my black coat an' Stetson. "I gotta talk to someone about all this, y'know? Release all the stuff that's been held up, lighten the load."

'Who do you want to talk to?'

"You know who."

'Are you sure about that? What if she finds it difficult to look at you later on?'

"Then I guess that's that, the chances o' bein' with my crush get crushed, an' I move on."

'But you won't.' He knew from experience.

"You're right, man. I'll just pretend."

Jackie's house was squashed between two bigger ones, like a kid holdin' their folks' hands, an' if anything, I felt pretty damn small myself. I knocked on the door a couple o' times an' waited, not fussed about the rain makin' us wet an' causin' my hair to glue to me.

"Who is it?"

"Me – I mean, us. It's Cain right now."

I heard her unlock the door, an' then she opened it, wearin' an undone white dressin' gown, showin' off her pyjama bottoms an' blue shirt.

"Cain? Why are you here? Do you know what time it is?"

"Hey, Jack-Cat, I'm sorry, it's just that we – that I needed to talk to someone, 'bout some personal stuff."

"It's to do with what's been going on, isn't it?"

"Kinda. It'd be better if we could come in an'… talk, ya know?"

"Okay, come on."

It felt so warm inside, the 'drips' an' 'drops' an' 'plinks' o' water comin' off us made it feel intrusive, the last thing I wanted to be.

"Are you thirsty?"

"I'd kill for… I'd love a beer, thanks." I picked a bottle o' cheap cider out o' the fridge once we entered the kitchen. I was surprised to see, on top o' the kitchen table, a white one-eared kitten, thin but fluffy around the chest, talkin' to us in little 'mews'. The sight o' cute animals would have me gushin' over 'em, but I felt nothin'.

Jackie picked it up an' stroked it, the little fella purring like it was given a sensational massage. When she talked to it, it wasn't like between a pet and its owner, but a more personal, matter-o'-fact discussion.

"Julian, what are you doing up at this hour? You should be with Adam and Ellen. Come on, get plenty of rest." She pointed to a small pink fluffy bed in the corner, filled with two other white kitties. Julian 'mewed' again, his lil' yellow eyes glancin' over at mine.

"Don't worry, they're friends of mine," Jackie answered. "Now come on, off you go, be nice and snugly with your brother and sister." She put him on the floor, where he wondered off to bed to explore more o' the kitchen.

"I've had these little fellows for a few weeks, and they're little troublemakers. I swear, it's like they don't even understand me. I know that they're babies, but still, I was learning to talk at their age. Being on an alien planet is weird. No offence."

"None taken, Jack-Cat. Anyway…" I took a huge swig o' my cider; it was too sweet for my taste, but what the hell, I needed the booze. "Gotta talk."

Jackie nodded, and sat down on one o' the chairs by the table. "Alright, then. Whatever it is, however bad it is, you can tell me."

I spent a few sour minutes lookin' into my bottle, which was transparent, attractive, filled with more sweet, useful stuff than me. Can I even envy a bottle?

"A long time ago – we're talkin' six to seven centuries ago – Davey-boy an' I were travellin' along in England, one foot at a time. Back then, I wasn't the same guy you're talkin' to right now. Sure, I'm a jerk, I ain't sugarcoatin' it, but I wasn't as chatty, sensible or thoughtful in the War."

"The War?"

"The Hundred Years War, Jack-Cat. I wanted to fight, to bleed, to feel pain an' death an' deal it to others. Sayin' that I was just violent, *that* is sugarcoatin' it. I *was* violence, every second o' every day we were spent chained together. Davey-boy had to carry the burden o' my existence for hell-knows-how long. To him, I was a demon, a monster bred to butcher left an' right with no shit given for anyone but myself. An' you know what? He was right, now that I think about it. Dean told us I was meant to kill, I was made that way, with a Voice ringin' in our ears, tellin' me, orderin' me to kill humans, an' I barely had a mind at the very start, so it worked."

"By the Saints of Tranamus… you mean you were programmed to do that? How cruel! It's monstrous." She was startled alright, her eyes wide with horror and bright with the help o' the kitchen lights.

"Yeah, preachin' to the choir there. Yer safe, don't worry. I've been neutered, so to speak. Anyhow, we were in England, an' we ended up bein' a knight for all our troubles. We musta

286

saved some knight through flashy fightin', I think; the details get messier every year. So they found out we was two guys in one body, there's a huge panic, but then it's decided that angel or demon, we knew how to kill a man. Davey-boy's fed lies that the French are in need o' dyin' on account o' goin' against England an' its King, who was God's Number One Guy."

"His number one guy? Is that what humans really believe in?"

"Used to, with them bein' backwards-ass, filth-covered idiots at the time."

"I was going to say that that's what my people believe in." My face was struck red.

"Oh. Okay, I'll bump my head on the way out. If ya turn out to be a princess, I can't afford to piss off the Holy Royal Jack-Cat Clan. Had enough royal families tailin' after us as it is." I cleared my throat, desperate to get back on track. "Speakin' o' which, the King pretended to be a nice guy to us, if he wasn't. Tough lil' teeth o' mine pokin' out as I tore into meat on the table as we talked; musta been hard to hide his disgust."

"How long were you in the War for? The whole hundred?"

"No, just thirty-seven years, an' we don't regret it. It was easy for me at first, cuz I loved a good fight with lotsa blood. Davey-boy grew more an' more concerned that he was on the wrong side… o' the world, that is."

"I can't imagine how you both felt after all those years. I've been in my fair share of fights, but to spend all that time on a battlefield for something you're not even sure of, it's enough to give me nightmares." The uncomfortable shuffle an' starin' at her knees made it all the more apparent that she wasn't used to stories like this.

"Good thing ya didn't have to live through it," I assured her. I almost smiled, but I knew it'd be a fake one, an' she would too.

"And to think, wars happening everywhere over things that can be so petty…"

"Nothin' we can do about it, eh? It's cuz o' our... experience that we refused to get involved in any more, just concerned with savin' innocents. On that battlefield, there were friends who weren't friends, just labelled that cuz they were on the same side, beautiful fields and hills soaked in people's innards, countless innocents, morals and values twisted, everyone sufferin'... world gets pretty bad pretty fast. The Voice fuelled me through all that like coal in an old train, but as it wore on, I started to get – an' I can't believe I'm sayin' this – bored. Not disgusted, not annoyed, not pained, just bored. That's when Davey-boy an' I agreed to find a way to stop this thing drivin' me to maim, an' it's worked for the most part. We wanna find out who made us like this, trapped like this, get answers."

Jackie clasped her hands over her mouth while her eyes (so big so sharp so lovely) were slicin' through mine, wider than what they were before. Fear, nothin' else but that. Ya can't mistake it for anything else once you've seen it on yer enemies' faces, no matter the subtlety. There weren't no bulgin' eyes, no wide revealin' mouth, no red-pink discolouration in her ears; I just had to see it in her slit pupils, an' I felt like leavin' the room to save her from gettin' even more nightmares. But I couldn't, even though she was too good for me.

"Sorry if this is too much for ya, Jackie. I ain't experienced in sayin' all this to someone. It's creepy for you bein' in the same room as a movie monster, am I right?"

She removed her hands an' said slowly, almost like she was lost in a dream, "I don't think you're a monster, Cain. I know what it's like to have blood forced on your hands and look at them in shame, but you were someone else. As you said, it was that Voice that made you do it, and whoever it was who put it there. I don't blame you for anything you did before."

My eyes sprang wide open, mouth hangin' like a goldfish, stupid-lookin' an' speechless. Jackie went down the same road as me? Okay, not the exact same one, but enough to get a very similar view o' yourself. I still saw her as better than me, even before I asked her for details; I just had to know.

"You – I had no idea, Jackie. I here I was mopin' about my problems. What happened, if it's cool to ask?"

Jackie closed her eyes an' breathed in an' out, clearin' her head as she recalled. When she opened her eyes an' talked, fear was deeply sown into her voice, pain from years ago hangin' offa every word.

"It happened when I was a child. I was coming of age, and there was a passage of right for that, mandatory no matter what. The adults – my parents and an elder representative of my people – took me to a forest beyond the domed town I lived in, lying past the single locked entrance. These great big forests separated us from the other towns and big cities, filled with so many different people. I was only eight years old, so afraid of failing the event, afraid of what I might do. Mother said not to worry, I'll be fine. Once we were in the forest, they chanted how this, for the young to fend for themselves and kill in the wildlands, was in honour of our primitive ancestors, like Julian, Adam and Ellen over there. Then they made their way to the town entrance, intending to leave me behind. I grabbed my father's ceremonial robes and I cried and cried to him not to leave me."

"Please tell me they didn't."

"He said they had to, because it was tradition, and he looked at me like I was a coward and that he was ashamed."

I nearly broke my bottle as my grip tightened around its neck. I didn't know if they were alive or not, but the need to punch her parents coursed through me as naturally through the air in my lungs and the Voice when it used to rattle in my head constantly.

"I spent an hour by that door once it closed. I was all tears and fists, calling out to my parents, but it sunk in that they wouldn't come back for me until the morning, using my scent to find me. On my own, hearing all the noises, all the voices of things I couldn't see and didn't want to see, there's no worse fear for a child. Under any other circumstances, a child would have enough hope to imagine their parents to arrive soon, because of their love. Only the glow of the small lamps by the side gave me some tiny comfort."

"Do ya think they love you?"

Jackie stared at her hands with disgust curling her lips briefly before she looked back at me. "To this day, I convince myself that they still do. Some children on my world get used to the distance they're bound to have with their elders and just move on with life. Others don't, especially after the coming-of-age event. I was still by the door when I heard the sound of twigs snapping nearby. I turned my head towards the darkness, trying to adjust to the night – which I would five years later – and trembled at the sight of a lastur, a large bird, twice my size, one of the most ferocious creatures on my planet.

Black feathers sheltered it from the darkness, but the outline caught by the lamps told me it was as broad as the door. The white feathers that crowned its head distinguished it as an old but experienced hunter. Its tough silver legs, the snap of its crooked beak, those piercing blue eyes; it was ready to pounce at me and tear me into as many pieces as it liked. I stood up and had my back against the wall. My heart felt like it was about to give out at any moment. Fear got me by the legs. Then it lunged at me. I jumped out of the way and it crashed into the door. It was dazed and I kept telling myself to run away, so I blindly dashed into the forest."

I pictured the whole thing in my head like a movie, almost distracted from my case by everything she told me. "Holy hell, that's like a horror movie. How'd it turn out?"

"It was five hours of hide-and-seek before it ended. I was tired, the adrenaline forced me to stay awake. I was so hungry, so thirsty, but my survival came first, and I hated the whole thing. It was like a nightmare made reality. The lastur would always feel my presence no matter where I was. Finally, I was cornered inside the base of a tree trunk, the lastur's head stuck in the hole leading to it, trying to bite me greedily, inches away from my face. Crouched, terrified, desperate, it was only then that I resorted to using my claws. I swiped at it in a blind panic, got it in the eye, and another along the head before I accidentally sliced its throat. The creature died with a sick gasp – oh God, I can still recall how dirty its breath smelled – and its one remaining unbloodied eye fixed on me.

"The shock crept in eventually, and the blood and skin wormed and stuck under my fingernails told me that what I had done had actually happened. I had been forced to take a life when there wasn't any reason for it, no matter how justified it was in everyone else's eyes. Yeah, it was trying to kill me, but if I hadn't been sent out into the forest, it may have lived for a few more years. And what if I had died? Did my parents ever wonder if that was possible, or were they too arrogant or optimistic or just plain stupid? All those thoughts were woven into my head through the rest of my time in the tree trunk, and they're still there, even if it's just a throwaway thought or if I'm asleep.

"Sleep. I wasn't lucky enough to have that luxury at that point. It was impossible with its face and feathers and blood so close to me, eyeing me, wishing to still get me in some way. When I was found and taken back home, all the hugs and praise and smiles my parents provided me couldn't stop me from reliving that moment in my nightmares for the next two weeks, only then, the lastur won, tearing me and picking at my bones. I guess, in some way, it won after all."

She closed her eyes tightly and then blinked a few times before wiping away the tears.

"God, I can only imagine how tough it musta been for someone yer age. Big ol' night terrors for a kid so small. How did it feel…to kill for the very first time?"

"It…" She stared off, mind all over the place as she pieced her answer together. "It was relieving, at first. I was glad to be safe before I realised what I had done. When I wasn't suffering from bad dreams, I was plagued with thoughts of whether or not I would end up killing again, and who would end up torn away by my claws – family, friends? Since I was forced into having to kill, my imagination branched off into other scenarios where I'd be forced to take a life. Every day at school, there wasn't a face I'd look at without picturing them with their hands squeezing away at my throat, or trying to bash my brains in with a rock or a pole. Every day I'd be forced to kill them in my mind, and feel the same way as I did that one night. Even eating dinner with my family was hard."

My skin grew pale and cold. My brow creased as I had difficulty imaginin' any of this happenin' to Jackie – her face was too pretty, her smile was too pretty, all of her was to pretty for somethin' so awful. "Did it ever stop?" I managed to let out, despite a lump in my throat.

"It never stops. I can't even look at anyone at work and see them with good intentions."

Somehow, my face dropped lower than it did before. "Jeezuz." An' then, the closest question to my heart, ready for the answer to tug an' stamp it out into a red pulp. "Even— even me?"

The slightest reluctant bob of her head agreed. "I'm sorry. Nothing can be done about it; therapy, drugs, mental blocks, they might as well not exist. Even you're not as much as a lost cause as me, right? At least you've been able to move on to some extent. As for me, I can't hold down a relationship or social life."

"You ain't a lost cause, Jackie, I mean it."

"You don't. It's sweet of you to say so, but—"

"I mean it. I don't lie about this kinda stuff, an' I don't lie to someone I love."

For a sec, everythin' froze. Kitties were sleepin' and snugglin', yellow kitchen bulbs strong an' bright against our skin an' the shiny kitchen countertops, our mouths shut, unsure o' what to do or say. Time slowly breathed back into the room.

"Holy shit, did I just say that? That I... I... you? I did, didn't I?"

292

Jackie whispered, "Yes, you did," her face just as surprised as mine.

I sighed. "Well, at least that's distracted us from our woes for a while. Is this a bad thing? I can't tell. Never really…loved someone before. Really weird circumstances."

"I'll say," again in a whisper.

"Want me to leave? Don't wanna trouble you no more. Be on my way." I got up, red, light-headed (from embarrassment or cider? Riddle o' the ages), slightly pissed, had to look around a couple o' times just to remember where the door to the hallway was. Before I could take a step in the right direction, Jackie's voice spoke up. She was light, calm, strong, just as powerful as she was when she bulked up. She carried comfort, a warm comfort that made me feel like a child.

"No, you don't have to go, Cain. You're still welcome here. After all you said, I don't think of you any less, and I'm sure you can say that same for me too. I'm not looking at a monster right now – I'm looking at a man."

Never realised how beautiful her eyes were up-front. So bright, so detailed like paintin's.

"Okay, Jack-Cat. I'll stay for a bit longer. Thanks."

"Good. You're welcome." When she smiled, I felt like I was caught by her fangs. "Do you want another drink?"

"Ain't finished my first one, but sure."

"Double good." She grabbed one for me, an' one for her.

We talked for a long time, an' I didn't leave her house 'til mornin'.

Chapter 23

Shifting Along

The next day featured an unusual little guest appearance at IISEP HQ – Brad walking a cuffed Slaml and Gib, still in their Laurel and Hardy shapes, to the building from his much-more-usual parking space, his face frozen into a scowl. Cain and I found this out first-hand, having just made our way to the place when Brad had pulled up and forced them out of the car, the duo complaining all the way.

"Give us a chance!"

"No need to be rough!"

Brad was having none of it. "Rough is all you get after I caught you spying on me and my wife at home," he let out with a strained, almost whispery voice not to let his anger rise to shouting.

Naturally, we couldn't let this go unnoticed, so we went over to them. "Hello, there, gents," I said, tipping my brown replacement Stetson as I did, though it didn't feel as good as having dear old nostalgic red instead. "I see you wrangled up some trespassers. Did they give you any trouble?"

Gib and Slaml shifted their troubles over to us, telling Brad (no, begging him) to let them go back into the car or to rush them into HQ, their voices high, loud, desperate like we had them at gunpoint.

"Quiet," Brad commanded, and they were. They gave us weak smiles and waves (well, wiggling their fingers up and down like they were exercising them). "Not really, David. Came across their car perched up by the pavement in plain sight of the living room, peering in with binoculars."

"Guys, there are other ways to watch telly, like buying one," I said, throwing my best joke at them. No one laughed.

Brad continued. "I shot their wheels with my hand, and they were too scared to run."

"We were only doing our job," Slaml muttered. "Mr Gregory said he'd paid us extra if we checked up on you. Double, he said." A crack to the rib from Gib's elbow led to his turn to talk.

Gib's tiny moustache wrinkled as he moaned. "Stashing us into that bunker was too much! We're claustrophobic."

"Then you should have turned into flies and amused yourselves," Brad shot back. "Come on, in you go."

Slaml whispered in Gib's ear, "We should try that some time."

"I assume," I said uneasily, "that you've taken a few precautions? If Dean's targeting you and, God forbid, everyone at the facility…"

"Yes. Jane's decided to stay at her sister's until this is all over. These idiots don't know where she is, so even if they somehow get away, there's nothing new to relay to him."

Gib cleared his throat. "Mm-hmm. 'They' have names, you know."

"And I don't care."

"Fair enough," Gib whimpered.

*

Slaml and Gib sat in the interrogation room, unsure, uncomfortable, unhappy, un-anything. Frederick, a professional interrogator with the power to know when someone lies, sat across them, his wavy blonde hair and its one curl sticking out as the only light colour in the room and blessing him with a slightly angelic appearance alongside his baby face.

The interrogation itself lasted for about two, two-and-a-half hours, mostly due to the duo's fumbling. For instance, Frederick asked them why they'd taken up their current forms, and they winded up giving him a biography of their previous forms and asking him if he'd never watched any

Laurel and Hardy films, a conversation that ate up ten minutes; to say nothing of the frustration that burned behind us, Dwight, Jackie (her face a little red when she saw us) and Brad, who twiddled with his robotic hand in an attempt to occupy himself. His tranquillity gave all of us the heebie-jeebies.

I rang up Emily when I exited the room some forty-five minutes in, letting her know of the current events and that it might make it easier to get a hold of Scarlett easier, which felt like a lie despite the honesty of my words.

"I want her back so much," Emily uttered. She sounded weary, tired. How much sleep did she get last night?

"We know, and we will."

"Will you, though?"

"Emily, you don't ever have to doubt, and you know that."

"I had a thought the other day. It was wrong of me to have it, and I don't know why it came to me, but it did for some reason."

I was apprehensive, but I pressed on. "What was it?"

"It was... how things would have been so much better if we never got in touch again, back when I was in uni. If I hadn't recognised you, bugged you until I learned and still wanted to learn so much about you. Scarlett would be safe, we'd be going out to lunch or seeing a movie and just being happy to be with each other. It's like no matter what, there's something dark always following you two, like it wants to get in the way and ruin everything and everyone."

As she stopped, I took the time to get rid of the tears and tried to not let her know that it was hard to bear hearing the truth. "I see."

"Don't hate me for this. Like I said, it was a random thought, it didn't feel like me."

"We get it. The worst of times bring out the stuff we never expected to have. Don't think for a moment that we hate you, because that's not true for one moment."

"Okay. Thanks for keeping me up to date, you know?"

"Any time. Want us to see you at some point today?"

"I'm fine, I'll hold up. Besides, the fellas guarding my place keep me from being lonely. Bye, boys."

"Bye." I didn't want to hang up, but I did. I wanted to forget about Slaml and Gib and just talk to her and see her face until we had a lead and worked everything out. She was my best friend and, in spirit, daughter, and while it killed me to hear her words over the phone, I still loved her. The day I would stop loving her would be the day Cain and I finally die. Hopefully we would be able to save Scarlett before anything… irreversible happened.

At least Slaml and Gib's foolishness brought a faint spark of amusement. They apparently had a history of enjoying and copying the styles of comedic groups, especially duos, and proceeded to shapeshift into a few when asked; Abbot and Costello; the Marx Brothers; Ronnie Barker and Ronnie Corbett, and the more recent (as in, a decade ago) youth-faced talents of Jason Blessford and Tony Perkins. Their impersonations, physically, vocally, stylistically, were spot-on, even providing their own jokes, which they had a habit of practising when home. When asked about their true forms, however, that's when they drew the line. It's been so long since they started their Earthbound integration to check out the locals that reverting to it would be… I can't believe they said this… alien to themselves. They had gotten quite used to being in human shapes nearly every day, apparently.

Brad left the interrogation viewing, emotion seeping through the cracks of his wall-like face.

"Off to anywhere, Brad?"

"Shooting range," he gave stiffly. "I have to practise my aim with this hand."

"Wouldn't it scorch the targets?"

"Not if I dial back the power input to its lowest." He pointed at a small series of black buttons on the back of the shallow imitation-flesh, each one with a number from one to six.

I shrugged. "Relieving stress, then? I don't blame you."

He left without saying a word, flexing his fingers with every step.

Once again, Slaml and Gib knew nothing of Dean's whereabouts, despite Frederick's heavy mention of the kidnapping of a mother and daughter, and said daughter's current imprisonment. They only knew that their payment would be the biggest they'd ever receive, and that their only means of contact came from blocked phone calls that would ring at the end of each day. Any attempts at tracing the money via bank account was met with the details withheld at his insistence (a rather annoying bank feature brought into effect seventeen years ago).

Until the next call, the two were to be detained at HQ. However, they were quite aware of the consequences of their actions, so rather than have them spent six to seven years in an IISEP cell, Cain and I decided on a more agreeable and productive approach with Dwight's permission.

We swapped places with Frederick and gave the shapeshifters a lengthy spiel about the benefits of working for the IISEP; to be among fellow star-travellers; exchange cultural knowledge and practices; marvel over the extensive library, especially educational videos; get paid with more than enough money to end their worries (after all, the pay is *very* good); be a part of the Christmas office parties; get a parking space; have donuts on Tuesdays.

In no time at all, they agreed, their false faces smiling as the four of us discussed every little detail of the job's perks. They'd be the first shapeshifters under HQ employment, and hopefully the most useful.

Well, one outta two ain't bad.

Chapter 24

A Little Chat

Dean called later that afternoon at four o'clock, in the midst of an early Chinese takeaway dinner. The caller I.D. recognised it as 'Scarlett', and from there came the need to talk to her, to force him to put her on. Neither Cain nor I spoke at first when we answered, determined to hear what he had to say.

"Hello, there, my little bounty hunter. Seems you've taken in those bumbling oafs – I should never have hired them. For shapeshifters, they're not very chameleonic. But that's not really important, to be honest, because I've got some good news for you, and I just know you're going to love it. You can't say no to this, it's a limited-time only offer. What's that? Say something. Don't tell me you're tired or even falling asleep, boys, or else you'll miss out big time. Then again, if you do, that means I'll have more moments with that red-haired little skank."

Fire burned in my voice. "Speak. Now."

There was a light chuckle. "My, my, that got you going. Were you afraid of what I was going to say at first, or do you just want to hear me talk for as long as you want? Something tells me it's the latter."

"Only in your dreams. Tell us, what's this 'offer'? You're going to hand Scarlett back, aren't you?"

The air of a game show host struck him – we could see him in our mind's eye, grinning with every word. "*Ding ding ding!* Congratulations, you got that right! Yes, on tonight's show, your prize is one terribly traumatised teenager who comes with her own broken wrist and bruises on her chest! Isn't that something? To receive it, please meet up at Balance, the Mexican-Italian restaurant in town, where our own Daisy Philadelphia will be to hand the brat over! And as an added bonus, you get to wine and dine with the not-so-lovely Daisy, but beware: her stomach knows no bounds!"

"Much like your eagerness to cause chaos."

"Oh, you're so kind, Mr Short. Tell me, do you always feel the need to attach yourselves to others? They're mortal, they'll die no matter what you do. One moment, they're fine, blink and they've been buried for decades. Follow my advice – see them as throwaway toys, it's so much fun that way."

"And then we'll be like you, which will be one heck of a cold day in hell. We've more a penchant for saving, not destroying."

He sighed in delight. "God, I love it when you go full-hero on me – you're so melodramatic, like you've been studying comic books."

There was a substantial amount of truth there. But dammit if I wasn't going to let him know he was right. "Oh, as if *we're* the only dramatic ones, Mr Gregory. You pack so much ham into everything you do that it's amazing that you haven't suffered from long-term stomach pains."

With that kind of insult, I thought he'd respond quickly. Instead, there was a good five seconds on silence before Dean finally let out, with a great belly laugh and shout that nearly blew the phone's speaker, "*AMAZING! HA HA!* You've *really* been holding on to that one for ages, haven't you?"

"I've been saving it for tossers like you."

"Consider it a success, David. Best insult I've ever heard. In fact, I'm quite honoured."

"Start a fan club or somethin'," I groaned.

"Now," I said, "back to the more important matters at hand, unless you want us to carry on turning our insults into a playground war."

"Very well," we heard Dean agree with a hint of annoyance. "The brat'll live a boring human life with some bad memories thrown in, courtesy of the good people you killed from the Hundred Years War, but at least I'll be free of her insufferable attitude. Kids these days, nothing but pampered smart-asses. As for the meet-up, make it eight-thirty tonight. Sound good?"

"Capable. Put her on."

"Can't. I have to prepare her for tonight." His final words oozed like dark honey. "Ciao, boys." He hung up, and we lost our appetite.

Chapter 25

Daisy

Brad drove his Clio through the town with barely a word, his grip on the steering wheel all too careful because his latest hand's strength; the fingers had dug in too deep, leaving a pretty awkward series of holes in the leather. Cain and I sat in the passenger seat, the silence between the three us uncomfortable. We were near the restaurant's location, give or take a minute. As we cut through the road while the sky was dark and shining with a few stars, I felt the need to speak.

"We'll be there soon, eh?"

"Yes."

"Can you… do us a favour?"

"What is it, David?"

"I know it's only for a little while, but can you protect Scarlett until this thing tonight ends? We'll call you when we're done."

A small sigh. "Very well. I'll bring her over to headquarters."

"Thanks. Emily's there, so they won't be apart for much longer," I said, only to help reaffirm this small piece of happiness to myself. Cain had no need of it.

'Gonna get to that food chick, get closer to Dean and GET ANSWERS NO MATTER WHAT,' he thought, circulating it in a loop through the ride the way you'd catch yourself unwittingly singing your favourite song over and over. Not the best person to be in the car with, but there you go. As long as he didn't blurt it out next to Brad, the uncomfortability wouldn't rise any further.

"You both care about Scarlett a lot, don't you?"

"Well, yeah. She's my – our best friend's daughter."

"I mean that you care about her more than what would be considered a given."

"You're right, Brad. We're old, you and everyone else are young; you end up seeing those close to you as family. We've never been a father, never knew if it would be a bad idea. Sometimes, I regret not going through with it, but I still hold back. In a way, we see Emily and Scarlett as the kids we never had. You lot at work are great, we've even got everyone down in a family tree as a joke."

"I see. Just wondering, what relative am I?"

"The standoffish uncle."

Brad gave a little smirk, quite an honour. "Very apt. I approve."

"Have you… ever thought about having kids?"

There was a brief silence between us, before breaking it with, "Jane and I thought about it, not entirely sure, like you. But since the accident… it'll take time to get back to that stage, if ever."

God, the uncomfortability rose like crazy, all the way to boiling-under-the-collar. "I'm sorry, Brad."

"Don't be. Focus on your issues. Speaking of which, here we are." The car slowed to a halt, the restaurant opposite the passenger's seat, and Cain and I got out to meet Daisy.

There she was, standing at the corner of the building with her body pressed against the brick wall like plaster. Her black hair was still in a bobcut, and her red lips gave off the feeling of cherries. Judging by the crossed arms and checking her watch in a huff, she had been waiting for us for quite a while. Her tight jeans showed off her wide hips and thin legs, while her black-and-white striped shirt was tucked in and realising more of her slim figure.

As we went up to her, her head swayed in our direction and caught us, causing her face to light up with a small as she left the wall. Her mouth was motorised, stretched out by her smile and opened and closed rapidly as she chewed vigorously and greedily on some gum.

"Finally! You took your time, gentlemen." She raised her arm for a handshake, the hand stretched out as far as it could possibly go. The fingers were spread out in a way that looked like you'd strain them with effort, but with her face hungry with eagerness, they must have been relaxed instead.

The hyperactive energy booming from her voice, whimsical as it was, gave the impression that she had not grown up. "Hello, I'm Daisy, Daisy Philadelphia, and I am twenty-six years old and it is very nice to meet you, Mr Short and Mr Cain." This was all said as she continued to chew her gum rather noisily, though I had to admit she seemed experienced in doing so.

Taken aback by her politeness, I shook her hand. "Hello." She had quite a soft grip.

Cain wasn't exactly pleased with this, his opinion ringing angrily in our head.

'Fratenisin' with the enemy?! Screw that!'

Not wanting to disrupt things, I took to a mental comeback. 'Better a shake than a slap,' I retorted while Daisy shook our hand excitably like a small child, until she nearly had full control of my hand, even if she didn't know it. With that, I said to her in a neutral voice, "Where is she?"

Daisy's face darkened, worry spreading and reminding her of the situation. "Please, go to the alley. Follow me." She slowed her chewing to a halt and shifted around the corner into the corresponding alley, shadows consuming the space between brick-laid walls. I eyed Brad's car and nodded to indicate that Scarlett would come soon, before wandering into the darkness after Daisy.

'If the kid's hurt, I'm gonna do the same to that stick-figure bitch,' Cain thought in a feral growl that brought back too many bad memories for the both of us.

'I'm sure Jackie would like you then, Cain.'

'Why, you—'

'As much as I or Emily would want to, unless Daisy is as bad as her company, we do nothing, okay? Chances are, we might take it too far, especially you.' I turned my nose at some vomit that had dribbled along a wall before drying up.

'Hey, what did Jesus say – eye for an' eye an' all that?'

'Actually, it was "turn the other cheek".'

'Dammit, Jesus, why ya gotta be like that? Screw it, I'm takin' artistic license.'

By the time we reached the end of our inside discussion, Daisy had led us to her car, a red Mini. She opened the passenger door and led Scarlett out by the hand, the teenager's eyes covered by a black blindfold.

Daisy muttered to her, "Come on, dear, there we go," with sincere care, her accent slipping into French for a very brief moment. "The blindfold will come off in a moment."

"Is… is he… are they here?" Scarlett whispered. The fear in her voice, the utter dread, told us that something was wrong. The blindfold was an odd addition, but then we recalled that Dean had shown her what he called our worst moments, and the screams that Emily described. Oh God, the things she must have seen, the terrible things. Our stomach went everywhere.

"Scarlett," I called out softly, "we're here."

Cain went up for a quick, "Yup".

She shuddered. "Thank you." Daisy guided her to us with an arm gracefully around her shoulder before we took the girl's hand, which was met with an icy gasp.

"Don't take the cover off, for her sake," Daisy warned us. "She's seen a lot, and it would help if you hand her over to your friends first." Not a trace of dislike in her soft, smooth voice.

I nodded, frowning. "Alright." Keeping my grip steady, it was my turn to be Scarlett's guide-dog as I let her to Brad's car.

"Guys," Scarlett said, her voice so close yet distant in its panicked bluntness, "please don't try to talk to me. I can't bear to be around you. But I don't hate you; I'm scared. The things that man showed me, they're right in my brain. I'm on a battlefield, fighting people with swords and arrows

305

and…then you kill me, and you look so *wrong*, like a monster. And it keeps happening again and again, but the details are different. It's like I've got these memories that aren't mine, a ton of them. I can see them right now, in the dark. I just want to see Mum again."

'That ball-bustin' bastard's gonna pay!'

'Calm down, Cain.'

'Next time I see 'im, I'll rip his body into so many pieces, he ain't gonna come back for round three! An' then Tranue an' Daisy, they'll know too late that ya don't fuck with—'

'*Cain.*' My voice boomed in our brain like thunder in a storm.

That settled things. He was quiet for a second, and when he spoke again, he sounded small and apologetic, the way a child sounds when their parents tell them off. 'Sorry, David. Got too carried away there, y'know?'

'It's alright, Cain. Just relax. When Scarlett's with Brad, she'll be safe and sound.'

'But her lil' scared head. She's rememberin' the last moments o' the guys we killed back then, that's fucked up, an' don't even know how that's possible. How're we gonna—'

'Selma,' I suggested with ease.

'Right, got it,' he said, relieved.

'Hope to God it's not anything like the Voice,' a thought that made me want to hit myself for shattering the near hundred-percent hope we held on to.

Once we exited the alley, I stood behind Scarlett and removed the blindfold. Brad got out of his car and made a gesture signalling her to enter this safe zone on wheels.

"Take her to Selma," I told him. He accepted this with a nod. And then it came to Scarlett herself.

"Go with him. You'll be back to your mum in no time. You'll be home and in your bed and fall asleep listening to Alice Cooper in your ears. Then you'll have a nice lie-in and the two of you can go out to dinner and forget all this when you smile. The last couple of days will feel like seconds rushing through your mind. The days with your mum and dad, they'll be eternal; you won't forget them."

I imagined saying all of that to her when she crossed the road and got in and stared at us as Brad drove off. In some way, she probably knew it. The worst part for them was over, at least for now, mother and daughter together again. With heavy shoulders, I stretched our aching muscles and turned around to find Daisy looking at us, drying a teary face with a handkerchief, its body covered in tiny patterns of a mouth eating ice cream.

"Thank goodness she's away from him, poor thing," Daisy said before clearing her throat and tucking the cloth away into her jeans.

"Yeah," I sighed. My voice was weary, tired with stress. "So, what's the plan from here again?"

"Well, Dean wanted me to fight you – or 'challenge' you, as he called it – but I'm not one for violence." She resumed her habit of noisily smacking her lips with gum; I could see the worn-out wad as it bounced from tooth to tooth, a giant creased up ball, flashing with light pink, that had no doubt lost its taste.

"I can imagine. You were quite nice to Scarlett and her mother. For that, I'm very grateful."

Daisy shrugged. "I try to be nice when I can, which is most of the time," she said between chews. "Is it okay with we eat here?" She pointed at the restaurant with wild excitement, her rising voice matching that of a young girl. "I am incredibly famished. Haven't eaten in twenty minutes."

"What did you have beforehand?"

"A couple of burgers from the McDonald's up the road. Trust me, my metabolism is crazy. I need food, like, right now."

I rolled back my shoulders. "Fine, then, we'll have a bite."

"Great! Thank you so much!" Without warning she leaned forward and kissed us on the mouth, complete with

307

tongue action… and her gum slipping into our mouth. Ew. I tore us away from her, taking a good step back.

"What the he—" I stopped when I realised that the gum was still in our mouth, resting against our tongue, and took it out.

Just as I was about to throw it aside, Daisy took her palm out and pleaded, "Please give it back to me. That's the last piece of gum I have on me. It calms my nerves, plus it never feels stale."

I placed it into her hand, at which point she sent it back into her wide, needy mouth. Double ew.

"What the hell was that about, anyway? I say yes and you just snog me?"

Cain burst forth, riled up and teeth bared. "I got a girl on my mind, lady! Might even hook up with her." With that, he popped back into our head.

"I'm sorry," Daisy said meekly as she blushed, again letting her jaws make a stomping sound with her gum. "Hunger gets me really worked up, makes me quite, um, excitable."

"Uh, okay," I said with a very mild understanding. We knew appetites could get to you, make you desperate, hasty, frustrated, but this was unheard of. Maybe it was due to her high metabolism, but we could hardly imagine someone getting so starved that they'd warm themselves up with a bit of lip and tongue action. Still, she was honest.

Yeah, she looked fine, but if it ain't Jackie, it ain't worth kissin'!

Probably the nicest thing Cain's said in a while.

"Anyway," I said, "do you really fancy this restaurant? It's expensive."

"I'm not fussed about the money, just food. Mexican-Italian places sound so divine." She rubbed her stomach lightly with her fingertips as she let out a small breathy moan. Man, this woman was practically orgasmic from just the thought of entering the place. I wondered very briefly with Cain how she felt about baguettes.

"If that's what you want, then fine." I made sure to open the door for her – ladies first, after all, even if it's old-fashioned (then again, we were pretty damn old). She giggled at this gesture and jumped on the spot, attached with more giggles and a 'yay' before bouncing into the building. Were those burgers she had filled with sugar, or what?

The lady's childish eccentricity was quite surreal, like she was some children's cartoon character created by a load of coked up animators with a hint of Speed. Cain and I played around with potential names for a TV show with her – 'Dazzling Daisy' and 'Glut Gal' were a few contenders, though as we'd learn, the latter was very much appropriate and well-deserved.

Chapter 26

Got the Stomach for It?

Seeing her eat was a feast for the eyes. There was a feral and delightful pleasure in her as she gorged herself on everything the menu had. I am not even kidding, she ordered every item, food and drink alike, off the leather-bound six-page menu in such a casual manner that it was clear she had done this many times before. Cain and I just had a Coke that hid in the corner of one of the tables we sat by. We had been at the restaurant for an hour and a half by now. It was absolutely insane.

Spaghetti swirled into her mouth as tomato sauce decorated the corners of her lips, her eyes scanning the army of food converging on the two tables, evidently hungrier than her stomach could boast. As she gulped down the pasta, her mouth was assaulted by another helping, and this time she paused to actually taste the rich sauce that it flowed in, letting out a heavy moan.

"Dis is gooh," she mumbled before swallowing.

"If you're enjoying it, it must be, right?" I could only stare at her with amazement; specifically, confusing, stomach-churning amazement as she proceeded to send her fork into overtime and have it cram as much spaghetti and spicy rice into her as possible. Her cheeks bulged out at their fullest while she went through the tiring task of chewing the food to their absolute tiniest... and washing that down with three Cokes, like vodka shots.

"Wow. You, uh, you really weren't kidding about how hungry you were, eh?"

"Mmm-hmm," she replied with a nod, recovering from her soda-drenched throat's fizzy assault. "It's nuts, but I love it. I get to out-eat anyone, enjoy all of *this*. Where's the fun in wanting to get so full in such a short time?"

"I think it'd be in your wallet, or whoever else is paying," I quipped, with a little smile.

She snorted and let out a brief giggle. "That's really funny! That was meant to be a joke, right?"

"Yup," I said, somewhat flatly, slightly curious of her question.

She chuckled once more. "I'll have to remember that. I've tried coming up with some jokes about myself, but I'm not really that much of a comedian. I love funny stuff, but I don't think I've got the creativity for it, you know?"

"I guess your mind's hungry for something with a bit more flavour in it." I pointed at the many plates scattered around, compared to the tiny island I had, comprised of a Coke can and glass.

For the third time, Daisy laughed, this time letting out another snort. It seemed that she could laugh at just about anything; I'm hardly a master of comedy, more of a novice if anything. Observing the demolishment on her plates, I finally asked her what Cain and I had been wondering to ourselves.

"Have you always been like this, Daisy?"

"Nope," she replied as she wolfed down chicken strips in a barbecue glaze and salsa dip. "I didn't get to be like this until I was nine or ten. Kind of a private matter." Once she devoured every piece of chicken she could see, with her mouth glazed in different sauces, she moved her seat back and observed her belly, which had definitely grown since she sat down. No longer was it small and tight, nearly underweight; instead it had stretched out, reaching past an average waistline with a bulk of fat very much present, making it a round, squishy ball that stood out awkwardly along the rest of her thin body. It looked like it was trying to consume the rest of her frame. Daisy rubbed it, feeling how much it had grown, and patted it in triumph, with a small belch escaping her.

"All that food was delicious," she sighed, licking away the sauce across her mouth greedily. "And there's still a few

311

portions left. I don't think I'm ready to give up just yet, though. I need *more*, so much more, but I feel like I'm straining my normal limits. Well, as normal as I could be."

"My God," I muttered under my breath.

'What the hell?' I thought.

I was struck by that one word as it pricked our ears. "I'm sorry, *normal* limits?"

"Oh, I have this little ability to expand my body, inflate it like a balloon, if you can imagine. In the least, I can make my stomach even larger, give myself more of an opportunity to stuff myself."

"And at the most?"

"At the most, my entire body blows up into a massive ball. We're taking ten feet high, ten feet wide, my head, hands and feet just barely poking out."

"That's… quite something, Daisy," I let out in stilted surprise.

Her fork dug into some more rice. "I'm wondering, Mr Short, can I talk to Mr Cain? I don't mean to be rude, really, I just want to talk to you both."

"Okey dokey," I said as I sipped my Coke. "Here we go."

I took over, idly starin' at my drink can before makin' eye contact with the girl.

She sound all nice an' cheery, it felt a bit odd to me. "Hello, again, Mr Cain." She gave me a lil' wave, still holdin' her fork.

"Hey there. Just call me Cain."

"Are you having a good time?"

"Meh. You seem to be… having a really good time."

"Yeah. What's it like, being you?"

"Borin', mostly. Days are long, night are long, fights too short for my likin'."

"Hmm. Do you really like to fight?"

"I'm a natural. I might lose half the time, but I like to think I'm good at what I do." Track record's shit, anyway.

312

"Well, at least you try," she said just as reached for her nearest soft drink.

I struggled for words. "Yeah."

"I want to know," she said casually, "what you're like in bed."

"Wha-wha-what am I like? I'm, uh..."

Well, this was gonna be awkward if I told her the truth. I wasn't much for sex; too nervous to actually go through with it, let alone see a woman's... uh... important, unspeakable parts. I had to come up with somethin' believable, somethin' that definitely wasn't the concoction of a dumbass tryin' to impress a woman.

"...I'm, uh... yeah, I'm practically my own rival in love-makin'. I'm so fast that as soon as ya take your pants off, you're probably already pregnant. And I'm strong too, just poundin' women like a boxer beatin' at a punchin' bag – no bed is safe from me. Or floor. Or ceiling. Or anything with walls, for that matter. I have a tendency to break things. In fact, most of the damage done to my house is from all the sex I have. I just *give*, *give*, *give* like I'm fuckin' Santa Claus. But I do it in my own way, mixin' up a load o' techniques to create a style so interestin' and perfect that it'd be worth dedicatin' a whole sequel to the *Kama Sutra* just to explain it. In short, I'm a sexual Bruce Lee."

She looked at me like I was a weirdo. "What?"

"I... might've been exaggeratin'. No offence, but like I said, I got already got a girl in mind."

Daisy let out a snort an' a chuckle. "Oh my god, you read that wrong! I'm not into all that icky stuff, no, no. I mean, how do you sleep in bed? Do you lie on top of the sheets, or under? Me, I love to hug my pillow like crazy. I'm just interested in learning about people, that's all."

Idiocy washed over me. "Lady, you are nuts."

"Compared to my associates, or to the man who just called himself a 'sexual Bruce Lee'? Did you think I wanted you to give me a one-inch punch downstairs?"

I blushed. "Oh, right. I'll, uh, head off, then."

"No, please, I was just as—"

Switch.

"—king."

I sighed. "I'm sorry, Daisy, but Cain's a bit shy sometimes."

"No, I'm sorry. I shouldn't have asked him that." Those big eyes were genuinely determined to make up for it.

"Don't worry, he's like a teen. His ego will recover. Anyway, I think it's about time we went over our... mutual friend."

Her fork waved us a 'no'. "I'm sorry, I just – I just need to eat, okay? All of this stuff, with that kid, the stress really gets to me. No offence, I know it's a big thing that's hit you all – it's personal, after all – but I didn't know Dean or Tranue was gonna do all of... that."

"So, had you known beforehand, you wouldn't have gone with it?"

"Right on the dot." She nommed on three prawns at once. "Sowwy abow dis," she managed to say with a full mouth.

"Don't worry. You seem much nicer than that Tranue friend of yours."

"He's always had a... violent streak. The white-coats really got to him; I'm lucky I'm able to hold on to being nice." She grabbed a fistful of prawns, her hands seeming to act on their own accord, trying to feed her with anything she could see, even more so, and started shoving them into her mouth. I guess her stress-eating ballooned into stress-shovelling, so I just let out a light huff.

I wanted to call her out, but there was somethin' fascinatin' in her ability to eat; girl coulda entered eatin' contests.

When she went for our Coke, that's when I put my foot down (or hand on the glass) and she accepted defeat with a nod and putting her hand in a 'sorry' gesture, before resuming her feast.

"Who are the white-coats?"

She groaned with a mouthful of spicy rice. "Not now. I wanna relax, not think back to them."

314

"Okay, okay. Whatever it is, I'm sure it's big and very unhappy."

"Yup. I just want to enjoy getting really full and try you out."

Oh dear. That didn't sound good. "T-try us out?"

"Uh-huh. Mr Short, Dean's gonna ask me if I went up against you two, and trust me, he's very good at seeing right through me."

"If you don't, what's the worst he can do?"

"Make me wish I was still with the white-coats." For a moment, she broke off from her eating, staring at the tower of food on her plate with all appetite temporarily lost. She sighed before resuming her task with a plateful of pasta, mouthful after messy mouthful.

"Why do you stay with him?"

"Because of my... because of Tranue. We've known each other since we were kids; I can't imagine being without him. I wish he was just as loyal to me as he is to that piece of garbage."

Memories cropped up of those Cain and I had known locked in their own little personal prisons, wanting to leave but still drawn back to it. Even we had suffered that, despite our longing to forget it. To know that she was experiencing this kind of pain made me feel the old sly fingers of uselessness stroke down our back.

"I understand how you feel, Daisy."

"If it's okay with you, I'm gonna have dessert now. There's still so much I want to try out before we leave here."

"Knock yourself out, my dear."

*

Daisy plunged the last spoonful of ice cream into her mouth and held back a sigh of content until she swallowed it. The corpses of the entire dessert menu – including three tiramisus, six pancakes mixed in with cherries and

315

blueberries, four kinds of sundaes – were scattered across this little dinner battlefield. Her belly was even bigger, like two basketballs stuffed down her shirt; her jeans must have been elastic, as it seemed to naturally stretch along with her. Her wide smile and stomach patting expressed her content all too well.

"Ah, that's it. I'm done. I might have eaten past my limit, but it was worth it. Are you feeling full?"

"No, we're alright. We haven't much of an appetite tonight."

"Oh, I could have given you some of mine. I hope I didn't put you off – that usually happens when I eat out. I can handle it a lot, but not a lot of people can handle me." Her face was red and she removed her hands from her abdomen. "Sorry, you must think I'm a pig. Dean says that about me too. But I can't help it, it's what those stupid white-coats did…"

Daisy's words were drowned in sobs and a broken voice. Wiping her eyes and clearing her throat, she took a deep breath before speaking in a much calmer, in control voice. "I'm… I haven't had a chance to talk to anyone like this. Him and Tranue, they won't really give me the time of day."

I placed my hand gently on to hers. "It's okay, it's good to open up. We can talk about this later, if you want." I gave her a reassuring smile.

She smiled too, her eyes so big and shiny. "Thank you, thank you very much. Mr Short and Mr – and Cain, I just need to go to the toilet." With considerable difficulty, she rose from her chair and went off.

'Ah, great, are we gonna start a chat show about people's problems now? Why are we puttin' up with this kid?'

'Because she's a nice person. Being with those two have left her a bit troubled, and I want to help her.'

'After all the years I've been with ya, I thought I knew how to be a hero, but now I'm kinda lost. Let her sort this shit out for herself, or are ya gonna hold her hand like some moddly-coddlin' nanny?'

'It's good to be fortunate to others, Cain. Let's leave it at that.'

'Fine, as long as she's payin' for all her crap.'

I eyed one of the robot waiters, his artificial skin pale to the point of being ghostly. "Excuse me, can I have the bill, please?"

"Yes, sure thing, sir."

Three hundred and seventy-five pounds; less than we expected. I paid for all of it by card, much to Cain's… intense distain, shall we say.

'You fuckin' dick!' Yeah, it was quite a questionable action, but I have a compulsion to help those in need.

Daisy waddled back to her seat, her added weight making her groan and the chair creak as her rear pressed against it. Her face had died down to its natural cream colour, no tears in sight. She let out a small huff, and everything was back to normal when she smiled, friendliness in full shine with those red lips. "Hi, I'm alright now. I think I'll pay for all this now, if that's okay."

"I've already done it," I informed her with a thumbs up and a smile of my own.

"Really?"

"Really." I winked.

"That's very kind of you."

"No worries. And by the way, I don't think you're disgusting, Daisy. If you have to eat, then eat. It's not your fault if you're hungry."

"Th-thanks. Do I look alright, like this?" She prodded her protruding gut with one stick-like finger, the girth making it look like it was going to pop with pressure.

"Yeah, you're beautiful, no matter what. Hell, there are even some people who enjoy gals with a bit of weight on or an appetite, so you'll please all crowds." I winked at her, and somehow her smile was even greater than before.

The three of us and her abnormal abdomen exited the restaurant and stepped into a much darker outside, far more stars sparkling like diamonds, the sky almost black. Daisy tugged our sleeve, and as I turned to face her, she pointed to a further part of the street to her left.

"There's an alley down there, we can use that. It's a bit dirty, but I don't mind."

Odd choice of location, though considering a lack of more immediate and easy options, it made some sense. There weren't any big abandoned buildings nearby (the closest to that were old rundown houses at the edge of town) and Wolf Park wasn't exactly ideal after last time.

"Fine then," I accepted with a nod. "What is it with us and alleys these days?"

"What?"

"Nothing, just reminiscing about a few friendly faces. Look, Daisy, you don't have to do this, you know that?"

It was her turn to give a small nod, this one laced with regret. "Sorry about this."

"Don't be, my dear. Come on then, let's have a workout. It'll be good for digestion, anyway." Even if it was a small exchange, this was probably the most affable pre-fight conversation we ever had.

The alley was, for all things considered, clean-looking, even if it was a bit dark, but we could tell that there weren't any traces of puddles around, and the walls were far enough apart to create a decent mini-battlefield, a good twelve feet or so along a path of thirty, leading to a carpark. We stopped once we were concealed in the alley's depths.

"Ready?" I asked her.

"Ready," she confirmed. "Right, I'll set things up. I'm gonna inflate myself, so you might want to take few steps back." We did, and then it began.

Her stomach started to expand even further, growing with unnatural quickness like a balloon. Her jeans stretched

318

with it, unsurprisingly. She looked to be nine months pregnant (well, with food) in a matter of seconds, and she was still getting bigger, her shirt unable to cover it and shrank as the gut started to encompass her body. The jeans were covering up the bottom half of the belly, which was now a four-foot orb and showed no signs of slowing down. She grew taller, her small scrunched-up shoulders broadening and hips widening, reaching past normal human proportions like she was trying to block up the alley, and any evidence of a skeleton beforehand was rapidly diminishing. Her chest rose up, her breasts enveloped in the swelling mass of her increasingly-rounder body, helping to form a perfect sphere from top to bottom with her stomach and sides. My skin shivered as I thought that she might explode at any second.

Daisy's face started to change as well; her cheeks, quite thin and hollow, proceeded to puff up rather quickly into two balls, and her quaint nose and eyes and lips remained fixed on what turned into a large bloated parody of the mistress. A chin or two developed, pretty subtle compared to the rest of her. Her arms and legs were filling out, developing into flabby cushions before being absorbed into the rest of her, the only visible remnants of them being the hands and feet, those (admittedly) gorgeous shoes and red fingernails sticking out, adding to how her body had expanded almost exactly like a blowfish. Her head poked out at the top, smiling those cherry-coloured lips in the middle of those doughball cheeks. By now, she was a perfect ball measuring at ten feet in diameter, her clothes still covering most of her body, save for her large, bare stomach, her belly button almost as big and deep as my hand.

"I think I'm gonna have a ball with you," she said with a giggle.

"Do you feel okay, being that size and… shape?"

"Oh, yeah, I'm okay, just feeling pretty full, in a good way." She closed her eyes and sighed in delight.

There was no way either of us could contemplate any of this, least of all her comfortability. "Um, if you say so. What do you, uh, plan to do from here? You don't look like you're mobile or anything." In weirded (or weirded-than-normal) fascination, I poked her stomach; it was ridiculously soft, sponge-like, the finger plunging into it like a pillow.

Daisy let out another small giggle from this. "Looks can be deceiving."

"I'll, uh, make the first move, then?"

"Be my guest. I'm not in a position to punch or kick you right now."

Holding back, I sent a fist into her stomach, making sure not to cause her great harm. Our hand felt how marshmallowy her skin was in this form; the bounciness almost sent us backwards. The impact of the blow sent Daisy rolling back like a bowling ball, not fast but enough to go down a fair portion of the alley, considering her size and the assumed heaviness. She came to a stop in a matter of seconds, her back against us and her feet up in the air. Then with just as much force and speed, she dashed towards us; I tried to slip by one of the walls with our back to it, confident of avoiding her even in this narrow space. Much to our surprise, she anticipated this, growing even wider in no time, the brick walls shifting her body into an oval shape yet not affecting her speed, and we were pretty much flattened as she went past us.

Turns out she wasn't as heavy as I thought, not like a wrecking ball or anything, more like a big beanbag, but the force of her going against our body and sending us to the concrete was enough to hurt like hell all over. "Agh," I groaned, trying to brush off the pain surging through us as I got to our feet. "You bounce right back, huh?"

Daisy shrank down, now fully circular but reduced to a six-foot orb, which somehow looked more comfortable to me than when she was ten feet. At least she didn't haven't to worry about stretch marks. "Sorry, did I hurt you? I wasn't sure if you were able to dodge that or not." Her sunken-in face looked so worried.

"We're fine. One-all, so far." I rubbed our throbbing temples.

"Just tell me when you want to stop."

'I dunno about you, Davey-boy, but all this talk is startin' to sound really weird, even suggestive. Or maybe that's just me.'

"It's okay, just give us an update when you're destressed. Come on."

With that, the girl shrank back down to her normal, thin-as-you-can-get state and then had the impulse to come at us like the bloody Road Runner. We couldn't prepare ourselves for a sharp flurry of slaps across the face; I think a couple did our jaw in, made it feel broken. Once there was a break, I gave her a flick on the head (well, the fringe, technically, but it counted) – a massive, annoyed 'OW' rang through the alley, and then one from me when she replied with an even harder slap. We're amazed we had the strength to feel our mouth, much less move it.

"Right," I just about managed to utter through clenched teeth, "I think we've worn out slapping for the moment."

"I'm almost done now. I think I know how to spice this up – throw me into the air," she suggested enthusiastically.

I went bug-eyed for a moment. "Why?"

"I want you to kick me around, like a one-man volleyball game."

"Wh… okay, this is starting to sound a bit masochistic, Daisy."

"No, I'll be fine as long as you don't go overboard." There was a slight sensation of childishness in her voice that led me to believe that this was an activity she had wanted to do for years. That or she really *was* masochistic.

I held her up by the hips (we all felt a bit uncomfortable with that, especially Cain) and tossed her upwards with as much strength as possible, sending her to the very tip of the buildings alongside the alley. When she reached the peak of

321

the throw, frozen in the air for a moment in time, she inflated herself again, returning to her previous ten-foot ball shape. Daisy descended, and bounced slightly as my fist hit her. The weight wasn't too difficult to manage, especially when getting used to it with every blow, so I made sure to keep up with her and ensure she never left the alley.

'Cain, do you fancy having a go? You can barely feel anything.'

'I'll pass – she's fuckin' huge! I don't wanna pop her by accident!'

'Suit yourself.' Despite how exciting it started to get, I knew that we – or rather, I – would have to convince her to help us. Here we go.

"Look, Daisy, about all this. Come with us back to headquarters and you'll be safe from Dean. I mean, he's hardly Adoptive Parent of the Century. You'll be with people like you, those who wouldn't be seen as 'normal' per se."

Daisy looked at us, puzzled and amazed – her wide eyes and raised eyebrows were battling to solely express one. "Others? What kind of people? What are they like?"

"Various. We're talking vampires, werewolves, aliens, magicians, typical stuff you might know from pop culture."

"And the non-typical stuff?" she managed to ask between bounces, never letting the thick BONK sounds against the ground interfere with her curious tone.

"Even more various. Robots, glowing people, things from water, things from earth, things from swamps, things from the dark… really, just a lot of things. What do you say?" I avoided touching her this time, letting her land one last time.

As Daisy's body touched the ground, gently rocking back and forth to a halt, her puffed-up face was locked in concentration, eyes glancing left and right, thoughts bobbing back and forth as well, before that too ceased.

"Alright, I'll go. If you say I'll be safe, then that's that. Besides, if Dean did care about me, we'd have been far away from him long ago," she said as she quickly deflated back to normal.

"Great." I walked up to her with a smile, and it felt relieving to see her respond in kind. What started out as a relief quickly swayed into a mildly toned-down cocktail of that and awkwardness once the lady swung her arms around us like we were a big teddy bear. The sudden physical contact, those thin arms wrapped all over our frame like a secured ribbon, and the sweet flowery perfume that made me think of roses, was pretty surprising, to say the least.

"Thank you so very, very much, Mr Short and Mr Cain," Daisy whispered in delight, almost sounding to be on the verge of tears.

'Um, Davey-boy, I don't like this huggin' thing right now...'

"It's... okay, Miss Philadelphia. Now, why don't we make our way over to HQ, hmm? Not that I don't enjoy a good hug every now and then."

"Oh, sure, sure," she rushed out as she let go. A sudden queasiness grabbed her now, causing her to groan and place a hand over her stomach. "Ugh... I don't feel so good. I think I should have given my tummy time to settle before doing this..." After groaning once more, a low, deep belch escaped from her, sounding like she had been possessed by a growling, ferocious demon, much to her embarrassment.

"Why don't people ever listen," I joked. "Always wait thirty minutes before turning into a human pinball. Forget swimming, *rolling* is the real food caution."

Chapter 27

The Unseen Enemy

Scarlett had trouble trying not to squirm, flinch or express any remote form of discomfort as Selma focused her energies on helping her. Selma's designated room for private psychic activity, which was white with a desk and two chairs, was a lot easier than being among all that collected psychic energy from her and her workmates. Bad enough when you have a boatload of unpleasant centuries-old memories of dying crammed in your head, you don't need to go through wearing headgear to prevent an even worse headache. Their eyes were closed, Selma's fingers pressed against Scarlett's temples, connecting their minds like ships docking together. The young girl's hands gripped the psychic's shoulders for an attempt at comfort, though I think her nails digging into them weren't helping matters.

"Please, try to relax, sweetie. I know it's hard, but the more distressed you are, the harder it will be to get rid of these memories."

"All the fighting... he's – they're killing me, again and again."

"Not you, Scarlett, not you."

Sweat trickled down their heads; a first for Selma, so this must have been one hell of a challenge. Cain and I stood by them, back to the wall, biting our lips, feeling their combined stress (we weren't sure if it was just from what we were seeing or if their emotions were spilling into us on account of the operation's pressure). Emily was outside the room, looking through the window, sitting on a chair with her ears covered and face down.

'Davey-boy, I wanna leave. Can't stand watchin' this. Too painful.'

'Same here.' We left the room, trying hard not to glance at the pair and say anything, and sat next to Emily, somehow gaining the courage to talk to her.

"It'll be alright. It might not seem like that right now, but give it a while and she'll be fine." Standard comfort talk, it's a shame I had to rely on that.

"Yeah, thanks," she let out. She lifted her head, took her hands away from her ears and smiled at us. "I'll be there for her, at least in spirit."

Spirit? That didn't sound right. "I'm sorry, what? What do you mean? You're here for her right now, outside that room. You'll be by her side through all this – right?"

"Of course I will." Her smile, it didn't look natural. Was it how her mouth stretching out didn't lead to her cheeks rising? Or the eyebrows not lowering? Or the slight wrinkles around her eyes refusing to pop out and stay like etchings? Was it in part of how her eyes, which fell flat of shining so bright as they always would? An off smile, almost as if she was faking it, which would be unlike her, especially in such dire personal matters. It put me and Cain on edge, wary of what she'd do or say next.

"Emily, I need to know – are you feeling alright? Do you need to get some rest?"

"No, I'm fine," she answered, never dropping that unsmile of hers. "I had that thought again. You remember it, don't you?"

I nodded, unsure of where this was going.

"I had it again and again, ever since I was told Scarlett was let go. Life without you, no worries, no old enemies of yours intruding on our normal lives, no memories of death floating in my baby's head, no traumas. She'll be free of them, but not of what she recalls. Then it blended in with another idea, working off of each other; dying to escape this."

Emily wasn't herself. She was too strong to think of this, even with all the stuff she faced from her childhood. These weren't her words, these weren't her musings. They were, as we pieced together while she spoke ever so calmly, Dean's. It made sense; if Dean could send memories of the dead into Scarlett, as impossible as it sounded, then why not send suggestive thoughts into her mother? Doing so would be an easy feat. Perhaps it might have explained a good portion of her depression and worries, nudging it more in the direction he wanted her to go, emphasising it gradually.

He had been playing with us, he was there where we couldn't see him, hiding in a person's head, twisting emotions, both hers and ours, just to take another stimulating stab at harming our loved ones from behind the scenes. To go this far, when we thought he couldn't breach the barrier any further…

I placed my hands on her shoulders with care, not too soft, not too firm, but enough to let her know we were taking her with the utmost seriousness.

"Emily," I told her slowly, "you're not you right now. What you're thinking of, however rational and logical and good it feels, is something that was planted inside your head."

"Don't be silly," she said. "No one can force me to think things like this."

"Not unless you've been conditioned. Dean's been screwing with your brain, leading you in this direction. We need to get you fixed, now." I rose, taking her by the arm, and was about to open the door to Selma's room until Emily used her free hand to shuffle around my coat and snatch Bob from his holster. It was too quick to stop her, so when I turned around to face her, the revolver's barrel was pressed against her head, and her smile remained, fixed like a statue.

"Oh God, Emily."

"It's fine, everything's fine. One pull of the trigger, and I'll be gone. I might try and make sure Scarlett can't suffer anymore, that way we'll be happy together." She flexed her trigger finger, cementing her statement.

Our mind was blank, unsure of how to approach this. If we made a move towards her, she'd pull the trigger and blow her brains out, or do the same to her daughter first. The shock we'd feel of her daughter's death would give her the time she needed to take her own life. We wanted to move, but we couldn't. We wanted to grab the gun out her hand, but we couldn't. We wanted to be her heroes, two good men, a redeemer and a saviour, twin guardians, but we couldn't. The horror of the moment got to us, took us by the limbs and mind and forced us to watch. Here was a woman caught in a battle neither she nor her daughter were meant to be in, used as a weapon by a ghost from the past, looking at us with a contorted alien expression, enjoying what she about to do. Her eyes were hollow, we could tell, as though she was already dead. Our thoughts merged into a fast and feral stream.

'That won't come to pass that won't come to pass she'll be fine we'll make damn sure of it no one else has to die no one no one especially not them Dean will pay no arrest no cell no laughing that he won no he will pay if not with his body in pain then with his life yes his life a life he wasn't meant to return to a life he's used to ruin others we might kill him even if the girls are fine he must die so this nightmare ends the day is saved and we can get on with our lives he must die he must die he must—'

We stopped, ground to a halt when we saw her smile briefly falter and one of her eyes twitched. No, not a twitch. She was winking at us.

"Emily, why did you stop smiling for a second?"

"I didn't." Even if she sounded assured, she was confused by my question.

"So... you didn't wink either?"

"No," she replied, again confused. Her body was acting in a way that didn't register, unaware of what she was doing while focused on her task. Our thoughts were immediately cast back to one way of looking at this. When you've spent a few decades in an oddball place like the IISEP, you get to know a lot of things. One of them is when someone under mind control is trying to alert others that they're aware of what's going on and fighting off this double-consciousness. Normally, the person wouldn't rush back into control, but instead perform little acts here or there that would go against what's controlling them, say making a signal with their hand, until they've gained enough strength to push it aside. Was this Emily reaching out to us, buried underneath but determined, like someone waking up in a grave and attempting to dig themselves out of it?

'Davey-boy, ya think that's true?'

'I don't know. Let's see.'

Over eyes scanned every part of her like a hawk, ready to pick up on even the slightest of hints. "Emily, as hard as this has been for you, tell us, can we help you? Are you still a woman of reasoning? Please, let us know."

"I'm perfectly fine, David. I don't need any further 'help' from you." Despite this, her mouth twitched, trying to open, and succeeded in moving enough to say, silently, 'yes'.

"Okay, good, that's very good to hear. I can tell that you're aware of what's going on and know what to do. You're strong, and in control." We had to keep her talking until any help arrived to restrain her or she managed to regain enough control to stop this. Throughout this, I switched between looking at her face and the gun.

"Just wondering, Em, can we have one last conversation, regardless of subjects? Like a pick-and-mix blend of questions? For old times' sake."

"Fine."

"Is that a new haircut?"

"No." No response from inside.

"Looks nice, anyway. Cain, tag out."

I asked her, "Would ya like a cup o' tea or coffee?"

"I'm not thirsty."

"A snack? We got a vendin' machine, they do chocolate bars, biscuits, lil' bags o' sweets."

"No." Still nothin'.

"Not even a last meal. Wow. Well, I got nothin' right now. Tag out."

Time for something more direct. "How does it feel to have your finger on the trigger?"

"Good." My eyes focused on it more and more.

"I'm guessing your aim's good too? Ever worked on it at a gun range? If not, I'm worried that you might end up shooting your foot if you fire it now."

"I never miss." Her trigger finger twitched.

"But we'll miss you, and so will Scarlett and your ex-hubby and all your friends, should you go through with this. Everyone will be sad, and you don't want that, do you?"

"I do." The finger forced itself away from the trigger by an inch, edging towards the trigger-guard.

"What's your favourite colour?"

"Red."

I glanced at my coat and her daughter. "I believe you. Were there any places that you wanted to go?"

"Tokyo, Spain, Las Vegas, Ireland." The unsmile started to diminish with every word.

"What's your absolute favourite memory? Or memories, if there's loads. It can be a top ten list."

Her finger gripped the guard, slowly veering towards the handle to reunite with all the other fingers. "Being with you that night, all those years ago as a child, safe from Dad. The moment I laid in bed with the man I would call my husband. Holding Scarlett in my hands. Hugging and kissing her when I wished her good night." Her arm dropped, Bob facing the floor. Emily closed her eyes, took a deep breath, and looked at us. The shine was back in her eyes. I took Bob from her and put him back in the holster. Once that was done, we embraced Emily.

"You did great," I told her, relieved.

"Nice goin', kid," I slipped in.

"Thanks," she whispered before letting go. "I knew what was happening, but I couldn't stop what I was saying. I don't even know when it stopped being me and started being… him."

I gave her a pat on the shoulder. "But you stopped yourself from making the worst mistake."

"I'd never… want to do that to myself or Scarlett. He messed us up, and I don't want him to get away with that. You both need to make sure of that."

I nodded. "Will do. Come on, let's try and make your head completely Dean-free."

Chapter 28

Childhood Lost

The following is a recording of Daisy's words during her interrogation.

"Do you have any gum around here? Just so I can relax? Oh, okay. You guys really need some in your vending machines; I vote for Hubba-Bubba, Spearmint, Bubblicious… I hear there's actually a stress-relief gum, chewing it helps you stay positive, isn't that great?

Sorry for talking a lot, mister. Gum's kind of my favourite thing.

I've known Dean for a long time, since I was a girl. Benjamin's known him just as long – I'm sorry, I think your people are more familiar with Ben by his name 'Tranue'. That was my idea. When we were kids, he wanted a really cool name to suit his powers, since he loved comic books, so I played around with the word 'nature' and boom, he's used it ever since. I kind of regret it now, it sounds silly in hindsight.

Benjamin and I grew up together in a little town on the outskirts of France. It was wonderful, I remember it so clearly. The streets were paved with bricks, so smooth that you wouldn't believe it. The houses were connected to each like one great whole, we knew every person, every street, every little patch of land, it was so simple and lovely, like a wonderful painting. Sunlight hit every corner, but the heat was never a problem. Benjamin and I would stare at the river for ages, whether we were sitting by the banks or the bridges and get lost in how it flowed. Sometimes we'd throw pebbles into it and wish really hard before they plopped into the water, and we'd keep our wishes to ourselves, no matter how hard we teased each other.

There weren't many trees around, but they were usually very old ones – climbing them was like a big action movie scene, or scaling a mountain. When you're small you think you can do anything. Benjamin was always able to reach the top without falling, not once, and he'd let out, 'I'm the tree god!' at the top of his lungs. Everyone complained about it, but I didn't mind, I'd just laugh. We were having fun, and it was fun to be around him.

His father was an old-fashioned shoemaker, he always took it upon himself to keep up old traditions, even custom-making shoes or mending old ones to make them look new. I suppose my parents had a more professional vibe. Mama was a teacher, Papa helped writing pamphlets for people. We all saw each other as one big family, and I love to imagine that we really had been one.

Oh, yes, the white-coats. We were nine years old when they came – no, their people, all in black masks with handcuffs and things that stun you – electric batons, maybe. It was night, pitch black, when they took us. Not just the two of us, not just Mama and Papa and Benjamin's father. They took everyone in town. It was the best time to take anyone, swarming over the town like a plague while we were all in bed. They burst into our houses with door-rams, and the shadows turned them into big, featureless monsters. Mama and Papa tried to fight them and I was scared, crying, trying to get away from the men but they knocked us out.

By the time I woke up, everyone had been put in designated cells. Neither Mama or Papa were with me; I never saw them again. Watching them being assaulted while protecting me, that's my last memory of them and I wish it wasn't. When the scientists, the white-coats, came, they injected me with some kind of red liquid and left. Turns out they were administrating everyone with this stuff, a formula that rewrote our DNA, in order to observe the effects, see if any of us reacted to it differently. That's how I got my powers. I like to think that I drove them up the wall with my hunger coming back every five minutes. They had to increase the numbers of meals they gave me per day. Once I was full, my stomach would get too big for my shirt, and I had to unbutton my trousers to be comfortable. I had to do that every time the white-coats gave me food. They didn't want my clothes to burst off and they couldn't tell if I'd end up as a blob if I kept eating, so they had these special clothes made for me. Some kind of hyper-elastic, that's what they said. No matter what size I was, they'd always fit me. Yes, even the ones I'm wearing now. Twenty-odd years later and they still fit – great, huh?

My ball form was a nice surprise, even if at the time I thought I'd explode if I got too big. No, I don't think there is such a thing as 'too big'. While I was full one day I put a lot of thought into what happened if I ate too much, got really fat, viola, I was a living exercise ball. It took some time to properly control it, especially when sorting out my thoughts of 'thinking about it' and 'being it'. The white-coats nicknamed me Violette Beauregarde, after that kid from those Willy Wonka movies who turns into a blueberry, saying that and my love for gum suited it well. Personally, I don't see. I don't even like blueberries!

After a while, they started to clump some us together into joint cells. Whether it was fate or not, Ben was my cellmate. He told me that those who survived the side effects of their powers were either taking it well, as much as you could do, or they broke down, went mad. He'd seen or heard some of them when he was escorted to my cell. Jeanne was screaming, yelling out that his skin was on fire. I hope it really wasn't. Tony could turn himself invisible, though he had trouble trying to do so completely; last anyone heard of him, parts of him had vanished completely, some were shown as bones, layers of skin were missing on his face, organs were exposed, and skin was missing in patches. We were tormented with dreams of what Tony looked like, getting closer and closer to us, asking for help. Angeline, a nice old lady, she had the ability to access people's memories, or would have if it hadn't backfired on her; she *was stuck reliving her worst memories in a loop, barely able to talk to anyone. She ended up a complete wreck. Phillipe's body could stick to surfaces, perfect for Spider-Manning up the walls to avoid the white-coats.*

This must have lasted for a few months; it was hard to tell when you lose track of the days. People started to go missing – maybe the white-coats got what they wanted out of them or figured they were walking failures. As the days kept getting longer, hope was slipping away. But as long as the two of us stuck together, we were able to hold on to it for just a little longer. We'd try and pass the time by playing games or imagining that we were still back home going about our lives.

Benjamin has always been protective of me, yeah. He promised me that he'd never let anyone harm him as long as he was around. That didn't last when Dean won him over, though. When the white-coats came to our cells to take us away for more experiments, he'd throw himself at them and summon pillars from the ground to keep them from getting close to us, while I'd inflate myself to make sure I was too big to fit through the door. Ben wanted to use his powers to get out, but we realised that saving everyone trapped there would be too much for us to handle. We were kids, not superheroes.

We met Dean there. No, we'd have known if he had been in town – like I said, we knew everybody. Apparently, he found out what had been going on and decided to stop it. He stormed the facility, security had trouble stopping him, even with all their firearms, so the white-coats thought it'd be best to... remove the evidence. Alarms were blaring, red lights flashed around us, people were scurrying, white-coats and security personnel and prisoners alike. There was gunfire, I don't know if it was from 'removing evidence' or if it was because Dean was nearby. Two men in heavy black uniforms came in training their guns. Ben stood in front of me, but I had no idea if he was going to do anything – we'd never prepared to be faced with guns, so we froze on the spot.

Dean blasted them from behind before they had a chance to pull the triggers. Seeing them drop was horrible, but Ben was more at ease with it, even kicking them in anger. The first thing I noticed about Dean was his thick, scruffy face; he was grinning at us and the men in uniforms, there wasn't a moment where he dropped it. He rushed us out, grabbing us by the hand, telling us he was our saviour come to sort out the bad guys, and even back then I didn't believe it.

No, he never rescued anyone else. Maybe we were the only ones left alive, or he wasn't interested in anyone else. I guess our age might have had something to do with it, a couple of kids in a bad situation, willing to listen to a kinder person, or one pretending to be kind.

He told us about Mr Short and Mr Cain, calling them old friends he wanted to meet, and that he was tracking them down for the time being, so we had to move constantly before settling into England.

Life with Dean was easy at first. Food on our plates, clothes laid out, beds to keep us warm and safe. Moving past the separation of our parents was a completely different matter. Nightmares, little pieces of life reminding us of them, seeing children under care of mums and dads. Ben may have accepted our loss years ago and I don't know if he's lucky for that. Dean always praised him and encouraged him, but never me. I guess he kept me around for my powers, and that my being girl ticked him off. He said something about his mother trying to push him to be 'normal', whatever that was, and he didn't like her for that. If he was actually a nice man, I would have sympathised with him. All I want to do is—

Frankie, I'm afraid I'm going to have to stop here. I'm going to stand up now.

Don't move, for your own safety. Please, Frankie, I mean it.

Because – don't turn around.

Because Benjamin is standing right behind you.

Chapter 29

I Think the Interrogation Room's Full

Well, this was quite a shocker; we went down to see how Daisy's interrogation was going, and found the room occupied by security guards training their energy rifles at Tranue, Daisy facing him with fear or surprise (flip a coin) and Frankie unconscious on the floor. With all the times Frankie's been knocked out by intruders since he's been around, I'm slightly more surprised that we haven't got any defences in the interrogation room other than security guards who turn up with the help of a button under the table, or from involved staff members viewing it. I blame budget cuts.

Now, some might say that having Tranue at gunpoint in our territory would be a good thing, stun him should he attempt to attack or flee. To those people, I refer them to Wolf Park and that he'd just slipped into a building and knew exactly where to find Daisy, so headquarters was practically his new toy. I wished that we wouldn't have to fight him across the entire facility; I'd hate to get the bill for the damage.

"Sorry, Tranue," I said as I slipped between two of the black-armoured guards. "We don't do visiting hours here. You'll have to wait till she leaves, but I reckon she wants to stay."

"No, Mr David and Cain Short, I'm the one who should be saying 'sorry'. I'm here to take her away." He tried to take a step towards Daisy, but the energy rifles' high-pitch whine as they locked on to him forced him back, but he smiled, playing the rules of this game for a little longer. "Your workplace loves those things, huh? They were pretty annoying last time."

"Yeah, they've been pretty handy beforehand, and I'm sure these latest models will prove to be even more annoying on your person."

He cast his attention over to Daisy, who stood with her back against the wall, frozen as she locked eyes with her childhood friend. "You're not taking me back to him, Benjamin. I swear to God if you do—"

"I know you don't like him, but you don't have a choice. We owe it to him to stick by him after all he's done for us."

"For you, more like," she corrected him, her voice lower, darker in spite of her innocent appearance. "He never liked me, you must have known. You were like a good son; I was just a pig."

"That's not true, Daisy—"

Suddenly, the fear projecting from her vanished, and in its place brewed anger. "You mean you never noticed how he looked at me with those eyes, like he was disgusted to be near me? Where were you when he started beating me and forcing me to be quiet about it, threatening to hurt me even more if I told you? Or did you not just care about me anymore? Why couldn't you have seen it earlier? What did I do wrong to make you ignore me like that?" Her voice was strong, loud, boiling in her memories as she recounted them. "How could you give your word to protect me when we lived under that bastard's roof all those years?"

Tranue's mouth drew open and closed before he had the chance to say anything; clearly, he had never anticipated the acid in her words. Once he cleared his throat, he managed to reply, the smugness and determination he had displayed earlier left him as he spoke softly. "Daisy, believe me, I never meant to hurt you, I never meant to break my promise. I just wanted to pay Dean back for all the good – no, all the opportunities he provided us. For God's sake, I owed him for letting us see sunlight again! He meant something to me the moment he saved us that day."

Daisy revealed, sharply in her burning words, "I wish every now and then that we had died there, instead."

Naturally, this was more than a little intense for us. Cain commented on this in our mind, 'The hell am I watchin'? It's like a fucked-up soap opera. Can we change the channel?'

'Cain,' I told him, trying to concentrate on what was going on, 'not now. If she keeps talking to him like this, we might be able to resolve this non-violently.'

'There goes my stress-relief plan,' he grumbled.

I turned over to the head of security, the (literally) stone-faced Salor Romen, and whispered in his ear, "Can you please tell your men to decrease the energy volume? We don't want him getting too hurt." Salor gave us a nod, his yellow eyes strong and slightly disturbing, before signalling to his men to adjust their guns' settings.

Tranue, despite acknowledging security around him with a glance, was more occupied with Daisy's stinging comments. He clenched his fists, though it seemed to be more for regaining strength than to intimidate her. "So, what are we to him, then?"

"Weapons to be used against Mr Short and Cain, that's all. The fact that we're people was a happy coincidence."

"Why do you want to stay here? How can you trust these people? For all we know, they could be just like the white-coats."

"I trust them because they treat me like someone rather than something."

Tranue's face dropped, a gulp clear from his large throat. "*I* do, Daisy, and don't tell me otherwise."

"Don't take me back to him, Benjamin. Don't." She took a bold step forward, and so did he, her anger diminished. Anything could happen in this moment as they grew nearer and nearer to each other. Would she get through to him? Would he carry out his 'rescue' and lead us on a destructive Benny Hill chase? Tension thickened with every sound, whether it was a footstep or simply the act of breathing.

Tranue was the first to talk once they were within arm's length. "Don't make this any harder for me, Dai—"

His rather poor choice of words was countered with a slap so powerful that it swatted his face to the side, the force just as loud as gunfire. It wasn't a warmup for de-stressing her, nor was it applied to someone who let her do it; it was born from stress aimed at a friend she had once held dearly. Even we thought it was unexpected.

"Benjamin... you don't have the right to say I'm making things hard for you. You came here because of his orders like a good little lapdog and didn't consider that maybe I was happy to be away from him? If you decide to go back to Dean, tell him I'm not budging, understand?"

Nature's number one son touched his cheek and lowered his head in shame. Raising it a second later so that their eyes met, he told her calmly, "I do. I guess he'll have to find someone else to tell him, then." Eyebrows were raised all round by that statement.

Tranue's voice was warm, sensitive, letting him smile as he thought back to simpler times. "Remember when we used to throw pebbles into the water and make a wish?"

"I do," Daisy answered him, trying to hold back a smile of her own.

"I wished one day that if I ever did anything wrong, anything that upset you, I'd find a way to make up for it. This I promise to you: I will right what I did wrong." He faced us and security and declared, "You have the right to detain me. I won't fight you, you have my word."

As gratifying as that sounded – to me at least, as Cain was moaning and cursing at this in the living room of our psyche, wishing to put a foot into the TV – I had to be sure in order to extinguish any doubt. "So, you surrender, then?"

"That's what I'm saying, yes."

I sighed, relieved. "Okie-dokie, then. Ladies and gents, you can relax now." With that, all the tension in the room deflated as the security force lowered their rifles. "Now, Tranue – or Benjamin, whatever your preference – if you can please follow us, we'll give you some new enchanted clothes, for you stay here; they'll prevent you from using your powers. Think of it as a supernatural straitjacket of sorts. Oh, and can someone please work on waking Frankie up? I'd like him to be conscious when Dwight congratulates him for not dying for the umpteenth time. He should get a bigger pay rate, the poor fellow." It was weird being authoritative for a change; the last time Cain or I had a sense of authority, we had taken up babysitting.

Tranue made his way out of the room gingerly, his huge hands desperate to connect with Daisy's for her sake. And they did.

Chapter 30

Revenge, Wild West Style

We didn't drive Emily and Scarlett back home till two in the morning, their minds now cleansed of Dean's influence and tired to the point of exhaustion, nearly nodding off a few times. Sending them back ourselves wasn't necessary, but we couldn't refuse the idea, as seeing them off personally would make the night's closure fulfilling. They thanked us, smiled and went indoors to finally sleep in peace. We all felt a little bit happier.

First order of business after that: drive back to HQ and stay there. Yes, we weren't far from home, a good five minutes or so away starting from Emily's place, but we needed to be in the workplace as soon as possible in case we learned anything new, pyjamas and bedsheets be damned. Hard to tell if this was practical or insane. Then again, we were being dragged down by stress, tiredness and a dash of obsession (considering the circumstances, the latter probably explains it the most). We went back to HQ, where we learned that Daisy was still up, talking to Tranue in his cell. Before we could think of anything as we sat down at our desk and closed our eyes, we were swept away by our dreams, recalling the past once again.

1853: Putting the Castrator and his gang to rest. Back in the shed in which Dean had performed his 'calling' on us, we wait until we are fully healed before starting our escape by pushing our strength to its limits. We are neither one nor the other in this moment in time, but one in body and mind, operating swiftly with no arguments either side. Despite the initial impression of futility in pushing our arms and legs away from the ropes binding us and the strain of it against our skin, our restraints give in and loosen, allowing us a brief moment of pleasure in freeing ourselves. Our shirt and trousers are dirty with sweat and dirt and age and are insulted by the holes spread across them from Dean's torture and the shoot-out with his gang preceding it, but that doesn't matter now. It's time to take out this bunch of petty lowlifes.

We notice a knife and poker lying carelessly on the floor, and we adopt them until the time comes for other weapons. The knife's small light body in our right hand, blessed with the power to cut through the air gracefully with a few quick swipes; the poker's long dense physique in our left, ideal for ending affairs with a blunt closing statement. There is a dreadful beauty in each of them, and to embrace them together in this desperate glowing hour for justice and revenge magnifies that a hundredfold. A savage mindset, true, but it's better to go into battle armed with what you can get than to rush into one empty-handed.

The window and cracks of light at the edge of the door tell us it's still daytime. Can't afford them the luxury of having any more fun with our body. Rather than rush through it and make a spectacle of ourselves, we open it slowly and peer from the doorframe. To the left, a view of the pale cream rocky valley far ahead, the great jagged teeth of mountains lost in the grass and forest and waterfall that roars with life. Unlike our captors, we appreciate the marvellous spectacle. To the right, a house that, with its peeled wooden skin and awkwardly squashed body, feels determined to establish itself as the root of early alien decay in this wonderful land. At the right-hand edge of the shed, Jebadiah Frost, a stocky man with shoulders broad enough to carry even Dean, stands with his back away from us, scratching the unwashed tuff of hair on his chin. Shame he has to be looking away from the waterfall – he would have had one hell of a beautiful view in his final moments.

Now for a pre-emptive strike. With no shoes, it's damn easy to catch someone from behind unawares. The poker bashes his head, sending him to the hot dusty patch of ground, and to prevent him from reacting and alerting others with a yell or gunfire, we let the knife check out his skull for a few seconds. Cutting his throat would have been easier, but we're feeling retributive, and to be honest, it would have lessened his pain. His revolver makes things easier once the knife is stashed in our pocket – sure, we only have six bullets to work with, but it's time for an upgrade. There's an initial disgust in holding it, Cain's 'up close and personal' warrior code seeping through, though it fades once the reminder of our position kicks in.

The back door leading to the kitchen doesn't take long to reach, and a warning sign appears as we hear the singing of Bill Stead, his broken voice apparently good enough to keep the windows by the sink from shattering. Okay, now let's move on to a home invasion, give them a real shock. We bust through the door, causing Bill to jump and stare at us in dumb surprise.

"You have a talented singing voice; you almost charmed us out of killing you." We aim and pull the trigger... only to break the plate he's holding into tiny pieces.

"That was my best plate," he shouts before brainlessly throwing dirty plates at us. It's more annoying than effective. A second bullet ends his kitchen madness.

All that's left is Albert and Dean. They must know we're out for them now thanks to the noise. The living room, dull and brown with a fireplace and complemented by a few chairs and a table, is empty...if you disregard Dean and the chair he swings at us from behind the door and whacked us over the head. It's our turn to fall and be shot at, Dean's small revolver blasting our left hand, causing us to let go of Jebadiah's gun, and then a second bullet pierces us below the knee.

"I saw from upstairs you taking out ol' Jeb. Never liked him much. Don't need to wonder about you offing Bill either." He sounds awfully grateful.

"Glad to see more of that wonderful partnership we admire," we say through the scorching pain.

343

"Yep, it's so wonderful that I made sure Al didn't interfere with me handling you. Guess I can't call this a gang if it's just one person now."

"Well, it defeats the usual idea of one, so we're inclined to agree."

"Gotta admit, at first I thought you was nothing special, but now I can see you've got some damn fine balls on you." Let's not ponder what he really means – it hurts to think about it. On the other hand...

"And we have to admit," we respond with a grin, "that you've got some too." One good swift kick to his pair of miracle-workers gives us all the time we need to drop our poker, reach for our gun with our good hand and blast him in the stomach, sending him to the floor. Getting up is difficult due to the bullets hibernating in our hand and leg, but we get there thanks to the poker. "Right, time for a little baptism by fire to help you along the way to hell."

We grab Dean's chair and feed a bit of it to the fireplace, letting the flames swallow it gradually before throwing it towards its brethren and the table, allowing the fire to spread violently and somewhat beautifully. Stepping over Dean's bloated body, there's the sense of satisfaction in ending him and his friends. Unfortunately, it's tarred when his hand suddenly squeezes at our bad leg, leading us to turn around with a sigh in frustration.

"I'm... not through with you," he growls, probably unaware of how hot it's getting.

"Sad to say this, Dean, but you'll have to find a new toy." Another good swift kick, this time to the head, does him in, enough for us to stride out of the house, dropping all of our weapons now that they were no longer needed. After all, they're not actually ours, just conveniently borrowed for a moment or two. Just because we were killing them doesn't mean we couldn't give them back.

As we limp away, there's a weight off our shoulders... one that'll reapply itself some two-hundred years down the line. But for now, the great fire's glow thinks otherwise.

344

Chapter 31

Hauntings

Waking up from this memory-turned-dream would have been easier without seeing a pale-red spectre's glow from the moment we opened our eyes. Steve McCaden was walking soundlessly through the workplace, the low light of his body (such as it was) standing out as the only form of illumination in an otherwise dark room. Chainmail, iron boots, shiny breast and shoulder plates with gauntlets that could punch a man across the room – add the fact that the claymore he had in life was strapped to his back and you had one hell of a fierce looking knight. The thing is, the thick armour that blanketed him wasn't actually armour, it was just him manipulating his appearance so that it looked like he wore such a suit. Still, got to give him props; he knew how to scare the shite out of someone, even if he was a big softie. His beard hung low against his belt, a wild mess of hair for only the truest and boldest of manly warriors…or if he wanted babies to grab it and cuddle it like a pillow.

Beside him were two figures, smaller and younger than the middle-aged Scottish juggernaut. Alice and, surprisingly, Chris, talking with him with the kind of enthusiasm children would have when meeting Father Christmas (we met Old Nick once or twice, great drinking buddy). Alice we understood, she worked in Paranormal, it was a given for her to be up in the morning trying to sooth her bubbliness, but why was Chris tagging along, especially at this hour?

"…o' course, ye usual giant Death Jellyfish is very tricky to fight in close quarters. I had to keep slicin' me claymore every second to stop it from shockin' me."

Annie sounded like the air was being sucked out of her as her face swirled shock and suspense. "How did you beat it?"

"Simple – I got it out o' the river and forced it on to the bank, then once it plopped on I flung me sword into it. Deflated like a bloody balloon, it did; no blood, no ectoplasm, not even a lil' man operatin' it, sayin', 'Don't looka the man inside the jellyfish.' *Boooof*, it went. Ended up usin' it as me rug." Steve let out a great booming laugh, his beard swaying like a pendulum as he did.

Chris was amazed and confounded in trying to picture the tale, which wasn't helped by the squinting he gave when he removed his glasses to rub his eyes. "I… my word, Steve, that's incredible. Absolutely incredible."

"I hope so, I tell that story all the time. But that's nothin' compared to the time I faced off against the Monster Pigeon o' Little Barrow, the foul thing. Ah, Dain, lad."

The great ghost's head turned to us, referring to us by the joint nickname he gave us. Chris gave a small wave and a smile and Alice had trouble holding back her excitement, belting out, "Hi-hi-hi, guys!"

"Hi, everyone," I greeted them, managing to work up my own smile in spite of the dragging sensation on my eyelids.

Steve commanded the turn of conversation with a friendly, "How's existence? Still wishin' you were like me? I hope not, you'll get awfully bored."

I chuckled, wiping my eyes. "Existence is providing us with more and more distractions every day, Steve. Seems you've got some fans to keep you company on your night shift."

"Aye, a fresh audience help me feel alive again, especially when they're wee ones. I think yous know this new fella, Christopher." He tried to give Chris a gentle pat on the back, but the force of it sent the boy to the floor. "Oops, sorry, lad. I forget me strength sometime."

"It's okay, Mr McCaden. I'll live." He got up, managing the wallop to his spine.

"Hah, you'll notta lived if you hannae heard o' me wrestlin' with the Chameleon Cat o' China, fierce kitty-cat, for true."

Feeling washed with tiredness – our watch said it was 4:30, two hours' sleep so far – I massaged my eyes while I spoke to Chris; Cain was too knackered to even say anything in our head. "So, Chris, what's up with you, then? Things going well with Alexander and the rest our fang-filled friends?"

"Alright, I guess. I talked with Alexander over some steak – turns out he really does like it, so thanks – and… well…" He cleared his throat, struggling to talk. "Actually," he explained hesitantly, trying to break it to us politely, "I'm having trouble getting completely, um, comfortable around them, so – so I talked to Dwight about letting me check out Paranormal for a while. Need a break until I feel ready to brave it with the vamps, you know?"

"Oh, right, I understand. Doesn't it feel weird to be transferred to another lot of dead people? Or should that be undead, since they're not in the afterlife? No, wait, that's for zombies and vampires, not ghosts; they're in actual bodies. Whatever. Sorry, Steve, not sure if I offended you there."

"It's alright, mate, I cannae grasp some o' the lingo meself. Reminds me o' when I fought AZ the Word Master an' his terrible traps; the frustrating Alphabet Maze; the gruelling Terminology Tunnels; the confusing Slang Swamp; the perplexing Thesaurus o' Doom—"

"Yes, thank you, Steve," I interrupted in a calm tone, ensuring the discussion didn't diverge into another one of his stories. He seriously needed to get them published in Spirited Ghouls Magazines (where the dead can provide interviews, news articles and works of fiction – some have even submitted ghost stories).

Chris talked as if Steve had never spoken, his voice rising in excitement. "That had occurred to me. But I find spirits more interesting, to be honest, what with the whole 'life after death' angle and what they can do. Alice and I interviewed a few before meeting up with Steve, it's—"

Alice swung an arm across Chris' shoulders, not noticing how his face shuffled from a smile to an awkward glance in her direction. Naturally, her own excitement was fast, thick and mad, a verbal chainsaw. "Yeah, it's been fantastic talking to them, obviously I did a lot of that, but doing it with a newbie around my age is even more fantastic! And we haven't even checked out our latest guy, this knight from some really old war, calls himself Peter Straw, he's totally nuts, going on and on about finding someone from his time called—"

"Peter Straw?" I belted out in shock, moving away from the desk to get closer to Alice. That name, we hadn't heard it in years, much like Dean's, but this time there was no confusion. We had known him prominently, professionally, personally, an ancient dark memory dosed in pain and regret, gathering dust, though the recent light shining our old wartime sins wiped away the age and made them feel new. We switched back and forth as we tried asking Alice questions, our voices harsh but not cruel, loud but devoid of anger.

"You said that, right?"

"A knight, Peter Straw?"

"Was that really his name?"

"It couldn't have been anything else?"

The poor girl was unnerved by this, twitching and flinching as she faced this manic performance. "Yeah, yeah, that's his name, Candy Cain."

"With a light beard?"

"Low voice?"

"Asking for John and Cain?"

"Or the English Angel or Devil?"

Alice answered all of these in one. "Yes!"

Realising that she was now scared, we calmed down quickly. "Sorry, Alice."

She took a deep breath before asking her own question. "Are you telling me you knew him?"

I phrased the answer as: "We were workmates, you could say."

Another way of putting it: we killed him.

So, you know, good vibes.

Chapter 32

An Old Face

We were escorted to the graveyard, which gave us (well, me and Cain) chills considering the early hours of the morning and lack of sunlight yet to dawn through the windows. The graveyard was Paranormal's way of putting some souls stuck in the physical plane in hibernation when they were bored, inactive or trying to get some semblance of rest in their disembodied state. It consisted of a large hall occupied by giant rows of shelves, like a library, each one organised by dates, species, planets, star systems, down to the tiniest of relevant details, filled with small metal balls inscribed with the names, birthplaces and, with exceptions, years of birth and death of every person. At least there weren't any problems with space, though one employee assigned with adding a new 'grave' ended up accidentally sending six rows' worth of graves to the ground. Good thing they're incredibly durable.

Alice removed Peter's new home from the 1300s section and showed it to us; it read 'Peter Straw – Nottingham – DOB 1341' in a shining gold font, almost angelic. "Here we are," she said before setting it to the floor and pressing a tiny switch on top.

Peter shimmered into existence, rising out of the ball and going from a red wispy collection of energy to a man in his thirties standing in front of us, the ball lying by his feet. Like Steve, Peter's assumed look was that of the armour of his time, chainmail and metal hiding the thinness of his chest, arms and stomach, thick boots matching his toned muscular legs. His hair was long and greasy, shaded in crimson given the nature of his red-coloured state of being, as well as the flecks of hair across his face that formed his beard.

It was difficult to hide our disgust towards him; our head wrestled with thoughts of anger and curiosity, the desire to yell at him for the gall to look for us and dread of what he wanted to do with us shook around madly. To look at a man we had once considered to be our friend, only to find what he was really like… there was an ugly thought of wishing he could live and die again until he learned humility and regret.

The first thing Peter did upon seeing us as to stare at us in confusion, even as he said our names. "John? Cain?"

"Yeah," I said reluctantly, the confirmation feeling like poison. Cain instead popped out for a few seconds to let out a low feral growl.

Peter examined our clothes, primarily the red coat, and cracked a grin. "You were never one to dress normally. I have missed that, as I have missed you, my dear brothers."

"We're not your brothers, Peter."

The spectre's smile ceased, and the faded friendship in his voice was blended in yearning and nostalgia. "But you were back then, Jonathan, on the grounds of battle against the French. Oh, what joy we had there."

"That's behind us now. We've moved on. There's been a resurgence in reminding us of those times, from a man who's made it his mission to haunt us."

"And his name is Dean Gregory, is it not?"

"You've met him?" Somehow, probably the timing, it didn't feel much like a surprise.

"In an uncomfortable turn of events, yes. He tore us from the Beyond, Jonathan."

"Tore *us*?" Now *there* was a surprise.

"I know not his means, but he removed myself and many others from those days in Hell. By the Name of Our Lord, the pain when he had done so was worse than when you damned me to oblivion, or indeed worse than its torturers."

Alice, her eyes bulging in shock, replied for us. "Holy shit. How could he do that? To actually snatch so many people from the afterlife… it's unheard of."

Peter faced her. Despair and terror choked him as he went on, his recount strained and bewildered. "Child, you have now heard of it. Upon stealing us, robbing us of continued existence, I was almost desperate to tell him not to send me back. I witnessed him place fellow sufferers into contraptions shaped like men but made of metal, with blank faces and small red eyes. Once each man's essence was trapped in those things, the faces would adopt theirs, flesh atop those monstrous frames, and they would be his puppets for the game he has planned. When the time came for my entrapment, I gathered all my strength to break away and find you. And now I have. Help them, brothers, help them to ensure they are free from both his cruelness and the Beyond's."

Picturing this tale was easy enough. Agreeing with his request was another matter entirely. For the time being, mind unsure, we went along with it. "We'll try, Peter. Do you recall where he did this?"

"A large house, what he called a warehouse."

"Would you be able to direct us to it?"

"Yes, though I must warn you, he has offered some of the damned revenge against you for killing them, and those who had since moved on from ancient grudges are forced to comply – he had enchanted their steel bodies to fight you even when the nobler ones had other ideas."

So Dean had taken spirits from the Beyond, specifically the Hell fragment, and placed them in robot bodies. How long had he been doing this? How many people had he ensnared? Judging by the expressions garnered by Alice, Steve and Chris, they had been thinking the same twisted questions.

"Peter," I finally said after much thinking, "I'd like you to tell us everything, absolutely everything, about Dean, anything you might have noticed, and everyone you saw.

352

Follow me, we'll let you meet up with Daisy Philadelphia – she was with him until now, but it's likely that she might not have heard about your predicament." I carried his 'grave' and strode out of the graveyard, our old associate following us uneasily.

*

"My God," Daisy exclaimed, the shock from Peter's story hard enough to stop her from purchasing more vending machine snacks, her collection residing on one of the many chairs beside her. "That's— that's horrible! You poor soul."

"At least we know Dean kept it to himself," I assessed, "not that I suspected you, of all people."

She reached for a chocolate bar in her collection but withdrew her arm. "And he's been doing this for years? We lived with him and we never found out…" She bit her lip in frustration.

Peter kneeled before her and said with practised gentleness, "My lady, I do not blame you or your friend for our capture. It was the work of a madman defiling the laws of life and death, however horrible they are. My hand will treat yours with the fair touch of compassion." He tried to hold hers, but I shot that down with a cold "don't", and he complied.

"It's odd," Daisy said, "but I can't recall where Dean lives, and neither can Benjamin. That Frankie man of yours can back it up, when we finished the rest of the interview. It's like, the moment I thought of it, it was in mist. No matter how hard I try, it's too far away to recall. He screwed us up again, didn't he? If I… if I had the chance to kill him, I'm not sure if I had the guts to go through with it."

"Daisy…" It was hard to not want to hug her.

Her pain was soon overshadowed by the strength in her voice. "If you're going to that warehouse, I'm coming along. I want to make up for not about any of this until it was too late."

"Very well. I suggest you get some sleep now, you must be knackered. We'll lead you to a room to get some sleep, okay?"

"Okay, thanks." She got up, just about managing to carry her loot. We reckoned a potential sugar rush would hamper things for her.

*

Having Peter around us, his former friends and murderer, was awkward, yet we agreed to let him check out HQ to see what it was like. We traversed empty corridors for the following hour, ideal for Peter as a walking nightlight, and especially ideal for him to initiate a conversation he wouldn't start amidst other company.

"How have you been, Jonathan, for all these centuries?"

I had trouble shifting through the different things I could say – boring, depressed, philosophical, suicidal, helpful, good, outdated – and I eventually responded in a flat tone, "I've been around, thanks for asking. It's David now, by the way."

"Your lives and names must rival that of both your allies and foes altogether. What have you been doing since my death? Following the path you committed yourself to, I hope?"

I shot him a venomous look, informing him of my displeasure of the subject with my sharp eyes.

"Obviously not, it seems," he concluded. "May I ask why?"

"It got to us. What we did across those years, it made us realise that it was all pointless. Why kill for hundreds for land, why kill for God, why convince yourself that what you're doing is for some greater good and call yourself a hero?"

"You have spent many a day reflecting on this, to which I say, we fought to defend our country and Kings because

354

we were theirs and knew our rulers were wise in what they did and believed in."

"We were pawns foolish enough to serve, don't you see?"

"I do not, Jonathan, David, or whoever you call yourself. Unlike you, I firmly believe that I am a good man, someone who appeals to his leader and tries to make the world a better one."

"All those lives we snuffed—"

"People who opposed our Kings and Lord! So, I am not a fool, brother, but rather it is you. A good man stays to fight and protect those he cares for, not run away and hide in shame."

"We do fight for loved ones, Peter, that's why we're in this mess in the first place. Unlike *you*, we have dignity and honour, values that went over your head when your arrogance swelled it."

"I have them," he retorted.

"Is that why you forced yourself onto the wife of a man you had just slain?"

Pride and attempted reasoning burst from his voice. "He had insulted me, if you recall, so I had every right to punish him. As a defender of England, it was only natural that I took his wife as my own."

The memory curled in our brain in one stressful angry ball. "If you had been exposed to all the cultures that we had seen before and after yours, you'd understand that your attitude is barbaric, downright monstrous. A woman is not yours when you kill her beloved; they're not objects or living fancies."

His eyes grew wide as a thought struck him like the very blade we used to kill him. "Is that why you refused to let me touch that young lady's hand back there? Ridiculous. If men have no right to own women as theirs, what is the point of their existence other than to produce children?"

It took a great deal of strength to stop Cain from bursting forth and thrashing him with all his might. "Primitive thinking, Peter. You'll find that nowadays they're equal to men."

That knocked the wind out of him. "What a mad world this is. It may as well be Lucifer's work. What made men decide to let them be—"

"Wait a minute, wait a minute. It's just hit us: you're taking your death rather well, all things considered."

"I learned to forgive you, my brothers. Years of torture at the hands of demons made me realise that how you ended me was a quick mercy compared to the ways they dispatch poor wretches. There were moments where I felt that my actions proceeding it were less than just, and, I must admit, a part of me, a slight one, believes it. You did what you felt was right, just as I had."

"Oh. I see. I don't know what to say, really. I guess, 'thank you'. Have you, um, ever had any regrets?"

"My last action, given what that led to. Another is being unable to push my goals toward finding someone to truly love, rather than bed for a single night of indulgence."

"Really?" I asked in astonishment.

"Yes."

"Well, now that you mentioned it, it's not hugely important, but I sort of loved you."

Peter stared at us in confusion. "What do you mean?"

"I mean the way you would love a woman."

Words couldn't describe the shock on his face. "You loved me in such a way?"

"Um, yeah. You were the nicest friend I had during the War, though your growing ego killed it in no time. Nowadays, we'd call it a turn-off."

"Another of your inhuman eccentricities," he remarked calmly.

"Always had a way with words, Pete – the kind that would get the crap kicked out of you. Love like that's commonplace too. You're a fish out of water, really."

"What a strange new world."

"'That has such people in it'. Shakespeare. Smart, dirty playwright, good brawler. Look, we're awfully tired, so we're heading back to our desk for some sleep. What do you want to do?"

"I shall wander this place, though I will be sure to be near you. Rest easy, my friends." It was still odd to hear this man call us his friends, just as much as it was for me to refer to him as having been an old friend. As we left Peter in the barren corridor, grave in hand, we felt the heavy shadow of our past grow light.

Chapter 33

The Devil's Punishers

Assembling a team for the warehouse raid as a bit of a hassle for Dwight. The majority of ghostbusters employed by the IISEP were unavailable (we're talking seventy percent here) due to having their hands full with other cases, leaving only thirty people, mostly experts, to join us. On the one hand, they had all the equipment they needed to remove ghosts from any possessed bodies; containers with globs of what was labelled 'expel gel' for close encounters; two-handed blasters that trap them in crystal prisons; grave-balls that automatically lock on to and pull in individual spirits (great for light, quick containments when things get crowded).

On the other hand, we didn't have much of an idea of how big Dean's forced-draft army was, so for all we knew, we faced a good chance of being outnumbered. But now wasn't the time to fret. We had resources (well, as many as could be spared), so chin up, eh?

It was ten in the morning, and the sugar from vending machine snacks had failed to keep us awake, hence the three or four empty energy drink bottles parked on the desk. The computer didn't have any games on it to pass the time (Cain missed the days of playing Minefield during breaks) and our phone's games weren't filled with anything particularly captivating.

The last couple o' hours were what I called 'Wild Boredom'.

The lack of sleep wasn't really a problem, but Jackie's wish to involve herself in this operation for our sake was one for Cain. She was brave and strong enough to look after herself in a scuffle, but what they got up to that night together made him more sensitive to her than usual. Oh, and

Steve decided to tag along and provide some help because... well, either he was looking for another adventure, sympathised with his fellow spirits, or he was bored.

Peter led our six-van squad and my car out of town, through the wide lush beauty of the countryside for the best part of an hour. Flat yellow and green fields were the new streets, and trees were standing proud as nature's buildings. The fresh air was a hell of a lot healthier to take in than the stale odour of Chelnsworth – for the first time in years, we could actually smell other things. Eventually, we went through a narrow road deep within some woods and made a few turns before finally reaching a clearing that led to another yellow field, with a large grey warehouse standing tall in the middle.

"There it is," Peter stated, caught up in fear while we stared at the building, its dark dull complexion sticking out against its colourful backdrop with what could only be described as an unnatural presence.

We cut through the field as the yellow flowers waved in the wind, and parked around the entrance up front, a door wide enough for two of the vans to fit through. It was hot outside, the blazing sun not really helping, but we got used to the clamminess during the ride. Good old Bob the Revolver slept in our holster, ready to do his job; the busters drew their crystal blasters; Dwight, Brad and Jackie had their fingers on their stun guns; Steve wielded his broadsword, and Daisy was ready to become a ball at any moment.

The entrance was locked, just a small sturdy one fixed on the side. I just shot it, simple as that. Everyone gave me an annoyed look before the blast's echo died down.

"What? Nobody had a key."

Brad told us, "I was about to suggest I blast it off."

Oh. "Oh. Right. Sorry. Dwight, don't bother paying me today."

The door slid open with ease. Daylight crept in, and we followed, noting the sick, stinging smell of metal. The air was stale, damp, filled with corroding warmness that slithered all over our bodies. Peter was the first to enter, trying to brave it but failing as his face dropped from the view before him. The bare steel bodies filled the warehouse in rows of ten on the further half of the ground floor, tall and still like metallic statues. The hands were clenched into tight balls, toes flat against the concrete, broad shoulders and thick torsos gave the impression of a well-built physique. Every one of their bone-white faces, from what could be seen from afar, were reflexions of the unfortunate souls trapped inside – fat and thin, young and old, clean and scarred – which made it unsettling when viewing the rest of their lifeless-looking bodies. Their optic sensors were cold red balls, a mannequin's glare. Beside the entrance was a stairwell leading to a platform that spread across the entire building like a spider's web. Large machines of various shapes and sizes occupied both sides of the ground floor, and though it was fruitless trying to figure out what they meant for, it was easy to assume they had a hand in helping Dean.

Peter raised an arm in their direction as he stated, "There they lie, encased in those devil-worthy suits of armour. You can free them, can you not?"

"'Course," Alice answered, her tone refusing to fall flat against the sight of things. "We'll just pop 'em in the graves and send them back home, if we can. Shame spirits don't carry money, or we could charge them as supernatural taxis. Don't worry, guys, I'm joking!"

"How are we going to handle the robots?" Jackie asked. "Even if we manage to secure the ghosts, Dean could just stuff more of them back in. And there's so many of them…"

Brad clenched his left hand. "Blast them. Leave not so much as a scrap behind."

"Don't tell you're enthusiastic about this, Brad," I wondered. Cain and I thought back to Constantine from

Cain's brief time in the bar, and even though the artificial life-forms before us were probably not sentient, a part of us refused to let Brad destroy them.

"I'm being practical," Brad responded. "Plus, it'll be a blow to that fool."

Dwight butted in, his voice low and smooth. "Gentlemen, I suggest we approach this one matter at a time."

Daisy took a few steps forward, her brow creased and mouth wide open in shock. "All those people, stuck like that. It looks so horrible. I want to help them."

"You will, Daisy," I told her. Though she didn't smile, the small nod she gave made it clear she appreciated our words.

Before we could cover a third of the area, Dean suddenly materialised in front of us, appearing with the sharpness of a finger-snap. He was dressed in a smart blue suit that hugged his bulky frame, a black shirt, red tie and dark Italian shoes that complimented him. Not exactly casual material, more like the sort you'd wear at a party; seemed that he was the host.

"Hello there, my dear guests," he let out, spreading his arms out as though he was welcoming a circus audience (or that he caught a really big fish). "I'm glad you finally got here – I was worrying whether or not you'd be too early or too late. Doesn't matter, though. We're in the third act now, my lovely players."

Steve addressed me and Cain with loud curiosity, dampening Dean's entrance. "Is he always like this, lads?"

"Pretty much, yeah."

"Christ, I thought I was too dramatic."

Dean snarled in Steve's direction. "Ah, I see you brought Macbeth along. I'll have fun making you my new toy." His hatred then bubbled away when he noticed the broadsword. "How are you even holding that blade? I thought ghosts were intangible."

"I made a promise to a lady many years ago to confront all sorts o' creatures, one adventure after another, to eradicate all evil. My sword is bound to me for all time."

"Hmm. How dreadfully dull. You've got guts, though, unlike that coward over there." Dean pointed a finger at Peter, declaring, "The brave knight who ran away, even though I offered him a shot of well-needed revenge."

Peter stood his ground, his voice bold and firm. "I do not wish for revenge, demon. No, I wish to free those enslaved by you!"

A grin curled across Dean's mouth as he chuckled. "Demon! How flattering, sir knight, but I'm afraid I'm just too evil for Hell." His attention turned over to Daisy, and the snarl resumed. "I thought a weak little flower like you would have crumbled into nothing by now, Daisy. But you had the nerve to betray me, you selfish pig."

"I'm not afraid of you, you bastard," she shot back, filled with the same energy that helped her deal with Tranue.

"Once this is over, you will be." The grandiose flourish he wielded before then returned. "Anyway, David, Cain, I enjoy your efforts to actually try and get one over me – it's downright adorable. It's almost a shame I'm not really here."

I groaned, already weary of his talking and boasting for the day. "You really get off on using holograms, don't you?"

He smiled. "But of course! After your old war buddy scarpered, I figured there's no way in hell I'd risk coming back here in person to finish things off."

"How long, Dean? How long have you been snatching people from their resting places?"

"Not as long as I've loved you in my special way, sadly, but long enough. Like their casings? Not sure if they do, but it's the toughest I could afford. I focused their programming on slaughtering your friends, even if they don't want to."

"It's sick," I exclaimed.

"Creepy fuck," I growled.

362

"Would you expect nothing less from me? I've even given them a team name." Dean spread his arms out, his smile broad as he breathed in the atmosphere he had carefully built up. "I call them... The Devil's Punishers!" With that, he lowered his arms and his voice resumed its more casual bounce. "What do you think, a bit too much? It felt easier to say than some of the others names I nominated. 'Ghosts of the Past' was a very close second."

"All from the War?"

"All I could find, sadly, and I searched very high and very low. I only had a limited supply of these shells, and only so many of your little battlefield bonanza buddies, so I had to fill out the rest with some souls from more recent times, a few even going a couple of decades back. Got Nazis in one row, Klansmen right behind them (they'll love you, Dwight), 1920s and 1930s gangsters who happened to work for me, samurais, hunters and a few molesters. Oh, plus the occasional drug dealers here and there."

I cocked our head, both amazed yet confusion by one little omission. "What about your old friends, Dean? I thought even you of all people would have appreciated the chance to get your long-dead mates beside you, it could have made your revenge all the more fulfilling."

Dean chuckled. "Why should I have brought those idiots back? I'm alive, they're not. They wouldn't understand how much this means to me, how I want you for myself, not for a bunch of slack-jawed fools who always got on my nerves. As much as I'm compelled to avenge them and give them a chance, this is more about me."

"What, really? We couldn't tell; you've been so subtle up until now."

He ignored our little remark and continued. "In any case, there'd be no real point to it – I'd send them back to the afterlife once their purpose was fulfilled."

How is it possible someone could show how much more of an arsehole they could be? Maybe I had set my standards in regards to evil a bit too low. "You know, it's nice to see you're a very… considerate and compassionate person, Dean, but it hasn't warmed our heart enough to stop us."

"Well, there goes my number one plan," he said with a smirk. "Anyway, do you like my little assortment? It's quite impressive in variety given the somewhat limited scope in size. I'm a bit disappointed I couldn't give it a more apocalyptic edge, know what I mean? Something fire-and-brimstony to amp things up. Shame that even the demons I found weren't interested; they've been in a civil war since that Rhasadon the Destroyer fella left them, and when they knew he bit the dust, they got too afraid to come up and meet you."

Our pulse quickened slightly from the sheer mention of Rhasadon as we instantly thought back to our confrontation and near-death all those years ago. "Jesus, even you know about him? This is getting ridiculous."

"Lemme guess," I said as I popped up, "ya also knew we killed 'im before them demons told ya?"

"Of course! I set the whole thing up. I learned of him in the eighties, told that kid where to find the Box and waited for the outcome of my challenge – either save the world or watch it get torn apart and live with the guilt. You passed wonderfully."

"What the he– Why? Does the world mean so little to ya?"

He shrugged his shoulders heavin' his weight as he replied nonchalantly. "Less than little, I'm afraid. I think Dwight here didn't think about who tipped him off about youse and your ghostbusting hobby for Dead Fred. I wanted to see you rise so you could fall even further."

"So…we owe our job to ya?"

"You're welcome, boys," he said in delight.

My part o' our brain felt funny tryin' to process this, so I retreated into our head an' let Davey-boy resume the talkin'.

Twenty years' worth of fantastical experiences, exploring the unknown powers and secrets of the world, were now drowned in a dark and bitter taste, like white chocolate trapped in a Turkish delight. "Oh my God…"

Dean lapped that up with, "I really wish I was. I haven't got enough ego to back it up, but I'm a dab hand at manipulating mortals, wouldn't you say, my subjects?"

His head turned to face Dwight, and a roaring sense of self-righteous supremacy flashed in his wide eyes and rang in his voice. "Great to finally meet you, Dwight White. Never known any niggers with that surname before, nor any who survived meeting me."

"Welcome to the exception, Mr Gregory," Dwight shot back, his deep voice unable to hide his contempt. Past injustices from his childhood could be felt in his words.

"You won't last long, though considering your successful career – and employing my two favourite men – I'll give you special treatment. You're a broad bastard, but you'll break soon enough. It'll be fun to count how many broken bones I'll give you, you black punching bag."

Dwight snorted. "I doubt it. The only one who's going to break is you, Mr Gregory," he said, keeping his cool, as difficult as it was for him.

Dean's attention was ground to a halt when he noticed Brad amongst the group, gazing at his hand with surprise. "I thought Tranue turned your hand into a charred pulp."

"It got better," Brad answered in his usual stoic fashion. "Upgrade."

"Oh, is that so? Nice to see you've gone to the effort of preparing to lose yet another hand, and to me no less. What an honour, eh?"

"You won't get the chance." Brad flexed his hand.

"Ouch, you're a hardass; I like you, I'll kill you last. But still, technology's wasted on replacing something as minimal as a hand. Better to have it save your life. Look at me – I nearly got killed in a housefire, my saviour patched me up, and now I'm a two-hundred-year-old cyborg. *That* is beneficial, Brad, not like a hand or, say, a leg."

For a moment, Brad's voice dropped, ebbed in confusion and fear. "Leg?"

"You think your wife forgives you for what happened to her? I can tell by her face that she wishes you nothing but pain. So blunt, so uptight, so withdrawn – no wonder she blames you."

Brad refused to respond to Dean's jabs, recovering his hardened face as he went on. But even still, he curled his left hand into a fist.

I stepped forward, desperate to intervene. "Hey, why don't you focus on us two right here? Don't tell me you've already dumped us?"

"I'm sharing myself amongst all of you. Brad, you have no idea of what she thinks when you're away: 'Why did he suggest it? I didn't want to go, we knew the risks, but he was so enthusiastic, he practically forced me to say yes. If I hadn't submitted myself to him, I wouldn't have fallen and felt the world spin and hurt me, cry out as my ankle twisted, yell as my kneecap shattered and leg bend and warp itself. The bone broke through my skin like it was trying to force itself out. I wouldn't have needed my leg to be replaced and feel disposable, or hated him when I was confined in bed. He got off lightly with his hand, but he's used to it – he lost his heart years ago. But that's okay, because I'm his wife – I have no choice but to love him, in this prison we call marriage'."

With that, the silent well-built wall Brad had forged for himself crumbled with the weight of Dean's words. He screamed in pure hot anger as he fired at Dean (forgetting that he was here via hologram), blinding red beams of light coming from every one of his fingers, almost as if he turned his rage into a weapon. They went straight through Dean and exploded against the invisible wall that revealed itself as a rainbow-coloured mess behind him, shrouding the ghosts in the machines for a few seconds before hiding itself from us. The intended victim remained perfectly calm and composed.

"Amazing, Brad! All it takes is to widen a few existing cracks and your wall comes tumbling down," he said triumphantly.

All of us were taken aback by the sudden appearance of the wall, like a successful horror movie jump-scare. "You set up a forcefield," I said with surprise.

"Well, I don't want anyone coming in and messing up my work, do I? David, Cain, let's have a chat, two-to-one. Meet me on the platform." He disappeared and reappeared instantly on the platform above, looking down at us like the mastermind he thought he was in that overheated brain of his. With the twists and turns he had manufactured, we're surprised he didn't get lost in the details and had to write everything down.

Cain and I gave everyone an uneasy smile, trying and failing to be reassuring before ascending the stairs. We wanted to make a quip to relax them but nothing came to mind. The building's great volume gave each step a loud THUMP that echoed. Our eyes made it their mission to stick to Dean as we held onto the handrail. We stood opposite him in the middle of the platform, his hands buried in his trousers.

"What do you want, Dean?"

"I want to give you something, to make finding me a little easier." One large hand came out and stretched itself towards us, palm facing upwards.

"...I think you've forgotten how this 'giving' thing works," I said, confused as I observed his beefy palm.

"Let me borrow your phone for a second," he commanded.

"I'll let you borrow our dictionary first."

His temper rose as he gave off a fake smile. "Do as I say or you friends will suffer." What a smooth talker he was. With no other choice, I handed it over to him, at which point he took a small device out of his other pocket; it was a black metallic cube, shiny and weirdly beautiful, the top face glowing with a tiny blue screen and decorated with several coloured buttons. Placing the mobile on the screen, he proceeded to press several of the buttons with quick, masterful ease, and from there a high-pitched squeal rose and caused our mobile's own screen to flicker for a few seconds. When all was silent again and screens were still, he threw the phone back to us and we just about managed to catch it.

"There, I've punched in my address," Dean stated. "It's been reprogrammed to direct you to it, and all means of communication have been disabled."

Charming. "What a lovely 'upgrade', Dean. Ever thought about opening up a mobile service?"

"Your sarcasm won't do you any good now." As I turned away and started to walk back down, he declared in a raised voice, "I wouldn't bother doing that, by the way."

I faced him again, uneasy. What was he up to now? Options swirled in our head. Did he want to fight us on the platform (as weird as it was since he was projected through a hologram)? Have his prisoners do the work for 'im? Set the whole on fire, or make it explode? How about all of that, just to be extra annoyin'? "Why?"

"One of the little buttons I pressed on my lovely little gadget set up a forcefield around the platform; you can't go back whether it's the stairs or a flying leap."

The bastard, he trapped us! "I think we've spent enough time here, so let us go now."

"Alright. See that door behind me?" He aimed his thumb past his shoulder, pointing to a door at the very end of the platform – it felt like it would take a mile to walk to. "That leads to the outside. You can go."

"An' leave our pals to rot?" I growled, barin' my teeth with an' already red face and yellow piercin' eyes as I took over.

"Don't worry, they'll have something to do while you're gone. Consider this place a playground for the kids."

At first, I had no idea what he meant, but then the pieces clicked together quickly. "You turned off the forcefields downstairs, didncha? When ya fiddled with our phone?"

"You're right on the button there."

I turned an' yelled, "Guys, get ready! No forcefield down there! No! Forcefield!"

"Idiot, they can't hear you. They'll get the gist in a second." Just as he was about to press another button, I swiped a claw at his black box – but my hand went right through it, an' he succeeded.

'Shit, it's not here. Stupid, stupid idiot,' I cursed.

The 'bots started to move; first the heads o' the poor bastards looked around, irises an' pupils red, then the rest o' their bodies as they settled their attention on Jackie, Brad, Dwight an' everyone else. Lips moved on both sides, faces stoic, unsettled or excited like an emotional parade. I gripped the railin', an unwillin' audience member. Jackie tried talkin' to me, an' I had only one idea what she was sayin' – "come here". I bet she realised we couldn't join her, an' the worry on her face agreed with me.

"Dean, stop this," I begged him. "Why do this to them? Why not us?"

"I want your past transgressions to be paid in blood, and I think it's more entertaining when done with your friends."

The ghosts-in-the-machines broke into a run, arms an' legs flowin' in unison, an' our guys only had seconds to react. Everythin' went by so fast. Jackie activated Muscle Force, throwin' her enlarged body at her attackers, claws slashin' into 'em, her tail sometimes caught by steel fingers. Steve's sword sliced through metal with no problem, though he tried to gain distance between swings. Brad's finger beams struck like Thor callin' down thunder, but it was hard to keep track o' all the dead people surroundin' him. Daisy swelled up some twenty, twenty-five an' started to knock 'em down like bowlin' pins; those that leaped onto her bounced back to the floor, but whenever they hit her, she ended up bein' their beach-ball. The ghost team's blasters sent out streams o' bright colours that enveloped the spirits in hard blocks o' crystal, their bodies blurry an' glazed. Whenever the robot bodies turned to scrap, the faces o' our past shot outta 'em like fireworks, only to get sent inside the grave-balls before they could escape or

369

possess. But there were so many, almost endless, like a swarm o' metallic bees, an' only so few o' our friends…

"You know," Dean said, revellin' in his fun, "staying here will only make it worse for you, though you can stick around for as long as you want."

My grip on the railin' clamped down, warpin' it outta shape. We were angry – no, I was way angrier than Davey-boy, unbearably mad at myself for bein' useless, mad at Dean an' his tricks, mad at them ghouls in their prisons… an' I was afraid for everyone, especially Jackie. I couldn't think straight, just watch an' feel powerless.

'David! David! Tell me – tell me what I should do.'

'We have to get out, Cain. If we hang around here, we're not helping them.'

'But she's down there.'

'Let's go.' It was hard to admit, but he knew what was best.

'Right, you're right, let's go.'

I let go o' the railin' an' locked eyes with Dean, an' warned him as I pointed a finger at him, "We're comin', an' we hope to god yer ready for us."

The fucker smiled. "I've always been ready. Question is, are you?" He pressed a button on the cube an' vanished, leavin' the exit in plain sight. I dashed to it, coverin' the distance in no time, resistin' the urge to look back, an' found myself out in the open, face caressed by a light breeze as I stood on a flight o' stairs. I hurried down an' got into our car, focusin' on the directions the phone's automated voice gave us as I drove off. We wished they didn't lead us to another dead end.

Chapter 34

Let's Get This Party Started

Dean's house was twenty miles from the warehouse, across another field in an open road, far from another other houses in the countryside. There was a wooden gate between some bushes that led to the place, with a cemented pathway winding up to the building. Given the haste of things, Cain's skills behind the wheel meant that we went through the gate veered on and off the grass and the hard grey carpet Dean had set up. The house was – actually, 'house' didn't feel right in describing it. 'Fortress' seemed like a snug fit; a large square slab of stone that stretched across the field like a virus, its roof flat and windows scarce, at least two on each side. A pale blue garage door stuck out on the right of the white front door, both of them tiny compared to the giant they were a part of. Hundreds of floors looked to have been squashed together to form this place – if everything turned out well, it'd come tumbling down like a Jenga tower.

Cain just about managed to apply the brake and stopped us from crashing into one of the walls.

"Right, let's do this," he said with burning excitement as he turned off the engine. He took a deep breath, but didn't budge from the driver's seat.

'You okay, Cain?'

'Yeah, 'course I am, just coolin' down from the rush.''

'Mmm-hmm. Mind if I take over from here 'til you're ready?'

"Sure, man."

I got out and removed the sports bag I had stuffed in the trunk, its weight immense due to the small collection of weaponry knick-knacks I had stored the night before. Walking up to the front door was odd. Granted, we were entering enemy territory and it was the only viable entrance (unless you were a mole-person who could dig into the place), but since we were 'invited' here, I was plagued with the idea that this was a twisted party or sit-down filled with drinks in plastic cups and snacks in hundreds of bowls and paper plates with napkins. I was about to knock when the door slowly opened with no one in sight to reach the handle or greet us.

'Wow, I bet he uses this place as a haunted house on Halloween.'

"Yes, a door opening by itself is truly the stuff of terrors," I muttered. "What's next, dimming the lights?"

One of two uneasy steps led us into Hell… it wasn't half-bad from initial looks. A large hall spread across every single angle, leading to a magnificently polished staircase that split into two; a few tables and chairs were by the side, draped in white; chandeliers presenting a lovely glow; rooms left and right by what looked like a mile away from the front door; black and white tiled floors. But upon focusing on the finer details, it was clear it was still Dean's home. Decorated on every wall were sketches of me and Cain in various positions and situations from many years ago; fighting against gangsters in New York in the 1920s; confronting the Ripper in Whitechapel; conversing with societies of old during the Middle Ages, ones of magic and secrets that were no more, and saving innocents as a bystander in the wars since The Hundred Years War. His knowledge of these encounters, such detail in recreating them as though he had been there with us, even before his birth, filled us with so many questions, so much disgust and horror, that one body wasn't enough to contain all of it. Even our castration had been depicted, complete with the pain etched on our face and Dean's own greasy satisfaction. The beauty of the house was superficial, like something out of a catalogue, lacking any sense of soul or warmth beneath the floorboards or in the corners of the rooms.

And then the lights dimmed. I drew Bob out of his holster on instinct as I looked around, unsure if we were going to be assaulted in the dark. Thankfully, that wasn't the case. Unseen light sources focused on the top of the staircase, where Dean descended, eyeing us even when we were nearly lost in the shadows.

"There you are," he bellowed with gusto, pointing one thick finger in our direction. "You really kept me waiting, my little bounty hunter."

I locked eyes with him, trying to steady our cool. "Miss us already?"

"I always do. Oh, David, Cain. You're what drives me forward every day, living my life so, and for that I'm grateful. Holograms never make me feel like I'm actually with you, they don't bridge the gap between us. My dreams never ease my longing for you, it's just another night of waking up alone in the dark, clinging to a memory I wish I could meet again. To touch, to admire, to violate, to have my revenge for all the wonderful pain I felt all those years ago. Being with you two as I am now, in person, makes me tremble." Having finally reached the bottom of the stairs, the room's lights were back to normal, ending his most recent dramatic flair. He took his time unbuttoning his blue jacket and draping it on the stairway post, loving the atmosphere he had so carefully framed. He'd been waiting for this moment, preparing everything in little or huge ways, regardless of the people he drew in and used. None of them mattered, they were pawns that had served their purpose and were now forgotten. One thing was for certain – we were finally his, and he would not waste it blindly rushing in and spoiling his victory.

Dean's barrel-like chest strained the silver buttons on his handsomely-tailored shirt, and his arms were more like tree trunks in their thickness. He raised his fists and put one foot forward in a mock-boxing stance, preparing himself for what was to come. "Please make the first move, boys. After all, you're my guests, and I'd hate to be a rude host."

'Better take the offer while the takin's good,' Cain told me.

"Don't worry, we'll make it an explosive one," I said to both Dean and Cain, putting Bob back in his holster. I rested the sports bag on the floor, silently contemplating what to arm ourselves with first before unzipping it. An automatic rifle, three revolvers with explosive rounds, a double-barrelled shotgun, several grenades, and... yes, that one was perfect. After a moment, our hands accepted the grace of one particular weapon and pulled it out. Starting off with the grenade launcher felt right. It took two hands to manage the grip, aim and weight of the ten-inch six-round steel chamber, filled with alternating standard grenade and incendiary rounds. The crosshairs were too small for my liking, practically unnecessary – as long as we were staring it right down Dean's thick smug face, it didn't matter. One pull of the thick silver trigger and he'd be (hopefully) sent to the floor.

Dean grinned. "Nice toy. Love how big it is."

"Thanks. We brought it along just for you; I was tempted to wrap a little bow around it."

"How thoughtful."

The air was stiff, caught in the anticipation of the moment. The launcher was raised, Dean right in the centre of its aim, and all that was to be done was to shoot. Breathe in. Hold it. Breathe out. Our finger slammed against the trigger. The round was sent racing through the air; Dean met it with a manic smile and a punch with his right hand. The explosion came in a great roaring light and a thick smoky cloud, piercing our hearing and ripping through the house like a wave. Cain and I were pushed to the floor and tried to get a hold of what just happened while a whining noise rang in our ears. Getting up, we kept our focus on the pillar of smoke as it started to settle, waiting for Dean to rear his head.

'Punchin' a grenade? The hell's the matter with him?'

'Maybe he wanted to show he wasn't afraid to face it head on,' I speculated.

'He'll be lucky if he's got a head after that.'

Before we had time to raise the launcher, Dean burst through the smoke in one large superhuman leap, his right hand worn away from finger to bicep, revealing a bare blue metal mockery of a skeletal arm. He made it into a fist and swiped it at us, striking our jaw with the bluntness of a truck, causing us to drop the grenade launcher. Dean picked it up effortlessly with one hand and threw it far across the hall.

"Like I said, nice toy. And that's all it'll ever be." He hit us again, this time with his left hand, but as we fell to the floor, we rolled to try and create some distance before standing up again.

I tagged in an' got my claws ready, circlin' Dean like a tiger waitin' to find the right time to strike. At first I wanted to tear into his chest, ruin his shirt, even if it was just to spite him a lil'. But then, thinkin' o' that reminded me o' when I sliced his throat; despite never actually hurtin' him, it only healed when he mended it back together with his hands. So what's the one place he'd probably have the most trouble reachin'?

Dean was a fast puncher, I'll give him that. The air's disruption alone as I dodged each hit by a hair's breadth packed enough force to nearly knock me on my ass. He swung a right jab, but bein' quick on my feet, I was able to drop an' scurry around an' make my way behind him. Before he could respond, I sliced deeply into his broad back as far as my fingernails could go. I tore through his skin as easy as a curtain. Apart from noticin' how every muscle bulged under that tight shirt, I could feel that hard metallic core o' his body, it was like wadin' through a mountain o' pillows only to be stopped by a stone wall. If it didn't hurt him, it'd hopefully cause him a few internal problems down the line. I dug in some more with my other hand, just as deep, just as rough. He yelled out – did I strike a nerve, or was he just frustrated? Either way, it made me an' Davey-boy as happy as a herd o' grass-guzzlin' sheep.

"Like that? I coulda been great in the back-stratchin' business." My body actin' on its predator instincts, I leapt onto him, clampin' my legs round his stomach an' started clawin' at his pecs as best I could. Boy, his groans told me he didn't like that! A sick sadistic glee burned through my body. I was red with joy, and it wasn't unwarranted. "Gonna turn you into scrap metal, buddy."

"I – beg – to – differ!" His hands suddenly rose up an' grabbed me by the throat. At first he was gentle, I got a caressin' vibe, but then it roughened up, his fingers dull forceful daggers.

"The hell ya tryin' to do?"

"Getting a load – off my back!"

Uh oh.

"Uh oh."

He flipped me over like I was a ragdoll, an' I crashed to the floor, back takin' the full brunt o' the blow, practically bent outta shape. I wanted to get up an' regain advantage, but his foot stomped on our chest, pinnin' us down with ease; the longer it was there, the more it forced itself through our ribcage, an' the harder it was the brush off the pain an' talk. Dean's face, a pissed-off shade o' red, towered over us upside-down.

"You ruined my favourite shirt."

"Looked a bit small… figured ya needed a new one. Wouldn't kill ya to lose weight, really." I ain't one to admit it often, but I can be a total dumbass sometimes. His foot agreed with me.

"I have to say," Dean said with a venomous snarl, "as much as I hate them right now, those claws of yours are impressive, Cain. Your designer did a good job working on them. Then again, he had all the time in the world."

"I ain't… sure if I should be… proud o' that."

"Shame his weapon got a bit rusty thanks to a weaker, softer personality. He'll probably consider you the first draft, iron out the flaws with the next model."

"Ha! No one's gonna replace me an' Davey-boy – there's only one o' each."

"Oh, you'd be surprised, Cain. Still, that's in the future. For now, let's settle on sorting you out."

Managin' to work through the grindin' agony on our chest, I grabbed Dean's foot an' exerted all my strength into pushin' it away. He wasn't gonna let that happen; his weight shifted into forcin' it down harder on us. I drew my head back to see how far close his other leg was – just enough for a strike.

Taking over, I whipped Bob out of his holster and fired a few rounds into the calf before shooting him from every possible angle – head, shirt-torn chest, stomach, his prominent foot. The force of it caused him to step back, giving us the chance to get up. One hand rubbed our chest, the other replaced Bob with the stun gun, our eyes and aim fixed on Dean, who alternated between us and mending his bullet wounds, pinching them quickly like he was dealing with mosquitoes. His shirt was split open, dragging tears across his chest with the torn skin revealing, instead of blood, glimpses of blue metal.

I pulled the trigger, and the gun's wire-like cord shot out and landed right inside one of the chest wounds. Electricity jumped straight into him, and now, to our surprise, his screams were of a man who had long put off pain, and its reintroduction was more than a little shocking to him. We got him! We knew his weakness, thank God! To hear him suffering, to be the ones to seriously hurt him in a glorious reverse, it made us happy; if it wasn't for his grabbing the cord and tugging it out with a fair amount of effort, we would have kept the trigger pulled until any trace of life was extinguished. He pulled the cord and the stun gun leaped out of our hands, dangling in front of him before turning it into scrap, squeezing and crushing it the way you'd screw up paper into a crumpled ball. Pretty short victory, really, and it was hard to tell if we could afford a more permanent one, especially with how his wide eyes shone with revenge, and parts of his body twitched in unnatural sharp spasms.

"I think we need to drop a note to HQ on the quality of the cords: straight steel sounds nice."

"That hurt," he growled, throwing the deformed gun aside.

"Good, must have been quite a jolt," I said, spewing out a joke on instinct. "Glad to see you're not completely invincible, then. Your friends should give us a miss if we can take down their best man for the job. Come to think of it, be a good host and answer this: what's the *other* certain thing they want back?"

Dean's unnerving movements ceased, and those piercing dark eyes gazed at ours, before saying in a stern, cold voice with arms spread out, "This planet."

Confusion ran rings around our brain in haste, with thoughts of 'oh dear' and 'oh shit' on top of it. These people wanted the Earth *back*? Who the hell were they? More than just a little surprise, that's for damn sure. "This planet?" I echoed back.

"Imagine: you know that somehow and someday your world's going to be destroyed, so it's absolutely vital that a new one's found to carry on your civilisation. You spread out across the stars searching for the right planet to inhabit and call Home 2.0 – right gravity, right atmosphere, right climate. It has to be perfect, completely devoid of other races. So you plant a beacon on it, knowing where to find it when the time comes."

"…And they came here when life hadn't started yet," I took over, trying to fill in the rest. "That means we were made to wipe out any chance of life on this planet just to secure it for them. Sacrifice one lot of people for another. But why were we conditioned to get rid of only humans? And how could they know about them?"

Dean's throat thumped rhythmically as he chuckled. "You're on the right track, sweetheart, but not entirely there. Let's not get your brain too worked up just yet – that's for later." He took advantage of how mind-blown we were to leap forward and deck us in the face. We couldn't react in time as we fell and had his left hand gripping our skull, nearly digging it and rupturing it. There was a small sting in our neck, some kind of injection, and drowsiness soon reigned. Our arms went limp, our legs turned into wooden planks, and the pain of Dean's fingers grew dull and unnoticeable in the wake of our need to sleep. Very quickly and passionately, our eyes closed, and dreams opened up to us.

Chapter 35

Unveiled

The moment we woke up, hell ran over us. Our chest was crushed from all sides, making every breath small and sparse, and big throbbing lumps covered our eyes, so opening them was an invite to torture ourselves just by blinking, which was especially annoying because we couldn't even see where we were in Deanie's Playhouse. But the room did have lights, the orangey-red glow in our eyelids told us. Our arms and legs were suspended by something (rope? leather? chains?) that tightened to immobility, so our wrists and ankles ached and moaned over how uncomfortable they were. No smells to provide our surroundings – I really wished flower-scented air fresheners for some reason. A dry well summed up our mouth and throat; as far as we knew, our tongue was close to falling off.

Oh, an' we were naked, nothin' left unseen. God, I thought o' how bad this was gonna get. Couldn't help but think back to all those super fucked-up torture porn flicks I heard about – no saws, drills or whips, PLEASE. At least gimme a backrub with sandpaper, that's all I can take.

As you can tell, Cain was trying not to panic and was completely fine. In my case, I was more focused on re-examining what had happened. Flustered, reckless, stressed with taking down Dean immediately, unsure of how everyone was doing back at the warehouse, pressed for time. Result: some superficial damage towards him, and we got knocked out and, judging by our face and chest wounds, pummelled before we woke up. Great, another exciting turn of events in the ever-growing cock-up department. No real plan other than 'good guys beat bad guy and make sure everybody lives' – idealistic, overly-optimistic, idiotic. Still, at least Dean didn't have to target anyone else to get our attention. He had us all to his cruel, cruel self.

Speaking of which, our gracious host came to us with the sound of a door creaking open and closing like some creepy ghost house, and a few heavy footsteps that took their sweet time.

"Enjoying your stay here, boys?"

"Hey Dean. It's going alright. Couldn't get us a seat, could you? Only, we're feeling a bit stiff."

"Good." He was so close to us that we tasted the satisfaction in his words. "I want to make sure you're as uncomfortable as possible." Two thick fingers stroked the bruises over our eyes, and he continued as we twitched and winced in pain.

"S-stop," I pleaded.

"In my own time." A massive hand grasped our throat. When I tried to move my arms, he increased the pressure. "The drugs I gave you a few hours ago have dulled your strength. You're my plaything now." He withdrew his hand and I gasped and attempted to breathe as deeply as possible despite our chest pains. The fingers got bored of our face and started to slide across our shoulders and arms.

"I never realised how toned your muscles are. Such broad shoulders, too. A much better body than any of the most recent victims of my little 'hobby'."

I gulped. "Are you going to do that now?"

"Hmm. No, not right now. I'll talk to you in a bit, about what you really are."

"What we are? The whole truth, then?"

"Yes indeedy. It's time to take the cap off of these big old secrets. I'll tell you when I'm ready – I have to be in the right mood, especially when sorting out my instruments for later."

Curious, I came round to ask, "What, you're a musician?"

"Oh, no, my friend, not those kind of instruments," he explained.

My face dropped with disappointment; that woulda been an okay breather. "Oh. You bastard." I slinked back into the shadows to let Davy-boy take over.

"Ain't I just? Give it a few hours and you'll be all healed up, just to be mentally and physically torn all over again. Don't think that any of your psychic friends will find you; this place is well-guarded against psychics. See you in a bit, my special pets." There were more footsteps, growing distant, then the door creaked and closed, leaving us alone again.

It was hard keeping track of time in this bound sightless state. An hour, two hours, a day? For all we knew, only a few seconds had passed. It's like being in the queue in a busy supermarket. However, we could feel the swellings go down and our chest regain its strength, enough to blink without feeling pain and breathe freely. A game of 'I Spy' was in high demand, mostly from Cain, but then the obvious occurred to him and all was silent on his part.

The door soon opened and Dean's footsteps greeted us before light burst into the room thanks to a handy-dandy light switch and a powerful lightbulb. The room itself was quite small, around the size of the average living room, with Dean's frame making it downright claustrophobic. The damage we had given him was undone – there were no signs of shredded or bullet-riddled clothes, no exposed metal bones or unpeeled skin. Chances are he hugged against a wall to mend his back, couldn't see him having any more 'friends' to do it for him.

On one side of the room there was a small wooden table, a stool and a curved knife as its companions. On the other side, a metal helmet rested against the wall, its body a dark grey block with a thick chin guard dangling at the bottom. It looked like – no, it *was* the same device that had been strapped onto me/us in the memory we received, no matter how hazy it had been.

"You brought us some headgear, Dean? Not our style, but it's the effort that counts."

"You won't be trying it on just yet," Dean stated, his eyes scanning our body. "First I want to talk about your past."

"Ah, you're gonna take the bookmark out of that now, eh? Very well, Dean, enlighten us. Why do they want to wipe out humans, and how do they know about them?"

"It's a little complicated, but here we go. At the moment, they don't even know life's floating around this little shithole of a planet, nor do they have the notion of wiping out anyone. Their world is still intact, so they're fine as it is. The aliens – they're called the Norians – who gave me new life and configured you, are from the far future, give or take a millennium or two, living on Earth in a conjoined society with humans."

We were stunned, our eyes wide open and mind blank for a moment as we reeled in this information. Time travel. Admittedly, that never occurred to us. We'd seen and done too many things to not be aware of temporal tricks, so we were quick to accept it.

Time travel. I fuckin' HATE time travel, so confusin' an' weird an'... already my side o' our brain was hurtin', an' Dean hadn't done anythin' yet.

"Wait, so... we're from the future?"

"Bingo," Dean confirmed with a grin.

"Oh God. What's going on there – what's going to happen in that time?"

"First contact, rocky start, but sorted out in the end. Nearly everyone on both sides get comfortable with each other, even producing interspecies relationships, complete with itty-bitty hybrids. Of course, there's also opposition on both sides – 'we hate the corruption of our species', 'no purity among us anymore', 'this is our planet, not yours'. The guys who we're tied to are part of those factions."

"Sounds heavy. I hate to remember being there myself – I hate political-social arguments like that."

Dean let out a giggle. "I watched it all on recordings, nearly bored me to tears. I felt like I died all over again."

"But what I don't get is, why time travel? Okay, we get the idea, they want, or wanted, or will want to make sure that when the Norians head back to Earth, there's no unexpected neighbours, but why not do something more practical? Come to think of it, managing a time machine must've been expensive as hell."

"From what I've been told, starting a war would drain their resources and just complicate things. It's only the minority of both sides that hate each other, so starting a fight wouldn't be in their best interests unless they were suicidal. What would be the point in damaging a planet you reserved as a back-up with no additional back-up in mind? And besides, think of the damage – mountains shifted and clumped into small rocks, radiation washing over the land, craters littering the cities, massive insurance claims."

Being the fountain of information he was, I decided to sum up his answer as, "So basically, 'don't have a war, it's too complicated'. I tell you what, Dean, that'd be a great anti-war slogan."

"I swear I saw a bunch of posters and banners with that saying in the sixties. Anyway, someone like you, with the best qualities of both species, would be the perfect ironic genocidal assassin."

"The best of both... we're a hybrid?"

"Yes. Well, I wouldn't call you a natural one, though, not from what I've learned, but a mix nonetheless. Think about it, all the people you killed, even when you were doing your best to be a hero, or your worst. You helped slaughter thousands of humans and had no real idea what you were sent for. They told me to say thanks – you did a good job."

Our brain sank into our stomach, slowly and painfully as we went over this. Justice or revenge, saving or damning, we had been serving the Norians simply by going about our shared life. The Voice had been our greatest bane, and still we were fighting it, still we were trying to reclaim our humanity, unaware we had been fighting for the fate of the future. Was our time in this world, all the happiness and love and friends, worth every drop of blood and corpse we stood over, as far back as the early days?

All my life, I never thought it was like this, not this big a scale… god, what the fuck kind o' person was I?

As we contemplated Dean's words, he slipped the headwear onto us, tightening the strap just that little bit harder, though by this point we were too deep in thought to care. "Now, enough talk for the moment. This little present of mine, it's not just a great accessory. It's got a nice home movie on it. Want to see your daddy? I'm sure you'll point out how much you take after him, Cain."

Stepping back, he took the stool and placed it in front of us, taking his time to sit down as he refused to break eye contact with us. He took out the same remote-like device he had used back in Wolf Park, fiddled with a few buttons and our eyes were plunged into darkness.

*

We could no longer see Dean, but instead, security footage took up our field of vision, the colours washed out and the quality somewhat grainy.

A vast lab, its walls grey and lifeless. Glass tubes present themselves on the side, containing green liquid that bubbles away, and various other machines and monitors litter the place. In the middle of the room, a young man lies down on a metal slab, unconscious and naked, a metal helmet gripping his head while an older man observes him, smiling from a control panel. The prisoner's face and body is ours, from what can be made out – he is us, yet at the same time he is not. The older man's eyes shine yellow, his pupils slit and a pair of fangs stick out in his glee. He wears a black uniform that clings to his thin figure, covering his hands and feet with red lines down the side. A few moments later, he glances at one of the panel's readings.

"Excellent," he cries out in a voice frail yet determined to cling to the strength of his fading youth. "The mindwipe's done its work. No memories in that head of yours, my friend. Empty, but not for long."

Pressing a few buttons on the panel, a jolt is sent through the young man's body, arms and legs moving erratically as though electricity is racing inside him, yet he does not waken nor scream.

"In a moment, your mind will be replaced my voice, a perfect copy of my own will. My ideas, personality, memories, all of me will be inside you. I will live anew," the man gloats, revelling as he twists the captive's brain. "The Norians will reclaim their rights – I WILL it to be!"

Just as he reaches the height of his experimentation, a loud booming voice, female but artificial, fills the room. "ATTENTION, MASTER. I HAVE DETECTED INTRUDERS ON LEVELS FOUR AND FIVE."

"What? Intruders? How did they get in? How did you miss them?"

"I SUSPECT THEY CAMOUFLAGED THEMSELVES, MASTER, THROUGH VISIBILITY DAMPENERS OR DEACTIVING MY DEFENSE NETWORKS ON THE PROCEEDING FLOORS."

The Master, as he is dubbed, grits his teeth. "BETRAYAL! That must be it! Asmish, *activate the* Proxnir Wave *on Level Six – I need more time!"*

"MASTER, THE PROXNIR WAVE *IS FOR DIRE SITUATIONS. IS THIS SUCH A TIME?"*

"OF COURSE it is! They CAN'T take this away from me! They WON'T! I will set right what once went wrong – I swear it, on the lives of the GREAT NORIAN EMPIRE!" He moves away from the panel and the footage cuts to another side of the lab, revealing a large black machine that dwarfs all the others; an arch with red runes etched into its grand metal frame, as though it is some ancient otherworldly force

providing immense help to the man's realm of technology. It lies against the wall, the hole reflecting the lab's grey colour like a pool, but as soon as the Master flips the appropriate switches and dials on the thick rectangular panel alongside the arch, a red glow surfaces and crackles violently while the runes burn bright like the sun.

"There we go. Now for the coordinates." He punches them in before running back to his subject, leading to the previous camera angle, examining the panel for the mental rewrite. "Oh, Achman's Bane, it's taking too long. Thirty percent complete. Come on, hurry up!"

"MASTER, THE INTRUDERS HAVE TAKEN THE WAVE INTO ACCOUNT AND PROTECTED THEMSELVES FROM IT. THEY ARE NOW SIXTY FEET FROM YOUR POSITION."

The Master reluctantly stops the process and removes the helmet from his subject. "No time, no time, no time. Must move, send him off, heal the Empire…" The still-unconscious body is dragged over to the arch, slumped to the floor as the Master heads over to its connecting panel. "Yes, definitely the right period. Those apes won't see it coming. Pre-emptive strike, yes, yes."

A sound off-screen – a door forced open, crashing to the floor, an explosion? – and voices yell at the Master.

"Doctor Sacratus, stop where you are!"

"You're under arrest for conducting illegal experiments and attempted terrorism."

The now-identified Sacratus dashes over to a nearby table and grabs the pistol resting on it. He shoots wildly in the directions of the intruders while getting his experiment to his feet, the two of them dressed in the red glow of the massive machine. "TRAITORS! Traitors, all of you! By Mensur's Arrow, you will pay for your betrayal! I'll set things right, just you watch!"

Gunfire from the unseen opposition races past him like blurry lightning bolts, every hit lowering the quality of the footage for a few seconds. In the midst of conflict and shouting, he raises the captive to his feet again, sending off a blast at the police frantically, and uses all his strength to push his guinea pig into the great red light of the machine, and so the young man vanishes – we vanish, leaving Sacratus alone as he continues his defence, his manic fury replaced with a smooth reassured smile. As if to dampen his victory, the authority's gunfire strikes the panel, birthing a shower of sparks and electricity crackles wildly around it and the portal; Sacratus' anger is renewed, as though his very pride has been destroyed in the damage, left irreparable.

A group of officers, their bodies and faces clad in cold blue featureless armour and carrying silver rifle-like firearms, swarm him. The police read through what could be made out as his rights amidst his rabid rants condemning them, though that changed once they placed a clear see-through helmet on him – he instantly calms down, his acquisitions dropped and replaced with silence. The footage switches over to the lab entrance, where the door lies flat on the ground, and the police escort him out, though as they do, there is a trace of smugness around the corners of his mouth. Victorious even in defeat.

*

The footage died in a black wash, and for a moment our eyes had trouble readjusting to normal vision. Dean still sat there on his stool, his great arms now crossed. He looked like he could have killed for a bag of popcorn. For a few seconds, our mouth and voice felt non-existent. We had heard and seen everything, but our brain was continuing to process every little detail by the second; the words, the actions, the meanings. To have been told our purpose fell flat when viewing the footage, glimpsing the shadow of our past and the future of Earth and its people, both old and new. We had been the tool for someone's sick mission, the

388

ultimate in evil, and the sheer scope of the operation grew in our mind like a tumour in place of the Voice.

'Jesus, Cain,' I thought, 'that was… unsettling. I never thought that we were used like— Cain, are you there, mate? Answer me.' I could tell that, in the depths of our brain, there was a cold emptiness lying where Cain was. 'Where are you, Cain? Come on, don't freak me out here.'

'Don't wanna talk,' he said, and I was both thankful for a response and worried. 'Need to go over this.' The coldness in his spot returned.

I was going to be alone, now of all times, of all places, with the worst person in front of me. This was the first time I was met with a Cain who was shocked enough to isolate himself from me, and that scared me.

Dean, oblivious to our inside chat, spoke first. "Speechless, boys? I thought so. Gotta love how the cops misfired and hit the time machine – I blame sloppy training."

I found the strength to respond, trying to act unfazed from the 'home video'. "What happened to the machine?"

"It got broken, genius. Not completely useless, just faulty. You view fragments of history in certain locations, like watching TV, but when it comes to actually travelling back, the exact coordinates are slightly random, and you only have a few minutes to frolic in the past before you have to head back or else you're stuck."

A broken time machine? Now that was an odd development. That would at least explain why none of these rogue Norians or anyone else decided to pick us up as early as possible when things didn't go their way. With this problem, it would also mean that it would probably never be repaired (or hasn't been repaired, or will never be repaired – bloody time travel tense troubles), otherwise we'd have been nabbed already and have centuries of our life undone. That's the annoying thing about time travel, you never quite know if A goes before B, if breakfast, lunch and dinner go in that order, or if the worst moments in life happened because some git went back and changed a few things. Knowing Dean, he'd have added some more torture to this by not including a diagram.

"Right, let me guess," I said, piecing things together as best as possible, "they took you to the future, patched you up, and dropped you off some time after the house fire, a couple of years or so? Maybe not even in the same country as before, so you might have had a wacky adventure or two trying to get back? Is that the right answer or am I allowed an extra guess?"

"I can tell the years haven't worn down your thinking cap, bounty hunter. I felt like I was in their world for years, probably was, for all I know."

"It's a good thing they don't have customer service, then. God, I hope they don't. That Doctor Sacratus – or 'daddy', as you call him – he must not have been willing to divulge any info on how to fix the machine. He's got to be pretty proud of himself, breakdowns notwithstanding."

Dean chuckled heartily. "Oh, the man's got quite the ego, I can tell you. But his side, The Great Restoration, they're not the only faction involved, none of that black-and-white shit. When word got out about his tampering with history, loads of other groups rose up with loads of different ideas of how to approach you. On one side, kill you for history's sake, needs of the many and all that, or to prevent others from getting their hands on you and dissecting your beautiful augmented body. Then we got the 'family-friendly' options: give you a peaceful life in the future, maybe undo the changes made to you, or leave you as you are in the past – after all, if the good doctor's plan had succeeded, then the future would've changed instantly, or so they seem to think."

"I had no idea we were so popular."

"You're not the only big names, you know. Ever since I was taken out of my time, all these groups wanted me to do damn near everything for them, even stuff that went over my head. But I whittled it down to the two best options at the time; drag you back to the future, or kill you here and now." He emphasised 'kill' like it was a sweet he had dreamed of eating for so long.

I hated to ask, but I had to. "Which one will you go for? Have you already decided?" Our heartbeat strummed so fast that I feared a heart attack was just around the corner.

Dean stood up and leaned towards me, his face close to ours. "Yes, I've made up my mind: I'll do neither. I'll have you all to myself, damn what they say. We'll just keep to ourselves, move across this world, invisible to everyone. No matter how long it'll take, we'll dodge them. No one can get in the way of my love and hate for you, or what I'll do to secure it, my little bounty hunter." He caressed our chest with gentle fingers before sliding them down our abdomen. "I'm going to have so much fun tearing your body to shreds over and over. My dreams will be realised." His hand went lower and the softness faded as aggression took over.

I tried to keep a brave face as I felt his uneasy touch, unable to drown out my forced moans. "Dreams... fade, Dean."

"That may be, but they always seem to last forever, don't they?"

"Only makes me want to... wake up even faster from this nightmare."

He gripped our manhood, nearly squeezing the life out of it. "Beautiful. I'll lop it off, and then once you've healed from that, I'll give it back to you in my own... special way," he revealed with a large, monstrous grin.

"No..." Seconds were starting to turn to years as he held on.

"Yes. It's been my favourite fantasy for decades; it has to be fulfilled, with or without your consent." The grip tightened, and I yelled. Before our throat could grow sore, he let go as quickly as he handled it, and all the life and pain and relief Cain and I had accumulated for millennia rushed into our groin in great drumbeat throbs.

"W-why did you let..." I tried to ask, my voice weak.

"I don't have the right equipment at the moment. Using that knife over there wouldn't feel appropriate. No, I'm thinking of something more grandiose for this little reprise. I'll be gone for a while, but try not to miss me too much." Dean removed the device from our head and placed it on the floor before making his way out of the room.

"Hopefully," I said, "we'll die of boredom waiting for you."

The lights went off and door was closed, leaving me and Cain (or rather, just me) with the dread of what was to come.

'Cain,' I called for him in the darkness. 'Cain, can you hear me?'

No reply. The thoughts of Dean's upcoming game of 'Slice, Dice & Insert' were forgotten as I grew more and more worried for my friend.

'Cain, please answer me. Talk to me.'

He did, but his voice wasn't loud and arrogant, nor snide and witty and rude; it was small and afraid. 'I'm sorry, David.'

'Sorry?'

'Yeah, cuz I'm here with ya. If I weren't, ya coulda had a different life, a better one, been Raanan for years an' years, not cursed with a monster in yer head. I put ya through some terrible stuff, an' I'm sorry for that.'

'Cain, don't—'

'What've I done since I first sprang up? Kill. Kill the guys who saw you as their brother, an' ya got exiled for that. Killed people left an' right in the War... so many people... just because I was hungry for death, an' I never thought o' the consequences. Some nut decides to erase humans from history, an' I'm what he got. Hell, I ain't even my own man – just an empty-headed double o' his with an' order sent into yer head. There ain't one good thing I've done all these years compared to all o' yer heroics.'

'Come on, we've done a lot together, Cain, and in all that time you've grown. You're not a monster anymore.'

You know anger, pain, joy, love. I'm not living with a demon – I'm living with a friend, a brother. And I'm sorry for making it worse when we did that "target certain bad guys" thing back in the day. Not a day goes by where I don't feel like I haven't used you.'

'Thanks, man. For what it's worth, all the arguments, all the lil' disagreements, back an' forths, they don't mean anythin' – you are my best friend, an' from now on, we don't take each-other for granted, 'kay?'

'Right on, brother. You know, we've got quite a bit of time on our hands; I guess we might use that time for a few more discussions?'

'Beats dyin' o' boredom, I 'spose.'

The grand sight of nothing started to become our favourite view during our suspension, as well as conjuring up images of friends and foes alike in a desperate attempt of a pastime. When we brought up Emily, dressed in jeans and a brown leather jacket, her hair a lovely wavy stream, smiling and talking to us wordlessly, something hit me, like a chisel inching through our brain.

'She might have been planted,' I thought.

Cain's thoughts rang with confusion. 'Planted? Like, what, she was some sorta agent?'

'No, not an agent, or a sleeping one. I mean that chances are her life from when we first met her to when she was at university was arranged by someone.'

My old friend hesitated before he talked back. 'Are you fuckin' insane? That... that don't sound right, get me? I think yer part o' our brain's got 'crazy-in-dark' syndrome.'

'No, listen to me. How likely was it that Emily went to the same university as that lad with the Rhasadon Box?'

'Kinda likely, to be honest. Lotsa people around from all over the place.'

'Yes, true, but if we dig a little further, how likely was it that she, of all people, turns up on the same campus, in the same building, recognises us after all those years, and decides to help bust Rhasadon and is very accepting that demons exist?'

'Got me there,' Cain said, stumped. 'So… lemme get this right – you think that maybe one o' those factions in the future screwed around with her life so we'd turn out fine when Rhasadon popped out?'

'Perhaps. After all, according to Dean and that footage, we were sent back in time, and we don't know how this might affect things in the future. It makes sense that some of those groups would want to preserve history.'

'But if we got killed by Rhasadon originally without anyone to help, wouldn't he have fucked up humanity? And what about when the Norians turned up – if there's no humans, how would we have been made and sent back to… oh no, I've gone cross-eyed.'

'Yeah, it's not a solid theory. Bringing up the time paradox thing makes me seriously doubt Emily is someone's pawn. Then again, chances are we're talking about alternate timelines – going back and changing the past could create a separate reality that would have no bearing on the original world, so there's probably be two separate realities now.'

'Don't make our head explode, ya goddamn encyclopaedia!'

'Okay, okay, but you get my point.'

'Just about,' Cain grumbled.

'Still, it's all speculation. Sorry, I think everything that's been said today has started to make me pondering the wrong places.'

'I agree. It's just a theory. A big, bold, brutal, bullshit theory that needs way too many diagrams. In my humble opinion.'

'Yeah, too true, Cain. I don't want to see Emily as a puppet instead of a person. Let's… let's think of something else, something a bit more relaxing.'

'Before we get our dick cut off.'

'You're great moral support, buddy.'

394

Chapter 36

Showdown

Dean entered the room, breaking the darkness once more as he turned the lights on. His footsteps were loud and quick, his face screwed up in broad anticipation, red with joy. The white brick walls that were his teeth were stuck together as he ground them, and his voice grew low and excited.

"It's time, boys."

"Oh, finally," I said in faux-exhaustion. "I thought it was going to take forever for you to let us go. When we get out of here, we're gonna write a painful review on Captors.com. No tape over the mouth, no furniture, scant visits, not even the tiniest of tortures on our manhood to stimulate us. Terrible sense of horror or fear: one out of ten chloroform bottles."

"No, time to have my fun with you. Below the belt. Snip-snip." A grin overwhelmed him.

"Very well, then, take a bit off the top, make sure the hairs look stylish."

The grin vanished. "Don't think you'll be able to mask the pain. If you keep up your attitude, I'll give you some more of that drug, so expect your healing factor to be dampened."

That certainly shut me up. "Well, let's this over with then," I muttered, bracing myself.

"Now we're on the same page." He removed a machete holstered under his jacket, a behemoth of a blade glistening in the light, overwhelmed in a moment of awe as though he pulled Excalibur from its stone confines.

Oh, Jesus Christ.

Oh, Jesus Fuckin' Christ.

"I'd say this won't hurt, but where's the pleasure in that? Close your eyes and scream for me, my devils." His large right hand cupped our genitals, then squeezed them tightly. The surging, flaming pain concentrated there was tough as hell to shrug off – I gave out a loud, hard yell. I swear we heard Dean sigh.

As he raised the monstrous knife to do the deed, the lights suddenly cut out. Dean's hold on us ceased, almost reluctantly. "What the hell was that?"

Cain surfaced to crack, "Has someone not been payin' their electricity bills, Deanie-boy?"

"Be quiet," he whispered into our ear. We could hear him moving about, fiddling with the light switch, but it didn't work. He opened the door, only to find even more darkness, not so much as a flicker in the hall. "Strange, this has never happened before. What could have caused it?"

"I second the bill theory," I prompted. There was something different in the air, we could feel it, a new element surrounded us, though it was difficult to pinpoint what it was.

"Good thing I have a torch," Dean said, bringing the small blue light of a mini-torch to life, aiming it at our manhood and casting a frightful glow on his face. He made sure to bring the tip of the machete close to our pubic hair, seconds away from tearing into us. "At least I'll be able to see what really matters."

"I am afraid you are quite blind to that," a low, cultured voice whispered in the dark, slicing away the loneliness.

"What…who's there?" The torch turned away from us as Dean shone it desperately around the room in search of this intruder, peering it into what laid beyond the four corners of the room with no results. For all his knowledge of us and the IISEP, it was clear that the disembodied voice was new to him, this educated creature who was bold enough to reveal himself with a tasteful taunt. But we knew who this was, it was hard to forget, even with all those centuries behind us. He had arrived, of all people, which raised a few questions, but the most prominent one now was, what was going to happen? There we were, the four of us in the dark, and only one could call himself the True King of the Night.

"Where are you? Come out so I can show you how foolish you are in thinking you can take me on." Dean was sounding more irritated than baffled. He and the torch made their way back to us, the brightness causing us to close our eyes for a few seconds. "Alright, if you won't show yourself, then watch your friends suffer!"

The blade's movements were felt in the air as it was raised back to hack us up. Dean didn't get the chance to bring it down when a harsh force burst through and blew him across the room and out the door, his flashlight rolling to the ground as he was smacked against the wall. In the blink of an eye, the bulbs came back to life, showering us with a view of our saviour as he faced Dean. A great volume of white hair stuck out in regal splendour, combed and gelled into position with only a single curl hanging on either side near his pointed ears. The expensive black suit and leather gloves made it look as though his pale head was the only part of him with skin, and even then there was the question of how long it would take before decomposition sank its own teeth into him. His face was charming, a bold classic film star look, broad with a high brow, his lips and cheeks as though they had been sculptured. His deeply set eyes shone a warm shade of blue, inviting enough to lose yourself in them and let you be his if he wanted to.

"Please don't bother trying to get up and fight, Mr Dean Gregory," he said in his soft beautiful voice, "it is pointless to resist me. Give yourself up and I won't try to drain what little life you have left in your tinman shell. I so detest going back to those savage days."

Ever the defiant one, Dean got to his feet. "Who the fuck are you?"

"I am not surprised by your question, as vulgar as you phrased it. My name is Alexander, but you may know me by another. Aspects of my youth were written in a book by an old friend of mine. You've seen me portrayed by many

397

an actor across many a medium, none of whom were close to matching my true face. I may not possess an outrageous cape or widows peak, nor a rodent-like body or a red coat and hat, but I am the Call to Blackness, the Vein Gorger, the Cloak of the Night, the One True Vampire. The world has come to know me as… Count Dracula. You may kneel before me if you wish, but that will not be necessary – should you continue to resist, your body will lie before me, welcoming Death." Placing one hand behind his back, the sophisticated vampire raised the other in our direction, guarding us like an undead barrier.

Our captor took this in stride, working through a crick in his neck with a smug-smothered smile. "Oh, Dracula, eh? That's quite a kicker, I give you that. Always wanted to fight you; guess this'll be another fantasy brought to life."

"Unfortunately, my cybernetic child, you will not live long enough to enjoy it," Alexander replied, turning his open hand into a fist. A black glow swept over his arm, energy lapping like an ocean wave, its presence oddly soothing and casting a mild heat. With no hesitation, Alexander threw a punch, slinging the black substance off him into a large ball, hitting Dean straight in the chest and sending him through the wall he was pressed against in an explosion of raw, thunderous power, leaving a great hole in the wall that ventured into a corridor, leading to another hole that casted a black void. To see Dean as a pushover after everything he did was hard to believe, but it was also immensely bloody satisfying.

Our thoughts summed it up nicely:

'Holy…'

'…shit!'

"That will put you in your place, boy. If your body had been wholly flesh, you would have met the Reaper instantly." Alexander turned to us and flicked his sharp fingernails at our restraints, causing them to fall apart and remove themselves from us. After spending God-knows-how-long tied up like a sadomasochist's cheeky piece of art, it was so good to finally move our limbs and rub our joints.

"Thanks, Alex," I said with great relief. "You could *not* have come at a better time."

"It's good to see you unharmed, gentlemen," he said with a smile creasing his face. "Before you ask, your friends are fine. The warehouse was a success, all spirits were captured, and the forcefields were turned off once that happened."

Neither Cain nor I could sigh deep enough with this news. They were okay, thank God! "That's great to hear. Alexander, you're one hell of a messenger. How did you find this place? I thought it was psychic-proof."

"You seriously underestimate Selma's talents, my friend. There was initial difficulty in tracing your location, even with the great deal of positive feelings between your colleagues, but she was given a big enough boost with aide of... I believe their names are Emily and Scarlett, correct?"

"Yes, that's right! I... we need to thank them so much for that. Are you the only one here?"

"No, the rest will enter shortly. I am the first wave, to call it such. The new boy, Christopher, he informed me that you might have been in danger, and could hardly find a better opportunity in which to repay my debt to you."

"Wh-what debt was that?" Yeah, we were honestly baffled by that.

The King of the Night's face dropped. "Seriously? Five centuries, countless dinner conversations, and many a fight later and you don't recall?"

"Um... no, but I'm sure we'll remember it eventually."

"I'm beginning to regret saving you now. Oh, one more thing: I found these in one of the rooms in this corridor." The vampire sent a hand into his slick suit pocket and produced, amazingly, our underpants and jeans, neatly folded up, and put them in our hands. Hiding big items in ridiculously small containers – not exactly a common practice in the world of supernatural beings, but something

Cain and I had hardly seen in all our years, let alone from vampires. As we put on our newly-recovered clothes, he then produced the rest of them, shirt, waistcoat, socks, shoes, both our prized MIA and emergency Stetsons, and our especially long red coat. I put on our red Stetson and handed him the replacement. Just when we thought he hadn't picked up dear old Bob and his stun gun cousin, he had indeed, complete with holsters.

"Fangtastic! Is this one of your powers? I don't think we recall that."

"Just like you, my friends, I have an unusual taste in clothes."

Once we had embraced our second skin like a dad hugging his child, the three of us left the room. Taking caution into account, I grabbed the knife by the table that Dean had discarded for sake of his 'bigger is better' fetish, and doing so flooded us with déjà vu, making the blade feel twice as evil. Alexander went to the hole in the wall that was made by his energy blast and came out of it dragging Dean by the ankle, turning our mortal-slash-immortal enemy into a toy.

"Need any help there?" I couldn't help but offer my services, feeling slightly useless, especially after seeing what our friend had done.

"No, do not worry. Come, let us—"

A blast of lightning struck Alexander, consuming him greedily and cracking his skin until, weakened, he collapsed, losing his grip on Dean. It was then we saw that the cyborg was awake with an outstretched arm sporting a small metallic groove in the palm before disappearing. He stood up somewhat shakily, trying his best to grin and supress the twitches in his face. His voice was now cursed with electronic crackling and whirring that interrupted him and stretched his words.

"Talk about disappointing. You think –*kkk*– I wouldn't have some *ki-i-i-ind* of back-up system installed for situations like this? Old fool. Age has certainly raddled your

400

brain." A terribly hard kick was sent to Alexander's head. "Never mind him, though. If he's here, *the-e-e-ere's* a good chance your other friends are here, too, and I hate uninvited guests." His machete in hand, he shoved us aside and made a dash down the dark corridor.

Anger boiled in our veins as we went after him, raising the knife to stab him senselessly, our body shifting back and forth as we fought over which of us should hurt him first.

'He has to be stopped…'

'…gotta be stopped…'

'…at all costs…'

'…no matter what…'

'…we'll deal with him…'

'…wanna kill him…'

'…put him under arrest…'

'…kill kill kill…'

We heard the Voice – no, Doctor Sacratus – starting to creep back, flickering, skimming, whispering across Cain's psyche, demanding to live again, to fulfil his insane mission, to win and take comfort in that knowledge. But somehow, in the midst of blind rage and panic, we kept him under our thumb, though it wasn't easy as we pursued our more tangible enemy across the barely-lit corridor. Dean aimed a hand over his shoulder and a groove popped up before a concentrated ball of electricity sprung from it; we just about managed to dodge it, never dropping our speed as the chase continued.

"You're awfully quiet, boys," he shouted. "Got a lot on your mind? Being around me, I'm not surprised."

More anger, our head hurting as Sacratus' echo tried to re-establish itself. We got close enough to retaliate, swinging our knife across his back, trying and failing to create a big enough opening to use the stun gun on him, so we dug it into his neck instead. We must have hit a nerve along his mechanical structure, because he screamed and came to a halt. Good, we wanted him to feel pain. Keeping a firm grip on the blade, we got in front of him and punched and clawed at his big stupid-looking mug, fake flesh peeling off in pieces revealing the metal beneath as we sliced his neck and throat. In return, Dean drove the machete through our knife arm along the bicep, causing a hard-working limb and the sleeves it wore to fall off. It's pretty hard not to cry out when your limb goes bye-bye, but it can be done with enough experience. Our brain took a second to realise that our left arm had been hacked off, and we were washed with hot pain.

"*Nngh*— you bastard! That's our—favourite arm!"

"Oh, the pain on your face alone fills me with jo-o-oy," Dean exclaimed in orgasmic delight. "But before I can fill my house with your blood, let's start with your friends', shall we?"

"You'll…die tryin'," I growled, tryin' to push past the pain. "We'll— I'll make damn sure ya do."

"Are you? Alright, give me your best shot!" He raised the machete again, this time for our head, an' he seemed to do it slowly, probably to give us time to counter it just for fun. I ducked before we could do the headless-chicken act an' sent my one good (an' remainin') claw deep into the side o' his gut. I put all my weight into my arm as I threw the fucker to the wall an' forced his head into it, tightenin' my grip on him 'til we heard a few things crunch into that metal noggin'. Now for the fun part; runnin' and runnin' down that hall as fast as we could go, takin' pleasure in his clickin' distorted yells as his pathetic face got ground up by the wall's roughness, a good chunk o' his flesh feelin' the friction an' our scorchin' hatred for him. God, how I loved to loathe him, it made me feel alive.

As for me, it was satisfying to dish out karma on him, to dish out justice. Every second felt like an hour; as far as we were concerned, our will far outstripped our current handicap the same way Dean's own will outstripped his loyalty to his 'employers', or even the same way Doctor Sacratus' will outstripped the need for history to remain unaltered. All three of us were beasts, the outcome of

Sacratus' plans, I could see that now. The joy Cain and I felt in harming Dean was deserved or probably even sadistic, but either way we were going to end this game once and for all, no matter how long it would take to reach the result.

Once we reached a corner revealing a flight of stairs, we quickly released our hold on him, causing him to fall with a *THUD* while we pushed forward and reached the first couple of steps. What a rush. Dean was on his knees, trying to reconfigure his damaged face. How disgraceful he looked – we loved it.

"Come on, then, what's the problem? We gave you our best. Don't tell us you're already worn out. I thought Alexander was small-fry to you, but apparently, you were wrong for the first time in this joke you call a life."

That riled him up; he stopped fixing his face (now an ugly torn mess with lumps of skin piled here and there like a bad clay model) and found the energy to stand up, clutching the machete like it mattered to him the most, lunging at us with an animalistic scream. "I'm not worn out! I'm never worn out. No one – *nothing* – can beat me!"

We took a step back for each swipe of the machete, somehow finding our balance as we ascended the stairs backwards, trying desperately not to trip and tumble down. In a weird way, it was shaping up to be quite a workout, like something out a movie training montage.

"Really, Deanie-boy? Then how come you ain't hittin' us right now? An' what happened to all that respect, babe?"

"Be quiet!" He ground his teeth, his eyes turned red, his technique grew sloppy as he swung recklessly.

"Oh, touchy, isn't he, Cain? D'you think he's cranky, or that his emergency power-up didn't quite bring back all that's left of his brain? Probably both." The elevation was getting easier, as though the steps guided our feet automatically, yet the space between us and Dean was too small for us to get cocky (or cockier).

By this point, Dean was less the confident planner and more a loud, violent child, angry at the world and the people

403

he knew, defiant and selfish towards everyone and everything. The only thing he wanted to do, and in a way, what he was assigned to do, was to spread pain and delight in it. We cracked the exterior and seen his true self, and we were delighted in the pain we gave him.

"I will make sure," the madman yelled, "that you never hurt me again."

"Of course, if we said that, you'd call us weak. And anyway, you deserve everything you get."

Yet another furious roar. "Fuck you!"

I smirked at this. "I dunno, you don't seem like good boyfriend material to me – my old partners liked to be naughty in bed, not nasty."

With that, he pulled back the machete to stab us this time, and went for it. We were just able to sidestep it, and heard the machete tear into something. A door.

'Finally! I thought we were gonna find ourselves goin' up to Heaven at this rate.'

The revelation of bumping into a door after what felt like forever served a good distraction; Dean sent us through it with one great wallop. We crashed to the floor, leaving the back of our skull in agony and reminding us that we were also one limb short of being perfectly healthy. Turns out we landed in another great hall like the one we were in earlier, blessed (or cursed, given the owner) with many tables and chairs standing eagerly at either side. Rather than receiving another thrashing, instead we were given a much more pleasant gift – the sight of fifteen IISEP operatives wielding long-range stun rifles trained on Dean, coordinated in a strong row of fifteen. Standing in the cracks of their formation were Jackie and Brad, here to help save the day, thank God.

Just seein' Jackie made me feel safe already.

"Hey, guys," I said with something ghastly on my face that was meant to be a smile, "Nice of you to come along! Sorry for crashing into view like this, hardly a fitting entrance, or exit. Our host hasn't learned how to operate door handles."

"Just what I'd expect from a brute," Brad declared, flexing his left hand.

Dean smirked, unphased by this nifty little surprise. "You think this changes things? All of you will meet the same fate: dying at my feet, wishing you hadn't come." Given what Alexander said earlier, I wanted to cry out 'plagiarist'.

Jackie braced herself, her arms behind her back as she stared down Dean with her eyes small daggers wrapped in gold, her fangs unsheathed. "Dean Gregory, you are under arrest. Cease and desist or we'll be force to incapacitate you."

Slowly, very slowly, we got to our feet (which was slightly difficult when you can't balance out two legs, one arm and a stump) and kept our sights on Dean as we stepped back into the line of defence; protection is never an excuse for cockiness or lowering your guard, as we were unsure of how this would turn out no matter how ready we were.

Our friendly neighbourhood psycho snorted. "Honestly, I don't know why you bother making threats against me. No matter how tough you think you are, at the end of the day I'll outlast all of you mortals. Still, you've got balls."

A few rounds of blue stun rifle fire hit him before he uttered, "Activate shield", and a light green glow encased his entire body, covering him as a shiny see-through armour. He unleashed a flurry of his electrical palm blasts on the wall of operatives as they continued to fire, the dazzling bright exchange being too much for our eyes to bear, not to mention the crackling fusion of disruption in the air that playing havoc with our ears and the vibrations crawling across our body. Once the shots died down, all fifteen lads were down too, and they had hardly pierced his shield while his body twitched some more… and was a few feet closer in our direction.

"Th-they're n-not dead, for now." He grabbed one of the unconscious operatives by the ankle and swung him around like a club with monstrous strength, though we were able to dodge him, wishing to prevent any more harm to the poor guy or the others. It was hard enough for me and Cain due to being so close, Dean's shield made it difficult to figure out how to stop him. We were able to get behind him, but Dean quickly turned around and grabbed us by the throat with his free hand. A sudden energy blast from Brad's hand shook Dean a little, causing the green casing to flicker for a second, the shock rattling him enough to drop us and the poor human club he held savagely. There was no trace of pain aside from the now-standard facial twitches, so for him to let go was a testament of the power Brad quite literally held in his hand.

Brad conjured a smile. "See? Brutish, nothing more."

"Y-you damaged my shield!"

"How observant. And you call my new hand pointless." Brad adjusted the settings on his hand and another blast ran from his fingers, this one pushing Dean back bit by bit, one continuous red stream beating down on him, its glow and the shield's clashing in a blinding display, the effort in Dean's futile steps forward increasing.

In the middle of this, we looked over to Jackie and it was then, with the time and means to focus properly, that we noticed something – the whip she held in her right hand. A cat o' nine tails. For a second, we thought nothing of it other than an odd attempt at symmetry, a means to find a weapon that connected to her in some way. However, the red leather and the claw attachments on each tail tipped us off, and the presence of what was inside the whip was felt by us, clear as day – those who've used it before can sense it. Jackie had brought Aelurus' Tails with her, one of the most powerful and dangerous items in the IISEP's high-security storage; for her to wield it was a prelude to suicide. The look on her face indicated that she knew our realisation. I guess we were easy to read.

"Jackie, why did you bring it with you? You should know what using it means."

Dean shouted out in his great booming voice, "This won't change anything! You haven't pierced it just yet!" As if to say otherwise, the shield started to darken and fade.

Unfazed, Brad simply stared at our foe and replied with, "Exactly, not yet." Adjusting the settings once more, he called out, "Full power." The beam grew broader, surging with the full capacity of his anger, his frustration, his determination. The incredible force blew Dean across the hall, the tables and chairs hating the way their master zoomed past them, and collided with a statue that looked like it was miles away.

Wasting no time, Cain and I ran in his direction, calling out, "Brad, Alex is downstairs, make sure he's okay. By the way, nice work!" I bet he smiled at our compliment; we should have opened a betting pool for stuff like that.

Despite the numerous recreations of our adventures decorating the walls, the sadistic plans and dreams wishing to come true, the fifteen-foot marble statue of me and Cain (well, me) tipping our hat somehow topped everything he made concerning us. Dean was half-buried in its pedestal, black metal bent and warped around him suggesting there had been a plaque. The energy beam had caved in his chest, a great rift between his pectorals revealing charred blue steel and electricity surging in tiny buzzes.

"Seems like things are going monumentally well for us," I quipped, sporting a smile.

The machete finally fell out of his hand as he tried to lift it up, exhausted but unwilling to lose. "Well for all three of us, yes-s-s. It'll be better once your friends die – we'll— *kkk*—be able to fulfil our destiny together, just us and no one else."

Our smile was replaced by a cold hard stare, anger swelling up as we clenched our fist. "You know what? We've heard enough of you for one lifetime." Cain and I felt joined again, one being, one body and mind, focusing every emotion, thought, desire, semblance of power onto him. To be one, especially in times like this, made us whole. Our body shifted as we spoke, going back and forth with the smoothness of clay.

"Yeah, way more than enough, too much for anyone else to stomach. You talk about destiny, our destiny, yet you could've worked on yours, not worrying or thinking about us for one damn second. Maybe ya coulda turned yer life around – I mean, ya got into this shit cuz o' how much of an asshole ya were, so why not? Atone, save lives, get a nice husband, be an accountant, something to make this second life worth it, do more good than harm, and even if you failed, you would have still tried. Woulda, coulda, shoulda, what if, maybe, wonder, how about – they're words, important lil' words that show wasted opportunities, regrets, but o' course that'd go over yer head. We've come to terms with our past, the things that've haunted us for a long time. I've learned to accept who I am; I'll only kill when I absolutely have to, when there ain't no other way. See, some two hundred years, and in that time we've changed while you've been stuck in the same moment. We try and help, an' you just continue to cause chaos everywhere ya go."

What was left of Dean's face struck a smile. "Perhaps, but try as you might, neither of you have changed an awful lot. A do-gooder fool going through the motions and a living weapon with a troubled conscience. Vulnerable to a fault. Don't think what you do makes you superior to me. I'm here to help you see that."

"Oh, so are we know talking to the Noble Castrator?"

"No, just a reminder of the past... and a sign of the future, *your* future, and mine."

"Past? Yeah, we can get behind that. But future?" Punching him was an absolute delight, each blow peeling more and more skin off his face, twisting and bending the open metal and his skull. "You do not tell us – what the fuck – our future is! We are sick – and tired – and bored to tears – of hearing what you say our fate is! What we'll do with our

408

life ain't yer business – you obsessive – manipulative – sadistic – blowhardy – bastard!"

Dean was pushed further and further into the statue's base, marble and metal chipping off in shiny chunks. There were a few good fist-shaped dents, his eyes, hair and jaw caved in, resembling a horrific distortion of the human body laid out in a surreal painting. One of his eyes was starting to fail, switching between normal and complete darkness, like it couldn't decide. He tried to speak, but a garbled mess came out instead, words lost as any familiarity with the human voice was raped with electronic screeching and clicking.

Feeling satisfied, I twisted the knife further by telling him, "That should shut you up. Permanently." We walked away from this pathetic junkheap that had once been a man, and waved at Jackie as she made her way to us, the presence of Aelurus' Tails still unnerving despite the smile she wore.

I was ready to hug her, just to be comforted after everythin' that happened. Okay, that'd be an awkward hug with one arm, but what the hell.

Before we could draw any closer to each other, Jackie dropped her smile and belted out as she ran towards us, "Turn around, he's back up!"

The moment we swept back, too shocked to make a fist, Dean's arms wrapped themselves around us with such tightness that our arms started to bend and crush our ribs, muscles caught in one hell of a vice and screaming in pain. His face... Jesus, it was worse seeing it up-close. The mouth was a gaping hole with teeth either loyally sticking on, dangling or missing entirely; scant pieces of skin were along the eyes and cheeks; a jaw bent out of shape, a metal skull ready to kiss us with its cold lips. A strong stinking smell akin to nail polish burned through our nose, made even worse when he spoke.

"Kkkkk—don't—move—cat," he managed to croak out, his voice standing against a wave of static. *"I've activated my—self-destruct program. There'll be one hell—of an*

explosion. *If you aggravate the harm to my body—it'll go off a lot sooner."*

"By the Saints of— you bastard," Jackie cried out.

A tinny chuckle escaped him. *"Don't waste your breath. Two minutes—everything within ten miles will be lost in a crater."*

My voice was weak as he kept us in his deadly lock. *"What?* Sounds unlike you, chum. What happened to being with us till the end of time?"

"Running low on power thanks to you, critical damage— no way to recharge. If I'm going out, it'll be in style, taking you with me. Surely even you can't survive an explosion like this."

He was right, as far as we knew. Impalement, dismemberment, bisection, bullet to the brain, that's a usual steady week. Decapitation, blown to pieces, reduced to a fine ash or smoke, we daren't accept that in case our 'get out of death' card didn't hold up that well, especially if we're dealing with a massive explosion. For the first time in our life, we were scared of the very likely possibility that we were going to die for good.

I think Dean realised this, stretching his mouth out into a monstrous attempt at a grin. *"This is the best way to end things—otherwise you've lock me up for years—lie about killing me soon. To die with you—to hold you in my—our last moments—feels right."*

Jackie's voice cut into Dean's self-loving monologue. "Don't expect to win."

We looked over our shoulder (surprised that Dean's grip hadn't popped our head off toothpaste-style) and saw how firm and fierce she stood, gripping the deadly Aelurus' Tails. "I'll make you regret everything you've done, you monster."

"Go ahead, just try. As the host, I'm liable to grant the dead last requests. I've faced all kinds of lashings—my back was scarred before I was ten years old, so don't think yours will do any good."

410

"Dean," I said, very, very worried, "it will, believe us. That's no ordinary whip. It'll make what you received look tame."

I looked at her, my face feelin' long an' pale (seriously, how much blood had we lost by this point?) hers coloured red in determination. "Jack-Cat, ya know what that'll do to ya, dontcha?"

She nodded. "As long as I'm careful, everything will be fine."

"But ya don't know that for sure! Use it for too long an' yer dead! Think about this!"

"I have, Cain." She smiled at me, but it didn't ease our worries. Jackie stared at Dean and uttered the necessary incantations, loud an' strong. "Aelurus, Lord of the Whip, bind thyself to me and dispense thy justice!" Davey-boy took over to try an' escape from Dean's bearhug.

The handle grew longer, possessed by the vicious entity within, snaking along her arm and choking her bicep. Every one of the nine tails rose of their own accord, floating mid-air the way a person floats in water. A low voice, ancient and demanding and furious, rose from nowhere, speaking a language that was impossible for us to decipher. The whip was covered in a red light that brightened and brightened until flames erupted and spread along her arm, yet she didn't acknowledge any pain, just the stern look she adopted before, willing to do what she saw as the right thing.

A face emerged amidst the fire, looking at first to be a cat in the blurry view of things, before growing more and more defined as it stretched out; a twisted parody of a lion, its hair wild and flowing, with large lynx-like ears, teeth resembling great knives, the eyes great balls containing animalistic ferocity, and perhaps an ounce of sadism. The flames and face grew higher, nearly reaching the ceiling, and with it the rest of Aelurus' body was formed – even more vibrant wicked flames birthed the illusion of roughed-up fur, three tall limbs snaked out either side of its bulky frame, paws replaced with human hands and sharp black

411

nails, its swaying tail split into three with each one ending with their own clawed hand. To behold Aelurus in all its terror was to behold oblivion, destruction was guaranteed, no matter what.

It stared at us – or more accurately, Dean – and emitted a low growl. Aelurus was awake, hungry, demanding for a soul, ready and happy to 'play' with Dean, to claw at him, to terrify, burn and humiliate him beyond reason before its great scorching might. From personal experience, mortals and immortals alike don't stand much of a chance against demons unless they possess capable weapons, resources, cunning and knowledge…stuff that Dean was seriously lacking at the moment. Jackie's life force was being drained for every second Aelurus was active, and since the whip could muddle your thoughts the longer it's used, Cain and I wondered, with the countdown still in operation, if the demon might go against her wishes before this was resolved.

It leapt in our direction in excitement and adopted what seemed to be a grin. We worried that it might take us in pursuit of Dean as a hot blinding wave passed over us… but instead, only our favourite madman was swept away, his hold over us non-existent as his arms went through our body painlessly. Our ribs sighed with relief now that they were free, though the rest of our body throbbed all over in a cold prelude to yet another death as the results of blood loss started to creep in. Aelurus ran through the home of its new victim with the raw speed and force of a train, crashing through every wall it could find, thrashing across tables, chairs set alight as it strode past them, ramming through the marble statue and destroying it without a trace of its existence. Dean's screams were heard as he burned in Aelurus' stomach.

We looked at Jackie and what we came across worsened the chill in our bones. Her skin turned dull and pale, shifting to chalk-white while veins bulged along every muscle and blisters ruptured in a black-and-red flavour, bubbling hastily

412

like meat juices in a frying pan. The tummy she had perfected through dedicated hours of inactivity and snacking was met with a rapid fast, every inch and curve shaved off in seconds. Her shirt and trousers hanged loosely as her breasts, thighs and belly lost their shape and being. The cheek bones stuck out as her face grew gaunt, and the now-red glowing eyes started to sink into their sockets.

Our concern had us calling to her, Cain's desperation far exceeding my own. "Jackie! Jackie! Oh, shit! Can you hear us? Jackie! Jackie!" Shaking her by the shoulder did nothing except make it seem like we were talking to a puppet that was about to fall apart. Looking back at Aelurus, we saw how its many claws demolished brickwork and plaster as it ran along, while Dean's wails continued to haunt us and the heat of the creature caused us to sweat profusely. Things were getting way too hot here, and that's not even getting into the countdown. Come to think of it, how long had it been since it was initiated? Surely there wasn't much time left until…

Our answer came to us with a great BANG, wild arcs of electricity bursting through Aelurus' skin and sizzling the air, the demon itself ignorant of this mechanical indigestion, carrying on its pointless destruction as Dean's final, desperate scream was stretched and lost in a grinding sigh as the explosion settled and the internal thunderstorm died with him in what felt for a century passing us by. He was gone, dead at last, with no way of coming back this time. That scream wouldn't leave our head any time soon; to suffer at the hands of a demon like that and have your death prolonged in a warped last wheeze, it felt pitiful. With Jackie's life on the line, we were hardly in the mood to celebrate or shout "Yes!" with our fist in the air.

She was now bone-thin and nearly lifeless, red eyes flickering in the caves of their sockets, the whip stubbornly raised despite fulfilling its task. What the hell were we going to do?

413

I had an idea. It was kinda stupid, but fuck it, anythin' goes. I pressed my cold, cold lips against hers, red an' cracked with blisters, an' held her head with my one good arm. 'Come on, come on, notice,' I pleaded, fightin' through how uncomfortable it was to kiss her damaged lips, desperate to snap her outta this. Nothin'. Nothin' after ten seconds, more than I could handle, so I stepped back an' let the stress take over from here.

'Cain, why did you think that would work?'

'Hey, it worked in stories, didn't it? God, I don't want her to die, I don't wanna!'

'Cain, try and cool head, we'll think of something.'

'How can I keep cool? There's a big fuck-off flamin' cat roamin' around!'

I then jumped from scared shitless to angry the second I brought that monster up – Aelurus, this was all his fault! Demons always ruin everythin'. Now our head was poundin' as my emotions dominated me, roarin' out, "HEY, ASSHOLE!" I demanded his attention, an' I gained it; he stopped his rampagin' an' looked at us with his fuckin' ugly mug. Guess he's easy to annoy.

"Yeah, I'm talkin' to you, dickhead! You got her into this, you get her out of it! NOW!" Turns out Aelurus wasn't a master o' conversation – instead o' givin' us a sign o' obedience, he let out a growl an' braced himself, claws an' tails set on us an' ready to strike.

"Alright, then, I'll take ya on! We've beaten monsters like you before. Go ahead, do yer worst! I don't care, ya giant fuckin' pussy!" I even gave him the finger for extra measure. Now he looked pissed, red-hot pissed, the flames shinin' brighter, his deep growls soundin' increasin'ly personal.

'Cain, what the hell are you doing?!'

'Gonna fight the bastard, whaddaya think?'

'Oh, for the love of— I can't believe you're this stupid!'

'If this snaps Jackie out of it, then I don't care, David.'

Aelurus went an' pounced with that 'jungle-cat predator' ferocity, barin' his teeth like he meant to swallow us, pourin' out all o' his vileness an' parasitic need to take an' hurt in one long, explosive ear-rapin' roar. It was like bein' launched into the sun, the heat risin', sweat stickin' to our clothes, difficulty makin' out things an' breathin' was hard as he drew closer…an' before we could be gulped down quicker than vodka, the bastard dispersed instantly, snuffed out in a second, gone so fast I had to make sure I wasn't dreamin'. He just vanished the same way you'd blow out a matchstick – a big bulbous flame that went *puff*. The roar died instantly, leavin' the room awful quiet as we were left in a hall filled with wrecked shit.

'He's… gone.'

'That means she either broke away, or…'

'Don't you dare say it.'

'You know I wasn't going to.'

I wanted to turn around quickly, to reassure myself that she was fine now, but the fear o' 'otherwise' grabbed my legs so tight I had trouble breakin' away. But then her hand fell on my shoulder, the leathery finger pads cushion' the weight I felt hangin' over me, an' she shook me to be sure Davey-boy an' I hadn't died on my feet. It might as well have been her claws slashin' away at that grim 'otherwise', an' gave me the strength to turn 'round.

Jack-Cat – no, Jackie – was fine, her skin pink an' healthy again, demon-free eyes yellow an' back where they should, an' though she was still thin, her body was startin' to plump up, restorin' her to her rightful shape, like how her face rounded out an' hid the veins that crept up her temples. Aelurus' Tails rested on the floor, an' if it weren't for the fact they were hard to destroy, I would o' wiped 'em there an' then.

"Hey," she said, her voice kinda sore, weary.

"H-hiya," I said back, fearin' my ears were gonna burn off with how red they were. "Y-ya good now?"

"I think so. I might need to rest for a while; it's hard to even lift my arm right now. Sorry for that."

"Oh, right. Don't worry, it got the job done. I'll try an' help ya. You can rest on the way home, you look like you need it."

"You're one to talk, you're missing an arm."

415

"Eh, it's back there somewhere, it'll be fine. Actually, where the hell's Brad? He an' Alex shoulda come up right now."

Speak o' the goddamn demon, they did; Brad shouldered a tired-lookin' Alex outta the basement, the vamp's steps small an' careful. Dunno whether it's cuz o' the shock Dean gave him, or a mix o' how old he was, but it was a pretty rare sight to see Alex needin' someone's help just to stand.

"There you are! The fuck took you guys so long?!"

Brad sighed an' glared at me. "*You* try carrying a vampire who's been cheating on his blood diet."

"Oh. Fair enough." Alex was terribly addicted to the substitute blood packs at HQ, more than any other vamp, couldn't be helped. Our head was gettin' awful light alluva sudden. "N-now, if you excuse us, we have to die for a while. See you in a bit, guys." An' then we crashed to the floor as we blacked out an' our heart stopped. We wanted a nap, but this was takin' the piss.

Chapter 37

Let's Wrap Things Up

Somewhat unsurprisingly, Colin was in our face when we opened our eyes, though unlike before, when he garnered a creepy smile, this time it was a pout instead.

"Oh dear," he moaned, letting out a sigh as refreshing as the Antarctic, "you're awake."

It took just a second to realise that we were sitting in an armchair in a corner of the morgue, which was pretty weird. Don't get me wrong, it was a wonderfully stern chair with nice thick armrests, but the fact that our temporary corpse had been sitting there with Colin looming over us made us uncomfortable.

"Sorry to disappoint," I said as I rubbed our eyes as if we had been sleeping. "How long this time?"

"Six hours," he croaked. "I'm surprised you were as active as I'd been told; do you realise that any normal human would've been dead long before that chap you'd been after bit the dust?"

"Yeah, we do. Where's everyone else?"

"Oh, they're going through all that equipment they found in that fellow's place. Just a handful of items, but from what I hear, accessing it is like trying to break a concrete wall with your fists."

"Huh. I am not surprised. So, what's with the chair, Colin? No ice-cold slab for us? This is a bit too nice, even for you. Did you want us to feel nice and safe when we came to see you? Oh, you kind soul in a soulless room, you really know how to bring life to the place."

There was a sort of educational inflection in his voice when he explained, as though he was back to being a teacher at med school. "When I saw that all you lost was an arm, I thought it was best to give you something fitting to rest it on while it grew back. Believe me, I was very observant, and it was… wonderful, fascinating."

"Um, thanks for that," I uttered, flexing our new arm and detecting a slight numbness that would die down in an hour. I then realised that the shirt and coat sleeves of that arm still ended at the bicep, and sighed at the knowledge that we'd have to go out and buy a new shirt and custom design the coat once more, or hope that someone had found the sleeves and brought them back.

Spoilers, they did.

Jackie got a right seeing-to from Dwight about using Aelurus' Tails when she wasn't supposed to, what with it being a real dangerous weapon; however, he made it clear that in spite of that, she did save everyone's lives back there when no one else could, so he let her off with a very stern warning not to repeat wielding it again. She told us later on that even though she was far away from the whip (which was how she liked it) she could sometimes hear the low voice of Aelurus beckoning her to join with it again and be free of all her worries about intimacy and death.

"When I used it," she said, her voice wet with a sense of fear and longing, "it was like sheer bliss. I didn't have to worry about anything or anyone, just guiding Aelurus to the man I wanted to see gone. I saw things through his eyes and everything inside him, including Dean. As it kept going, I barely had a sense of who I was, but I didn't care, and that scares me. But I'm fine now, trust me."

Maybe it was because of the trauma, but she started to feel a little easier about being with people, especially workmates, and the chance to be close to whatever lucky soul she might have her eye on. Cain thought she meant him, only to realise that it wasn't the case before he could blurt out his assumption. I comforted him, my arm around his shoulder (metaphorically, of course).

We took Daisy in with us until we'd be able to find an apartment or such for her, but in the meantime it was nice having someone live with us, especially when she smiled all the time and her enthusiasm for food was blatant when shopping, taking as much off the shelves as her arms could manage. I helped her learn how to cook so her plans for pasta in chocolate-sauce and sausage and mash to resemble mighty castles was realised, so the three of us took turns every night sorting out dinner. As far as beginners go, she was quite creative in a childish way, and did a pretty good job with making sure the food wasn't under or over-cooked. She visited Tranue as often as possible during his stay in the cell – we asked as little questions as possible to avoid digging too much into a personal matter, but she always said, "It was okay," reminiscing about their lost childhood.

Emily and Scarlett found themselves getting a great deal of sleep for the next week, Scarlett especially thanks to having no one else's memories in her head except her own. They fancied a vacation soon, spend the odd week or two in the sun and forget their worries. Emily offered us the chance to tag along as a way to pay us back for helping them, but we declined – we stated that we'll be swamped with all these different cases for the next month, but in truth it was the fact that we had gotten them into this sorry mess that prevented us from engaging in a well-earned rest with what we guess we could call our family. In a way, I guess Dean had won - the words he had planted into my best friend's head as well as our own little independent bog of self-hatred were still there. It's difficult to say if Emily caught on to this, but she was a smart woman and we didn't doubt that, so when she said she'll think about arranging it for two months' time, I swear there was something in her eyes.

When we spent some time with 'em round their place one afternoon, Red an' I jammed to a concert video o' our great personal God, the Almighty Alice Cooper, may He Rock In Peace. Like I said, the kid had taste.

I told her my own lil' theory about him – y'know how he used to die in his shows – head cut off, hanged, shock in the chair? What if he was immortal like me an' Davey-boy, so his 'real' death was actually a cover-up, an' this is all part of a decades-long publicity stunt before he shows up nice an' fit so he could put on the most awesome series o' concerts in the history o' rock?

Red certainly liked it. "Ha, that would be awesome!"

As a guy who's made a career outta dyin' again an' again an' treatin' death like goin' to bed drunk at six in the mornin', I think my theory holds water. Or booze, if theories came as a pint glass; god, I wish they did.

We spent the rest o' the evenin' comin' up with more insane theories about stuff we liked; I think the kid an' I got on real well, she was like my lil' sister.

One night, as we rested in bed amidst total darkness, Dean stood at the end of our bed, healed and wearing his blue suit, facing us with a wide grin as he folded his arms smugly.

"Hey there, my little bounty hunter," he said.

I sighed. "Piss off. You're an hallucination, nothing else. You died and that's that."

"Is it? After all, I came back once, so why not a second time? There was never a body to be found; yes, I said it was self-destruction, and there was an explosion, but that could have been anything, couldn't it? And though I'm not really here – though come on, this might be a hologram right now – I still live on in your mind, because you can never forget me now after all that's happened."

"You're right," I admitted, the words forcing themselves out. "It'll be... hard to get the thought of you out of our head for a while."

"A while, you say. Try a decade or two. Or perhaps a couple of centuries, maybe several millennia down the line. What you count as a while, I can easily call eternity. Speaking of eternity, there's also that itsy bitsy piece of info regarding what's to come – you know, the Norians, the

420

humans, Kingdom Come starting to topple in the wake of extremists out for genocide and your lovely precious body?"

"We haven't forgotten. It's not exactly hard to ignore. We're just trying to take it in fully."

"Just think, there'll be more guys like me flooding in from the future; some wanting to save you and history, others wanting to bring you back and dice you up, a lot willing to wipe you out entirely, and let's not forget the idea that dear old 'Daddy's plan might be fulfilled one day. You won't be able to tell who's friend or foe – that'll be a challenge, won't it? Ooh, what a bloodbath! How exciting!"

"We'll find a way to deal with all that, and we'll do it as peacefully as possible."

"Ah, you say that, but do you mean it? Don't think I won't know when you're lying or unsure. This whole thing is too wide and powerful to fully comprehend, I'm surprised you haven't cracked entirely. Or perhaps you have, and it hasn't occurred to you."

"Oh, go back to Hell," I groaned, sandwiching my head behind the mattress and pillow in an effort to return to comfort.

"Oh, please," we heard Dean, "Hell's so boring. I'd much rather stick around here – you're far more entertaining. At least one of you is a little devil in your own right." He chuckled and then he was no more, allowing silence to reprise.

I think we captured the essence of Dean a little too well – even as an hallucination he was a smug prick.

"Well, that wasn't pleasant," Alice said, placing the 'grave' in her hand in the rack that had been compiled for the spirits in the warehouse.

Cain and I got up from the floor, rubbing our aching joints. With a recently-bruised ego, I was forced to speak on Cain's behalf as he rested in our head. "Too true there. We forgot just how darn angry some of those Klu Klux Krazies could be; I think from now on, we'll leave out the 'really bad' ones, just focus on the lesser criminals and lads from the War."

Alice shuffled through the rack, examining 'graves' for dates and names to know which ones to ignore. "Are you still sure about this? I mean, talking to all those guys is a pretty weird thing to do… and I like me some weird, but this is kicking it up a notch for me. You killed them, I don't think they're gonna be happy to see you again."

"Alice, we need this. Talking to Peter made us realise we have to stop running away from the past and face up to it. Pretty foolish to try and have a chat with nutjobs like the KKK or Nazis, really; hardly the best of people to talk to. The War was a dark time, and if we want to lighten its shadow even further, we need to talk to its— our victims."

"Wow, you and Candy Cain are, like, some of the angstiest guys I know. That's kinda hot."

My eyebrows jumped high in astonishment. "You certainly keep to your declaration of liking weird things, my dear. I'm sure somewhere out there, there's a nice troubled young man waiting for the joy you'll bring to him."

"Thanks. It'll be my luck if it's Chris – what a cutie."

"He'll be surely blessed, I bet. Anyway, not to rude, can we head on to the next poor chap?"

Alice pulled out the 'grave' of Nathan Jones, died 2013. The moment he saw us once he materialised out of it, he gritted his teeth. "You! There you are, you stupid-looking bastard! Take this!" He tried to strike us with his fists in a furious flurry, and when that failed, his legs.

Managing to dodge him repeatedly, I simply said to him, "Hello, Nathan, I just wanted to say I'm sorry for killing you. I intended to set things straight, but it's clear you have a different idea of going about it."

"You'll be sorry, alright! Shot me—in the leg—in that poxy warehouse! I used to be a kickboxer, coulda made a comeback!"

Not wanting to drag this out, I ended it with a swift kick to the knee. You can't really break a ghost's body, since they don't have any bones to break, but they can feel pain similar to what they felt in life. He went down easily.

"Sorry about that, Nathan. See you later… maybe."

Before he was whisked away into his grave again, he managed to let out, "Stupid-looking ba—"

Next, we tried one Matthew Hand, a chap from the War. He turned up in his armour, no helmet to conceal his dirtied boyish face, which stared at us in perplexment. "Where am I?"

"You are among friends, Matthew."

"You look— I know you! I perished because of you!"

"Please calm down, Matthew. Those days are long and distant now, and we are hardly the same people we once were. I changed, and for the better. I wish to make amends for what I had done to you and others like you. I am sorry, and wish to know you for the man you once were and forever will be."

After a long pause, Matthew calmed down like I told him to. "If this is the Devil's dark work…"

"It is not."

"Very well. I shall talk to you. It is… unheard of for a man to discuss things with his murderer, but I will allow you this opportunity to prove that you are another man now."

"Thank you, Matthew, I am grateful for your allowance. Now, let us begin."

Now that everythin' had been sorted out, we could actually kick back an' relax in the fabled relaxation room. The new pool table was installed, which I thought wasn't worth it when we coulda still used the old damaged one, but what the hay. Anyway, we sat down with Chris in one o' the booths, both drinkin' some watered-down soda (which was fuckin' disgustin', but Daisy had taken all the drinks outta the HQ vendin' machines an' most o' the good stuff at the bar, so needs must).

Chris asked us, "Fancy playing a game of pool? I've been practicing."

"Nah, doesn't feel like the right time, not after our... outburst. Still, I'm sure you'll kick our ass eventually, so I'm lookin' forward to that."

"Ah, right, okay. Fair enough," he said kinda disappointed, retreatin' by sippin' a bit more o' his crap soda. "So, how long will it take for Dean's equipment to be analysed? From what I heard, there was a lot of stuff."

"Dunno, really. Last time we checked, not even friggin' Master Touzer could use his best spells to unlock anythin'; not even the best alien tech in this era can crack it. We're talkin' seriously advanced shit here, I'm not surprised if we couldn't dig any further."

"That's a shame. All this future business, first contact with a species that called dibs here, factions on both sides mucking about with time. It wouldn't hurt to have some foresight, learn a lot more about it to prepare ourselves. Who knows what those groups have got up their sleeves?"

"I getcha. Davey-boy an' I need some more time to get a handle o' things, stop worryin' about what any of 'em are gonna do next. But trust me, yer talkin' to the wrong guy when it comes to time travel. I fuckin' hate time travel. Can't watch 'Doctor Who' without reachin' for the Anadin."

Just then, Jackie walked up to us, carryin' her own drink. "Hey, Cain."

"Jack-Cat, hi there. How's it goin'?"

"Fine, just need to relax a bit more after all that's been happening." She rubbed her right arm, experiencin' the phantom pain of Aelurus.

"Hope ya feel hundred percent pretty soon. Look, I just wanna say... about what we did the other night, at yer place..."

"Yeah?"

"I found it a tiny bit off."

"Oh, really?"

"Yup. It was a little painful, sure, but not enough to ruin the whole thing. I enjoyed how flexible you were, to be honest, especially yer tail."

424

She smiled as she thought back to it. "We had a good laugh about that, eh? So, you wouldn't really be up for it again?"

"Well, we had a couple o' drinks an' that made it better, but I think we should try out with other people 'till I'm bold enough for another go."

"How about doing it with a load of people?"

"Nah, that'll just complicate everythin'; imagine the mess."

"But that's part of the fun, isn't it?"

"True, but I prefer doin' it one-on-one."

"Fair enough. If you want me, I'll be sitting in one of the booths over there. Ta."

"Ta." I gave with a lil' wave as she walked off, noticin' how her tail moved playfully with her hips. I went back to lookin' at Chris an' saw him with his mouth and eyes wide open. "What's up, fella? You look a bit pale."

"Sorry, I just... um, from what you're talking about."

"Really?"

"What were you doing together that night?"

"We was just playin' Twister, that's all."

"O-oh, okay."

"Why, what did ya think it was?"

"I, um, I'm ashamed to say it, but I thought you might have had... s-e-x," he whispered.

"No, no, god no. Get yer mind outta the gutter. Just Twister, that's all. Mind you, it was naked Twister, but I don't think it changed the rules much."

Chris sprayed his drink everywhere.

"Oh, for the lovva Jesus' crib, man! I thought you were polite."

"N-naked?" he squeaked. "How could you— I mean, are you seeing each other then?"

"No; she said since we're only just startin' to get to know each other, we should see how we get along first before decidin' we got a chance together, y'know?"

"But... Twister?"

"Lemme lay it down, bud. Her people wear clothes, 'course they do, but doin' stuff with someone in their birthday

425

suits means that there's a certain connection between ya that others don't provide."

"Like romance?"

"No, I mean like sharin' the same rare point o' view or... actually, that's all I got so far for reference, but it's more basic friendship stuff than relationship stuff for her people. At least, that's I've got so far."

"Oh, right," Chris said with a nod as the info sank in, or just about. "That's certainly interesting. I never thought aliens could have such an open form of intimacy."

"Hee-hee, makes ya wish you got involved, huh? An' anyway, even if we wanted to get frisky under the sheets," I carried on, smirkin' as the kid's face reddened, "we can't. We're incompatible, to put it one way, bein' different species an' all. The closest we got to that was when we—"

"I got it," he cut in, "please don't say any more. The images, they're too much."

"Come on, kid like you at your age, probably had a cheeky thought here an' there. Okay, in all seriousness, I'm sorry, I'll stop, letcha talk wi' Davey-boy."

"Thank you," he said, hidin' his relief.

"Ah," I said, feeling pretty relieved myself as I sipped our drink. "Now I get to enjoy this openly. Wonderful. We need different flavours here. I'm rooting for vanilla. Which one would you go for?"

"Go for? Um, I don't know. Cherry?" He sipped his drink steadily.

"Not a bad choice, Chris, not a bad at all. Oh, I nearly forgot, Alexander told us about how you informed him we were in danger."

"H-he did?" Chris almost spilt his drink as his head jerked in mild surprise.

"Yup. That was pretty brave of you, all things considered."

His cheeks turned red as he talked. "Well, it was nothing, honestly. I just ran and ran and ran and then fainted right before I spoke to him. I've never really been an active person."

I raised my drink to him. "Still, you were a life-saver. We just want to say thanks for that. You couldn't have helped at a better time, trust me." Snip-snip.

"Thanks," said the boy, smiling properly for the first time since we met him. "I guess it's good to know some people, eh?"

"Very true. Are you still going to be in Paranormal for a while? Or going back to the vampires?"

"It's hard to say, really. I'll probably stick around for two more weeks; not because I'm nervous about... the vampires or anything like that, though I still am, very slightly, but just so I can experience more of what every ghostly goings-on has to offer."

Tipping my Stetson, I said, "Fair enough, my boy. Glad to see you're feeling better about our fang-filled friends."

"Um, so, with everything that's been going on, all the stuff you've endured, I hope you don't mind if I ask, what are you going to do?"

"The only thing we can do," I said, taking a sip of our sub-par soft drink. "Move forward, but not too fast. Let's try and take everything in in our own time, nice and slowly. We'll try and have a bit of fun along the way."

THE END

Lightning Source UK Ltd.
Milton Keynes UK
UKHW021850050321
379874UK00004B/789